Brixton Overcoat

Skee Morif

GW00417678

Searchwell Books

Published by Searchwell Books
PO Box 52175
London E8 9AX
email: editor@searchwell.co.uk

ISBN 978-0-9552841-1-3

Dedicated to:

Ellen and Elvie

Chapter 1

Gridlock, mile after mile. And a puzzling overcast; tall clouds that conceal something. Hard to make out what it is. But it's much more than rain. It could be a woman in blue jeans. Swallows veer past a dust-stained windscreen. And the motorway from here getting later all the time.

If that a woman up there, she blue. She could check the gridlock out. Or read scriptures, laze a while. Then laugh loud over cloud cover. Some drivers have sat-nav; they can scheme from here.

A Charlie Parker solo starts in one car and, soon enough, it takes over. Louder now. A loner sax. It pours out a solo to scud rain clouds away. Tempers fraying.

In this gridlock any Miles Davis track would calm things down. One driver yells to another, shouting 'Neanderthal!'

London Zoo only a shout from here. And quick, this a clue how a horse-fable can come out of nowhere. Some fables are nicer than cars. And somewhere, somebody knows why swallows ever bother with a city in August.

Jimmy shunts the wheel. Gets the kerb. Then inch. Slow, inch by inch. Climbs the kerb. Then scoot. In other cars, they don't like this. But Jimmy shoots down a side road. The motorway will wait.

It would be different at the coast. A day like today the sea big with yachts. Huge blue water. And the great thing would be masts taller than telegraph-poles, but not too heavy to run the whole ocean down. Someone ashore would be watching this. A blear loner would be gazing at spinnakers, seeing sails billow with salt breeze. But in a city gridlock, remembering sail is like a fairytale.

Chapter 2

Dank air gusts into London Zoo, a place with windows open but at the same time closed. A house cut by summer. And something else. Hard to pin it down. It must be flesh. Or it's cut perfume. It's a woman-like smell, just like pulling up in a country lane and getting fresh daisies on a verge. And with all that, only one thing is missing. Butterflies should be coming and going in the southerly trace of breeze.

Ten minutes in the zoo and someone would leave. Leave now. But the gridlock outside is too big. And cages are one business. But the thing with Jimmy is, well, nobody else black here.

Cheetahs do not pack well. Gazelles meant for these cats are out on the plains a whole hemisphere away. Cheetahs have their eye. With a nod to 70, a grown cheetah hits the speed limit before any Aston Martin. And from 0 to 60, it will outgun anything from Ferrari. But a cheetah wouldn't get out the blocks in a zoo. Mobile twitching, Jimmy turns away.

Woman after woman moving around. Woman too nice to let pass by. This zoo could be the place for a lone to score. Especially with the sky pitched like asphalt.

Thirty seconds into the first phone-call, lightning breaks cloud cover. Baby-blue, slashing, pale, wronged light, lethal. The mobile cracks.

"Minims in Britain _"

"*Minims*," Jimmy says, "it's called Minims now. Remember?"

"Sure, sorry about that."

"C-sharp is the thing. It was B-flat, but I changed my mind."

"Oh, right."

"Can you hear me OK? I'm at London Zoo. Rain anytime now."

"Minims, well_ "

"Sharp keys cut through weather. C-sharp zaps the lot!"

"Your line's breaking up, so let's get to the point. Minims, we like it Jimmy. We all think it's on the ball. But it's jazz, mate."

"Yeah, I know."

"Why get difficult?"

An elephant trumpets in the zoo. The mobile slams close. "What's difficult?" Jimmy yells.

"Jazz is not folk."

2

"Is it the theme you don't like?"

"*Theme* does not come into this. Jazz is not folk."

"Got something against jazz?"

Silence loads up, streaming the void. Silence swallowing the whole line like snakeskin. Jimmy knows the score.

"As it happens," the voice drifts back, more casual, obliging, "some of my favourite music is jazz."

"So what's the problem?" Jimmy says, sensing betrayal, but deciding to play along. "Think bebop will make a comeback?"

"Make a comeback? It's never gone away, you know. This is 1999 and, by the way, how old are you?"

"Twenty-four."

"How old?"

"Twenty four."

"Wish I was that age again!"

"Age is only the tracks you play. I think bebop was the thing!"

"Bebop brings it home. Max Roach is still around. He's one guy who keeps it safe."

"Yeah."

"Those old tracks of Max."

"The ones where he's in the band with Charlie Parker!"

"Classics!"

"Ever see Max play?

"Yes, yes. New York, Chicago, London."

"London?"

"Yeah. He was at the Barbican not so long ago. But we could talk about that all day, so let's cut to the chase."

"I know. You want to talk about the festival."

"The *folk* festival."

"Sure."

"The Millennium Folk Festival is about *folk* music, got that? There's obviously got to be somewhere for your _ "

"Any ideas?"

"Loads of gigs out there, pal, places where your _"

"Like where?" Jimmy says, vacant.

"Look!" the voice spits. "I've had just about enough of this. Try Brixton!"

Today was supposed to be a sunny August day. But the weather looks like a lame flip-flop already, like a flaked-out somebody that operates rented rooms. One year Jimmy rented from one. And every day she flopped on the stairs to live in a fashion magazine. For a while, getting past that on the narrow stairs used to be danger. Until one day she made her mind up.

The weather's big on storm-clouds now. But only two days back Heathrow was near meltdown, over 90 all day. Now rainstorms snatching southern England. And anybody that wants to get wet, well, they have the blear sky to grab at. Jimmy can tell. Even after a putdown phonecall some things are still the same. Wild animals here that are colder than steel.

A coach-load of Lib-Dem women collect and chat. They don't bother with the animals; the zoo is just a backdrop to them. To a loner, they look like sunlight on a wet pan. Chatty women looking open, but set, winnowing down. Paddy Ashdown quit as headman yesterday and these women getting clenched up over it. The unsmiling ones try to steady those with a damp question in their eye. One girl rubs and rubs her eyes, trying to figure why anyone would ever choose a zoo to strut. But everybody in a hold-zone here, killing time, sloping.

Paddy was the man. The daddy. That guy understands danger and paperwork. He can break a soldier's neck with his hand. But in the street he can tell a mile off, he can separate hurt from paperwork. Next to him most politicos are only little-sister noise; all they can manage is spit spiders on TV.

A squint of raindrops hangs in the zoo. Shadows are sighs on the ground. Rain. Summer rain heading this way; feral, wet, crazy, scat and scatting. Rain will fall any time now. And Jimmy walks on.

A bulked mid-ground shakes out with hay piled high on a cart but, getting nearer, the two keepers pushing it look lost. Sad, their voices getting lower than knees. Two sad keepers sorry about the failed foetus under that loose, lush hay.

Somebody takes a swig of air, trying to switch. But the air too bare, more like stale fairgrounds than air. Two slow breaths confirm it, slower this time. Yep. It would be cage-doors all day to dwell on Brixton. Jimmy knows. Arleene is sweet up the free motorway.

Today the M1 is rut-time. A motorway that's a dream of open miles. And a cubby on asphalt waiting. Today will be a great chance to win from rain lashing down. For Jimmy this is because of

4

Arleene, the tamarind woman up the motorway. She a blue boogie, a special, never talking talk. Cooing down the phone she said she'll be set this evening. And all tonight. But she was lost. For a while her name was in the wrong address book.

A wet motorway is a great place to sail. The wetter the better. A place where graphite becomes a washed lake, woman or no woman waiting.

Aquaplaning is for the few. For Jimmy, summer rain will rut the motorway today. And nothing can ever match that. Nothing is ever like water lashing the ground, whipping it to fever like a half-wild horse. The kind of rain hard to believe, like a herd of reindeer taking ground in summer. A herd that turns back to sweat as one. Or it backs off, cools way down with you dismounting and inhaling all the sweat you want. Or it stamps all over you.

Even Michael Schumacher backs off for rain, even him, the rain master. But setting sail on that black roadway, well, it comes from minding your business on a clear stretch. Your eye on gyre, or catching green country that's way above miles, or you could be singing a modal-song. And the road so silk. The wet road looks like your personal name down on it. Wet road pulling you closer all the time, sigh and sighing, shhh! Graphite, sweet like a jazz solo or woman ironing her clothes. Because of rain, the road can get like a mean river. And all because of sky-water lashing down. You check the rearview mirror. This a must-do. Quick, the speedo clips 80. Next thing, 90. One blink and you the man! Way past legal, grabbing out at that bad river. And then. And then.

It lets go. The whole thing lets go. It starts with the same dream of a speedboat. You float water instead of old road. Maybe you have four tics to live. Or ten to die. No clocks, no fuss. Only the rush. You clear this black water, or your bones will sing in your car-coffin. And hearing your bones singing you, even for half a bar, even for one blink, that can *not* be a bad way to go.

Jimmy grins. He knows aquaplaning by name: not aquaplane, that thing is tarmac-sailing. Quiet, his shoulders roll, head clears. The putdown phonecall was weasel. A dumbo. Stupid weasel in a graphite farmyard. Time to check the time.

In the asphalt sky, lightning divides like eels. Blue fire up there, laser eels twisting high because of how storms filched them from the ocean. Teeth clenched like a portcullis, a loner looks for the zoo border.

A keeper comes up to Jimmy. She asks if things are OK. Clearing his throat he hears himself mumble. This is a good-natured woman.

"Why the long face?" she wonders.

Jimmy shrugs. "Today is blues day."

"What?"

"Millennium blues."

Stock quiet in an instant, she starts to learn. Her eyes are kind. Quiet eyes, and calm. The zoo is her home from home. Eyes crinkling, she mocks the cloud. "Cheer up! What a nice day!"

"Yeah, nice as spice."

"Whatever it is, don't take it too personally. *Nothing* can be more desperate in August than queues forming for the winter sales."

"What?"

"Winter sales-queues, they're on Oxford Street already."

"Clowns?"

Laughing, the woman checks his eyes. "Yes," she says, "a bunch of idiots have already started queuing up for the millennium sales!"

Jimmy laughing as she turns away to hand a bunch of keys over.

Chapter 3

Everybody wants the rhino to move. 'Do something, rhino. What part of *move* don't you get!'

Jimmy at the zoo one hour and, with a world class gridlock outside, this rhino could mojo. Prove it is no sculpture. The tail will flick, one keeper says; a gaunt keeper saying a rhino is a kind of pig. A difficult pig, but actually more kin to horses than pigs. And far away and tropical, somebody tricks a hummingbird out of air. Not so easy with a rhino. Hard to see how this thing is part horse. But in a fairytale, Stephen Hawking could kick a hummingbird in a wheelchair.

Folk queuing for the millennium sales? In August? On Oxford Street? On New Year's Eve one store will give Pacific cruises for a quid each to the first thirteen customers. That's what the rumour says. All that is four months away but some people putting markers down already.

The woman-keeper answers with her eyes. Then she spells it out. One more time. "Winter vigils are starting on Oxford Street and that's so ridiculous in the heart of summer!" And, as she turns to walk away she slaps Jimmy's back. "Nineteen ninety-nine is only a number, my dear."

Jimmy used to check the bible. The whole millennium business goes back to the preacher. The big fuss going back to a solo man with a cross to die on. And nowadays bishops say he was God, no less.

This rhino? This is more like a pig than horse. A politico would want to milk the crowd here, preach some blanks, like try getting the rhino to move a rhino part. This is a lady rhino, so a politician would want to get down in her enclosure to milk away.

The gridlock outside is a knot. It's too near. And too far from the motorway. A zoo could be the place to work this out. Pig or no pig, kin to horse or not, this rhino is no joke. This military pig or freak horse flicks a tail now. At last, it moves something. Hard to see Lester Piggott or Frankie Dettori galloping a rhino in the Derby; that's what somebody says. But this rhino is a steroid-tormented lady with a slow tie. And rain will wash her stray milk away.

Penguins are flightless, lithe as wet marble. Calling them birds is only booklore. And the really funny part is by now they know why they get laughed at. They know the zoo, the slick space they slosh in.

Lighting a smoke, Jimmy half laughs. He can tell. Some little architect had a problem here. Whoever designed this penguin space had a bad illusion, had mermaid heartbreak. Some sad loner codged this place to cut a wave, but all he did was give heartache to a mermaid. Somebody should have told him. But the zoo put penguins round his fake wave. The architect did not understand the sea, did not know your hands should be humbly at your side when you look at the ocean. Your hands must not pencil mermaid private parts. The architect was a dry-land swimmer. And penguins do not get that. They know about the visitors.

"Hey!" Jimmy yells. Straightaway every penguin turns round. As one, they look up. Just like he the ringmaster. But they'd be better off not posing. Jimmy is no ringmaster. They could quit splashing round this mermaid place and front the cut of their penguin race: the hollow, the yellow teeth, the guffaw. Zoo penguins could face down the crowd. But everyone would freak. And that's because penguins are only wet toys in this place, splashing. But they know. Sometimes their little black wings shrug and look like weary arms. But they do not dance, never turn to the crowd to snap their wing and move their feet. These penguins never want to tap dance: shuffle-shuffle, shuffle-shuffle, one, two, three.

Maybe only because of checking the clouds, but somebody wondering about polevaulting. Pole-athletes are it. They grab the pole and take a tension. Inhale, then run at the whole sky.

Some of these animals could get away from the zoo. To steal away from here, a rhino would have to polevault. But even with a hundred tries a day, every day, a rhino would need a zillion more years on the planet to learn polevaulting. And rhinos are not the only ones that can not vault. Aching wet, penguins can not.

Quieter now, Jimmy turns to the penguins and says, "Hey!"

Chapter 4

To most folk, Brixton is some glitzy London place. Seeing it on TV they get a medley on top. Stuff like market-stall after stall, and shimmying inner-city fables. Caribbean, African and white. Grabbing at the time, Jimmy at the zoo ninety minutes now.

Tabloid TV crews roll to Brixton. They go for the drool. They want drool from the ethnic. So they check the street, unpack kit bags and walk around. TV crews go flexing to Brixton, never chewing gum, but mouths like fish wanting wet. That's the Brixton the official on the phone talked.

The weird thing was the guy himself. He knows good jazz. Jimmy could hear him snazzing it, snapping his desk with a 6-8 pro-beat, danger to the line. But the way his voice got rid of Brixton! That was a mucous mouth doing it; no way talking cultural high or lows, no way giving kind advice or bad. Not with phlegm in a wine mouth. That was woad talk.

Woad was the bluest dye. Bluer than blue sky. It was always more than dye when the army of Caesar logged it here. Centurions clocked flint-eyed Brits paint their body with the stuff. But when they told Caesar he laughed. The boss general had to see for himself. And it rocked him. But the shock did not last. Caesar was a man of the world so woad made him laugh. Seeing bloke Brits smeared with woad, and lady Brits smearing their body to check their cut in a stream, Caesar laughed. His Mediterranean tan flew, it almost blanked his diary. And 2000 years down the road that blue stuff is still around; not so cut, but just as sharp. Woad, blue as ever.

Low overhead the zoo, clouds look like zebras' eyeballs. Their slowed dream-state is dizz. And the animals. Animal after animal beating the air. And folk talking. Roaring and growling, trumpeting, snarl. And birds sly in a cage, singing.

Giraffes are the high choir in a zoo. But giraffes don't sing. Leaves are their thing. Leaves sing for them, green, green, sprinkling the open plains, the hot savannas singing of leaves. Being so long-necked is one sad business here. Without that neck, giraffes wilt like morning stars. Giraffes wired to air.

Wet, the M1 is graphite. By now, that highway should be clear. This is motorway time. A sister-like tarmac waits. And then. Jimmy

9

smiles, knowing this is Arleene time. Arleene is the owner of tamarind. A day'n nighttime woman. He turns to go. But on bad ground. Doubt, starting to worry. This worried man can not shake a bad feeling. It's like a mange dog. A dog that talks. Cunning, the dog says 'Hey you, remember your tune? Yeah, that Minims. Well, it ain't no folk!' Jimmy kicks out. Minims is a jazz-opera, pooch!

If the dog could speak now it would tell what folk is. But this dog will not reply. And that's because the dog-tongue too busy. The dog-tongue licks busted ribs from where a boot cracked hard. Dogs hear higher notes than clouds make.

To Jimmy, jazz is the biggest folk of all. Anywhere with TV or a radio, nighttime Mongolia or Shepherd's Bush, Cape Town or Chicago, folk know jazz straightaway. Going past the rhino with a fresh cigarette in hand, he's getting away from here. Heading to the exit. Nobody ever kicks a grown rhino to death. But any bozo can breeze into a pet shop, traipse round and end up with a hamster.

A jacket would do it here; even a scarecrow coat. Something to button. To pull together with. Laces loose, Jimmy looking round side to side. Summer or no summer this place is cold. Brixton could be some kind of bootlace.

Arleene will fix this. Jimmy's had no contact with that woman for a year, so this time it must be broad daylight. No sneak moon boogie. Not tonight. Arleene wants tonight to be homing night. So it will start from broad daylight, heaping from the moonlight. Arleene knows the score. She will not get uppity. Jimmy will bring the long motorway. Tonight she gets a long black motorway with voltage tensed by miles. Arleene will pull that danger, whisper low.

Jimmy at the zoo exit as a furrowed woman gets near. She comes up to him, stepping quicker, hurrying with twin girls, small, freckled. A camera pouts in her hand. Will he take a couple of snaps, please? Her red hair looks easy, let go, lax, will not tire all day. Hair that's easy and belle-red. Her hair changes light round it like a red hello. The camera in Jimmy's hand now and her eyes seem happy but deep-set, soft as moss; eyes laced by regret, this redhead woman is clinging to something. Five paces back, and the viewfinder changes everything. The woman's hair is a haystack on fire.

Squinting, Jimmy confused about where's where. This zoo could be anywhere. Flecks of drizzle wrangle halting summer air.

Chapter 5

Leaving a zoo without checking the lion? Tigers are bigger than lions, but more catlike, too much like a pet. It's hard comparing lions with a woman.

Gridlock is not the word for the roads. So what's out there is iron. Rain stalls. One minute the clouds shape up and cut clean, then later the same clouds get stark. This is painful. Especially for somebody at odds, canning round, quiet, wondering. One thing is to figure how weather works, or read it in a book, like exactly how clouds fling apart then close. But now and then things just sort of shape in clouds.

Overhead the zoo, the clouds look like a woman now. Well, that is them to somebody like Jimmy with a woman in mind. But not just any woman. And no way the wisp, the gaunt kind. These clouds looked that way a while, looked like gaunt women with elbows every place waiting to shrill. But now the clouds look like a round woman, a large lady, the kind of heavy woman who sings trad songs or, if she croon, dreams out jazz standards at night; a lady huge enough that her dress stalls an albatross on her belly.

Jimmy gets out a smoke. And ambles back into the zoo. Unfinished business there. Must see the lions. Must talk to them.

London Zoo is a big-city place. It's got a name that says 'Big me up by day.' And yet. This zoo paves a way for folk from every place. Rhinos make bad bacon if fried.

Thunder grabs the ground. And the sky holds on. The tobacco is bitter. Bitter smoke cropping, gnashing. A keeper says smoking is spiteful; smoking is not allowed here, the keeper says.

Jimmy cold, ignoring. Then again. *Callous* is one word. Teeth clenched, smoke billows from his lungs. It's the zoo. The reason why anybody ever comes to a zoo at all. Could be it's rapture of steel. But this zoo brings back too much. Bad recall. For Jimmy the putdown phone call was woad. Arleene will definitely understand, but no agony-auntie would ever tell a fortuneteller 'Try Brixton!'

The clouds could not be bigger now. This gaming rain can not wait. Big water in the sky. Sky water biding time, waiting to do it here. And nothing can match rain for being callous. Some days rain hangs around, kills time in the sky. Or it looks down and sees only prey. But mostly, rain nice. That water tinkles. Rain can be cooling like suntan oil.

Chapter 6

Lion! The ground latch. Cold, latching ground. Two lions ahead.
And one blink to move in. But a cage is there. For a blink it was
only lions. But they inside the cage. Steel round them. They in a
steel room. But a loner's whole life yanked through the cage.
Somehow.

So, this what lions look like up close! The gaze of the male lion is
a butcher's gaze. Visitor is only meat in that eye. And the mane.
The lioness paces her space, pacing. Granite wears that eye. The
lens is sure. Her eyes are clear as honey. But her gaze is more than
her mate's. That steady lioness eye whispers, saying 'Fear torture!'
With no fooling round, she'd suck your bones while you bawl the
sky out.

Nothing domestic is in the cage. And nothing cross. Nothing like
a ball of wool footing an old woman that gets cute in her chair. A
secret collects in the gaze of the lioness. All moves depend on that.
The next move. But the steel of the cage looks good. Reminding.
And reminding the lioness. Yes, a different space for lions here. But
something is a message. A note is at the lions' cage. Hurt welling
and blood floods the back of their watchers' eye. Lions hear zoo
birds singing in a high cage.

Jimmy steps away, looking round but knowing less and less. This
zoo would be huge if it wasn't for traffic outside.

Giraffes don't mope a lot. That's what one keeper says. But elephants do. The keeper laughs, saying elephants get sentimental.
This guy laughs to throw a big question. Making him pay would be
neat.

In a zoo a rhino is not the kind of thing that bothers. Rhinos only
go rhino. And lions don't mind callous meat. Even water is no help,
not here. Penguins are so water-longing that they cozy up to anything. Penguins see the sea in any old puddle, clean or dirty. But
seals are bad. Not conning a predator in the ocean, all that seals do
in a zoo is poolside party-tricks. Their eyes dampen air like cold sea
plums.

To Jimmy, that putdown phonecall was only the most recent
thing. But who to tell? Nobody to talk to. They always know the
score. Or they never quite believe. Now and then one up-front one
will cut to the chase, saying 'You're welcome to go back where you

13

came from!'

Going your business some place like Oxford Street, your face is on a thousand CCTV screens. But if a lion walked that same thoroughfare, tarmac would fly.

A woman's hand moves. Her hand moving on damp steel. The hand meets Jimmy's on the steel. But the woman gazes the cage. The hand is near and small. Whose hand? Better see this woman's face.

Jimmy wants to ask it. Ask anything. Ask the woman if rain will come this way, or ask the time, even some stupid thing, anything so she will turn round. But just by thinking it he gets to see her face as she turns. And now the woman! She lets go of the lions.

Before swinging full round, she gets Jimmy. This woman can see in one take. Her eyes fix his. Amber in her eyes. And heed.

Some people looking at this woman will see only mixed-race. This bothers Jimmy, making him sorry she turned round. She looks too gashed. What brings her to the lions' cage? She is two people, a two-ness all over. Maybe she the other side of a bad night. A night with no mercy. Has she walked from a pitiless night, from some guy pushing too hard, too hard, and too long. Or she could have walked from bigger than that. Maybe she's run from something in her belly that somebody does not want. Somebody like a bad, angry guy.

As she turns round, her mouth smiles. "Wonderful, aren't they?" she says, off-hand, nodding at the lions.

Jimmy knows she does not want him to speak. The looks they exchange tell him that. So he turns to the cage, turns to the lion hunger and steel. Something to reach out for in the cage but he turns round again and looks the woman over, wondering. Maybe she's here to go after lions with all she's got. She stands so still. Only the trillion microcircuits in her body move, circuits that whir away silent below a loose emotionless suit.

Some people have lions in their eye. Jimmy did not know that before today. Everybody gets the same TV. They get a drama where the camera pans wide to pick up lions lying around or yawning in shade, or moving cubs place to place, or doing the lion groom. But hungry lions are a dread sight. And the greatest part is always when a hungry pride gets going, calculating, connecting to death, tacking, sectioning, cutting down a savanna that is as heart-stopping and

14

tawny like them.

A summer day but Jimmy is cold here, feeling cut off. Even from the woman standing next. Her suit is a black shade of grey. This like-two woman in a near black suit that is so set by the bare arms of everybody in the crowd. Now she closer by half a step. Hoarseness is in her voice but only a semitone away.

Jimmy turns to the woman. "What's your way to deal with a put-down? A racial."

Quick, her face pops. Her face pops like she's been hit, like it was a rhino in the question. She will not turn round. Afraid of getting hit again. Whatever she should say, she makes herself hold back from. Her lips a cage. Her lips dither. This woman having steel lips that confine something that wants a chance to leap, one chance to get away. Her lips are full zipped. And, big surprise, she turns to face him. Her face is blank. And for too long her eyes look pointblank. A knowing face. But still withholding. Her brows crimp.

The woman nods at the lions. Facing them. "Don't forget where you are," she says. "You're in a zoo, don't forget!"

Jimmy will not think. For a second he can't tell. Is the woman answering him, or talking to lions? Her suit could mean a trip to Oxford Street. Or maybe she shopped there already, walking along, going past beseeching eyes of blood-drained mannequins.

A thick crowd at the cage now. Everybody should relax. But there's nothing to recognize. No gladness, not even fear. No nerves. No amazement over lions. Nothing but blank for tawny to paint on.

This is love. A loner wanting lions, to see their eyes and watch their moves and lion stillness. Their loom is the colour of just-washed hay. Hard to accept the same loom gets red with blood every time they eat. But that is a price to pay. The two lions brace together and, in all this, only a sneeze ticks by the cage.

A huff from the crowd. Something raw but human, indigo, jealous. Somebody saying you can not be jealous of something in a cage. But the mane of the lion is handiwork that never happens any place except by thunderstorms on savannas.

A flurry of raindrops in the air. It nags away, a swish that taunts the yawning air. Something will happen here.

Somebody watching the lioness, quiet watching. Her gaze shifts from the crowd. The honey gaze dapples air then gets back to the crowd. A clumsy child moves. And straightaway! The lioness wants child meat. A spray of drizzle shrugs from her lion shoulder.

Nobody saying zip at the cage. The business is lions, the mane mystic. The hushed crowd sees a heavy mane turn from them to leave them to gaze, to watch. And this is part to do with reverence and part to do with getting jealous. This the kind of quiet a congregation makes before closing their eye. His heavy lion gait shovels him sideways. Then sideways again, over to the lioness. Who pays her any mind? This lioness has seen the whole thing a thousand times already and even counts watchers arriving in ones and twos. By now she knows. No, she won't get to kill them. She knows her space.

A ribcage is in the cage. What's left of it is at the back of the cage, fluorescent white, stripped bare. Nobody in the crowd knows what it was. And if a chair was by the cage, nobody would sit. Rumble.

This is thunder. Rumbling thunder blunts the dreaming air. The two little twin girls get anxious with their mother, the woman with bright red hair and a camera. It's going to rain, one twin says, and they don't want to look at lions anymore. The woman fits Alice-bands to their hair and promises ice cream.

One keeper talks. Nobody asked him, but this keeper says when the weather's too hot the lions get ice-lolls in the zoo. *What?* Yes, ice-lolls! You mean, like vanilla or chocolate? Blood, the keeper drawls. *Blood?* Yeah, blood. He explains. Lions don't want to feed if the weather's too hot, they don't want meat to eat in the heat, they want to drink. Lions like ice but there's got to be blood somewhere so vanilla or chocolate wouldn't do. So the zoo makes shafts of ice; about the same size as this, the keeper says, extending his arm. The redhead woman steps back, thinking of lions licking arm-sized ice laced with blood. She takes another step back, a redhead woman looking at lions and that ice-loll strange.

Lightning strafes the overcast. Lightning flickering down to drowned marble eyes. The sky tears apart. It runs laser to laser. And quick, everything turns to a meeting place.

The like-two woman is afraid. Her hands smooth creases from her suit. "That lightning," she pants, "it makes the zoo seem like it's up on a cinema screen!"

"Yeah," Jimmy nods. "Like one of those old silent films you can't turn away from."

16

The woman's eyes do not follow the arc of Jimmy's. His eyes long for heavier clouds. Hers prefer the cage. Jimmy checks the time.

A nervy clearing is where her mouth was. "There's something childish about you," she says, eyes set with iron.

In a way this lightning could smile that. And, on cue, the psycho lightning smiles. Lightning smiling slick and high. The woman's hand is a vice on Jimmy's arm. Her hand wants muscle from his body. She spooked. Thunder explodes. Thunder in her head. He does not get any sense of his other hand. The lion's mouth is empty. Thunder mowing the ground. And Jimmy holding the woman. The missing hand is holding the woman in the near-black suit. But the strangest part is that he won't look at her face. What's she want?

And then. It's over. Three, four seconds. Lightning and thunder gone. Nobody talks. Blear all over. The light fades to twilight. And a strange scent in air; strange, but it's really only the scent of scared air. The hardest thing is air. And two lions no longer wanting to kill anything that moves.

They turn from the crowd. They at the back of the cage, set, quiet, and, with a quiet glance the lioness squats the ground. She ignores the crowd. But her eyes remember. And now the lion connects her. Secures the join. And humps. His lion teeth claim the nape of her neck. One woman says the lion's mane looks like a city umbrella. Nobody knows what to make of this. Part of it is the lions don't want to waste time, getting it on because of sudden twilight. The keeper says lions will mate forty, fifty times a day when the lioness is in season.

Jimmy checks the time. Arleene is up the motorway, far, waiting. But it's nice chatting to the like-two woman. He knows if they ever meet again somebody will be there to talk what happened at the zoo. Somebody saw the whole lion thing. A whole crowd saw it. And that's something to be glad for.

Heart thumping, the woman asks why. It's kind of hard to explain, he says. And she touches him, softly, saying the way the lions got it on was only like any longtime couple in their living room. Shy, she smiles. Drizzle cuts the air. The big rain can not be closer. Jimmy wants to ask the woman if they will meet again, but she's gone.

But there's always lions. He wants them to look back one more

17

time, to swap gazes, eye to eye. The woman is half the zoo away taking bad weather to two keepers. And Jimmy mulls over her phone number he did not get.

This time it's time to go. Maybe the lions will remember.

Chapter 7

Jimmy alone in the carpark. Seashells clatter the glove-box; these things are solo, half-forgotten, got on one lost trip to the coast, a handful of nacre that's as tender to look at as a woman's smile. And five music tapes, a chewed-up old map and a pencil. And very old tobacco.

This tobacco can not smoke. It's in bits to hell. No Rizla paper in the car. Lightning strafes the sky. This tobacco could be all that's left in a desert world. The shells want to explain. They were left behind. One shell looks like music, not for somebody's hand, so the way it fits is by pure chance. Like dice. Whatever lived in the shell, well, it listened the whole ocean round it. And the magic is how it compiled itself by bearings from the sea.

The engine starts. Clutch bites. The steering wheel turns. But quick. Another feeling; voices saying 'All roads to Brixton.' Nothing is what it seems. There's only one place a loner can be. And that place is the poles. The North Pole maybe. You really can *not* be some place in England. So you're looking at polar bears and the temperature is 50 below. Just like at the North Pole, a thousand ways to go from the park gate but where will Jimmy go? Rain veers. Rain, the water bitch. The engine dies.

Rain! Rain jumps the limber green as flocks of birds hurry across the low sky. And somebody jealous of bird lightness. Not jealous of birds being light. But jealous that birds know where to go. A Charlie Parker tape plays. Jimmy's eyes close, slow. Rainwater falling, slate and grey. And seashells in a glove-box far from the ocean.

Something. Not a dream. It's somebody, tapping. Tapping hard and now. Not exploring. This is no blind one with a cane. Somebody at the driver's window.

Jimmy wide awake. The rain gone. Goodbye sky-water, say hello to the sea! Rays of a new sun tweak the zoo carpark and, through the globules of water on misty glass, the woman who was beside him at the cage. The like-two woman, watching.

Her lips part. "You OK?" she says. Her mouth softens and, quietly, she repeats herself. "You OK, everything alright?"

"Must have dozed off," Jimmy yawns. The window winds down part way and his eyes open full. "No sleep last night."

"No sleep?" she smiles. "Well, that's OK then. Just a bit of a nap, something to top-up the daydreaming? Listen, back there it was like you wanted to do an Androcles with that lion."

The window winds down all the way. Jimmy blanks. "What do you mean?"

The woman shucks rainwater from her hands. The seat pulls upright. But this is easy. Even a raindrop knows what this woman is getting at. Her gaze tells him she understands. Some women can read Jimmy. And this one can read the wet carpark. He was asleep maybe ten minutes and, all told, been away from the road two hours. The gridlock will be gone. He hates naked emotion. Part of the survival game is emotion cut, stuff that must never get loose. And now he holds back. And watches the woman's eyes. Her decision about him toys with her mouth. She will make her mind up. She weighs the invitation one more time. Her eyes say 'You sure it's only to sit and talk?' And, weighing him still, she smiles her easy smile and heads round the car.

"Lorna Stanley," she says, getting in the passenger seat.

"Jimmy-Lines."

"Jimmy *who?*"

"Jimmy-Lines Dell."

"Nickname, right?"

"No."

"What part of the world is it from?"

"My birth certificate."

"Jimmy," she says, like tasting the name, "and Lines, as in lines on a page?"

"Well, it was to do with travel. Dreams of travel."

"Lines?"

"Yeah. Latitudes."

"Like the equator?"

"Something like that. My old man had a thing for places. Kind of a weird story."

Lorna's lips twitch, then press to a smile. "Crisp, meeting you."

"What's in a name? Hey, they might have called you Molly."

"*Molly?* No chance!"

His eyes in the woman's and, normally, this would be enough. But the weird thing is him having nada to say. She suspects this. It annoys him. But he knows. This package in the passenger seat is a

20

lot more than babe in a suit. This a woman. One that will not slow it down with small talk. Quiet, he nods.

She turns to him. "Tell me I'm way off the mark, but you looked desperate back there. Anything wrong?"

Jimmy should relax. But something dims in the woman's eyes. Something like self-denial. And the way her eyes just take the right amount of light, all she wants is talk.

His hands grab the wheel. "Me, desperate? Like how?"

"Like you'd *die* if you couldn't get those two lions out of there."

"And you wouldn't?"

"The poor things! God, the elephants. Did you see the elephants? And the giraffes. The whole affair."

Jimmy weary. But on guard. He knows where this chat could lead. So the best thing is to back off. Maybe it's only her suit but he knows that if he will meet her again it must mean better go easy now. And it's pointless trying a chat up, everything about her tells him that. Something always going on in the mid-distance with this woman, even face to face. Maybe the way she sits. She looks as ready for take off as a robin on a twig. Only a fool would scare this thing away. "What's the big deal?"

"The deal is freedom," Lorna says. "Ring any bells?"

"Come on, most people would set those animals free."

"And me and you, we have our hands tied, eh! I've probably got this all wrong, but, well, you know, _"

"Hey, go for it!"

"It's like you'd want the lions to thank *you* for it."

"Me?"

"Yes. In a word, you."

"Thank me for what?"

"Getting them away from that cage."

"What's that supposed to mean?"

Lorna's fingers wrestle the clasp of her shoulder bag. A wrestle fidget. Finally, the clasp jumps open. "You don't get it. Not a clue what's out there, have you?"

"I'm not in somebody's classroom, am I? You a teacher? Or is it animal rights?"

Softly, Lorna's hand glides to Jimmy's arm. The hand is light, up from a kind heart. A simple hand. Not a prop. Not from a song. Not even like a falling leaf. Her soft touch moves over to his fist. He can

21

tell. This woman's lived a life.

"Got a man in your life?"

Quick, the hand pulls away. Like from fire. Her whole body pulls sideways. "Woah!" she says. "Slow down, man! One step at a time. Relationships and things, anybody can do those, you know, have a great time. But it always happens. Come breakup time and it's always 'How did I *ever* get into that?' Makes me sick!"

Jimmy saying nothing. This woman confuses him. In one way her hand was only like the touch of an aunt, some relative, someone close. But she is not auntie, not a relative. Who this woman? A campaign junkie? She talks like prophets talk, mostly about the zoo, that this place started in 1828. London Zoo was where liars used to come to study exotica; doing that was the sure way to get called a scientist. The general public didn't come here till 1847. To Jimmy, Lorna could be talking bible here. But only a Noah could get the animals out. She sucks her teeth, grabs her bag.

"Caged lions," Jimmy groans, "all they do is run their rails."

"What else can they do? They're in a zoo, true or false?"

A Charlie Parker track starts. This is Ko Ko. Lorna winces as the volume turns down. His eyes ask if she wants more volume.

"Rails?"

"Lions and rails," Jimmy says, "that's how it's going to be for a long time to come."

Lorna's eyes cut through the car park. And Jimmy wondering how old she is, thinking she as much as thirty. But she could be twenty five. Her suit hints at a toned woman-body. The body troubles him. She turns to the carpark again and points to her car. Somebody could reach over and run a finger over this woman. Even more to her far-away sideways than in her full frontal face. But she turns round. Again. Then.

Mystic pathway! Man with rivets for hands grabs steering wheel! On a rainy day with a man missing a specific woman, or just any old day, what Lorna's got is the real thing. Her skirt rounds on mystic flesh. The cloth of the near-black skirt is from another faith, like spun by an alien seamstress, far from penance, spooking. The near-black of the cloth is scarier than a soundless night. And she fires up, eyes blaring, talking of lion cubs, the kind of life a cub at the zoo gets born to. But Jimmy can not listen. Man with rivets for hands gazing, can not hear what mystic woman saying.

22

Parker's Mood plays on the tape, quieter now. And even in the poky quiet the tune wells up. Jimmy asks the woman if she ever grooves to Charlie Parker, the flights on sax, the mission solos more. She wonders if that isn't Charlie playing on the tape. Yes, somebody once gave her a John Coltrane CD, and the liner notes mentioned Charlie Parker. It's the improvising, Jimmy says; that's the thing. Charlie P the man, way ahead! Ahead? Of what? Charlie is ahead of classical, ahead of jazz. You can even see those Charlie solos. Solos you can see? Yes, blues but not blues. What? Blues carry jazz, flies it and always gets back. *What?* Charlie's solos always get back, Jimmy says again.

With the woman in the seat beside him, haunting but not aware, something happens. Jimmy wants to find her. This is not her body. Not anymore. This is the story in her eyes.

"What do you do?" she wonders.

"What work I do?"

"Bet I can guess. It's music, isn't it? You're a music man!"

"*That* obvious?"

"A mile off!"

"Well, yeah, music it is. I play piano. Jazz mostly."

"Jazz?"

"Yeah."

"Come to the zoo for inspiration?"

"When stuff goes haywire, music is it. But sometimes I don't even know what it is."

"Music?"

"Yeah."

"Come on, music is music!"

"Well, yeah. I suppose."

"Music is music!"

"Yeah, I suppose that's why it's out there. Yeah, even when there's stuff up to here."

"Music man," Lorna gently intervenes, "what's wrong?"

Jimmy fumbles for a smoke. But none there. "You really want to know?"

"Talk to me!"

Some people can not confide. Difficult for some folk telling what is way down, even to someone close. But something in this woman's eyes, something she understands. Jimmy knows she can

23

not know the half of it. He would have to ask how she knows. How can she know the sickening that starts in a man's head and percolates to his balls.

"It's all pent up. There's this bad genie, pissed off, ballistic in a bottle."

Worry in her eye, she turns to him. "What's caused that?"

"There's always stuff to deal with. A load of weird, weird stuff."

"You mean racism, don't you."

"Yeah."

"So," she sighs, "what's new?"

"Ever seen a rhino polevaulting?"

"Polevaulting?"

"Yeah."

Lorna's ochre face turns pale. Slow, her head shakes. Her breathing chops. She turns away. Hands wringing. Her lips mime, then say, "Rhinos, polevaulting?"

"Yeah."

"*Polevaulting?*"

"Running with a pole down the runway, like a jet plane."

"That's terrible!"

"Yeah."

"There's so much pain in that. Rhinos polevaulting?"

"Yeah."

"Makes you want to laugh if it wasn't serious. *Dead* serious."

"Laugh if you want," Jimmy shrugs.

Lorna's hands set the strap of her shoulder. "Guys like you can't cope. I've seen it before. I think it's flake-highs."

"What?"

"Flake-highs."

"What's that?"

Pulling her skirt below her knees, she steadies herself. And wipes her forehead. "British guys get it," she explains. "British black guys are the worst."

"Flake-highs?"

"I've met guys who _"

"Yes, but what is it?"

"There's been one or two guys that, well, they're guys at the bottom of the escalator then sorry at the top."

"Flake-highs?"

24

"There's another word I could use."

"Posers?"

"Eunuchs!"

On the tape, Charlie Parker soloing on Yardbird Suite. Somehow this solo seems like nobody's ever heard it before: far, desolating, reaching out, wailing through wet weather. A dab at the volume switch and the music gets the volume it needs. The wet carpark draws near.

When the track ends, Lorna and Jimmy sit back. Wordless, spent. Two silent people looking numb past the wet windscreen. She is lonely, wanting somebody to talk. But in Jimmy she would have the wrong man. The one thing Jimmy knows about himself is he is no talk type. And as for being a listener, well, that is for guys that don't compose.

Lorna's breathing is low. Then it rises, slow, rising and swells, then it falls. She wants to tell. Far more than Jimmy wants to confide. *Flake-highs* sounds like a mind thing, he says, saying it could be like a tower-block tumbling down, or the title for a fairytale; but it rings a bell. How did she know?

The physical thing for Lorna has gone. Now Jimmy must know who she. Anything, starting with where her life. Simple things will do it, like why she wears a winter suit in a summer zoo.

"Crafty stuff," he says.

"What?"

"It's a doddle to tuck into lengths of it."

"*What* are you talking about?"

"Some of them don't bother with colour," Jimmy nods. But tired of playing around now, he grabs the woman's shoulders and twists her torso to face him. "There's no winks, no nudges, none of that stuff. Some of them listen to jazz and know the snazziest bop."

"Who?"

"The hypocrites."

"Who?"

"Hypocrites have all the moves."

"What?"

"Things can be going OK, great even, but when push turns to shove, well, they jaw."

"What?"

"They jaw," Jimmy says.

25

"*What?*"

"They expect you to be from Brixton."

"Brixton?"

"Yeah. Some days, it gets like a ton of cement on your back. You never feel it?"

Vacant, Lorna quietly turns away. Her tongue is dry. It swells her mouth. And that's because she knows. Staring down her hands, turning them over and over, doing hide & seek with her palms. And then her eyes. Her brown eyes settle on green things past the windscreen. Still saying nothing, not with her mouth. A kleenex pops from her bag. And now she wipes the glass in front to clear the mist. Then reaches over, careful, wiping misty glass in front of him. And all the time her bag hugs her thighs. Now her hand reaches into it and brings out a postcard. Quiet, she writes something on the back, jotting, hand shifting like a wasp on heat; heedful writing. Her hand dithers as the card passes to him. The postcard shows the Tyne Bridge in Newcastle.

Across the carpark the woman with the red hair waves. She is one of the last to leave the zoo. She and her little twin girls wave goodbye from across the wet carpark and Jimmy waving back. The woman and her kids going home to remember. So much to talk. Way into evening they will talk what happened at the lions' cage.

Rain stipples the thin carpark space. Only three cars are here now. And sunlight wading through. Jimmy checks out the postcard in his hand. It's brand new. Lorna must have meant to post it from Newcastle but he won't ask. And suddenly, without a word, not even goodbye, she steps from the car. Woman going headlong, crossing the carpark already and never looking back.

"If you want to know," Jimmy yells, calling after Lorna, "those lions got me thinking. It should be me and them. The lions and me, on our way to Brixton!"

Chapter 8

The car knows where to go. But instead of to Camden, then up through Highbury to the motorway, it laps Regent's Park; going round the Outer Circle again. Sometimes millionaire apartments go by.

The folk here have their story to tell. Every dwelling that overlooks the park is only a stone from the zoo. And the order here, the reserve, the quiet. And the green. The nighttime fizz in these apartments must be a buzz, late night partying and hearing elephants trumpet or knowing lion danger near.

Jimmy's old car takes one more lap round. But things were sharp in the zoo. Things were clear cut. Steel and cage was there. Steel was clearer cut than this roadway.

Finally, the car turns into Albany Road. The motorway is only five miles away. The festival organizer was a crafty guy. He talked folk, but meant something else. To Jimmy any of the usual race words would have shrugged off by now. But Brixton is new. Sociology professors swap socks over Brixton. They know that if England is the green and pleasant, then Brixton is the part with a lion on the estate. White liberals going for nighttime to Brixton and even live there, sweat the same sweat, wouldn't live any place else. But nobody ever steps up to say 'Enough!' No bishop. And no astronaut.

Whack! Bile, thick, acrid. Spewed like bad wine. Whack! Gut wanting to home the garment on a one. Whack! This the Brixton overcoat.

Going to check a cool woman, someone as warm as Arleene, a honey lady, nothing like a Brixton overcoat can be near. A serious shower must come first. Then two hot baths, searing. Then a swim in the ocean.

Jimmy can not help it, not here. Not alone, mulling. His fingers twitch. The ocean is big water. To float it or have it get like riding sharks in a bay. The ache, the shrugging of the sea on a quiet coast. Or the opening of a door with a woman opening it late into night. And far up the motorway, Arleene waiting.

Chapter 9

Autumn is quiet in the leaves. Autumn a little late this October. But getting set for bluster, arriving a little more in a leaf per day.

This morning two trains crashed at Paddington. Eight people died. At least eight. Being on rails meant nothing to them. More than two hundred injured but more counting, more dead to log.

Someone was alone in a flat, alone at the 8th floor window of a north London high-rise every day, flat broke and wondering. Seagulls soared between the tenement blocks. They soared again today.

Great blues singers get the reddest red. And hit bluest indigo. But some days only a guitar can cut it. A blues guitar can get past indigo. Electric blues, soloing higher than gulls can fly. Or crows.

Listening the blues and considering, testing the blear autumn breeze, Jimmy is sure. No more playing for money. Playing for money breaks the soul of some players. So no more studio work. No more hustling on stage. Playing for money is smiling-the-smile. Even Eric Clapton repeats on stage. And that's because the deal out there is doing it because of habit; even Eric borrowing his own old clothes.

Jimmy checks the coffers. Things starting to squeeze. Money down to one week's supplies and life a razor line.

You wake up and take a shower, check the time and get to the station on time to get a train, something on rails all the way, a sure thing. That's what you do without a blink. Then something like Paddington happens. And the ordered world jumps out the bushes.

The only thing through Jimmy's window is the concrete of tenement blocks. Some days even the sky can be like heavy cement.

The windows are shatterproof. Glass here is like bullet casing more than glass. On some bad tenement days the windows have the speckled look of salt. And though seagulls go past sometimes, the ocean is too far for salt spray. Or the wind can grab ocean meniscus to dump on a high-rise window panes. Tenement in concrete. And seagull conceit.

Funny enough, it was only after the first news of Paddington that someone in the tenement weighed stuff. Each life tucks in a tenement box and every box is like an ocean-going container on a grey quayside. Only fatal livestock can be some place like this; cattle lowing, not knowing, waiting that last shipment out. This could be Peckham or Hackney, Lambeth or any place. But Jimmy in Tottenham.

Then the dogs. Tenement dogs bark too loud. They bark at night. *Bad* dogs, psycho mutants, deadeye machines. Barking that sends out far to night. Aural indigo in a dog pack.

Other noises here start with quarrelling. Shouting that flares any time, day or night. That is one thing. But the really bad part is music. Some folk in the tenement only hear their music when it gets too loud for anybody to listen it. And that happens all the tenement time. Noise so loud that nobody can hear what gets said, can not hear some honest thing, or person afraid, exactly what must get said quietly to be true.

Jimmy is OK on the 8th. Everybody calls the 8th floor Neptune. That mock is always a joke. And that's because the building's got ten floors; the tenement block is like the solar system, somebody said. Mercury is the first floor and Venus the second, then on up past more planets till the top floor. The folk on the 10th floor got left out; they have to deal with every kind of alien on scary nights alone.

But the noise in the block tells of bad earthbound: war cries, human fire, zoot flames, war cauldron, stuff blaring through concrete three levels away. Where are gulls going when they swoop past? They mistake the sight of tenement windowpanes for open water. Seagulls soaring and getting the ocean from mean vertical glass.

A half bottle of malt tells it. It tells Jimmy. The score of Minims runs its own race. This is crochets in the beat breaking off then falling, then giving way to minims in refrain. Twelve bars of refrain. The organizers at the folk festival. Dem? A big mistake! Minims is rhythms where crotchets get outpaced by the beat. But dem seh jazz a no folk.

Jimmy talks to a malt bottle. 'Who *them*!'

Britannia's lips are stone. No black man her friend. No black man her son. But one day the lady will exhale. She will breathe in and out. In, out, in, out, and bang! That woad-emotion will slop like rain. Britannia could care. The lady might shed a stone tear. But crochets in the street get scoreless; guys restless and tooling with the gun or knife. Younger and younger.

Sunday, and the same surrender. The same people going to

29

church. The same old thing. Weary black folk going headlong to their god. Singing in their little church. Singing that makes them not so sad. And they read scripture. And listen the sermon. And pray. But their god never saying nada. Or their god whispers low, making it too hard for them to hear. So they believe the pastor. Their god speaks to the pastor in a language only pastor can know. Or so he says. And they believe him. They put money in pastor's pocket. At one little black church the pastor had flying lessons then bought a helicopter from church money and the churchgoers said 'Thank God!' And only a few years back a black pastor got caught leaving Heathrow, tall with a Stetson, hauling a suitcase of cash.

Some guys get a gun to point with. Last month one guy zapped a younger guy because him wear de same make of dark-glasses, cramping dat cold street eye.

Chapter 10

Jimmy visiting at noon. London Zoo and asphalt for clouds in the sky. Today a cage-bar is what what. Cage, a room for wildness mullioned by steel. Later will be Arleene; Jimmy will check Arleene tonight. But as much as for the lions this zoo is for penguins. Here, penguins ignite a wet cabaret. And yet. In one bad dream somebody got a sight of lions going home to the plains. Talk is, some nights the keepers here toss a live cow in with the tigers.

A one-off girl coming to the penguin space. Jimmy clocks the girl as she clocks him. He could laugh. But only half laughs, nods, thinking of a penguin cabaret. The girl's eyes check the penguins. Her eyes say 'Dive!' She will not understand, but Jimmy won't care. The flip-side back. Brixton back. His cigarette burning on the ground. And quiet, his feet click. Not feet that tap-dance, but quickening feet. Chasing spit from fire.

The girl's eyes are clear. Bevel eyes. But not smiling. Jimmy tries a smile. He knows she knows. The bevel eyes of the girl know. Turning from the mirror in her face he wants to get away. But the wet penguin-space saying 'No way!'

Jimmy a music man. Saying *composer* could make music seem cold. But it should be easy to get a song here, a tune to grab a zoo day. Leonard Bernstein would have done it. Nobody moved on jazz opera since Lenny. He'd run the cheetahs and mull the whole thing for just one minute before getting a sliced theme; a jazz theme way down the road from West Side Story. Bernstein would see deep at a zoo. He would have called it loud here, yelling *Cage Side Story*.

Or Mingus. Charles Mingus with a right hand of thunder. He would tear this zoo apart. Elephants would chase the shock wave. Hands big as industrial lifting gear, but Mingus dead, built in de old ground. And Lenny polishing city clay.

Bevel-eyes on guard, the girl bites into a toffee-apple. Jimmy lights a new smoke, and already phased tobacco stacking like a black brassiere. The girl like she from a song, like from Lennon and MacCartney. It's hard, him trying to pin her down. Or even guess her name. She a Michelle? No, she too set for that. And not Julia. And no Lucy. Her bones are not fused to fossil fire. This is not a girl scratching her groin. Maybe she the one the guy in the song wanting to hold hands with.

This it! Jimmy checking it. She Rigby. The bevel-eyed girl is Eleanor Rigby.

But this can *not* be. She solo, something about her saying she dreams in fairytales. In a card-pack she'd be the Ten of Diamonds. To Jimmy, her laugh is F-sharp, so song, elliptic. Her name should be Mona. No way she is not Mona Rigby. Somewhere in the zoo a lion growl.

The girl slings the apple core. She 21, maybe 23. A girl like this can go any place. And maybe she's up for jazz. Some other loner would tap her shoulder, light, asking if she walked from a convent. But Jimmy checks the time. Maybe this girl only here to gaze at people going by. Lonely people. But if that's all she doing, a watcher, polite and plain, but only a counter of lonely people, then that would like that madness down Oxford Street; she'd be head of the millennium sales queues if she only a watcher here.

Mona spools the penguins. The way her heart takes to them she would live wet. She girl-bugging Jimmy. Quiet, he checks the time. Again. Wants to get away. The least of it is Arleene. Arleene waiting up the motorway for Jimmy. But something about the bevel eyes of a girl on a zoo day makes it hard to walk away. Her bevel eyes stream over penguins like a searchlight.

Getting closer to Eleanor's pretend-daughter, his throat clears. "The, er, millennium festival, I think it will be like a woman on new year's day."

Mona right. Then left. Quick. She turns right again. Not sure. Somebody talk to her? Not easy to set such eyes, not as before. Those eyes are not searchlights. For a flicker her eyes could chase sparrowhawks through countryside. But her eyes decide on Jimmy. Realizing this a chat-up, a sly one, she smiles. A searchlight smile on her puzzling face.

"It was you, wasn't it?" she says, trying to read him. "You said that!"

"Yeah, me."

"Where's it come from?"

"What'd you mean?"

"Festivals. How the hell can festivals be like a woman!"

Jimmy wanting to answer. But talking lets him down. It's the girl's question. Her question takes him by surprise. Her lips get in the way of what he could say. Her lips testing him. She waits, want-

32

ing something. 'Answer me!' her bevel eyes say.

"Well," he laughs, "everybody checks festivals."

"You a festival-head, carnivals and all that?"

"Festive stuff is OK. The ones with fireworks do it for me. But the big one, that'll be new year's day. Guys goggling at gunpowder in the air. Makes me think of handrails or a woman, yeah, something to haul with out the cold."

"What?"

"Handrails," Jimmy says, "or women."

Mona blinks. At sea, young, glazed, dazed. "Look!" she says, annoyed.

Jimmy laughs. "You want me to look at you?"

Brows hooked, her bevel eyes blink. "It's the way you talk. I mean, *nobody* talks like you. Not even close. I've never heard anybody talk like you before. What's this about?"

His shoulders heave. Half-heave. Then set. Set high. The girl's head levels with Jimmy's shoulders and he wonders if she was a little taller or less plain if there'd be an animal's mother to deal with. "From your face," he says, shoulders curled, "you're lagging behind what you want."

"What I *want*?"

"Yep."

"Hey, what's this about? Are you a fortuneteller?"

"Fortuneteller? I don't believe that stuff. You?"

"Then what are you saying?"

"It's your eyes. You're a serious woman but you have a long way to go. There's things you don't know."

"Nobody knows everything. But I'm sure *you* do!"

"There's keepers," Jimmy half nods, "and there's what gets kept."

"The animals? They have a great time."

"So you say."

"They obviously get looked after. It's about conservation, isn't it? Zoos keep the rarer species going."

"Politicos talk that stuff, hammer it. You never hear them? Hypocrites talking happy democracies, stuff that'll never hack it. There's always knee-deep bull to wade through. These animals are a sideshow."

"If not the animals, what were you thinking?"

"I was thinking, well, you know what I mean."

33

"No!"

"I was thinking things, the way things pan out."

"Like what?"

"If it wasn't for these penguins, I wouldn't be here in the first place."

"The bit about the millennium, what's that about?"

"It's where the hypocrites arrive."

"Oh, that!"

"What more can I say? What did you want me to say?"

Elephants can not run. They always walk. They can get the speed of a horse. But even then the elephant is walking fast, not running. A giraffe can run all day long. But a lion can not do that.

Mona smiles. Quiet, her bevel eyes smile. "Tell me about fireworks. You like fireworks."

"And I like women, right?"

Shy, she grins. "Yeah, I can tell."

"You can tell?"

"Yes. You play the field. It's all over you, you wicked!"

"Wicked?"

"Yes."

"Why?"

"Oh come on!"

"Where're we off to?"

"Tell me all about women."

"Well, wicked is not where I would start."

Mona's head shakes. "Then start at the start."

"The start? Where's that?"

Weary, the girl wilts. Suddenly slimmer. And quiet. Slow, her bevel eyes check the cloud stack. "Can I ask a question? Why're you always looking up at the sky? What's it about? Got your magic carpet on its way?"

"It's the rain," Jimmy blinks. "Rain makes me think of nakedness."

"Clouds, I can handle."

"Magic carpets?"

"Yes, I could even do a few magic carpets. But not kites. Anything but kites!"

"The millennium itself is only a kite."

"What?"

34

"Kites. Not much to say about stuff with strings attached."

Mona looks round. Deeper dazed. This the weirdest day in her life. She looks round again. A quiet journey starts in her eyes. Jimmy knows. This is man-travel. This what happens when a woman gives a man good luck. Travel it, girl, travel it!

After a minute Mona's back from her journey. Got the answer. Her lips lick. Lips that set and, before she tells, the look in her eye makes Jimmy worry what she might tell.

"Kites scare me," she says.

"I don't know how kites ever got into this."

"That hoo-hah about millenniums! So silly! It'll be hugely expensive, fireworks and all the rest of it. And the fact that nothing will have changed will be a *horrible* let down. You'll see."

Wooden, Jimmy knows the girl disappointed; she expected more from him. But she knows nothing about him.

"What's going on?"

"How d'you mean?" he shrugs.

"What's this about? If you want to ask me out, why not ask me?"

"Well, yeah, you are it. Beautiful."

"*Not* beautiful."

"No, seriously. You are."

"Look, I'll have to go in a minute. You interested or not?"

Jimmy tries again, low this time. "With music," he says, "composing music is there all the time for me. Music gets places kites never reach. And it shakes the crap out of kite-flyers, chucks them round like rubbish in a hurricane."

Puzzling, Mona steps back. Elephants can't run, they only walk? And soon, she's giggling. She giggles the kind of private time where a secret adjusts. This goes on a while. Sometimes her eyelids move as if dreaming and, next thing, she must know where Jimmy will go after the zoo. He can tell; she a serious woman, a worrier, not the kind to carry cement on a building site. He tells her that jazz his thing. And she already knows that most people have never been to Brixton. But he won't ask why she's scared of kites; no time, not for the jolting answer she might give.

"People can come from only one place at a time," Jimmy says.

"Where does jazz come from?"

"The scent of jasmine in a brothel."

"Jazz?"

"Yeah, it can come from any place. Anything. You could be catching a bus or notice somebody scared."

"What?"

"Rivers always have some place to go."

"Rivers?"

"Yeah."

"Why pick on rivers?"

"Ask your coach-driver."

"What?"

"The coach-driver brought you here. But he must get you back."

"Look, I haven't got a clue what you're on about."

"Try a man and woman," Jimmy grins.

"What?"

"A man and lady, doing the business."

"*What*?"

"There's only one best place they can go."

"I've never come across the likes of you before. Never!"

"A man and woman have one great place to be alone."

"And where's *that*?"

"The river. Any river."

"Because?"

"Rivers go down to the sea."

"What?"

"Yeah, they meander down. Got to get to the sea."

Calm now, Mona's starting to love the zoo day. She laughs. "The banks of the old Thames, that must be the place, then!"

Listening the girl laugh, Jimmy could close eyes here. She makes him almost change his mind over Arleene. Fresh linen back at the flat and this girl will never carry cement.

"How did ever Brixton get to be like it's my name?"

"Be serious!" she says.

"I'm not serious?"

"No, you want a chip on your shoulder."

Jimmy extends a cigarette. Mona's lips pucker. She's never smoked. But something about Brixton worries her. Looking quickly round, she will try explaining. Jimmy lights up.

She is no poet, but tries. "The Thames, it's so _"

"Dolphins swim in the Thames," Jimmy says.

"And poo floats on it. Half of London's raw sewage breaks into

36

the river after a bout of rain. It's something to do with the drains, clapped-out old drains from the nineteenth century."

"Yeah, I saw something on TV."

"So *that* river is definitely not the place for a smooch. Gross!"

"Well, you could always get people away from the city. Send them somewhere else."

"And dead bodies float in the Thames. Charming!"

Somewhere in the British Museum, a manuscript in Nile papyrus. One of the pyramids holds a mortgage on the solar system; that's the talk going on between two guys beside Jimmy and Mona.

Mona says she works in PR. Why a job like that? She says PR means mastering lots and lots. Like? Oh, everything from chainsaws to fashion. Quiet, Jimmy turns away. Checking the wet penguins.

"What are you thinking?" she says. "Say something!"

"Like what?"

"Say you mean it."

"Mean what?"

"Chatting me up. That's what this is, isn't it?"

"Hey, dolphins are great."

"Stop it!"

"Dolphins are beautiful as you."

"If you don't stop, then I'm leaving!"

"The idea of dolphins going past Tower Bridge and, well, _"

"Swimming in poo?"

"Yeah."

"That's life," Mona shrugs.

"Yeah, that's it. So hard to take."

"Yes."

Jimmy stubs the smoke. "Next time some idiot talks crap about boatloads of immigrants, tell them about the Thames after rain."

"Immigrants?"

"Yes."

"They come in by the planeload these days."

"My father's an immigrant. I was born here but some days I feel exactly like an immigrant."

A nervy cough escapes the heart in the girl's mouth. Quiet, quiet, very sorry, her bevel eyes are hazel mist. Her voice lowers. Her eyes are older. Quiet eyes. "Sorry," she whispers. "Honestly, I'm

37

sorry. I know what you mean."

Jimmy hates this. Hates to see the girl get cut. He should get her
back on track. Like maybe even get her away from here. In pain,
her eyes search the penguins. Quiet, he says her name must be
Mona Rigby. But her head shakes. No, she says, her name is too ordinary and it would be too big a letdown after Mona Rigby. Not one
eyelid bats as Jimmy tells her his full name. And, to test her, he
admits it. Jimmy admits being a predator, got a woman waiting;
grinning, he says the woman is far up the motorway. Mona asks if
the woman black or white. Jimmy says there's other options and if
it wasn't for Arleene he could spend the day with a Mona Rigby.
Blushing, she turns away. Shy, smiling.

Laughing quiet, but a woman's whole life in her quiet laugh.
"And after the zoo," she shakes her head, "we'd go back to your
place?"

A loner could listen a laugh like this. The girl's laugh so close.
Yet more far than near, like at sea. But Jimmy can tell. Fairytale or
no fairytale, she loves the sea. She can sail or crew a yacht. Go solo
or navigate. Somebody like Mona can go the whole ocean alone, or
get there with somebody galloping her like a mare. Jimmy wants to
get her away. But.

Her friends get back. They've done their excursion and want to sit
on the coach and chat, but now her friends are back. Closer and
closer, they gathering round. And tug. Jimmy steps back. They
tease the Mona girl away. And all the while they know she's not
ready to go. But they eke her with them. Her eyes say she can not
go, not yet.

Quiet, she looks over her shoulder. Looking back already. Jimmy
wondering if her friends thought of Brixton, seeing her in the frame
with him. Sad and too torn, her bevel eyes saying goodbye one final
time.

"Sorry," she says, moving away with her crowd, "got to go. Hope
you get there, you know, wherever. And good luck with it, whatever!"

Spit cut the ground. Jimmy grabs a smoke, watching the girl fade
to her crowd. Her home crowd. He will never see her again. Elephants can walk as fast as a horse can gallop. A quiet nod, and
Jimmy alone by penguin water. Checking the time.

Chapter 11

In Keats' poem, autumn is for watching weather play. But autumn can be beat up or flat copper, and shedding a leaf for dead-eyed folk with garden shears. If the sun gets too ripe it will not set on a greengrocer's stall.

Today the jobs' pages dried up for Jimmy. From now it's no ganja. Spliff time elides. Even cigarettes must cut way back. Charlie Parker did that business. That guy was sax over air, the oxygen fiend. He moved to journey's end with no set percussion and no fuss, just a tenor sax and autumn swirling a leaf. Charlie inhaled just one time and, all these years down the road, he still tags weather; every leaf belongs to him, every leaf faltering or fluttering like sail. His life was a swathe of Paddington train-crashes.

For one hour Jimmy plays Drifting On A Reed. Maybe because JJ Johnson is on this track with Charlie. JJ was the first guy to bebop trombone. Funny thing for a piano player, but trombone was the first thing Jimmy tried to play. And it was never the lung power, the monk-like to bulk with Olympic lungs, or even the way Jack Teegarden talks whisky from the slide. It was the clown side to playing it. One day Jimmy jotted a reason down on the back of a record sleeve. 'Playing trombone,' the note says, 'is not the kind of thing most people could do and keep a straight face, not while a room full of nice looking women are looking at you. So it's piano from now. And piano means you don't look up halfway through a solo and catch people reading your life.'

The playing on Drifting On A Reed is a neat conversation. Jimmy thinking of Arleene and that day she was going down the street two years back. Drifting On A Reed plays like that chat with Arleene.

'Well,' Jimmy said, and it was one autumn day like today, 'mmm, what's your name?' Arlene saying nada, did not reply, her head holding high, she was way too proud. That day was easy in autumn leaf so Jimmy tried a new tack, pointing at leaves. Arleene was trying to move fast but could not get away. So she turned round. But then surprised herself. Because, well, all of a sudden her lips smiled, her heady lips said 'OK, so you want to play, so play!' Jimmy laughed. Yep, getting to play that woman that same day. And Arleene can play. Every now and then it's play-that-woman time. Play note after note, note, note.

Jimmy being a music man means things can never be like two trains colliding. Not at Paddington, not any place. It's three days since the first ambulance got to the crash scene. Now some slick railroad official with a notebook is making a tally, writing the dead and talking weasel. Industrial cleaners are at the crash site still. A big industrial sponge wipes that caked blood away. 31 people dead, 400 wounded. One train, and it is a bad business. But not two. Not two trains. Not on rails.

Nobody is good as Bud Powell. Not on bebop piano. On Drifting On A Reed, Bud Powell keeps set with Charlie P all day. To those guys it didn't matter if it's cars or women, or a room of women, or only autumn, a blue note was there.

Someone said angels could be real. If angels are out there then they can carry a condolence message. Angels can pull weather like a woman. They can assemble sunshine. But music can do that. On this track playing one more time, Charlie solos a message through the sax.

Last week should have been rehearsals for Minims. And there was a hot midnight gig. It would have been good money for two days work. But Jimmy did not show. He was alone, standing at the window and wondering.

One job advert stands out. It's in the sales pages today: *£1000/week. No experience necessary.*

A girl's voice jumps down the line. The voice sounds like she can hurdle. This is new. But for Jimmy it's hard work trying to make out what she says. Her voice sounds like a whisky woman, like a true singer, a voice moving from swing to ballads with no delay. Money will not count here. Not compared with the voice. For Jimmy the thing is only about the girl's voice now. Maybe she's heard Astrud Gilberto sing, but she won't stop gabbing. She sounds like a hurdler reading post-it notes on a running track. Or maybe she's set in Piccadilly Circus, bouncing a trampoline, like with her mobile in one hand and knickers waving high in air.

Finally, finally! The girl out of breath. And when Jimmy asks for the gist, she swallows. But in a blink she's gearing, ready to start all over. Looks like this could be a waste-of-time job. But that's not what she says. And, oh, nothing else is like it anywhere; this is a once in a lifetime opportunity, loadsamoney, *gorgeous* benefits,

40

but, no, she can not say what this means, not at the moment, but nobody sane would pass up meeting some great people, *unbelievable* go-getters.

Jimmy is not looking for a career. And that's why the whirly girl got to talk. Well, mostly. He will go to the interview and size the size of the money. But it was the voice. Must see who owns it, a voice that jumps like a water-hose in a hot town square. The girl's voice is like Brazil, a coast town in Brazil where somebody sits for a lifetime seeing women walk. Coast towns like Belem in the north, or Porto Alegre down south.

Maybe this explains Astrud Gilberto. For a long time Jimmy used to believe Astrud was black, singing the way she sings on tracks like Vivo Sonhando. Or the way she croons The Shadow of Your Smile. It was a big surprise seeing that picture of a white woman on a CD. A white woman with ocean in her voice. And rum. But that is Astrud.

The voice of the phone girl makes Jimmy get set. Music waits for a voice like that. Maybe she a singer already, a jazz-lone, maybe a little down on luck, but crazy, making ends meet by temping the phone. She wants it to happen. Behind that hurdling is a great music eye. The girl wants to prove her cut. Maybe she sings in a nightclub already. Somewhere safe. But her voice is set with hills. Or maybe she's got roots in Jamaica, like maybe her parents come from there. Or maybe she all white, English white.

Chapter 12

It was 1975. The single-blade disposable razor arrived. And in London, the National Front set a huge street demo against Britain integrating with Europe; they waved their banners and beat their drum, chanting 'Get the reds!' Nathan was welding steel in Liverpool dry dock, working 6 days a week.

Nathan had brought a map from Jamaica. And that map was how Jimmy got named.

They folded it in an old dictionary that they still have in Liverpool. But why they bother keeping it is one story by itself. The map fell to the ground two days after he was born. It was never more than a sketch, line upon line connecting Jamaica to England. A straight-line map, cut on a longtime while Nathan was whiling away in Kingston in the 60s.

Jamaica got independence from England in 1962. But to some Jamaicans it was like sitting round after a crash. Nuf worry. Nobody know what happ'n. One day Nathan draw de line dem by han'.

It was money. Or it was education. Any England was a better life. For Nathan it was only the money. Pounds sterling used to carry class those days. But it was timing more than anything. The time was right to quit the sun.

Nathan was a Jamaica trumpet man. Nobody could hold a key better. Just like Dizzy Gillespie, what key they wanted was never a problem. He was cut for jazz. But England was not the best move to make. White guys used to fly to Kingston all the time, looking for music this, getting a deal for that; smart guys. Something was happening with Jamaican music and that's how they got Bob Marley. Eventually. But back then Jamaican music was more trouble to the English than music coming out of America. Jamaican music more African than blues or jazz. And mostly because of Bob, eventually, Jamaica music got naked with white folk in England.

Ska? Way before Bob. *Way* before. And blue-beat. Rock-steady. And guys like Prince Buster. But when they talked session-work to Nathan, it was guys getting paid ten times more in England than Kingston. And if it wasn't for bad luck Nathan would be ace today. In the 60s he was a hungry man in Kingston, and nobody could see more than one step at a time.

But side by side with the money was negative news from England. Race flared up in Birmingham, London, Manchester, race. Ructions over housing and jobs. When the word from England was bad, it was a bad alligator all day. But one theme got back to Jamaica. It was English folk an' dem animal; a England dem have dog in a de house. In the house? In a de house! Not the yard? No, de house! Some English folk would spend twenty minutes in a pet food queue but never two seconds to shake hands with a black man. Wanting to arrive in the middle of that was a weird move. Nathan and his generation admit that now. But that is history. Or so the man says. Nathan was set for the England idea and some of that racial business was not that true anyway. He says that now, being cool, wanting to make out he was never too big a glutton for punishment. He will be here till next year. Nathan will be sixty next year. And sixty is not old in Jamaica.

In the 60s, America was the big other place to England. But big time segregation was there. Redneck yankee keep dem dog in a de backyard, not de house, but black man still ha' fe back down to white. So England was the place. Even the Atlantic did not figure. Crossing that sulking ocean was no problem, crossing it the other direction that African slaves had crossed it.

One day the whiling was over. Nathan made it over the water in summer 1965. Harold Wilson was prime minister one year already. Jimmy was born in Liverpool ten years later while Harold Wilson was doing a second stint in Downing Street.

Nathan was 35 when Jimmy was born. It was to the 17 year old daughter of a black family from Liverpool. And right from the hospital Jimmy grabbed for music. That was clear. Home was a small council house on the Wirral and Charlie Parker was playing on the Blue Spot with everybody milling round, looking. They knew. No way this boy would ever want to be governor of The Bank of England. He was a music man already.

The next thing was a name. And that's was when the ruction started. Noise, getting a name, shouting.

One side of the family would choose a name and play around with it a while. Same thing for the other side. Everybody looking for the best name. And the first best name was Moses.

Moses was a name with mission, somebody said, it was from water, from the warrior part of the bible. But Nathan trumped that,

43

saying the boy better get called Miles. *Miles*? Yeah, a name out front. And that was that. Well, that's how it was for the hour. *Miles*? No, dat too white a Englan'. Everybody knows Miles Davis but in England somebody getting called Miles would have to squeeze a lemon to get near the sun. A black guy getting called Miles would get laughed at here; white folk would laugh at black Miles. So Nathan built a spliff. He was going through a Dizzy Gillespie and Art Tatum phase, so *Dizzy* and *Art* got up there as two. Then it was Cannonball. And Ellington, Thelonious. But folk would not understand somebody getting named any of that in England.

Then they tried *Kingston*. Kingston Dell was it for a while. It had a shout. Loud or slow, it had a shout. But. After a while they knew. It was too far loose in England to get called after some Jamaican place; too backward looking. A dat dem seh.

In the end it was going to be down to drawing lots. But then the name got solved. The right name was set. It was the map.

It happened by pure chance. The map dropped out of the dictionary and, quiet, everybody was stock silent. Nice quiet. That little map was on the ground and everybody quiet. This was bigger than luck, somebody said; it was how it should be. And that was it. Because after all the shouts and shouting down, the coming and going, Jimmy got named after lines on a wishful map. Jimmy-Lines Dell. And Hendrix was part of the credit. Or blame. The whole business is only lines in the sand. But Jimmy going along now.

First thing was a music degree. Learning fugues and counterpoint was some of the neatest directions anywhere. That music degree was way up there. But the whole academic thing kicked off with theology. Yeah. Hard for anybody to believe, knowing Jimmy, but theology was it at the start. That theology stuff still comes home. But after a year of it there was nothing but jester ground, nothing to think. It was OK to swap the course, and Jimmy went straight off to music. The music department was rational. 'Why music? Why now?' the admissions dean asked. And Jimmy blinked, saying that theology was just a bunch of marking time. The dean nodded, saying that anybody can get a machine to mark time; even a budgie can set a metronome to mark time, she said. That music degree was the best thing to happen. Working on Bach was the best part. And now if only one advice Jimmy can give it must be that anybody wanting to compose should check Ellington as much as Bach. When it

44

comes to music for money, that is session work. And one-gig bands. But the real deal is composing. This is special. Composing is for nervy people, the ones down the road even to their own shadow.

The rest of the way has been up and down. Nothing to write home about. Nothing far enough out front. Stopgap job after job, ants stirring when the money dries up. But travelling is the full ten by ten. And woman. And just because of the wildness that happens, that stuff never ever gets written home about.

Next is the grey place, the in-between, the hypocrite snake. And running up and down eight floors of a loud tenement. Taking the lift gives the tenement a pose. But sunlight triumphs in the sky. The sun is never tame. By checking out A Brief History of Time, Jimmy knows that now. And some days somebody can get as far inside a quiet woman's eye as sunlight.

Jimmy's generation got the vote when John Major was prime minister. But John was only two slow left feet, somebody that should have been testing lettuces in a factory. He was never the kind to crack a maths puzzle or score a rugby try, or gun a rally car through ice. To Jimmy's peers, John should have tried cricket umpiring, or gone after that lettuce job. John says he was born in Brixton. But he never had spit to say about black folk that walk hand in hand as a family on the pavement.

Now Blair, the bible boy. He been gigging the Dispatch Box two and a half years already. They say he can play guitar. Word is, some days he puts aside his law books to pick up a Buddy Holly songsheet and strum Peggy Sue through and through.

Chapter 13

Yesterday the girl on the phone said the interview assumes suits and ties. But Jimmy will go anyway. No suit. And no tie. A northerly wind gusts the streets. And autumn looking like a bout of flu. For one whole hour only traffic to chide. Taking a chance, he turns off the high road.

This is a tree-lined avenue. A sudden quiet. Everything is reserved here. Nobody would ever connect this easy place to traffic. A straight roadway. The avenue whispers by in a blaze of trees.

The trees are different. A few show off by glistening. But all have something deeper than being a tree. And that's because the people in the avenue love them. Jimmy moving it, looking them over like he was invited. The avenue says 'Forget the interview, stop the car and get some quiet. Look, see!'

Isaac Newton was on the radio earlier. It was that status thing Isaac had with Leibniz, the huge maths between them. Looks like Leibniz was right. He was ahead of Isaac in some things. Leibniz said how even the smallest thing will have the whole vision of the world. But Isaac unpacked a prism one day. And a laser in his head flashed. 'Good God!' he must have said. The prism in his hand un-twined light. Then carded it like wool. And that's because all along light was only a weave. That's what Isaac could see; all along light was never white, it was a weave of coloured thread. Lovelorn, shy in front of the naked universe, Isaac looked bleary at the prism. Then fondles it some more. Then ambled to one window to scan. And clear tears from his eye. Isaac knows that nothing can be the same again, the sun especially. The sky was no longer virgin. Isaac seeing light was truly mystic now, even more than a woman, and he started a song to the star. He wanted to undress light one more time. All it took was a prism in his sweating hand.

The car stops. Jimmy checks. Fingers tap the steering wheel and quietly click. Must have been a buzz seeing light get close, beautiful and naked. A wide grin and Jimmy's voice starts: 'Hey light, don't be shy. Take off the rest of it! Come on, I've seen it all before. What, you want me to turn the light off?'

The piece on the radio did not put the story that way. Jimmy bolt upright, laughing. Everybody knows what happened to Isaac under that apple tree one day, but the radio philosopher covered that
46

ground one more time. Then it was the turn of the prism.

Looking round, checking autumn in the avenue, Jimmy knows the story's been only half told. Newton could have done things with autumn. That's because lots more leaves fall than apples. A trillion leaf for one apple. And most women would want to talk autumn more than apples. Even Eve. So Isaac could have arrived at gravity quicker. Like if maybe he was out walking a headstrong woman one autumn, a smart woman. Way smart.

The woman would say, 'Something or other obviously accounts for leaves falling, but light is deeper.' Quiet, Isaac stops. Sulking now, he would ask why. 'Dear Isaac,' she'd say, 'don't think I'm trying to be Eve, oh don't think I want my private little Eden, but it's not normal to pull light down like little apples in a garden.'

And Isaac say, 'But I am Newton!"

'But of course!' she say.

Isaac growl, 'Here, take this little prism. It will remind you.'

'Remind me?' she say. 'Of what?'

Sweating, Isaac would say, 'Well, I can run the whole cosmos round. Because of gravity and, yes, this little prism, the whole universe is only a coach and horses to me, a mere machine. Here, take the reins!'

A cigarette in Jimmy's hand. Music is here. Somebody could do opera over this. They could call it Newton And The Woman. That Mozart could have done it; Newton's thoughts must have reached Wolfgang. Or maybe he would not have bothered, maybe supposing he was bigger than Newton. But Isaac must have left a note somewhere, a neater equation stacked, showing autumn connecting to what makes apples fall. To any muso, even a simple as the Presto from the Divertimento plays the same ballpark as how gravity hangs the universe.

Jimmy wants to touch. One bay window in the avenue is high with autumn, bronze leaves troubling the rim of a glass vase. The cigarette lights. Jimmy flat broke, should be hurrying for a job interview but this place is bigger than that.

After the avenue the rest of the journey is a blur. Somebody else would head straight to Newton's tomb to check what was said there but Jimmy shoots the car into an air hole. And the CD volume high. The road is clear, moving along, muso scatting.

Then a weird sign. It cuts the roundabout. The logo does not boast. But it wants to star. Somebody bolted this sign over a dizzy stairway. And that was a definite moron. The sign comes straight down from a grinning door that somebody believes looks prophetic. A metallic orange sign, saying, *Homes, Homes & Homes*.

Chapter 14

The girl at the reception winks. To Jimmy she looks like the wine-bar girl that always waves. But this girl is the hurdler, the one on the phone yesterday. She guesses who he is. Maybe because of the no tie. Her eyes tease. She is not content here. She nods when asked if she ever listens to Brazilian love songs. One empty seat is in the reception area.

Her heart will harden. Behind the reception desk she learns the tease game, too fast. Suddenly her voice does not matter to Jimmy. Too much is in her eye already. She's maybe twenty six but should get told why teasing is a bad mistake. But Jimmy will not climb bitch-mountain to preach, saying he is no painter.

Her eyebrows arch. "What's that to me?"

"A painter would take care of you," he says. "Out there there's ace painters waiting to get at the art in your face, that yearning."

"So what?"

His head shakes. Looking round the squat reception area, odd-job faces gaze back. Empty face after face. Most of the chairs don't belong in a reception area and Jimmy takes the one empty seat. But not at ease, shuffling already. This is nerves. Wanting to leave.

"Would you all like to come this way," a woman's voice says. She glides past the screen near the reception desk. She wears it well, wears a spick olive suit that wants to smudge the pale yellow of the screen. "I've kept you all waiting. It's been a terrible, terrible 2 o'clock, I'm so sorry! We'll just be a minute more, not to worry. We'll get acquainted in a minute. One little minute."

As one, everybody looks past the woman. They look at the wall clock. The clock shows twenty past two. This slick woman is a big dresser. But she does not connect. Most people here thinking she looks like a TV chat-show host. Paparazzi could film rolls of this woman. And everybody getting cut by the loud tinkling; the woman's earrings make a baubling noise. Big globes, these are the biggest earrings in London. On any woman any place else, earrings this big would be heartless.

Earrings clattering, she heads the way to an airy room. Most guys here already know. This woman likes it hot. She likes rhythm, hot and lots. A woman with these earrings, well, she could keep time with a rock-band. But not past limits. That's because with what a bebop drummer can do, or a bebop bass player, well, that's just too much bop for this woman to ever keep time. Then again. Maybe she's not for razzle. Maybe she's never got naked to real rhythm, hard or soft. Maybe she is eye-line, liking to look. And one thing is sure. She wants to get gazed at. Her earrings could be like ride-cymbals. Max Roach could set them clinking; 5-4 over 3-4, and, wait, syncopation, get dem ear tings ding! Maybe she's the kind of woman that goes to Land's End to watch birds migrate. Hitch a ride, woman. Hitch a ride!

Strict at the head of the room, she says, "I am Colette Core. I'm the sales manager at Homes, Homes & Homes. I started where you all are. And that's plain scared, apprehensive. I was a single mother, a little single mum with a part-time partner. Bills everywhere. That was six years ago. So relax everybody, I've been there. Please, relax. I'm on the board here."

Close as looking will allow, every guy eyes Colette. Her name could be Maybeline; she should have a country & western name. Something about the way she holds herself. This is cut to order. It will never block being a woman. She is huge danger. And every guy here likes that. She's maybe thirty-eight. But could be more. Her body holds her clothes to order. A bozo model practicing for years would not pull it off. But right alongside all that is something else. Colette is part tabloid. Her clothes come from good cloth, but they are a show-off. Her hips dip to spread on a table edge.

"Nothing like gender matters around here," she says. "We don't care where you come from. You, your parents, anyone. We want good people. Only people who can communicate. The first lesson is to know what our customers want. Are you with me? That's how we achieve our goals."

Everybody upright in a chair.

Colette sips water, lazy but wary. Her eyes cut to every face in the room. "Look," she says, "when I started here our turnover was under two million pounds. Last year, we did 14 million. This year we'll hit 16. Yes, that's 2 mill sunny side up! All the experts said you couldn't do it, the so-called experts, they all said it can't be done. Know what? I can't stand clever people. What do they know? *Anything* is possible! We're looking to share our success. Want to work hard? Yes? Then we want you! I mean, work hard *all day*! The rewards are here. Everyone of you can earn fifty grand a year, anything! Is there anyone here who can't work hard enough to enjoy a thousand pounds a week?"

A woman's middle-class voice butts in, calm but set. "What do we do to earn it?"

Everybody turns round. They must check this out. Must check out the completion in the voice. A class act. Her hair is close cropped. What's she doing here? She cropped that hair to get forgiven? What's she done? She a Schumann woman? Jimmy knows if she ever listens to jazz then it's Brubeck or Stan Getz. Maybe she can play some instrument, even piano. Or she can play lute. Something solo about her. Something bitter. Or she can make music instruments. Or the lute was what turned her into a cropped-hair, closing her eyes at home to listen Gregorian chants. But she's a class act, way out on her own in a room where women outnumber men by over two to one. Colette does not like her.

Cropped-hair tries again. "The person on the phone, quite a pleasant girl, but it was all very cloak-and-daggerish. Can't you tell us what the job entails? Could we start with how the earnings come about? I so need to know the facts."

"What's the problem?" Colette gags, her eyes are Venetian blinds. "Aren't you all salespeople?"

Thick quiet clogs the room. And somebody getting queasy, remembering a boat trip one night. It was on the English Channel. And on the way back was utter queasiness because of the water; looking at the wind on water was what caused the problem. The deep water was black, deep, deep black, its own creature, able to ride its own back. And only water can ever do that. Seasickness was on the boat. And a drunk shouted, 'Don't look at the sea! Focus on the stars!' And somebody shouted straight back, 'Where the fuck are the stars!'

The weather forecast this morning was satellite shots. London warmer than Athens, and Malaga hot all day. Then Sydney. In less than a year the Olympics will be in Sydney. And that means class, getting a chance to show who you. That is sports genius. Guys like Michael Johnson, Haile Gebreselassie.

This group-interview is getting like a queasy boat ride. Looks like the way to the money is over water. Only a minute back, the room was all Colette. Now it's dizz. Only one open-water swimmer here. And that is the old sales hand, a wary guy pushing sixty. This man

51

will have seen the likes of this before. Turning round, wry in eye, he is like the voice that cried 'Where the fuck are the stars!'

"Looks like we're wasting our time," he says, standing now. "The job advert said *No experience necessary*. The papers must have got it wrong."

Colette's hand shoots the air. "Hang on. Just a sec. There's got to be a mistake. Bet your sweet life if there's a mistake we'll refund your expenses. Yes, you get to get your travelling expenses. We'll have this sorted in a sec. One minute, no more."

As she quits the room the old sales hand whistles, slow. A whistle grabbing at the boss woman. Even the expert suit does not disguise the balance of hips. But 22 suspicious people quiet in a suspicious room where nothing is getting said.

Eventually, throats clear. Random chats start. Choking talk. But nobody walks. And nobody will talk of symmetry. What's that symmetry doing here? The doorway sliced it. It sliced Colette's woman symmetry as she went through it. She was made for pirates. A pirate taking a beach somewhere would take her body down. A pirate could heave-ho, row dat boatload body bay.

A rhythm in Jimmy's head. But the folk here won't care. Woman rhythm. Her rhythm lingers. Everybody worried by the room. Nobody here wants consolation, nobody waiting for transport fares. This is money time. That grand a week, now.

Folk in the room are a job-lot, weird people and hungry. Only halfhearted chats continue. Guff patched. Student types square off with middle-aged. Everybody going through hard times. One guy looks like a big time bank manager visiting a country fair. And some here are too mishmash to cut. Jimmy accepts that maybe he's the weird one of all. Some are under twenty, nervy, joking. Three big on grey hair. Some do not want to talk. And maybe only the cropped-hair woman is worth talking to anyway. One girl trashing the whole room just to take her coat off. She looks for something to see through the window. But only cars are out there, all from the up-side of the market, gleaming through a smudged afternoon. Jimmy's hand in his jacket, stroking the postcard Lorna Stanley passed him at the zoo.

Chapter 15

Colette moves one step before the spent man. This a drinking hombre, grey with a gait breaking down and jump-starts, short strides with no knee-lift, not the type that was ever fit. His aftershave chugs the room. Then the iced champagne grin. His gaze tells the women they already in his eye.

Colette turns to the room. "This is Mr Core. Our MD. He'll say a few words."

"Afternoon," the man grins, congratulating the room with sharp applause. "Good afternoon! Welcome, welcome. It's Clive Core. Clive. Apologies for the mix-up. All my fault."

Something wrong. Nice looking goods through the wall-to-wall window; picture-framed by burnished glass is a white Porsche and a red Maserati dovetailing a yellow Bentley in the car park. Then the easy tailoring on the woman. And bespoke suit on the man. But the place itself looks clunked, not talking success. Nothing wise is here. Nothing is reserved because of good taste. The Bentley could be green, blue or black, anything but yellow. And the Porsche could be silver, grey or black, and the Maserati blue. Everybody in the room sits back. A show is starting here.

Clive is a south London chuckle. "Homes, Homes & Homes is a byword for, yes, *homes.* Aha, ha, ha! Ladies and gentlemen, we are into home improvement. Home improvement on the outside and, yes, home improvement on the inside. Beautiful, or what? When I started this game I was running errands in a little architect's office. That was what, 40 years ago? We do your conservatories, your extensions and all your double glazing. You want? We do!"

No ashtray anywhere but the old sales-hand asks if smoking is OK here. The boss man steps back, rubbing at his cufflinks. With enough rubbing, those links will make a genie appear. The room expects a puff of smoke, magic.

Clive's head shakes. "To continue the good work, we're looking for some good people. The best."

Cropped-hair puts her hand up. "What's the job?"

"The job? Ah, yes."

"Is this about sales?" she says.

"Well now. That's why you are all here. The job is meeting our customers on their doorsteps, tell them the *great* news at Homes.

Ah, ha, ha! We're looking for marketing executives. But only the best people, mind! The ones with the dog's bollocks in their eye. They'll know who they are. Earn a lot of money, a *lot* of money!"

The old sales-hand smiles. "What's a lot of money?"

Clive steps to the man. "You tell me, my friend. Name me a figure."

"A thousand pounds! That grand a week in the advert would be handy."

"Want a grand a week?"

"That's why I'm here!"

"Well, you'll have to work for it. Ladies and gentlemen, there's only one trick in town. What you earn is down to you. Your bottom line is in your own hands."

"The more you graft," Jimmy says, "the more you make. Easy!"

Quick, the boss man quiet. Suspicion. Puzzle. He looks at Jimmy, weighing and weighing. Steps back. Hand to jaw. Weighing. "Now then, what have we here!"

"I believe in hard work," Jimmy says.

Democracy in his eye, Clive nods. "This man without a collar and tie, this man tells us he can work hard."

"That's how I've always made my way."

Clive pointing ironic to his neck. "You must have the balls of Branson, coming here without a tie! Never seen anything like it. Think you are Richard Branson, do you? That good? Sure of yourself, are you?"

"I never need ties," Jimmy shrugs. "I can hold my own without them."

Hand on chin, brow furrowed, Clive Core steps back. But only to study the lone without a tie. Jimmy in the circus-master's light. And getting rattled.

"*You,*" Clive says, halfway approving, "you will do all right here. Believe it, my friend!"

Jimmy turns all ways in the room, checking. Looks like him having no tie was not that big a deal. Cropped-hair winks. Clive ambles back to the room top. His circus eyes collect the whole assembly. Colette lights a smoke.

Clive slaps his hands together. "You all want money You all have a need. So let's get there together. You all with me?"

The whole room nods with one voice, saying a loud 'Yes!' And

54

straightaway a thick money wad jumps from Clive's pocket. He flexes the money wad. Flex and flexing. The room belongs to him, numb, in a cage.

"Anybody not sure what this is doesn't need to be here. Come, here's fifty quid, call it travelling expenses. Fifty quid each for anybody who doesn't want to be here. Come on, take your fifty qui. Please, leave now, no hard feelings. What, no takers?"

The old sales hand smiles. "We're still here."

"Well, OK! Looks like we've got some real winners here today. A, ha, ha! My friends, let's get ready to *rock and roll!*"

"How long," Jimmy says, "before we start getting the money in the advert?"

"That moncy?"

"Yes."

Following Clive's gaze, the room gazes at the carpark through the window. Gazing quiet.

"See that Porsche? That's brand new. Cash! Young guy from sales. Been with the company, what, 18 months? Only just turned 23 and, you know what? Earned 150 grand in 12 months! Frightening, a kid that age pulling more wedge than the prime minister. Our marketing executives do very well here. That's what commitment gets you. That's what we call success, the kind you can hold with your own hands. Wouldn't trust any other kind!"

The old sales hand lights a cigar.

Clive turns to the room. "That grand a week is down to you, my friends. And you alone. Ladies and gentlemen, want those things you deserve? Really *want* them? Want to show you can get 'em? And get legally, mind! Weekends in Moscow. Easter in New York. Your own property. A lovely new car. Aaah!"

Cropped-hair puts up her hand. She wants to be polite, but needs the endgame. One nervy cough, and she's ready. "What does a marketing executive do? It's not the same thing as a canvasser by any chance?"

Suddenly, the world going round anti-clock. The boss man wrangles his braces, eyes turned on the woman. Her cropped hair looking sandy in the silver blonde room light.

"*Canvasser*? What's that?"

"Well," she says, "if it's houses, then it's probably someone who knocks on doors all day."

"Oh dear, oh dear! Must be something wrong with my dear old ears. Canvasser? My friends, *canvasser* sounds like, well, it sounds like one of those screens you used to get at a lido as a kid. No, we don't have any of those here, thank you very much! Would be, like what, twelve Ford Mondeos in the carpark at Saatchi."

"So what's the difference?"

"Between?"

"Canvassers and marketing execs?"

The boss man's chin juts. His chin pounces from a Mussolini to a bear-fist. Proud at the window, his chin steps notch by notch. His right hand jumps to his temple and salutes the carpark. "Ladies and gentlemen, the difference is thirty-five grand a year."

The old sales hand clears his throat. "Why only fifty grand. Why not sixty?"

"Look," Clive nods, "we all know where this is going. See any Mondeos in that carpark? Look again, my friends. Any Escorts? No, and no! *Canvasser?* Do me a favour! At Homes, we're into what goes on in the mind. A marketing exec is someone of the mind. The mind, ladies and gentlemen!

"I'm not talking about academics. Our best sales guys, the best sales people, well they haven't got too much paperwork to speak of. But tell you what, some of them will go on to employ the best of them with degrees and what have you. And that's down to just one thing. That's down to *commitment*. Sexy, or what!"

"But what do we exactly?" cropped-hair demands now, not asking. "What do we *do*?"

Clive's eyes project the carpark. Everybody must follow the gaze. Everybody must love the slick hardware outside. And now he turns to the room. Hollywood sun in his eye. "Want some of what's that?"

"Who," cropped-hair says, "would say no to what's out there!"

"You will each do 500 quid a week by the end of your second week. But I'll tell you now, only the totally committed will stay the course. Only the best will pick up that grand a week. It's a tough old world. I'll tell you now, if you have any frailties this job will find you out. I must tell you, of the 20 of you here today only one will be around next year. Yes, only one. That's the bottom line. Only *one* of you."

Cropped-hair winced. "Which one is that going to be? The rest might as well not bother, go now."

"The fittest!" Clive yells, thumping on the desk. "Only the fittest gets the money! Couldn't be simpler now, could it? Man or woman, only the fittest. And it's all down to that Charles Darwin. Where would we be without him? Ladies and gentlemen, a quick hand for Charles Darwin!"

This is no longer about the job. A great show here. World class. A place with rabbits about to jump from a hat. And that carpark hardware. But Clive does not convince everyone. Eyes narrowing, face sweating, the boss man in reverie. Somebody mumbling, saying Clive gets all shook up by his own capacity, a talent that could make a good living in burlesque.

"Let's see, ah yes! Never underestimate what we're about. We're a growing company, top dog in the M25. But watch this space! You will all work in London. Those lovely, those millions of *lovely* homeowners. We're after them. We want them! Lovely people, *lovely* people!"

The old sales hand stubs his smoke in Colette's saucer. "What's the plan?"

"We have a nice little motto here," Clive beams. "It's a simple little thing. There's more readies waiting out there than any of you can collect. We'll show you how to crack it."

The old sales-hand coughs, pen shuffling his hand. "What's the motto?"

"Now, now!" Clive snorts. "No need for pens."

"There's nothing on these walls," cropped-hair says. "No logos, not a single word, no mission statements."

"I'll tell you what our motto is. You all ready for this? Our motto is 'It won't matter what plans you make if you don't own your home!' Get it? Coined that one myself. Nice, or what? Aha, ha! Remember it my friends. Let's all be happy, earn loads of mone*y*. Beautiful, or what?"

3 o' clock and a coffee break. Clive packed every miracle into half the hour. This is how Hollywood preachers pack LA freeways, folk hurrying to get saved. Today everybody got hired on the spot at Homes, Homes & Homes. And Clive said a full day's pay tomorrow, cash.

Colette splits recruits into groups and Clive slams £1000 in brand new fifties on the desk. The money carries its own light. £1000 lights a silver bloom in the room. £1000 sitting round at the front. Who the one? Everybody looking over every face in the room, wanting to be the one. But apart from the old sales head, nobody here has ever sold a thing.

Symmetry drives the mating game. One cut can ruin swallows' love-life. If swallows' tails get trimmed unevenly they will find no mate. Colette is a swallow. Guys here take the swaying as she walks the room. Somebody asks if she's related to Clive. And it's true. They are brother and sister; 18 years apart, she says, earrings tinkling.

"Hi! I'm Geraldine," the woman next to Jimmy smiles. "Looking forward to that lovely dosh? Spent it already?"

Jimmy takes the woman's outstretched hand. The handshake is like talk, like somebody with a stutter. He wants her to be tragic; the more stuff to a woman, the more tragedy there must be. Geraldine's eyes are bird's-egg blue. But no tragedy comes from them. Nothing holding back. She used to work as a translator. And now she gazes at the clasp of her hand in Jimmy's. And he knows. She would listen to clarinet music at night. Her hand pulls away.

Some people walked to get here. Some have arrears, mortgages and common bills like the community charge to face. Two do cocaine. It's the readies. £1000 in a wad of virgin fifties is no joke. Top football players earn ten or fifteen the likes of that every day. Seven days a week. Some earn more. But this wad taunts the people here. Everybody in the room getting cut by it. That £1000 is so set, get bespoke, ready to tuck into a pocket. Who wouldn't want to grab it? For Jimmy, nine or ten of those and it's run time! Well, for about a year. One woman says people do sales because of revenge. Somewhere along the line salespeople have messed up. It's not meeting people why they get into sales. That's the front, the excuse. And not even for money. The sales game is to blot pain. And social pain is the most painful pain. One woman says autumn makes her cry. She's better at work than alone at home. Vacant, somebody gazing the window. Clive's Bentley looks weird now. Earlier the car looked the kind of thing a pride of lions could gather round in autumn. The paint was the hue of autumn leaves. But out there in the cramped carpark now, the big Bentley looks like a dinner plate stained by mustard swipes.

Chapter 16

A huge flare-up at the tenement tonight. It was from Uranus. The police darted over the tenement block, taking site. One more set to pose. Their stab-proof waistcoats made them movie-tough, taking control, cold eyed with man but wanting tenement woman to view them as regular as any guy.

One thing is always the same. When this police business happens, you never doubt. And something serious enough every two weeks for them to bother turning up. They can kick your door down. Rush your closed time. Or jeer, looking for drugs or guns even where no gun or drugs can ever be. But catch one by himself and that a very different game. So different that young black guys only laugh; young guy looking in the eye of a solo robo-copper and more time only a puppy dog limps back.

The whole Caribbean is too far. Too much ocean from a tenement block. All the islands have their sun but nearly everybody is born in England these days. And it's easy telling the ones born somewhere else from the those born in England somewhere. They get back from the Caribbean and they always have a tall sun to talk. They talk a whole year about that sun there, how high the sun, how blue the sky. Women especially. Women get to Jamaica and never quite believe the tall sky. Or Barbados, St Kitts, St. Lucia, some place. Then they get back to the England tenement. And talk is the tall Caribbean sky.

The sky so blue, man, that thing so, *so* blue. And women will not talk what happens, the bad cut in a life, like how come all they have in the tenement is headache. And pain for a tall sky. The tenement sky here looks cumber than before, collecting clouds like paper.

Agnes is Jimmy's number one lady. She comes from Cape Town. Arleene knows about Agnes. Knows the whole thing. But Arleene only said, 'So what!'

It's Agnes' birthday next week. Her last letter was a twelve-page talk. She goes for a swim every morning and most evenings jogs three miles. Four miles. Jogging is because of something to do. That woman wants some physical thing, wants to get too tired to think London and Jimmy's apartment up on the eighth floor in Tottenham.

Agnes is having a neat time in Cape Town. This time of year Cape Town is like a crystal lozenge, the letter says. She's high on the new South Africa, loves being back and black. And the responsibility they give her in the bank. Nothing ever got said, but more and more Jimmy knows Agnes could be the one. But if she ever hears about Arleene, how Jimmy plays Arleene, Agnes would write no more.

Tonight Jimmy mulls the spiel at Homes, Homes & Homes. But nothing to think. Tomorrow will be give-it-a-go time. Grab the cash. Wad after wad. And maybe Colette wants somebody to paint that hip business with notes.

The lights turn off. Then the hi-fi. Jimmy alone, settling back, hoping for a rap blast from the flat below. Any muso could look-see that rap way, greet rap, stick it to the envelope. But rap is only for now. Rap is far from home. Jazz is for all time. Jazz is up with a tall sky.

Rap is closer to bulletproof than pain. It had to happen, one final jackhammer on the building site. More time, rap is not rant. Not all the time. To some people, rap is a kind of laughing-gas. Well, a wailing gas. Humphrey Davy got set by laughing gas in 1799. It was his first nitrous oxide trip and Humphrey said, 'My visible impressions were dazzling, and I heard distinctly every sound in the room, and I lost all connections with the external world.' Not long after that blast, somebody got painkillers and anesthetics from that same old laughing-gas. And now, 200 years down the road, black guys have rap to anesthetize. Kill pain.

On the outside rap looks like only bling. Some folk say rap getting bigger all the time, too big, wailing loud. But rap is cooler than mute. Because one day it will go. The pain will go. And that is because rap breaks something inside, something wanting the sky, some human thing, mashing down the human, destructing a place where somebody wants a tall sky to look at.

Sometimes, someone will get away from a tenement. Now and then somebody can burble at Oxford or Cambridge, then drive a brand new Merc round Marble Arch. But then they have a problem. Even with sky-high education they have a problem that can not get solved. Not right now. Somebody visiting the community after getting away, coming from the same streets as folk still mushing a tenement, and now they know. This the time to move on. And that

60

is the hard part. Somebody back to the community but only visiting, out and about some raining day, moving it nice and easy in their new car, maybe tuned to Mozart or Ellington, going through a few old-time streets, then a glimpse of a one, a onetime friend, shifting in the rain, some old school friend running down a 38 Routemaster at Dalston Junction. From inside the car is a numb knowing, moving to a different speed now. One somebody hurrying by foot and blear with rain. But the one in the car is breezing it, moving snug, windscreen wiper flitting rain.

Chapter 17

All the recruits show. Except one. Today is the new workplace, the new rock'n roll.

The reception girl wears a skin dress, snatch-pink, looking like she could shed Marilyn Monroe blood as she jigs round the reception area. She spins a shiftless smile, slaps magazines on the coffee table. This is one crazy dancer. Not who she could be. She's a stick teaser. By now she should know the deal between a dress and a body toy. Idling, somebody murmurs 'Wear it tight, bitch. Wear it!'

Colette calls from the salesroom. Doors to knock today and spiel to spin. And evident dogs in long driveways.

That £1000 wad is still on the desk, patient. Waiting still. Enough to run for. Then run from the madness. With that thing somebody here will clear their arrears on the community charge, or a car can get kitted for MOT.

Cropped-hair woman arrived late. Maybe she's seen too much in her life already; she definitely wanted to be the astronaut or deep sea diver. She could take a lute to space and while. But she wants to be by herself here today, only half nodding when somebody says hello. This woman hates being here, hates being preached at by the likes of Clive Core. And especially hated having to show hands.

All recruits had to choose one of two words that will describe them from now on. The first word was predator. The second was striker. And everybody showed hands for *striker*.

Role-play. Recruits will be going for the money today. And that means becoming a predator. Clive cranks the punch line. Oh yes, my friends, predators. Beautiful, or what?

From the role-play room, stippled sunlight through the window. Role-play is taking turns at being the homeowner. Colette tells it. But telling it like salt lemonade. But first, a coffee. Everybody take five minutes, OK?

Geraldine is next to Jimmy. She says hello and he nods at the money on the desk. £1000 a week is silly, she says; it's not real, not for something daft as knocking doors. Sighing, she says the money wad is vulgar. Jimmy knows this woman does not understand. Quick, he tells where he is. And the first thing she says is 'Go on the dole. Going on the dole will free up time for your music.' But then her vision hangs. No, somebody composing should do a job like this doorstep business; for a little while, at least. It is good to talk to strangers. That's why they're a stranger. Talking to them you can get a good feel for the life episode. Then she confides something. People on their own doorsteps, she says, are not the same people out and about; and that's got to be good for a composer, hasn't it? Jimmy shrugs. Like Philip Glass? Know about him? Yes, she says, that's it! In the dirt poor early days Philip Glass used to drive a taxi, and that was year after year in New York; he even did a stint as a plumber. Think of the hordes he must have met, and think of the endgame. What, like his Einstein On The Beach? Her eyebrows raise. Yes, that work of his came out in '75; the year I was born, she says. The way she turns and turns the wedding band on her finger it could melt down. Jimmy steps from the coffee machine, empties the plastic coffee cup and shoots the waste basket with it. Hard.

House prices will always rise. Well, more or less. And that happens penny by penny. Or it happens by huge pounds. Boom time now, Clive says, unfolding a chart. Because DIY is trendy again this a great chance for a pro to kick the granddads out of it! And the cowboys; give the cowboys a kicking, he says. Because more and more people work from home by bringing the office to the home, they want a true pro to take care of conversions and extensions. Homes, Homes & Homes is the place they should call. Clive grins. Geraldine whispers, calling Clive 'His Hollywood'.

Because of *style crimes* by people wanting to sell their home in a sellers market, that leaves a killing for the professional.

Clive is a plain man. To him the great business trick is not selling what people need. Not even what they want. The trick is them buying what they can find money for. Never matters how they find it. Borrow it. Beg. This guy is a raider, a cold-cut eye, quick to pick up on a wounded thing. And nothing in England is wounded as a furrowed Jones or Smith having a complex over their property.

But something has changed. Maybe because of seeing lions at the zoo, remembering them all the time, but Jimmy connects sales to blood. From the day of the lions nothing is the same. Already some faces in the room look like killers on the open plains.

Only one thing unites these people. Cold-blood hunger. And the money wad still on the desk. That's the prey.

TV is good at predators, good at big cats hunting in driving rain. Seeing predators in rain is the beautiful part. But just as they close for the kill a rainbow might appear out of nowhere.

Clive primes the recruits. Arriving at Homes on two legs they must see themselves in the simplest survival game of all. They all broke, all hungry now, yes? So, eat!

Something about a predator. Here maybe the game is getting paid for it. The people in this room want to kill. Knocking doors to set up folk for glass they don't really need, no glass is ever as cut. No bleeding as cold blood. Jimmy won't need a tie, Clive said. And that was a surprise. There was no racial. And not a word over Jimmy having dreadlocks.

As he looks around him, Jimmy's eyes impact the cropped-hair woman's. She is forty years old and just back from the Alps. But knows. She's guessed what he knows.

Chapter 18

"*Recession?*" Clive howls. "What's that? Sounds like what you catch from a lavatory seat!"

Geraldine blinks. "That's what the papers call it. Every housing expert in the press says professional home-improvement is in dire recession."

Rankled, Clive tugs his braces. The braces are like guy-ropes in a storm. "My friends," he says, "ladies and gentlemen, no negatives, please! No rubbish about recessions. That is so, what shall we call it? So sad. It is loser-speak. Look, let's be honest about it. Some of us wouldn't make a few bob if everybody was clued up, would we? If everybody was streetwise we wouldn't be here now. None of us. And I mean *none* of us!

"There would be no banks, no telly, no motorways, nothing. Know why? We would all be in animal skins, still living in caves, my friends. Now there's a prospect!"

"I don't see how that follows," Geraldine says.

Clive folds his arms. Lazing to the window, strides along it, then skips heavy. Steadying himself to speak, his cufflinks prate like wolves' teeth on a bone. "Geraldine, that's your name is it? Nice try, Geraldine. But no thank you very much!"

"What if they just can't afford a conservatory? If they can't afford it there'd be no point trying to persuade them, surely."

"Look, it's never what they tell you! What you've got to worry about is what they've got in their heads. That's the bottom line. You with me? Not what he's got in the bank, or she. Look at it this way. You have your house, a lovely home, what comes next? You have the biggest investment of your life, yes?

"Now listen! How do you *protect* the value of your property? Anybody? What, no takers? Well, now, what a surprise! You, the man without the tie?"

Cropped-hair butts in. "Could be a thousand answers to that. Personally, I think _"

"Own your own property?" Clive grins.

"I rent. A little flat."

The boss man claps his hands. "Well, now, how did I know that? Oh, deary, deary, me! Some of us sit on the fence in this life. Me? Well, you all know the answer to that! My friends, let's get back to business. Ladies and gentlemen, people will always protect their property. Only bullshitters live in sheds. But with a *lovely* Victorian conservatory, you have got tradition, you have a property to be proud of. And even your grandma's kippers could appreciate that!"

Cropped-hair can not laugh. And Clive is fed up with preaching. He rolls back his cuffs and elects Geraldine for the first role-play. Reluctant on her feet, she removes her scarf and prepares to be the homeowner. The willow green leaves her fingers and hesitates, then swoops, drooping to the ground.

"Really, we don't need a conservatory," she says. "No space. There's too little room in the garden as it is. And £15,000 is way beyond my means, honestly."

Clive turns to the room, winking a boozer-wink. Then spins back to Geraldine the homeowner. "Mrs Smith," he says, "times are difficult for everyone. We understand that. We've done our homework, believe me. And what a charming home you have! Beautiful place, you must be very proud! A tidy little conservatory is all you need. And what a lovely picture that will be. Now then! If we're talking value then the right conservatory puts 10, 15% on the value of this lovely property. For a beautiful home such as this we will definitely help with the finance. Tell you what, we will spread the finance, arrange a nice little package. Now, that'll be a big help won't it?"

"Well, I'm not so sure," Geraldine demurs, giving in as a homeowner. "You make it all sound so easy. By the way, what's the interest rate? How long would I have to pay?"

"Just a sec!" Clive yells. Standing back from Geraldine, he collects room daze like biscuits from a plate. "Everybody, pay attention to this! I want you to get what happens next. I cue the bit about a finance package and the punter gives out a juicy buying signal. Lovely! If that happens, *when* that happens, what you say is 'I am not qualified to comment on finance, Mrs Smith, but someone from our Customer Services Department will explain the details. What time are you at home tomorrow?'

"Everyone got that? You never ask the punter if they've got spare time, *never!* You ask 'What time are you at home tomorrow?' Better still, 'What time tomorrow will be convenient for you?' Everybody got that?"

Geraldine saunters to her seat. And gets the scarf from the ground.

She turns to Clive. "What happens after we make the appointment?"

The boss man struts a new Mussolini. "The kaycee moves in."

"The *what*?"

"Kaycee," Clive grins. Quick, he writes 'k-c' on the white-board. "Well now, let's see! In a word, a k-c is the dog's bollocks."

"A salesman?"

"Well, some words are never up to speed. Salesman? We could be here all day with that one."

"Then what is it?"

"OK, a k-c is a salesman of sorts. Yes. But not your average blagger!"

"But a salesman!"

"Give a k-c one whiff of the money and he's in there, close the deal! Ladies and gentlemen, you make the appointment and the k-c is your friend, gets you the money!"

"Yes, yes, but what does it mean? Is it Japanese?"

"Japanese? Do me a favour! k-c stands for *killer-closer*. Ah, ha."

"*Killer*?"

Disappointed, Clive's head shakes. "We don't kill anybody. Alright?"

"Then why use *killer*," Geraldine says.

"Because we kill their money, that's what! Slaughter the stuff! Aha, ha! Kill 'em without bloodshed, aha, ha!"

That marketing exec gets the k-c a foot in the punter's door. A k-c is a breed apart. The ultimate predator. Part cheetah, part wolverine. Dreamlike with purple charm, k-cs call themselves customer services managers. And nothing known to science will ever get between them and the money. A top k-c is the type that gets into the punter's house and straightaway strides over to their TV and switches it off. Then invites the punter to sit down. Inviting the punter to sit down in their own house, invite. Not every punter is a warmed-up mug, but then enough of them are out there as dead meat.

According to Clive, most punters have no sense of self; even in their own home. And tidy profits stem from that one fact. The biggest profits come from people who get disappointed if their little chat with a power-salesman is only talk; they are the punters looking for a star to turn up in their humdrum and quicken it with sizzle.

67

They don't know it, but they exactly looking for a k-c to call.

Now and then Clive hankers after the old days. Hankers after the time he was a k-c. Some days he ventures out and does the rounds, reacquainting with the kill.

One somebody with eyes shut here. And this is nothing to do with being squeamish. This a cut. what happens here in the role-play room reminding Jimmy of a dream. The dream is always a bleak place, a frontier, a stark place with slow-motion borders and wounded angels hurrying away on whisper-thin shoulders of other angels. In the dream the outlines of their face get visible but their eyes are impossible to see.

His eyes should open now, but Jimmy telling himself this sales gimmick at Homes is a good survival deal. And something else is here. Wicked, bloodless. This is no scam. There really is glass to sell. But k-cs lay into punters and take them down. Maybe it's the sound of *killer* in killer-closer. His eyes open. Something heathen here. But strange, welcoming. A cold but beautiful doom saying 'Come, this way, you invited!' It whispers 'No, do not walk from this.' Jimmy asks Clive if homeowners are anything like angels.

"What?"

"Angels, wisp-like things."

Clive's brow furrows. Boss man loose, hoarse. "What the 42nd Royal Fusilliers is a bloody angel?"

Clive's question makes the room laugh. They laugh way out loud in the role-play room, falling apart, laughing. The next move could be rolling in the aisles. But Clive does not laugh. Something holds him from the fun. His brow says he's worried.

The boss man is afraid, wants to brush the question aside. He's on a high tightrope between two tall buildings. A gust could kick him off. Frowning, rolling down starched cuffs, his links connect. Must explain. Yes, must say the right thing. Hand blunt to jaw, he says "What a funny question!"

Cropped-hair asks why.

"It's a tricky question," Clive frowns. "Nothing daft about it. A question like that, well, you don't get that everyday. Well now!"

"Quite a few people think homeowners are the church in God," she says.

Jimmy cuts in. "They say it's the murals of angels in a church that makes it work."

"*Angels*?" Clive coughs. "I don't know anything about them. But angels don't keep the congregation up to speed, do they! And come to think of it, listen, let's not get soppy. Angels can't look after business if they can't show themselves to us, can they!"

To Clive, the chase is on. A big bull's-eye is on every middle class house in England. A bull's-eye waiting to get aimed at. Even in London. Even the know-all city. And Homes, Homes & Homes is out and about. Taking aim, ladies and gentlemen. Taking aim.

Chapter 19

Hour of the money. Recruits gulp coffee and head out, going by van to get dropped on suburban street corners. This where it starts. This is where the prospecting begins, the gold trail. Only, no mules and shovels here.

As the afternoon rustles by, light and shade intertwining, cool daylight and quietness. Newton's remnants are in autumn leaves. Quiet is in the van, slow-motion in the street, and, after forty minutes, gold-brown leaves on silent lawns. Random. Beautiful. The van slows to another drop-off point.

Jimmy worried. Hard to think. His turn to go. But no homing signs. Not here. This place is not the kind where someone black owns any of the calm houses. Only middle class white people live in this quiet place. Only the seasons change. Lipped.

Time to go, but Jimmy too visual. That's how it feels. Having to walk these quiet driveways is getting nervy. This is no game. The folk that live here never have had anybody black knock their door. And Jimmy nervy. Not stage fright nerves, but like-a-child-again nerves, lone, not-wanting-to-go nerves. How come he here? The job advert said *No experience necessary!* but this the part where experience would do it. How to judge the blink when that first door opens? Best remember the role-play, get polite, say 'Good afternoon!' and show the Homes, Homes & Homes ID card. No adlib, just hit the script, get set in eye, ask if this is the homeowner. That's the easy part. But what if they see him through their curtain or CCTV, will they still open the door? Black, dreadlocks and no tie.

Geraldine can tell. Others in the van do not know. But somehow this blond woman understands, volunteering, getting out the van, saying she's happy to work alongside Jimmy. And he wonders why.

"Simple," she says.

"How come?"

"Because you're *so* going to be lucky."

"Think so?"

"I do. I do. You *will* get that grand a week. Remember it?"

Jimmy knows she knows The white woman knows. She saw panic over him. "Grand a week? Well, yeah, that's the plan. But you, what's the real reason you want to pair off with me?"

"I hate hypocrites," she says.

"Hypocrites?"

"Yes."

"And how are they?"

"Who?"

"The hypocrites," Jimmy shrugs. "What're they up to today?"

Geraldine smiles, shakes her blond woman head. A wistful but clear pair of eyes. "Frankly, there were little nudges about not wanting to pair off with you. I'm not into the nonsense of anything like that."

Nervy, but shaking hands, Jimmy thanks her again. Shrugging, this bright woman says it would be nice if they could just get on with it and not become little diplomats with one another.

"Never!" Jimmy says, tall again. "Best tell it like it is."

"Agreed!" the woman says as they step towards the first house.

Chapter 20

Like aquaplaning, doorstep canvassing is not for everyone. Not only because of the endless knocking and ringing, and polite paste on a face before the door. And not dogs rushing past the owner and wanting blood. Not even the postman miles. The canvassing job at Homes is about killing.

By the evening of the first day, four recruits have walked already. Cropped-hair was the first to step. She lasted half an hour and, from gossip back at base, she was halfway through a pitch then looked the punter long in the eye and said 'Forgive me!' They say cropped-hair hurried down that driveway, walking away from the good news she was carrying. Then maybe she went for a gin shot. Or shot straight home to look herself in the mirror, and maybe she saw sin bloom in her eye. Everybody agrees; cropped-hair was kind of weird. She was never the kind to settle for how legal everything is, that this canvassing game is a kind of show, that people want to get their doorstep feted, liking frolic there. Cropped-hair did not want to feed herself and the killer-closers this way.

A walk contagion. By the end of the second week, only 9 of the 22 starters are still out and about for Homes. The others could be anywhere. One or two are maybe grappling with Stephen Hawking's book on time. Cropped-hair could crack it.

Instead of A Brief History Of Time for the current title, this penniless woman maybe could grab her pen and change the name to 'Synoptic Time, By Time Changing In Respect Of Time.'

Jimmy and Geraldine are the top canvassing duo at Homes, ace-high in suburbia. The weather getting cold. And trees bare. They've been six weeks at Homes now.

Race? That business is never too far on the doorstep. And not only where polished pewter gleams. Mostly these folk have some band like Led Zeppelin playing the hi-fi and think Jimmy is the central-heating man come to check the boiler. Or a woman grins, quietly talks domestic, like baking soda because of the bubbling when water hits the powder, or asks if he can get the oil stain from her carpet. Maybe because they never had a black man on their doorstep before, but the race thing flusters them. And now and then a woman will flirt talk, and quite often she will know the line and call it quits. But from the bad longing in some eyes, even the bluest blue, a big herd of suburbia white women want to go with a black guy. Furtive and hard. That's one thing.

But three or four times every day Jimmy gets other race attitudes to contend. And that is the politics kind. But Jimmy can get even. Any racial, and that's the time to send in a k-c. Constipated folk making sending in a ruthless k-c a great kick. And then Jimmy will doodle at the keyboard later, imagining.

Geraldine never gets troubled by the predator game. For a woman who cries when Joni Mitchell sings, the lilt to Joni's folksy urban Debussy-influenced tunes, this kind of work should be unclean. Jimmy agrees with Geraldine on one thing. Joni Mitchell is beautiful to listen. But to Jimmy the job is acc. It's one way to get even. One evening after work they walk along and he asks how she can stomach being a predator.

Weary, the lady spreads her arms. "I *hate* the word. Predator is so melodramatic. This job is a numbness, an out-of-body experience."

"It's all legal."

"Well, yes."

"So there's got to be morals in it."

"Where?"

"Somewhere. Like in the contracts."

"Morals? Oh, we can all get morals. All it takes is a bucket."

"Your spit, or theirs?" Jimmy laughs.

Geraldine blares her angry-woman blare. And quick, Jimmy asks if she wants to exercise on the pavement. Why? To cool down. *Cool down?* Yeah, keep warm. Not amused, the woman checks her private space. Mostly she misses her husband.

Soon a small laugh starts in her throat. Head thrown back, she laughs out now. Her hands take to the air. Suddenly this is fun, a cute interlude; perhaps she'd even lob a basketball if one was here. Jimmy turns to watch her eyes.

Her head shakes. "Moralizing is what happens round nighttime coffee tables."

"Or the pub."

"Tell you a little secret. All my energies go into Brian, getting my head round the idea he might have gone for good."

"This job takes your mind off it?"

"Yes."

"Must be loads of other things you could do."

"Like what?"

"Anything would be better than this."

"Like?"

"Why not give teaching a go? Serious language graduate like you, they'd beg you to teach."

Geraldine's feet slam into the cold pavement. "I'd never teach!"

Grinning, Jimmy tries the reel. This woman could reel like fish. "You miss all those farm brochures and stuff."

"It wasn't *that* bad."

"Hard to see you sucking up to dirty great German tractors!"

"Not as bad as it sounds. It's high pressure language skills. Farm machinery can be so life & death. Operating instructions are critical. Got to get it right! Snotty kids in classrooms? Yuck!"

Jimmy scoffs. "I was thinking 6th-form colleges."

"Tractors, any day!"

"Imagine Clive's face if you arrived for work in a tractor."

She laughs. "This job is quick dosh, full stop."

"Well, yeah, but what about the other reason?"

"Other reason?"

"There's *always* some other reason."

"Listen to me, I won't play morality merry-go-rounds. No high horses, OK! Oh, hey, look, I didn't mean that the way it came out. I mean, can't we find something better to talk about?"

"Better than morals?"

"Morality is so, so subjective."

"There's bits to morality, bits like the Highway Code."

"I know what you mean," she says.

"Then why the denial?"

"It's that word, isn't it."

"What?"

"The biggest dirty word is *morals*."

"Lines in the sand."

"I draw the line with this job, believe me! Anything lower than this and I couldn't do it."

"This gig is only a step from the gutter."

"One giant leap for mankind, and all that."

Jimmy shrugs. The evening is not cold enough to deny Geraldine her Neil Armstrong line from the fist moon landing. A quiet nod, and he turns to the skies. "What's the German for gutter?"

"What?"

"The German for *gutter*."

"Where the hell is the gutter, anyway?" she says, brows packed. Her eyes check the cold evening streetlights. "I've heard of that place somewhere."

Jimmy knows. The gutter is the one place to hint at when somebody must feel better. Looking round, he could cup his hands and make them a megaphone. Why, she asks. He says it would be to shout 'Brixton!' out loud.

He remembers lions in a zoo, wondering what keepers do to keep them warm in winter. Geraldine turns from the houses across the road and, bright as a flame, asks about Jamaica.

She wants to know why so many black people bother staying here; she'd take the sun, yes, any day. To Jimmy, this is the dumbo question ever. And that's because ocean can cut people in two. And the half-moon overhead this evening is a lamp of means. But Geraldine could be innocent.

Jimmy wanting nicotine to flush blood. "Since when did I get a say in what's what?"

"What do you mean?"

"Jamaica."

"I don't understand what you mean."

"This is *your* society."

"What are you getting at?"

"How would the likes of me ever know where's where?"

"I don't know what you mean."

"Jamaica is not a bit of handy sunshine somewhere. This is your society."

Geraldine turns to the houses across the street. And regards them. Up and down. Up and down. Like just maybe they could know the right thing. "My society?" she groans, spinning round. "You were born here. The same way as me."

To divert the woman's gaze, Jimmy grabs a smoke. The packet is full. Time for a smoke. Time for a sear. Time to burn some bridge down.

As the match cuts to flame, he remembers Lorna Stanley. Dizzy for a serious chat last week, it was a quiet call to Lorna. The first call ever. But a weird call. Bad suffering was down the line. The only reason she was at the zoo the day they met was to see if lions know what a cage is. And at times she'd looked like the cage was only there by mistake.

Geraldine draws to the fire. Her gaze follows the fire as it sears the tobacco. She must ask something. So asks if she can ask a question, a personal one. Why, she wonders, does Jimmy not try a little harder to belong.

Jimmy lays the theme. Angry, example after example, talking Brixton, saying Brixton is a fault-line and black people have places they can never go. Not if too far from the likes of Brixton. Stephen Hawking sits down in a wheelchair and steers a route round the whole universe. But Jimmy six feet tall, able bodied, quick of mind, yet Brixton is a hold zone. Geraldine does not understand. She says she could understand.

Through Geraldine, Jimmy gets slice after slice of English countryside. Village places, hamlets, places where only a thousand people live, or few as a hundred. She has relatives and friends in parts of England where no black person goes, let alone lives. This had never occurred to her. No, not till now. Talking rural England, this woman talks and talks the sleep-like distance to stars. She does not know what the countryside can do. She does not know the hurt, not getting close, seeing it only on TV or grabbing at it from the motorway. Somebody wanting to walk down a country lane and maybe even chase a butterfly, but not getting stared at. But will get gazed at because they black.

Butterflies need the sun. And normal times will not fly without it. All it takes is a southerly air and those things flit the English fields all summer long.

Jimmy explains. "Black people only happen in London. Or Liverpool, Birmingham and the rest."

Geraldine wipes her nose. "Yes, I think I know what you mean."

"The black thing is simpler than people think."

"What are you driving at?"

"The only thing black people do is shuttle, move from one immigrant hotspot to another. Blacks use that other map of England."

"*Other* map?"

"The Ordinance Survey is not the only map. The other map is the black archipelago map."

"The *what?*"

76

"Ghost lines."

"Ghost lines?"

"Yes, ghosting it. Not living it."

"That is terrible. I mean, so serious."

"Yeah."

"Why do we never see this discussed?"

"Because it's so serious. Nobody will talk it out loud. You have a quarantine round the inner city, a line, something like city-states. Even simple things never happen for black folk."

"Like what?"

"Well," Jimmy says, "simplest things hurt the most.

"Yes, but what?"

"Things like not having a cottage."

"What's so special about a cottage, for Christ's sake!"

"A cottage overlooking farmland or tucked in the New Forest. The quiet that's there."

"What can we do?"

"We?" Jimmy exhales.

"We can change that."

"All *I* can do is take the money. That's why this job is great for me. I like this predator game. I can't sit and have a glass of sherry with them."

Geraldine's lips bale. O-gape, her mouth opens. "I don't know who you mean."

Jimmy shrugs. "The folk in those houses! Those people make a big fuss, always polite, but they don't really want somebody like me knocking their door. Except if I was the electrician. That's why I turn the k-cs loose on them. Payback time!"

Winter light is ancient. And sun zest in hard bluish-white petals shatter the moon. Maybe somewhere far away palm trees spread out in a message, saying 'Bluish seasons, intermittent.' And in some little street market, imported things bring fire to wear a gentleness.

"Hmm," Geraldine sighs. She turns away. Quiet, her hands tidy a bout of hushed applause. "Some enchanted evening!"

"I don't have to get preachy about it."

"Then don't! The priesthood would *so* not be you!"

"Somebody should mention it."

"Mention what?"

"The bullshit behind those doors," Jimmy says. In one bad torrent, talking no stops, he offloads a life to words. Hands weeping.

So, now she knows! Now this woman knows this racial. She knows it now. Knows it small. Knows from the other side. But she's spent. She's alone in a cold evening, wanting anything but race. Wanting maybe to think sheep and lambs. But now she knows.

"That chap," she says, "that little creep organizing the folk festival, at least he didn't tell you to go back."

"Go back?"

"You know, to, well _"

"Where I come from?"

"Well, _"

"To somebody like that, Brixton is bongo-bongo land!"

"Oh, not necessarily," she pouts. Quiet, her eyes gaze her feet. Her hands shuffle her coat. Turning to Jimmy, her throat clears. "The poor guy, he gagged didn't he? He ran out of ideas. It happens."

"He was talking woad!"

"Woad?"

"Little England."

"What?"

"The silent majority at home."

"But Brixton is *part* of England."

"Yeah, the spice part. Tropical condiments. Good for a laugh or a grimace."

"It's as much a part as any."

"Oh, yeah!"

"OK, so occasionally things are in the margins a little bit. But it's still on the same page, isn't it? These things take time. Take it on the chin. Will you let a spoilt spoof ruin your life? Your whole life?"

Jimmy chucks the cigarette. And watches the perplexed woman meet herself in a cold evening. Maybe she thinks far, like how nazis compelled Jews to sew the Star of David on their garment. But a Brixton overcoat? That business? Yes, it is two things. And the first thing is that it can not un-sew. Not now. And the next thing is what to do next.

"Look," Jimmy nods, "where I go, I go in this skin. Take a touch. Go on, feel my Brixton overcoat!"

Chapter 21

Playing dominoes all weekend. Mostly that's all Nathan will do these days. Hard to talk, sit, discuss. So dominoes happen instead of talk. Jimmy will not mention the canvassing job. Nathan would be too sad.

Bad seeing your father fumble. Nathan fumbling, looking for words. Scared. The man knows what he must say, but scared, wanting to say some wise thing, but scared of not being the big father, not wise. So Jimmy sits in for the ritual domino talk. And having a drink. And listening Louis Armstrong. Or Lester Young, Ellington or Art Tatum.

Sometimes Japanese music plays. Nathan brought back a pile of music from one trip to Osaka five years back. And he got given one of their bamboo flutes, a thing they call the shakuhachi. The plain niceness of this flute is hard to explain. The only thing coming close is *scant*. Or maybe a Samurai sword can compare. The scant, the louche beauty of that sword; you a Samurai going your business in the old days and you call on that sword and straightaway all your dreams get delivered.

As the dominoes collect and scheme, one man hears orphans in a bamboo flute. The other man crying inside because of sounds he can no longer get from the trumpet hanging on the wall. Nathan tries hard. But not wanting to think. So much music he would have played. And even now he still wonders what could have happened. What if it had been America instead of England. Top Jamaican guys went to America in the old days. Guys like Ernest Ranglin and Monty Alexander got it right; those guys upped to the States and got a good reception there.

Harold McNair. Harold skipped to England from Jamaica in 1960. And it was Harold here that was the final clincher for Nathan. Harold was another muso from Kingston, and at one time he got a jazz gig at Ronnie Scott's place. A residency. Harold was a boss flute player; not primal maybe, but bossing that thing. Now and then Nathan will play Flute And Nut, one album Harold cut here. And listening it with Jimmy, all Nathan will say is 'Man!'

When Nathan in a bad mood the dominoes are black, black. Down the years maybe two thousand games of dominoes have been played between Nathan and Jimmy. But even from the early times, the time living as one family under one roof, dominoes talked instead of talk.

Nathan is sorry about the hands. Arthritis in his hands getting more and more. Too hard to take. So pain is on two levels. He's still at the welding job but some days the pain gets so bad that he can not work. In England welding was only supposed to be the back-up plan. If the music did not work out, Nathan had a safe back-up plan. If playing music was just smiling around, smiling the smile and shuffling on stage, or doing mickey-mouse in a studio gig, then welding was always there. That was the calculation when this proud man first arrived. With music, all it was to take was six months. With welding, it was to be five years of grafting weather. But either way it was to get back to Jamaica and run clear. That was the plan. The money was only one side. Way beyond money, Nathan was a man of mission. America was still coming to terms with losing Clifford Brown. Clifford was 10 years before Nathan arrived in England and Miles Davis was the big man, edging Dizzy because of cool, so Nathan was thinking England was the place. On a good day he could take the trumpet places maybe only Clifford Brown used to take it, the speed, the tone, the harmony. In England the plan was to show them. But just in case, welding work was available on every building site.

Jimmy's mother married last year. And she is OK. Or so she says. She started out in a Liverpool orphanage and a black Scouse family adopted her. Even now nobody really knows where her birth parents come from. Talking about it she thinks a bit of England runs through her veins as well as Africa, like maybe Senegal. For Jimmy the wedding was the lady's happiness. He was all she had. So he was at the wedding because of that. At 41, she young enough to have more but will not go to that, saying she was born to have children with one man only.

To Jimmy hearing Nathan talk is the business. A broad Jamaica accent talking as your father. Nathan can do set English, or down-home patois. But either way a true Jamaican is always in the talk. And Jimmy can listen that. No matter what. Sometimes Nathan only saying this and that, stuff going on, ducking and diving in the street. But that Jamaica accent is what is really what, who really who.

One big thing now us what to do with locks. Wearing locks in

England. Nathan got rid of his dread one day. It was the first time Jimmy had ever seen the shape of Nathan's head. And suddenly it was time to get rid of his own locks. Time to travel the father road awhile.

Nathan says only genuine Rasta should manifest locks. The Rasta movement started in Jamaica anyway, and any Jamaican that shows locks in public England is a smalltime poppy-show.

A what? Nathan looks up from the dominoes. His eyes cut. A *poppy-show* is Jamaica talk for a fool, somebody that is a mascot but not knowing it. Any Jamaican away from the island can have locks if they use a hat in public. When you cover your locks, Nathan says, you show respect. And something else. Covering your locks means you have your bag packed, you ready to go. The same thing for the son of a Jamaican anywhere abroad.

Jimmy mulls on this. Nathan will not be told; to get through to him you have to use suggestions. So locks have something to do with lions? Nathan laughs, saying that is easy. Putting aside the domino talk, he says domestic cats are everywhere. Millions and millions. And panthers, tigers. But only a lion can have a mane.

Nathan talking overdrive. Missing the music he did not play. Jamaica made a big mistake, he says. Yeah, it was OK at the start. Jamaica taking rhythm from those American guys. You mean dance shuffles? Yeah, rhythm that guys like Louis Jordan handed down, rhythms that still set a dancehall alight. Guys like King Jammys used to build shortwave radios in Jamaica and listen to American rhythm & blues. That music got to Jamaica and, man! Guys tried it on guitar and it was the *ska, ska* chipping on guitar that turned into ska. And one day to reggae. But the boys on the island should have learned.

Ellington the boss. So listen to the Duke, Nathan says. Island tunes stack to jazz chords and, if more musician do dat, if dem do dat now, especially now, then maybe more respect to go round. Nathan laughs. Young city guys don't check the Duke. Mostly guys going no place. Except Wynton. Black folk can learn from Wynton Marsalis. And white folk. That's the way Nathan knows it. And maybe seeing gets easy for somebody with arthritis in their hands.

Chapter 22

For someone of colour, door-canvassing can be looking at woad. And that can be way up front. But often, woad hugs the ground.

If you black, some days your guard drops. And that's because things can be going great a while, the world moving easy, moving hour upon hour, the sun shining the same on everyone. And every star is the same nice at evening.

Then whack! Some word gets through. Whack! If anybody will believe, what happens is a word that can pack pain.

Jimmy will not embarrass Geraldine. Not by talking it. And mostly she knows the score by now. She looks in his eyes sometimes and asks what's wrong. But really she knows. And Jimmy turns away, saying nothing.

Talk is, it was Paddy Ashdown that named the whole thing. The talk is it was him who called it the *woad-game*. Before he got involved it, was only snide. Politicos only talked asylum-seekers and scroungers. But woad can be anywhere. Like under the bespoke suit of a studious individual, someone with long term influence, someone who in everything else might be having deep thoughts and appreciatively overlooking the Thames with a coffee. Or that thing is under the bleach-white summer clothes of a bozo quaffing lager in the pub.

Ashdown was no dude. He a serious guide. And that's the rub. It must be somebody talking life as well as death. Somebody that knows life can be flat death. Prime minister this, leader that, but when push turns to shove the leader must know more than talk. Instead of free speech to a race heckler, Ashdown's eyes used to narrow. Military eyes. Then he'd ask if woad smeared on anyone near. That's what people say about him. But maybe that is only fairytale. Or what they say can be true.

Ashdown was the English pappy. But he on the way to other business now. And he might even take down his military hand from a shelf. Hard to tell. But he could be relied on, a man of life and death, bringing death like a bullfighter, but too smart to fight a hummingbird. And in a meadow somewhere in sleepy England, a herd of cattle moves content past a compost saved from fire.

Jimmy makes up his mind. He agrees with Nathan. Showing locks in public England is a blunder. And insulting to true Rasta. Showing locks in public England is mimic-time. Dreadlocks inflation every place, dragging Rasta down. Duds mimic the sign of Rasta, but Rasta is humble human. That what Rasta-dread means. Nobody can ever mimic a nuclear warhead but any hypocrite can mash down the way of Rasta.

Nathan gets pissed off with that. To him, somebody that shows locks in the street is somebody walking with a big empty suitcase. And the bigger the dreadlocks in the street, the bigger the empty suitcase. The false-heads are the problem; and nobody laughs big as a false-head. False-head hear true Rasta talk 'bout Babylon but dem never understan'.

Nathan the same generation as Bob Marley. To him, dub is to blame for the mimics. Dub came along and was ace. But dub, man, now that ting ignore de high; dub knows but will not speak the high. Dub observe bad business in a de basement, like a million cockroach a breed, but dub shut de cellar door fe run back upstairs fe check folly.

Sometimes things get scary for the suitcase-heads. Guys like that have nada to say. If a mimic gets hit by a racial, they talk spit. If mimics get spat on then they claim England is Babylon, citadel of oppression. But dat? Only jive. Mimic talk the empty suitcase talk.

Some dubsters are not simple. Some are educated, saying dreadlocks have nothing to do with Babylon; not even religion, not now, not in the modern world. Dubster saying locks is man reclaiming roots from oppression. But Rasta no believe dat. A true locksman knows a mimic can do nada humble. False-heads always move around with the empty suitcase. But if somebody checks, then the mimic blinks. Mimic stutter, mimic shouting 'Birmingham!' or shout 'Bristol!' But if the question ever gets set, quiet this time, then the suitcase-heads can not reply.

Nathan's eyes mist. Just talking such things. Eyes the size of suicide. And Nathan should know. He was one of the first guys to have dreadlocks in England. That was the late 60s, way before the big dreading-up was fashion, way before any suitcase-head twisted a knot of hair then tagged along for the high ride. And that was because a locksman always had a packed suitcase. Always ready those days. Having dreadlocks was the sure way. From locks alone, everyone knew the score. It was plain. A locksman never came to England to grin sunshine. A locksman never wanted a house and car here only to fake forty years before age and a pension. And false teeth safe in a coat pocket.

Chapter 23

Black folk used to run for cover! It was a big divide. Black people seeing locks in England caused a huge divide in the 60s. And that is hard to believe now.

In the early days somebody like Nathan was just too black. Black folk never wanted to identify with somebody so black having locks. The older black folk run for cover! Nathan used to wear a hat but his picture from the Jamaica days was here. And black folk run for cover.

It was not till Bob was on the scene. Bob Marley was a guy that white folk loved because of that talent. And the skin tone. And the dreadlocks. And because white accepted Bob, black folk in England could accept a black-skin man having dreadlocks. But that was then. And not seeing locks now is plain impossible. True Rasta live a England but cover dem dread. Rasta content in a tent. But a suit-case-head is looking to glitz it, looking to bling out the Ritz.

New scissors in hand, Jimmy turns to the mirror. Scissors that will never get used after today. For a while it's only gazing. Slow minutes. A man watching and seeing the resemblance to Nathan in a mirror. The scissors will do the ceremony. Scissors gleaming, lethal, cold. But a friend. Scissors like hari-kari blades.

The first lock cuts off. The sad. But no going back. Not now. Nowhere to go back to. So, one lock at a time. Cut slow, cut careful. Jimmy cuts that suitcase away. Now something ebbs in mirror mist. The mirror getting like the open sea. In two minutes, a stranger on a misty shore. And one empty suitcase gets set aside. Suitcase no more.

Maybe it started at the zoo. Or maybe it was two women on their doorstep. Two hungry plum-voiced women were at their door one day. They did not want to talk glass. Not with Jimmy. They just wanted to be nice, but inside. Right on the doorstep one woman wanted to touch the dreadlocks, to fondle dread. She was the sly one. Her fingernails were blood-red. But the other woman just said her mind. A threesome, she said; fancy ten minutes upstairs with Genesis playing? And maybe Jimmy would have gone along with that. Thinking about that wildness was wild. But just as he was about to step into the house, Geraldine arrived through the gate. Just finished her pitch next door, she was coming to correct people she supposed were giving Jimmy a hard time. So now four people were on a doorstep. With two different ways to go.

In front of the mirror for a full hour after the shearing, a stranger. Watching. Checking it out. A different man. More serious. Less serious. More wary, less wary. Eventually, a relieved man looks back from the mirror. Disappointed, but relieved. The face is different. The bearing different. And at exactly six feet tall, this guy is nearly 2 inches shorter now. But no mascot, not now. If they need the man they don't need the locks. *Poppy-show* is a scared show. Jimmy talking a while to a mirror. Having locks was like someone else was always there. And another thing. Composing means people can not take you for the sermon in church they don't want to hear. And you the composer, nobody in a nightclub will squeeze your shoulder to say 'Play it, Sam.'

Jimmy knows. Eye clear and head clear of locks, things are different. Lorna was right. Guys zapping round and smiling the smile, wanting to go some special place. Or no particular place. But some can not pretend. Some do not know to pretend, don't even know the one pretending and so end up on mental-health drugs.

Flake highs is what Lorna calls that. A weird name, but it fits. Somebody knows it a mile off. In one blink they know the score. And yet. A thousand lives to get at. And even a thousand words will only be halfway right. That folk festival will be a kind of Passover. No room for jazz there. To them, jazz is a bad-mouth prophet. The organizer understands something like Minims, but still saying jazz and not folk. And because they alone call the shots, that makes it jazz, not folk. That's the way it is. What else can they do? They the folk that listen Radio 4 and go to the Tate. People like that expect tradition from a festival, saying the past is key to the future.

Deep into night, Jimmy at the window. Quiet, he lights a smoke. The night is far and near. It could sing. And maybe streetlights can sing as well as shine. But Jimmy sings the woad song, singing it: *Woad-man, yeah, you! You flick a switch and icebergs thaw. But when you look at waterfalls, even rain, all you see is deluge. That's all you want to see, all you want me to see, want me to see, to see. But more colours to jazz than blue, woad-man. Yeah, more colours than a rainbow could weep at.*

Chapter 24

More than twelve weeks since Jimmy meet Lorna that zoo day. He remembers her now and then. Some days she even compares to Agnes. Lorna works in mental health. She looked the business that day at the zoo, chatty but distant enough in her suit. And that suit was weird in the stammering sun. Cut cloth that was set, so near-black.

The Newcastle postcard shows abuse. It's been in and out of Jimmy's jacket and once a matchstick traced the phone number she wrote on it. But, so far, he has only ever phoned once. And that was nothing to do with Agnes.

Jimmy's got the blues. And that's because Agnes leaves being faithful up to him. And living up to that is too hard.

Lorna's brother could die. She's hurt. Hurt and alone. But not the kind of lonesome a night with man would fix. To Jimmy that day at the zoo is still strange. What happened there? He gets guilty over Agnes. But Lorna is not so close. Lorna is a set to some place. Especially a night like this. Jimmy knows. Lorna better stay outside. Nothing to do about her brother, but she'd better keep from his woman-hunger tonight. A Sunday night like tonight.

Locks cut off, but the ground is the same. Locks or no locks, Lorna would be a haul for somebody tonight. Jimmy saying 'Great if she was here!' Great if Lorna was beside him on the floor; she'd get some grabbing by now, hauling high with cushions. She was made for that. That woman is for stacking high with cushions now and then. Or pillows on a tenement floor.

Agnes? Why'd she leave her slippers here? What a thing! Why leave slippers in Jimmy's flat? Two crimson things. A joke. But Agnes is Agnes. She used to step from her shoes at the door then hit the shower, shower quick, then braid that hair. And that was always the same. Agnes and Jimmy talked one day about making the whole thing last, make what's going on between them go forever. Hair is a big thing to Agnes. One minute that hair wild. Then her head shakes and she talks. Then gets the jar of fourteen oils. Next thing is the neatest cornrows outside Africa. And only lightning is quicker than that. But she a hemisphere from here. She whisper. And dance. Agnes loves to dance. That woman move. And she can break-dance. Jazz is beautiful but unpredictable, that's what she whispered one day. Agnes a woman having rolled Cape Town r's when she talks.

For Jimmy being alone helps. You alone and you see some things right.

But the last clean sheet is on the bed. And Jimmy saying 'Agnes! Woman, you should be near!' The way she moved the flat. That woman did not just walk. Agnes rolls. That woman rotates. And mango bleeding. Jimmy remembering that roll, taking it to bring it home.

But Agnes is back in South Africa now. Too far. That day at the quayside was hard to take. The water was mist, like curtains to the ship. She'll be true, that's what she said on the mobile as the ship edged from daylight and sight. Might take as long as a year but she *will* get back to England; that's what she said.

Agnes better hurry back. Jimmy saying 'Hurry back! Woman, you gone too long!' And her blouse-black nipples can talk to sheets. Tonight they whisper to some lone dreaming.

Chapter 25

Geraldine knows a neat way to spite dogs. Or so she says, saying that feeding baked beans to tenement dogs gets them to calm down. Bad dogs shut their noise, all depending on the amount of beans you feed.

Dogs on Pluto? Attack hounds. Lethal by inclination. Most days they wait for their master to get back, the quiet guy that never talks, the one with the baseball cap low over his forehead not wanting to get recognized. Somebody reckons he was a big shot, a one-time big noise.

Jimmy tried Geraldine's trick with the tenement dogs. Seven jumbo-cans of baked beans got shoved down a cardboard tube through their letterbox. But the trick did not work for long.

After just one hour those hounds got set more than ever, howling the whole concrete, howling on their master to get back. And dust termites gnawed their eye. But Jimmy did not figure it. Tonight the dogs get diarrhea. Those bad hounds let fly. Nine feet up above a new shorn head.

Chapter 26

Christmas next week. Every house looks beautiful in suburbia. Happy lights are glowing warm. Some gardens have very neat winter-flowering shrubs, like Chinese witch hazels. These shed their leaves in autumn and are exquisite now in pale yellow petals. Looking them in the cold or getting close to them, a delicate perfume in the air.

Geraldine says 'Oh, look!' She buttons her coat. And adjusts her scarf. And then a minute of quiet gazing, looking at the ribbon-like petals. Then she turns to Jimmy, saying 'Oh, look!' But he turns away. Getting rid of the dreadlocks was one thing. But now a cynical man with not much to say; or so she says.

Say, what? What about a few ambitions? Like what? How about a few goals. Yeah? What about these houses, or ones like them? What about them? Houses like the ones in this road are up for grabs, Geraldine says, saying somebody of colour could live in one.

Jimmy looks again. Looking at the houses. House after house. The evening is maybe not too cold. He knows. It would be great living some place like this. Having a place here would be open-plan, wide, wide. And it would have a workout room with a rowing machine. But top of the list would be the concert grand; a Steinway, Ferrari red, hot. Something Oscar Peterson would make chant. Or Joanna MacGregor. She could drop by any old time to play Bach. Living somewhere like this means living alongside top heart surgeons. And deep theatre directors would be neighbours.

Geraldine says Jimmy can make it happen. While living in the tenement? That business is for now, she says, but living in a half million house would be it. Or a cool million.

Jimmy looks at Geraldine. Coolly now. Not sure. But as she gazes at the Chinese witch hazels in the cold evening light, her blond hair tucked into her coat collar, he believes she means it. To him she is one strange white girl. But easy enough to pull laughs. That day three weeks ago she saw him without locks and said it was exactly like young Denzil Washington. And quiet was in her eye.

But Geraldine can be wicked belly laughs. Earlier this evening she was fed up because of how canvassing is starting to wear her down. To cut the humdrum, she tried out a prank on a pompous homeowner. She got lucky, got gifted a sucker. A prim homeowner opened his front door with a Basset hound. To crank the prank she got the look right. She set the scarf to cover her hair, then narrowed her eyes. And got cool seriousness in a high-pitched voice. Then calmly looked the man in his face. And, instead of spiel from Homes, she tells him she's a grateful Eskimo. Who? An Eskimo. What? An Inuit. Well, now! Then she said she got a great education being in England, thanking the man for his taxes that made it possible, but now she's doing a bit of research so would he help? Well, she said, it's just a quick survey, a little questionnaire. What's the first question, the man asked. Quick, her voice upped an octave. Still doing the unblinking, she said her tribe was wondering if they could try a few igloos in London. London? Yes, in this street. *Where?* Well, as close to his house as possible.

Geraldine played that old city gent, worked and worked him, moved him round like a leaf; at one point he wanted to tie his tie even though there was no tie to tie.

And when it was over and the gent was back by the fireside, she was in the street the other side of privet. Laughing and laughing.

Chapter 27

Effectively, this is night. Saying evening would be bureaucrats. Somebody in a front garden is doing winter pruning and, because this is surgery, the wounds on the tree need special care to allow healing. Trees standing still, getting wounded.

The pickup van is late today. Canvassers chilling at the junction. The evening is like sugar in cold tea. It's either the pickup van or get back to base by bus. The van was never this late before.

Geraldine getting anxious. But she will talk of other things. Shivering, she begins a longtime question. "I've never heard anyone link jazz to folk. Why do you?"

Jimmy wonders if this is worth bothering with. But Geraldine is one human to make room for. "It's not easy," he says. "It's kind of hard to explain."

Somewhere in some airless observatory, bat frequencies are falling on some nerd's oscilloscope. And people going by quicker and quicker on the cold pavement. People going home to get warm.

"Try me," she says. "Start with jazz."

"You mean like what it is?"

"Yes. What is jazz?"

Jimmy shrugs. "Jazz is all about the blues. Ever listen to blues? Blues is folk."

"*One* type of folk."

"Good! So jazz, well, this is the part where it gets hard to explain."

"I'm not a dribbling idiot."

"Real jazz is half a step from blues. Only, in jazz you don't loop so much."

"I, er, don't get that. Run it past me again."

"With jazz you have to live it. You imagine the next moment and it happens. Got to get past repetition."

"And the rest of us live repetitive lives?"

"Well," Jimmy grins, "there's always somebody imitating, only living the past. That's not what I call living."

"Imagine or die?"

"Look at my hands. What'd you see?"

"Hands?"

"Yeah, my hands. There's things between left and right. You can

92

subdivide and subdivide."

"*What?*"

"Folk-music can get mistaken for the big racial," Jimmy laughs. Fingers clicking, his feet quicken. Shuffling side to side. Suddenly a scat, a track Clifford Brown called Joyspring.

Some of the people indoors will be looking forward to dinner. And checking the wine or TV schedule. Cozy, indoors, sipping coffee. Or ogling whisky.

After a minute Geraldine nods. Jimmy feels displaced, like between a smoke and smile. Looks like she understands, he thinks. He tries to light a smoke but the cold weather blows over the junction and both hands go deep in his overcoat. Her eyes say she understands.

Jimmy kicks a kerbstone. "Tell me why you do this bullshit job."

"Don't start *that* again."

"Why?"

"Because, because!"

"Because you get satisfaction?"

"*Satisfaction?*"

"Preaching at people."

"What?"

"Preaching of glass."

"Well, you know, there's something I should tell you. And what a story that would be on a cold evening! But it would have to be by a fire somewhere, with a glass of something. It's a long, long story."

"And you can't tell me the end part?"

"Feel like a bit of agony columns?"

"That bad?"

"Pretty much. It's, well, I must sort out something."

"Is it what's going on with Brian?"

"Yes."

"Like you must make up or walk away?"

"Well, it's not clear at the moment."

"Why not?"

"How should I know? Everything is so cut and dried with you."

"You been married three years."

"Three and a half! Straight out of university."

"And you want to *feel* married?"

"Well," she sighs, "of course."

"Why don't you visit him? I don't know the guy, but he's not hiding from you."

Geraldine tightens her scarf. And bites her lip. Every night the stars over England repeat themselves in orbits that repeat. The whole repetition takes thousands of years.

It's hard to talk her heart. But she tries. "I think it was pretty much irretrievable after the flop. We *so* wanted to keep our little agency afloat but the tide came in and we went belly up." Her voice lowers. "It was like losing a child."

"Go and check him. He'd like that."

"He's resurrected his PhD."

"Bright guy."

"IQ of 161. He dropped his PhD so we could set up the business."

"What's his thesis on?"

"Information theory. It could take another year."

"That's why, then. It's the other woman in his life at the moment."

"But *I* wear the ring."

Jimmy laughs. "You and me, we're the same age, but you're ten years up the road from me. At least ten. I don't know how you can do a bozo job like this."

"This stint at Homes is me on the rebound."

"A fine romance!"

"My adventure."

"*This* is an adventure?"

"What else?"

"Knocking doors, talking spiel?"

"Listen, morality doesn't come into it."

"It's sales morality. And that's no morality at all, basically."

"Well," she says, "I tell the punters the facts. I tell them a salesman will call. I never do rubbish about customer services managers. Never!"

In some of these houses there's bound to be the complete works of Beethoven in CD collections. And in one collection could be something on Hendrix, like a video at one of the festivals.

"I go along with it because it's how it works."

Geraldine shrugs. "Look, I've got to get away. Must think. Must do something."

"Why not give VSO a try?"

94

"Voluntary Services?"

"Yeah."

"Live abroad? For a year?"

"Yeah."

"A whole year?"

"What's one year?"

She skews her nose, narrows her eyes. "Can't wait to get rid of me?"

"Well, if you went somewhere it might help you think. Somewhere far."

"Hmmm."

"Not a bad idea, is it?"

"I suppose there's the Balkans."

"Or Afghanistan."

"Maybe. But I don't know a thing about what's happening there."

"Africa?"

"Well, I don't know about that. But why not? Somewhere like South Africa. Yes, might be nice to give South Africa a go once things get more settled."

Quiet, Jimmy looks away. Counts to ten. Slowly. Kicks into the pavement. Then counts from ten to one. Tries to light a smoke. But gives it up. Again.

"What's wrong?" Geraldine blinks.

"You want to get a suntan on some South African beach?"

"Politics! You should go into politics. No, not suntans. I'd just do the little things."

"Like?"

"Really want to know?"

"If it's about helping black people, I'd dissolve. "

"No, it's bigger than that," she laughs.

"Bigger, in their own country?"

"The difficult thing since I met you, Christ! Are all black men so suspicious?"

"What a big word!"

"You suspect, suspect! Everything. Me, everyone. Always on guard. Cynical. You never stop!"

Cars crawl, turning to turtle on cold tarmac this evening. Cars wanting to turtle, so moving in turtle motion. Some switch their headlights to beam. This is tarmac turtling. Cars becoming turtles to take a closer look at a man and woman at the junction. A black man, a white woman. Car after car wanting to turtle, slow them turtle eyes. And after every turtle-gaze the same thing happens: turtles decide to turn cars again; some shout their horn, then go off to turtle piss.

Geraldine never mentions this. Pretends not to notice. Hard for Jimmy to see how she understands. Someone of colour trying to get how come a middle-class white woman's got what it takes. Somehow, she knows this alienation. But Jimmy keeps the pain, gazing at Christmas lights glowing in the houses. The cold evening is a pain keeper.

Every house here warm. House after house, glowing, heir of every street in the country. A million miles of tarmac connecting every house in England. And someone can just up and get in a car to go any place.

And now, a cold lyric: *Black tarmac, come with me. Yes, you. You know me by now, know that cold archipelago.*

Quiet beside Geraldine, Jimmy mulls what happened one evening. It was a cold evening ten years ago and he was out with schoolmates doing carol singing. The look on those faces then! The same look on their doorstep face canvassing. Si-lent night, ho-ly night.

The van is too late this evening. The quiet houses make Jimmy think. Some people already know what could happen. The name of ethnic spots could change. Any immigrant spot could get called Brixton. Some small-time official could hurry back to a committee room and shout 'I've got it! We'll have lots of Brixtons!'

Jimmy trying not to laugh. It would be easy to laugh. Brixton-1 would not be a des-res place; only down-home blacks and white liberals would live it. Brixton-2 would have the best jazz club. But anything beyond Brixton-9 would be just too come lately, still collating, nervy, looking over its shoulder. While at the same time in the lily white countryside, mint sauce and hot dumplings pile onto lashings of beef, and early Genesis or Elgar play. This is serious. But who to talk to.

Trying to keep warm, he scans the road for the pickup van. And then notes Geraldine as she sears into evening landscape, her face etched by arctic light. The inclination of her body is the kind Hitchcock would have looked for, her specific English would be it for celluloid Alfred. Her whey face wracks with tension at the junction.

96

Jimmy finds it very hard to talk of racial with a white. Honest talk. "Why South Africa?" he wonders.

"That's probably where it's going to happen."

"Think so?"

"I believe so, yes."

"What's going to be so great?"

Geraldine tries her best smile. A sarcastic smile. "Guess what?" she says. "I didn't bring my crystal ball today. Oh, so careless of me!"

"Then just go for it, ad lib, make it up. I won't know the difference!"

"Can we stop now? Why are you so hateful? It's always the thing for *you* to talk of race, you want the moral high ground. But that leaves me with, what? Bursting into tears?"

One hot chat was at the party where Jimmy and Agnes met. She was avoiding everyone wearing gold, and was just about to leave as he arrived. Wear gold, and you leave town. Agnes would put every ounce of it back in the ground.

"It's culture," Jimmy says. "But I'll be honest, when I _"

"You mean I'm worth the truth? Well!"

"Look, when I think of South Africa it's white privilege. The old apartheid legacy is still around. I heard it's even in the grass, the sea. I'd feel weird going there. My girlfriend is from Cape Town and sometimes it's the same old."

Ages fascinated by English. She stayed at the party to talk to Jimmy only because he solved the puzzle: get from *gold* to *dust* by substituting only one letter at a time. After loud grumbling, scribbling away on a cigarette packet, embarrassed, annoyed, Jimmy cracked it: gold, told, toll, doll, dolt, bolt, boot, loot, lost, lust, dust. Agnes said there was a simpler sequence. But she smiled. And Jimmy was in.

"She's from South Africa? You've never mentioned that before. Black, isn't she."

"Yes."

"Where did you meet?"

"She did her degree in London. King's."

"Did she like it here? Oh shit! That sounds naff, but you know what I mean."

"Thought it was fantastic. London was a big city of lights. No racial insults, nothing."

"She gelled here, then. Oh, brilliant!"

"She got by."

"No, she didn't *get by*. She gelled. She obviously gelled with you."

"And I'm so hard to get on with, right?"

"If she can get on with you," Geraldine laughs, "she'd get on with *any* Brit."

"Brit? As in Britons?"

"Yes."

"*Brits*?"

"What's the problem? I mean, a woman from South Africa should know. She must have told you."

"What?"

"Didn't she say anything?"

"Like what? That there's black Britons?"

"Naturally!"

"Like who?"

"People born here. You're a black Briton."

Quiet, wanting a smoke, Jimmy gulps at cold air. "So you say, lady. So you say."

"Not what *I* say. It's a fact!"

Mentioning Agnes was a mistake. Agnes never said squat about anything called black Britons. Even on the phone when she talks of Brits, meeting them, visiting their monuments, she's talking white people. And when blacks talk of Brits, they mean the white man.

"How many white people talk that talk?"

"What?"

"You didn't hear?"

"Then what are you, if not a Brit?"

Jimmy's hands rub hard together, rough, trying to warm them. "How many white folk see somebody like me and say *black Briton*. I don't mean black British, I mean black Briton."

"Then who *are* you?" Geraldine grins.

Neil Armstrong stepped on the moon and was soon clearing stardust from his visor. But back at NASA, at base, on the earth, somebody was thinking 'Hey, Neil! Who you, now?' And Buzz skipping near the Stars & Stripes, grinned back at home in that lunar module.

"I dunno," Jimmy blinks. "Black, born in Liverpool. British."

"British!"

"Yes."

"So, you are a Brit. QED."

"Let's cut to neutral ground. If I was born in China, that wouldn't make me Chinese. If you were born in Shanghai it wouldn't make you Chinese."

Geraldine's eyes hesitate. Suddenly, what she wants to say hesitates. She can not say it. Her hand reaches her face. Her hand knows the face, steps of whey. The evening hesitates. Turtles could hitch a ride from the cold hesitating evening. The stars hesitate. And headlights hesitate from traffic hesitating. In the end, nothing is left that can hesitate. It could snow tonight. But chances are snow will hesitate one more week.

Geraldine's throat clears. "Briton is the noun," she says, "and British is the adjective. If you accept the adjective, you already have the noun."

"Cute!"

"What's the matter now?"

"I hate it all that grammar. I could wrap it round me and still freeze to death!"

"I was only joking!"

"*British* is what the BNP use when they mean white. Down the road from my flat I heard this BNP guy doing a sermon, and it was 'Britain is for the indigenous people of these islands, the English, Welsh, Irish and Scots.' He was a bright guy, a serious preacher."

"Come on, I said I was *joking*!"

"To me, a Brit is like a soldier in Boadicea's army."

"What?"

"I mean it. Brit is heavy-duty English. Like a baldheaded Tory, somebody like Margaret Thatcher."

A florescent light stutters in the front room across the road. The only house without Christmas lights. A tall woman walks to the computer desk and sits down. She does not draw the curtain, wanting it that way. The woman wants to be visible from the street. Standing again now, she removes her jacket and folds it on the back of the chair. And wipes the computer screen with her palms. Then takes a sheaf of papers and puts them in a drawer. And gets something from the floor.

Jimmy will not upset Geraldine. She's too good to him. And

mostly it is not her fault. But it would be great to get the facts, find out what is what.

Shoving her hands deeper in her coat pockets, she smiles a cool smile. "Thinking in the past again?"

"Yesterday, I got dealt a really weird hand from the woad-game."

"The *what*?"

"Woad. It still gets smeared on."

"What happened?"

Turning away, he remembers. "A bloke, a big red-faced guy said I can't be English. When I asked him why not, he said because my ancestors don't come from, I can't remember the name of the place, it was somewhere in Germany."

Geraldine gazes her feet. Hoarse, she murmurs, "Angleheim?"

"Yeah, that's it. Home of the Angles, right?"

"What did you tell him?"

"What could I say?"

"Didn't you say anything?"

"He was full of facts and figures."

"That's so shocking. So disappointing. Didn't think there was that much rubbish. That's interesting."

"Interesting, as in *jolly* interesting?"

Stepping in, she must see Jimmy's face. "What do you want me to do?"

"I don't know."

"Have I got a halo?"

"Your words, not mine!"

"So, I should shampoo my halo then head-butt a few diehards? Come on, let's hear it!"

"That's not what I mean."

"These things take time. Why can't you be patient? Be *patient*!"

"Patient, as in wait 50 years?"

"It will happen. You *must* believe it."

"So I should take a seat for now, right? Then make a nice cup of tea and wait a hundred years?"

"The sooner we get started the better."

"Then one day me and my neighbour will head off into the warm sunset together?"

"You sound like some horrid little drama you want to act in!"

"And my life is not a drama already, a tragedy?"

Arms flung in the air, Geraldine groans. Her head shakes. Quiet, resigned, she steps close and cups hands with Jimmy's to make a windbreak. The cigarette lights in the cold evening air and she looks him in the eye. "You're far too cynical!"

"Why'd you stop smoking?"

"Don't avoid the problem. Let's get back to *your* tragedy."

"What about a spliff, you ever do marijuana?"

Geraldine turns to scan for the pickup van. And somewhere a nerd or only Stephen Hawking is wondering why nobody from the future arrives to reveal a solution to time travel. In America, Ron Mallett tries for a time machine but it could take quite a while yet to get right. Then somebody of colour could get back, like maybe four centuries back, and pretend being a slave.

Jimmy taking nicotine in the old English evening. Lungs getting older and could die. But only exhale.

"I quit smoking," Geraldine sighs. "Not even cigarettes, not now. Gave them up. Can't afford them. And I *have* done spliffs. Satisfied?"

Across the road, the woman in the window turns from the computer and hurries from the chair. Now she's at the door, switching off the light. But forgets something. Back in the room, she's at the desk again.

It's hard to see the half-hidden sky over London. But talking to Geraldine makes Jimmy feel less cut off, liking to watch her eye, watch how she looks at trees. The way she looks at the warm houses on this road and night. Eyes that could even weigh the sky. Sometimes her eyes are astronomer eyes, seeing the big picture, understanding. And she knows names of trees he'd never know, like oleander and hawthorn, hollyhocks. This woman is a ransom, a keener of the outdoors.

"By the way," she says, "what's an uncle tom?"

This a big surprise for Jimmy. He drags on the smoke. Dragging hard, inhaling, dragging with no mercy, tobacco more than lungs will bear, watching the ember sear to him, trying to think, dragging harder. This the end point. The human terminus. The cigarette is a cypher. Nothing is left. Not even lungs. "Uncle tom?" he says, exhaling a billow. "Where did you come across that word?"

"What's an uncle tom?"

Trying for the best way to answer the woman, watching night

play her blond hair, Jimmy drags more smoke. And one more drag. Quiet, he nods. "Uncle toms are hypocrites."

"Who?"

"Grinning black hypocrites."

"Like who?"

"They're every place."

"It's not about being a tom cat, then?"

"No."

"Where's it derive from?"

"It started a long time ago."

"A long story?"

"Yeah. But the main part is where an uncle tom was a slave grinning from the master's house, doing the master's chores, cooking his food."

"Wiping his arse?"

"Yes, that's an uncle tom."

"Christ!"

"The other slaves were outdoors all day, minimum of 14 hours all day, every day, busting their guts in the fields."

Geraldine does not fully understand. Her eyes look for a place to set. Her eyes are busy with Jimmy's face. This woman studying a face like she's never seen him before. Her eyes are near, wanting something. But the more she stares, the more he could laugh. Headlights flicker. Headlights on Jimmy's face. Turtle lights flickering. And a woman getting evening from a face. He won't laugh. Her face is innocent. A clean face.

Backing away, Jimmy doubts her. So he must try, must find out. "Why not say blacks should go back where they came from, the ones that feel so hard done by here. Bet you think that sometimes."

"*What*?"

"You heard!"

"I have never thought in such terms!"

"Want me to jump off the world?"

"Let's get this straight, is that what you think?"

"Me, *know* to think? Since when?"

"If you think that, then it's the end. Is that it, is what you think?"

The front room across the street is back in darkness. Like the rest of the house. Except for one little Christmas tree alight upstairs, the house is black. And no sign of the woman anywhere. But then, she's at the front door now. A tall woman coming down the driveway, heading for the street.

Geraldine does not know the whole story. But her eyes are true. Jimmy believes her. Then again. Sometimes being black means being too trusting. And who will ask if half the Arctic on fire is still the Arctic on fire. He wonders about Geraldine, wondering if what she thinks is what comes from her mouth. But nobody will inspect this woman's mouth. There would be no gobbets of raw meat clinging to her mouth. Jimmy trusts her.

She tugs Jimmy at the overcoat sleeve. "Look at me!"

"No. I don't think you bullshit me. I believe you."

"Then what was all that about?"

"I never know. No idea where that stuff comes from."

"Then why say it, why say something you don't mean?"

"It just comes out. Hard to know who's who, what's what."

The evening sky is the same as the cold night sky here. And mute, a few stars reach out for who will look. And two people pace a cold pavement, numb in a minute of cold quiet. Without a word, they move from the junction. Christmas is less than a week away.

Recruits who stayed are well adjusted now. Everybody is a blood stained predator. Almost everybody, because Geraldine does not play the predator game. Everyday is measure day, weigh that lightning and pounce. Where weeks before was talk of tree-lined roads, houses to prospect for double-glazing deals, now talk is of predator tracks through docile herds. Deep tracks. Houses are not houses now. Those things are slow moving prey. And punters are warm and dumb, munching merry on muffin, content cattle chewing cud.

Chapter 28

This it? What, this? This is 2000? *Hugeness* was supposed to happen. Something way off the scale. Like a star-ship. That's what the fireworks mean.

A fireworks show on TV. Fireworks that look nice as night. Multi coloured lights that live. Beautiful fireworks. But not gentle as stars. And not as far. And nowhere near so kind.

The MC grinned. 'Ten, nine, eight...' then paused, sipping bubbly, then said 'four, three, two, one. Happy New Year!'

The river at Embankment reflects stars. But too faint. Stars are cut by fireworks. Tonight stars are an old lamentation drowned by water going to sea. And somewhere, because of a church cant, the preacher-man gets a look in.

Politicos are the ones. They the shrillest preacher of all. Already on TV one politician says this millenium will bring a fresh start. And stuff like that still cons people. Jimmy hates politics. Hate is not the word; even contempt does not hack it. Now and then he talks politics. But only with Nathan. Bishops are the main problem, Nathan says; those guys are all at sea. Bishops drop anchor in baptismal water and say 'The Lord walked on this.' Folk respect water. But politicians go for beer. And the great beer is their election. Hops, hops, hops. Nathan says politicians shake your hand only to raise their glass, saying 'Cheers!' Then as soon as you raise your own glass to sip, they already looking for your suicide in the beer.

The calendar shows '1st January, 2000'. Jimmy alone, cut down by malt whisky. A better calendar could be on the wall.

Counting years can never go away. But other places the big count could start from. Like with Jesse. Jesse Owens hurdled the skull of Hitler at the Berlin Olympics. And that was the very same year an Edward quit the English throne to wed a yankee dandy do.

Instead of 2000, the calendar could show 'Year 64, Owens Era'. But folk want to keep it celestial. Then again, counting could start from when Neil stepped on the moon. And Buzz. But who can win Olympic gold like Jesse? And politicians can not get into astronaut college.

Looks like the preacher-man was a muso. But people getting fed up with preacher. Preacher was a weird musician, saying how he
104

was a great cosmic player, Lord of the Sabbath. Then he upped the stakes a notch, saying he can play anything, anytime, and for all time. And promised to play the stars, get a galaxy to sing out. And folk turn their ears to the sky, but who can hear a star? A damp noise comes from a bell tower. It's the preacher-man tolling, still saying 'Turn the other cheek.'

But even weirder than preacher was preacher's mother. Some people can recite that part of the bible by heart. Preacher-man's mother woke up one day and was pregnant by her god. And not too long after preacher was born she started a common man's brood of kids. She wanted to heel the ground by testing her nipples; so she unloaded that woman milk to wailing mouths, fully human this time. And somewhere in all of that is a donkey. A donkey doing a package down the road. And that jackass still travelling, still coming. And someone in a blood-red Ferrari could stop to show carrots to a jackass on millennium highway.

Bishops light a light in church. And all because something out there always shines back. Day or night. But nothing is different. The TV shouts 'Hooray!' But Jimmy will not shout it.

The TV does not show music on the river. But now it must be sound checks at Embankment. The folk festival is tonight. But that does not matter now. And that's because Jimmy moving on, got more music to play.

Three days with no sleep. If a logbook was here, Jimmy would have a 3-day gap with no sleep. It would log alcohol jugged down. And log the meaning of that phonecall from Agnes. That call was for a whole hour. Agnes called from the southern hemisphere, saying she got asked again. But she turned the offer down. Agnes wants to boogie. The phonecall means she could marry to do dat right dis time.

Instead of sleep Jimmy will count lions. His eyes close. The last bottle of malt hauls up. Where's the wrapping-paper from the Christmas present Agnes sent?

Soon, tawny lion cubs file by. Day-old cubs nuzzle by instead of sheep and, in twenty minutes, one lion cub gets counted for every year of the past 2000. Honey-eyed little lions.

Alert, quick, Jimmy moves for coffee. And a yard of anything in the kitchen fit enough to eat. Right now anything would be better than counting a tribe of lions. Even sardines on stale toast.

105

Chapter 29

On TV the New Year's Day concert from Vienna. Having new year's day on a Saturday seems a wasted move. But the music is Strauss. Magic music. Melodies set to the Danube. Music deep over water. But something else on the screen. This is high art.

Ricardo Muti's doing a third conducting stint this year. Some people in the audience whisper how it is Lorin Maazel they like. Last year it was Lorin, and they wanted this millennium to be him conducting it. But Ricardo's doing great; that's what most people say, hushing.

A billion people have tuned in from all over. They listen to Strauss in Africa, Japan, America, in Europe, the Middle East and Australia. Folk from every place. Everybody gets a special on this TV show. Discipline is high. And that is the method of the whites.

Nine hours of sleep, a wipeout from two in the morning till near noon, but Jimmy finally awake. A spliff loops.

4 o'clock, and a bad call. This is Donna. The fuss woman phoning Jimmy. Wincing, he remembers Donna. Remembers how he was wicked to Donna one evening last year. For the first time he can see the whole thing. And if just one word must do it, that solo word is *desolation*. That Donna, that large lady got laid waste. Genghis Khan could not lay more waste than what Jimmy did to Donna last year. And seeing that, only now, after more than a whole year to think it, that is bad, bad.

Maybe it was not Donna. Through her body, Jimmy was maybe laying waste to something else. Like how England squanders: this insult and that, this setback, that spite, this door closed, or a door opened by hypocrites. And the church. Every false thing doled by the church, like the part in the New Testament where slaves must obey their masters in all things. And a preacher who was god, but played mortal blood on a wood cross; or was not god, but got his blood shed so his god would be content. And nobody today ever goes to church to ask why anyone should *ever* have a master in the first place. Or how come a priest lives in a palace, a priest living in a sumptuous place called Lambeth Palace.

That's what that weird evening with Donna was? That? That pillage? Maybe. But to have a kind-hearted woman on the end of that,

106

a singing black woman from the church. That is bad.

Donna phoning, the lady with her body as a house. She says she got the Christmas card.

And now?

Well, she can't stop thinking the good part.

Even after what happened?

What happened?

It happen last year. Donna was in the church choir and she get stoned by Jimmy. And now he knows. It was a survival business that happened between them. Donna disappeared in a sump. She always had too much to say; every day, every time, more gab. But the great thing was her singing: singing pure, singing full. Something was soft and always kind about that singing woman, maybe her eyes, something deep in that woman singing the church choir. So that evening last year Jimmy said it, well, asked her if she would check him at the flat. She was looking for something. It had to be affection. Donna was looking for tender things. But that evening last year, well, only stone grabbed that woman. Wicked wildness grabbed, a force-9 hurricane grabbing her down.

Donna is a large. A heavy lady. Hard saying how big she. Maybe near 17 stone. They call her Queen Donna because of size; that woman big as any lake. But not fat. Nothing was like a wet pullover in the laundry. But the days she fussed! Fussing that soaked half the London sky. But she always sung from the heart, eternally from the heart, every note full, note even, her voice like a euphonium, singing to sing. But she never got the timing right. It was the piece Jimmy composed for the church choir; every time she said 'The rhythm, the rhythm!' Fussing that the rhythm was always on the move. Look, she said one day, this thing is jazz, understand? This rhythm hops and skips all the time. And Jimmy said 'The rhythm, on the move? Where else would rhythm be?' Donna was not sure. And that was hard to take. Because she's a music teacher. There was no excuse. So that evening after rehearsals Jimmy showed Donna where to look for rhythm; that church woman got to see all the rhythm she could see. The personal kind. That evening was mist last year. Weird. The only thing is maybe that rhythm business was key. Who knows where stuff like that comes from? In one hour Donna got stormed, wicked, rough, a tempest, slaying, a hurricane, wilder than a lion killing in the dark. Jimmy owned all she had.

Even stuff she never believed. In the bible David was a great king and as a boy he dropped Goliath and later had 18 wives and a son named Solomon. Solomon was the guy with 300 wives and 900 concubines. But one evening last year somebody got from Donna all that Solomon never got. And when it was over Jimmy expected to get called *Maniac!* Or get called an animal. Even evil. But all Donna said was 'You are confused.' You're a wounded man, she said. Blankness was in the room. Jimmy was alone; so alone, she said. And him with nada to say. And when she got back from the bathroom she was humming to herself. And by now the spliff was burning good and Jimmy leaning back, smoking that high-rise herb. And watching yards of cloth fix to Donna's body.

Now it's more than a year later. It's New Year's day. And Donna calling Jimmy on the phone. Whispering, she says 'Happy New Year!' She's at her sister's place and three kids are snooping round so that's why the whispering down the phone. And what a serious turkey on the dinner table! Jimmy sprawled on a tenement floor, grunts 'Hello'.

Donna is going to Jamaica. She will go in two weeks. She could go for good. Mumbling, Jimmy says she should drop by before flying out; yeah, come for a shot of malt. But quick, something quick. This is bad. Cold quiet now. The woman's got something that was on her mind. She wants to hang up. This is New Year's day? Something else is here, and not even Donna knows what. Then the strangest thing. And that is Jimmy with a sudden feeling. A quiet, warm feeling for this woman. Drop by later, he says.

Donna's breath gets low. She wants something. But scared. From here, Jimmy will not speak. The next move must be the woman's move. Her lips damp the mouthpiece. A blindfold is on her heart. Eyes close, but eyes seeing a basin for sweat. But, well, yes. Donna says she can pass by tomorrow to say goodbye.

This is the first time Jimmy has ever chatted with Donna by phone. That bad evening last year floods back. The ache, the terrible loss. The loss still there because of how he mistreated her.

Chapter 30

Getting left out of the millenium folk festival is not so hard for Jimmy to take. Not now. Not after the way he treated Donna. And outside in the air, trees forlorn and a promise of snow.

A host of memories start. Things like family. And memories of longing. Stuff going way back. Bad, bad. Maybe this year will be better. This millennium year.

The first bad thing was that day at school. That was quite a while back, but it still hurts. Somebody painted a golliwog on the play-ground wall. And that still hurts. Seeing blood lips on that jet-black face, part cartoon, part vampire. It still hurts. It was a cartoon vam-pire; a cartoon was inside the vampire, for why did the golliwog grin. And a vampire was inside the cartoon, for why else did golli's mouth get big with blood.

Another thing was the name-calling. And learning to ignore it. Or pretending to ignore. The teen years were the bad part. The wise-cracks! Somebody should definitely have got their eye poked out for that wisecrack stuff. Then later the cold spite. It was from the guy at the factory, the boss man, the bozo that totally dripped school because of being thick, but now owns a factory and wants to settle a score by dealing spite to the low-paid workforce. That, and other stopgap jobs with morons ablaze. And even places where race words are scant, loud animal belching will be there that shows ex-actly what they mean when somebody black walks past a group of them. Or somebody black and innocent can enter a well-lit room and a redneck turns round and gazes at the light bulb, saying out loud that the room has gone dark; even in broad daylight, even with sunlight screaming through every window and door.

And the police. What a run they can be! Dysfunctional white guys using their uniforms to play games, winding down their police-car window to make monkey zoot, bonzo wearing police suits and say-ing you can not be coming from where you say, even when you show something that identifies you, even then, even when it's obvi-ous you are who you say, even then bonzo say you lying.

And if all that is just not bad enough, the worst part comes next: the civic, the mask you wear to pretend. You pretend you do not see the hypocrite mask that devious English wear when looking for something safe to chat with you. But when you discard your own mask, thinking it safe to be yourself because you sure who is real and who is lying, you can not conceal the cut; you know you're getting fooled again. The hurt of that is more bitter than bile. Bitter, bitter. All that, and a mile more. Some of it half-forgotten, all that bitter there and never going any place.

And the stuff Nathan talks about! Nathan and his generation have five hundred racials for every two acts of kindness that can get recalled. And if you tell somebody what's happening, if you make a stand, try only saying you're weary, had enough, then pow! Odds are they tell you to fuck way off. Or if they get polite, they say you have a chip on your shoulder. Or point to a moron sportsman on TV, a tried and tested uncle tom, then tell you 'Look at that chap who is black but always smiling, never complaining, just getting on with it. And, in any case, you are welcome to go back where you came from.' Dem do dat, all de time, matter-of-fact, end of story.

Chapter 31

Nathan on the line, calling Jimmy from New York. Nathan is over there rapping old times with Bobby Delaney, the tyro bandleader.

But it's the lyrics of Minims. That's why the call. Nathan remembers the music OK. In fact he just played Bobby the whole thing on trumpet but can't remember the words. Now Bobby on the line, wanting the lyrics, saying he could get interested to record Minims.

Jimmy's still shifting those lyrics round, still getting them simple, saying the music is the same and the theme the same. Yeah, the same folk-opera. Minims is for folk born in England. That's the theme.

Bobby laughs. Bobby says a theme like that is just one little size too big. That's because one theme can never fit *all* black people. Not in England. Not nowhere. That will never happen. Blacks learned that in the States, understand? Man, black folk will never see eye to eye on what needs doing.

Jimmy wonders. The bandleader talking the old black, brown and beige? Bobby huffs, but says yeah, saying that that stuff will happen to England too. Once a place gets more browns and beige, then most times the browns and beige will step away from black. Music must move free, Bobby says, saying jazz is not politics, and saying Ellington tried that reconciliation stuff and Mingus tried it, but who thanks them?

Then forget colour, Jimmy says. What? Where? Well, Bobby, think people with nowhere to call home. Who? People that maybe have never seen the ocean let alone belong to some place across it! That what happening to England right now? Yes. What? Yeah, people like that should have a fireworks day, have their own song. And that, Jimmy says, is where Minims steps in.

Bobby saying nada. Jimmy talks on, saying things are different in America. The black thing there is different, America is their home. Your home, Bobby.

"Kid, that is only talk down a phone line. Only talk!"

Jimmy getting urgent. "The theme explains the whole thing. The Minims theme deals with the blind lady and the child."

"Blind lady and child? What the hell you say? Blind lady, eh! She young?"

"This is no joke."

Longitude was the big problem at sea. Till John Harrison happened along in the 1700s. Shipwrecks happened the whole ocean over till then, because nobody had a sure way to know if they were going to China or heading away. Latitude was the easy part. Latitude was nothing more than lines from the sun. But longitude? Ghost lines on the map. Then Harrison happened. John happened along with a clock that synced the ocean. Because of him, any ship got to know where it's at. That's how Britannia got to rule the waves. That's how Bobby Delaney's got a back-story in America, folk picking cotton till it came out their ears. And Nathan deriving from folk slaving on a Jamaica sugar plantation.

"OK, kid. Yeah, OK, I won't mess with your head no more. OK, let's have it. This theme you have, it better be good, you hear me?"

Jimmy moves to the keyboard to hitch the phone. Hit's a C-sharp minor chord. Then starts the Minims theme: *The child looks at the sky, saying fireworks are at home. Sweet and low, the blind lady says 'Child, you describe it so well!' Fireworks at home in the sky makes the lady laugh out loud. She's easy, carrying the timing of minims in her head. In her head, her head. Tapping her cane, she's puzzling. She'd like to see colours of things, oh yes, colours, things no one can hear, but she won't think of that more, not the way things get ranked by colour under the sun. Blue things, purple, green, yellow, and oh, there's puzzles in huddles. The child wonders what sorts of puzzles? Oh, lots, lots. Like which ones? The lady sings it, singing, 'Minims, minims, minims!' Still singing, she tells of people who huddle: they gaze up at fireworks starry-eyed, up, alive, starry-eyed, starry. Weary now, sitting, resting a while, she tells the meaning of the puzzle: Folk huddle, but not because of the magic of seeing, no, no. It's because they only see like a Cyclops. She shakes her head, saying most people run from a proof. You hear them whimpering, eyes shut tight, oh Lord, scared of proofs, afraid, afraid! The child reckons circles are hard to measure. The lady seeks the child's face with her hands. Well, she says, yes, my dear, yes, alright, proofs can be hard sometimes, but it always gets there in the end, somewhere safe, very safe, safe like sunlight. The blind lady inches to her feet, cane waving to the sky. You know, she says, some folk expect other people to work for them, even work things out for them. And that's the start of every problem. Listen to this, she says, tapping the cane with both hands. Tapping the cane,*
112

tapping the cane, the cane. The child can see. Yes, minims can't be hearsay to someone blind. The cane is white, and that's for people to tell their condition, but the cane rhythm is everything, The minims' rhythm, minims' rhythm! The lady singing it, saying the rhythm of minims is the one rhythm that fits most things, even fits Parliament Square right in the middle of what was nowhere.

Bobby smiles. Down the phone line, and way across the sea, the bandleader smiles, gets the plot. "Hey, that's not bad."

Jimmy hears him turn to Nathan. To do something like the blind lady, Bobby says, man, that would be something! Nathan laughs, proud laughing. Then talk and flurry, stuff Jimmy can not quite hear as the phone hangs up.

Marconi and Bell should get music composed for them. Somebody should graft space-crackle to song, somebody with brains, like Pierre Boulez. Silence, ecoutez! Duke Ellington is somewhere still.

Five minutes, and Bobby back on the line. "Hey, kid. Minims is neat! No wonder they don't understand that over there. Handle it right and it goes places."

Jimmy must ask it. "Think you could give it a try, like even record it?"

"Yeah," Bobby laughs. "Why not. But look, hey Jimmy, me and Nathan go back a long ways, so don't mess up! Don't dream your thing away over there. Me and the band, we did Europe last year and, brother! The black people you have on TV in England, whew! Some of the ugliest mothers I *ever* seen. Nothing will happen there any time soon. Get the hell out!"

To Jimmy, this is a sign. Bobby Delaney to record Minims could not be better. This the best thing on new year's day. It cuts away from the slop from a fake folk festival.

Bobby's voice lowers. "Listen, the one thing you gotta watch is don't mess with the bible."

"The bible?"

"Yeah, your Minims is like from the bible. It's hipped far inside the bible."

"It's only the theme," Jimmy laughs. "I'll kick some shots into it, no problem!"

113

Chapter 32

Tuesday morning, 11 o'clock, 4th January 2000. Donna's early voice sings on the entry-phone. Three minutes, and this woman will be standing at the door. The scent of evening primrose hangs in the air. And a Duke Ellington CD playing on the hi-fi.

The flat is in great shape, but the kitchen a bomb. To somebody like Stephen Hawking the sky is only a beginning. A galaxy will go down an info tunnel, or a woman wear perfume before midday. Jimmy tucks away A Brief History Of Time. And gets back to the kitchen.

The cups getting a serious workout in the sink as the door knocker clangs.

What's this? *Who*? A whole new deal. Lips numb, his eyes say Wow! This is Donna? This woman? This can not be her. This a different woman. This woman limber. She definitely is not the same huge coming to the flat that evening a year ago. Now she's maybe only 10 stone, a poinsettia bloom.

Donna is quiet. She does not really smile. Her eyes check. She checks the details, the head, the eyes. From her eyes, she understands. She knows Jimmy walks alone now, on a mission, without dreadlocks or detour. She steps past the door and pretends not to see dishwater splashed over his cords. This the first time any woman has ever seen him this domestic way.

"Happy New Year, stranger."

"Yeah, I got rid of the locks. Been this way a while."

"Then happy new millennium," she says, eyes touring the room.

"What, the whole thousand years?"

"Loosen up!"

'You look great."

"Brought you some turkey. And a piece of new-year cake."

The flat looks nice, Donna says; the flat is tidier than she remembered. And it's more, well, sort of lenient. She won't do malt whisky, no whisky at all, not really. But hey, a bottle of sorrel is in her bag.

Biting her lip, she goes off into to the kitchen. And in one minute things in there getting a serious woman doing them. Jimmy's gaze settling on the old settee. Hands quaking, nervy, a spliff starts. Things to remember. Big things. Or try forget. Ganja lays on a to-
114

bacco trail as Donna comes back to the room. She carries a clean glass. One glass only. And quietly fills it up with sorrel. More washing-up to do, she says, turning from the sitting room.

This window next to the settee has never had a curtain. Excepting maybe for the other tenement block, there is nada to see; only a high-rise watcher could perv. But the settee. Man! This is where Donna got roughed the time before. The little settee gets Jimmy nervy, standing. Wavering. Remembering. The spliff ready.

Hard, figuring why it happened. He had not set out to crop Donna. But that pillage happened like out of nowhere. That weird evening last year happened by itself. She came back to the flat that evening after rehearsals and, to start, it was only him being at the keyboard doodling while she was on the settee. She sat on the settee while he played, playing inversions, wanting the right feel, lazing, playing around, random riffs, gospel riffs, Ray Charles riffs, music from the solar plexus of a wronged community. She did not want the ganja. Sitting quiet, she was listening the playing; dreamy playing, she said. So Jimmy played it. And smoked ganja, severe and quiet. And played it true. 16-bar music, blues, unguent blue-notes for Donna alone, the woman, not the complainer, for the quiet in her eyes. And when the music was over, when nothing was to play more, the player said nothing. Then realized. So said it was OK if she did not want to smoke, saying that some people can not handle spliff cut and, anyway, look, it was rhythm time. What? Yeah, de real riddim time come. What? *What?* The hour of rhythm, Jimmy said, saying this was the time for person time. Donna was cut down by shock. Quick, she upped from the settee to leave. But then. Everything changed. Donna bit her lip. And looked at Jimmy. And quietly she was not shocked now. But she sighed; I agree, her eyes said. His hands were faint. When him touch Donna, Jimmy hol' her close. It was difficult to believe. There was so much to hold. Then hold some more, reaching for was what, holding. Donna holding tight. Even the room was holding, the whole room. An' all de time she hum a gospel. And when she stopped that humming, took a step closer to look him in the eye. Then one full step, but standing back, checking, finding out. Then she said it. The music was great, she said, yes, she'd come for as much music as could get played but she'd guessed all along. Guessed? Yes, knew what was on his mind

115

and, no, no worries, a woman her size won't break. And then. The gap closed. And she said it one more time, saying again a woman her size won't break. Then it happened. Something snapped. It was as if Jimmy was waiting a whole life for that, one blink to get free, to cut loose, to know no obligation. Affection was in the woman's eyes but what happened next was nada to do with that. That whole thing is too hard to talk. Maybe only a tenement can hold the emotion to tell it. It was like a real woman was just too plain for Jimmy, too day-to-day, it would have to wait, maybe till he was older. Her clothes dropped to the ground. She backed into the settee. What a night. He got to rid what had been angry all the time. It was like from the ocean, but, really, it was only inside a body cave. Donna's body was her house. A bell was in the woman's secret dream. And she said it again, saying his playing was dreamy. But that was at the keyboard, playing blues, dicing gospel, reaching out. But now it was far as far can go. Far as a stone trombone. And that was bad. That evening was a stoning. It was with a stone trombone. And it was only because of one thing. Bad regard. Bad! Everything Jimmy did was down to bad regard. What name she called it, well. An' wid one whisper she complain. But not over no stone trombone. It was the window; no curtain on the window, she said. Jimmy turned to the window. And pulled out the trombone. And looked how that body-house get worked. Lazy by now, he asked who could ever see them all the way on the 8th floor.

That late evening early last year was one thing. Till now it was too much fog, remembering but forgetting. Jimmy does not know why it happened. Even now. Stone was in his soul that weird evening over a year ago. And he would have said sorry through the wall, out through the 8th floor window. But something was wicked by him; it wanted to play a heavy woman more. A battle waged that weird evening. And Donna was the field of dreams.

Now she's here. And looks great. Something is alive now because of how Donna looks so changed. This year really is 2000. But something wanting atonement. Donna is a lapsed Christian. She still sings gospel in a choir but has no real religion to cross her life. Not now. Jimmy likes that.

He remembers seeing her the first time. That was quite a while ago. It was one morning at Sunday school. He had just moved to

116

London with Nathan. And Donna was twelve, about five years older than him. And he liked her straightaway because of the gap between her two front teeth.

Now Donna here. Again. She divides the room with her woman eyes. Jimmy ashamed. She sips from the glass of sorrel. One sip is a lot, she says. Her eyes are clear, but want him to say it. Her eyes narrow. Jimmy can not believe her eyes. Donna gets close. Her hands approach him. Her finger tips cover his mouth.

"Say it!" she says.

Jimmy scared, looking to set a spliff. Wondering what to say. Sorry is a big word. But Donna must hear it. Somewhere a flower in a vase is by itself and, on a stem outdoors, that flower will have sisters glowing in a garden.

Misty eyed, his throat clears. "Donna, sorry about the stuff that happened."

Donna is nothing like before. She so set now. Her eyes say there's more. Jimmy pulls her from the ground and her hat falls. But then. A new mood happens. She afraid. Her eyes toll. It's bad news. She wants to talk. Something needs bringing up. Slipping to the ground and stepping away, she talks it the way things are. Spells the whole thing out.

Her life was all over the place since that freak evening. She was sick for a long time because of it. For a year she was even sorry for him. Then hate. Hate! Some days she wanted to die. But wanting him to die. Her eyes moisten. When she got his Christmas card all the hate came right back. She hated him all over. Jimmy can not talk. Quiet like timber, wondering. Nothing he can say. Somebody can go to a garden and cut flowers down. And who would leave them cut there, on the grass, not put in a vase? Even saying sorry is small-time. This is shame.

But maybe *shame* is not the word. Guilt is in the mix. The rest of it is too severe. And that's because Donna was wanting some of what happened. Jimmy knows she was looking affection, but all she got was stone. She wanted affection and stone.

Long ago the preacher-man preached by saying Peter was the rock the church will get built on. But 2000 years from that and the church falling apart. Pillar by pillar. Donna wanted wickedness. She wanted one wicked thing to quake her body, her house, her church; she wanted a wicked quake through it. And Jimmy stoned that

117

body-church, bulldozed it to the ground. And set fire to what was left. A year ago something in the woman wanted stone. Donna's body was her church then.

Why she here now? A lot going on, more than words can hold. More than war. Her eyes say 'Go for penitence.' Why has she come, Jimmy wonders out loud. The scent of evening primrose is faint in the air. Donna can not be sure. Could be ten reasons, even a reason she might never know.

But now she here? Well, reasons will not matter now. Not today. She will explain.

Her mother and father come from Portland, a green place up on north-east Jamaica. But more and more it looks like they will get old here. They will die in England. Portland is like Wales, she says, it has the same feeling of mountains and tumbling waterfalls. Only, it's warm in Portland. She will take a tape recorder to Jamaica and talk to old people, get old-time songs they remember, and tape the African words disappearing from Jamaica talk. She goes to Wales to get at Portland. Or going to Great Yarmouth is nice. But they have nothing in Portland like the great-crested grebe. And nothing is ever like a Jamaican hummingbird flitting in Great Yarmouth.

Donna sent off a DNA test in London. It can tell within a hundred miles where in Africa her roots derive. And all her roots derive in Africa. But the slaves got so diced. Tribe was rent asunder from tribe. The slave-master wanted slaves that could not talk their own language and, after just two generations, only a few remote slaves in Jamaica could talk in anything from Africa. But they have people in Jamaica, the Maroons in More Town can talk a language from Ghana. Donna could have roots in more parts of Africa than one. This woman is the colour of summer. To Jimmy, she beautiful as black olives today.

Jimmy has never checked any woman from the past. Nathan's advice was clear: a man dat go back to a flame is man dat 'ave no fire. But something about Donna. Maybe that's why Jimmy sent the Christmas card. It was a blank card. No emotion, not even his name. Yet she knew. Straightaway she guessed it was from Jimmy.

Something going on. The spliff ready to light and the matches irate. But Donna says no, no ganja!

Jimmy laughs. He reminds the woman. "Ganja is herbs, Donna. Ganja is head-lights all day."

She grabs the spliff from his mouth. "The rubbish getting smoked in England only coops up inside, it turns guys loose. So no ganja, not today."

And now her coat slips. Donna's hands folding her overcoat neat across the old settee. And a weeping sunset is in a Jamaica dress.

Chapter 33

Jimmy in Great Yarmouth yesterday. The ocean was angry and folk in thick overcoats. And gulls perched the seafront ledge, feathers puffed.

Getting there was touch and go. The gearbox scrunched the whole North Circular. But just the sight of the sign saying 'M11' and it was a go. It was a no risk, no sanity day. 130 miles each way, thinking, flowing, watching motorway signs loom and disappear.

Donna's friend is from Great Yarmouth. And invited her to a fireworks display near the seafront. But yesterday it was Jimmy on the motorway. And Donna on a plane to Jamaica. Maybe she gazed down at the ocean, thinking: one raindrop falls on a mountain and it will use five percent the potential energy in itself. That one raindrop will cancel a zillionth piece of the mountain away. The rest runs back to the ocean. The sun is the pulley. And now the Jamaica sun spreading on Donna today.

Jimmy was on edge; mostly about time and longing. And walked the beach a while.

Donna was right. Great Yarmouth has a big statue of Nelson. Horatio had a thing for Great Yarmouth. He sailed from the naval base there to taste ocean salt. Funny to think that that statue was up a full 30 years before the one in Trafalgar Square. Horatio Nelson, and pigeons; one hawk and a million city doves. Where those pigeons from? Falcons and kestrels are only toys now.

The seafront fireworks got cancelled. So Jimmy toured the coast road. Going from Hopton to Winterton, cut by every yard of winter beach. And solitude. Fifteen miles of solo sand taking a winter break. Somebody said hello. It was a lifeguard, part young and so ocean. And he turned and waved as she shouted back, saying the sea chose a bad day but windmills are only a mile inland. Traditional windmills are only a mile or two inland and working away. And Jimmy wondered what windmills have in common with the sea, and the lifeguard said 'Take a look!'

Lifeguards see water. Teeming or lost. They witness drowning. And see the newest seashells, catch the ocean sighing. Or see it panting on the shore.

Before heading back, there was quality time at a quiet restaurant. A polite place. Jimmy chatted with the polite owner. And tucked into a plate of scallops, artichoke and herb risotto. Next was an acre of steak & kidney pie, with fresh peas and tomato through red wine sauce. Somebody said 'Try cheese with apricot compote and walnut bread.' So Jimmy gave it a try. And all the time the sea was breaking on the beach.

Sediment was in the glass of wine. And two lazy, lazy cups of coffee. And a cigarette. And a giddy sight of gulls dicing the wing. It was hard for a tenement dweller to leave that place. But eventually, Jimmy was back on the road in a half-light turning evening.

Chapter 34

Donna is back in Jamaica . Back to religion now. And praying. She prayed as soon as the plane touched down in Jamaica. For some people what gets called faith was never the thing. It was pride all along. And Donna had a body always shy of what was in her heart.

Geraldine is glad. Homes is allowing another week off for the new year. But only because Clive wants punters' heads free of booze. No residual booze or mince pies must get in the way of the glass business. Geraldine is spending Christmas with cousins in their Hampshire cottage and she helped repair some thatching on the roof. And what a buzz, getting the right reeds to gel! And learning strange things. Strange? Yeah, like *liggers*. Oh, and *spars*. And *tarred cord*. Her shoulders never worked so hard. In fact, she could start life again as a thatcher. A bit of a Maggie? No, no! There's lots of other work these days, so most people don't bother much with the old crafts. But something about reeds, thatching is not all they do. Water is obvious. Papyrus comes to mind. And she went to a fete and won two old wood-block books on fishing. Then fell off a cooper's barrel. Bruises everywhere. But that's OK. And now she's half glad with her life. Well, for a while. But it's so relaxing before the open fire, sitting up till late and watching fire reflect on the parquet floor. And it is so beautiful outdoors, so cold with icicles and twigs underfoot. She's glad for winter. Glad for one barn owl. Glad for the garden gate and stillness of new snow.

Jimmy told Geraldine about Nathan, what happened on Christmas Eve. Nathan in New York, still laughing over the fight on Christmas Eve.

The run up to Christmas was weird. Jimmy and Nathan did a pub crawl, drinking and talking Jamaica, talking the ocean, mulling jazz. Nathan said 'Send a demo tape to the Marsalis brothers, Wynton the man.' According to Nathan, Wynton should be the one playing sax; Wynton could do more with sax than trumpet. And that's how the problem started.

Three guys from America drinking together next to Nathan and Jimmy. One guy wore a crown of a thousand scores, jazz scores; he could quote anything, scat or tap it, and said to Nathan he will buy the next round. Why? Because it's Christmas, buddy. And that parlay was the ace. The drinking was a whole oil-tanker sloshed down.

And a jazz rhythm tapping at the drink table that maybe was never heard before off a bandstand. Then more booze. And scat, scatting. Then one more round of booze. Then nothing getting said. And that's when it turned bad. Maybe it was the liquor.

The genius Yank started it, saying no American would ever piss on anything out of Britain. They can not play jazz here, he said, so how can they compose it, and, sure, some of the musicians in England are good, sure, but only as imitators, and yeah, some of the older guys are pretty fine, but give the younger guys a solo and, oh boy, they can not *play*. Nathan wondered about Stan Tracey, saying Stan is from London. But the three Americanos only laughed. Stan Tracey is one OK piano player, the genius said. Well, Nathan said, the likes of Sonny Stitt rated Stan.

Nathan told the genius that being a genius must be great, but being drunk and one genius won't cut it. So he better mind his mouth. And that cued the physicals. Heavy-duty.

Just a shot of millennium blues, Jimmy said, when the barman wondered what was going on. Quick, the genius leaned over. And head butted Nathan. Jimmy lashed out, aimed two evil kicks, evil mule. But then he got dropped by a trained elbow. And a beer glass broke in Nathan's arm, two of his ribs got zapped. But even with arthritis in his hand, Nathan handed down a bad penalty. Jamaican style. The law arrived out of nowhere.

Jimmy grins, remembering Nathan shifting down the road like a cheetah on fire. Even with two cracked ribs Nathan was moving it, saying 'Send a tape to Wynton Marsalis' as they split up on White Hart Lane. Two days later and Nathan in New York, laying low.

Chapter 35

Last night? Agnes was on the phone to Jimmy. Late. He admitted it. Admitted playing around; but only one small admit, no way the works. And not Donna by name. Every day before flying out, Donna was at the flat. Right up to the last minute., right to the afternoon of the night she got on the plane, that woman was living ten years her life in seven days. That's how it was. But she knows the score. And if things work out she will stay in Jamaica. The last two women in Jimmy's flat are far across the ocean. They can listen the sea.

One melody haunts Jimmy all the time now. A samba. This tune is like a hurtful woman and it's been nagging since Donna was at the airport saying 'See you!'

Maybe it was from that Brazil visit. Maybe it was from the north, like from Belem or Natal, or Recife, Salvador. Salvador? That place is mini Africa. Every Brazilian there black. Almost every. But they claim something big. Musos in Salvador claim all modern rhythms come out of Salvador. Even jazz. Yes, friend, even jazz. And samba, reggae, funk. Hard to argue with that, seeing one Salvador rhythm king scat and play. But folk in New Orleans would smile. And in Jamaica.

Ten million people got shipped to slave in Brazil. Ten million black humans. Samba was the dance that African slaves danced to fool the white man. White man thinking samba was stupid African. But samba was only dance up front; back of that was communication. Syncopation concealing secret Africa talking.

Two years back, Jimmy played jazz on the Brazil coast. And learned samba. Nighttime in Porto Alegre finally fixed it. Limpid sunsets and a beach that was set. Most nights was listening to weather, listening sea breeze run palm trees to a hillside and abide. Some people say palm trees talk. The more indigo a night, the more chance a palm tree will swoop to talk.

At one cafe they had The Third Man playing all night. The juke-box played it over and over. Somebody said Astrud Gilberto was there and she wanted that one tune played. And only that tune. But somewhere every night is always somebody watching The Third Man play. Or boozed to noon, they watch but only to hear that zither play one more time. The plot is lame to that zither: no scheme

124

at the border, no sluicing alleyway, no bootleg or betrayal, and no watered-down penicillin. Only a zither, that sideways shift. And the heartache; to hear Vienna in black and white, but it could be any place.

The tune nagging Jimmy does not rent emotions like that zither. And a girl. A special beleza was in Porto Alegre. A bad girl. She was way off the scale. Almond trees cut through evening there and the whole thing was coming along with that beleza body rolling like a brown guava in a tray. She wanted the touring jazzman, the one looking the sea all day. Jazz was easy in Porto Alegre. One morning the girl wanted to surf. Far from the city. Surfing, but not on a surfboard. It was on the inner-tube of a truck tyre. The water was turquoise and one mile deep. And the girl was the colour of fresh roast almonds. She laughed on the ocean. All the time on the inner-tube of that solo truck tyre, she laughed. From her, it was clear. Every laughing woman owns the sun.

Porto Alegre sunshine was on that almond body. Sometimes she magenta, sometimes she was ebony. Exactly the colour the sun wanted. Jimmy was drifting the ocean alone with the girl. She loved the water, but wanted the shore, wanted to get back to the small hotel up the coast. A watermelon was waiting.

To Jimmy that day was like Ocho Rios in Jamaica. That sea. Only the talk was different. The ocean was emotion. It was Portuguese that the almond girl talked. She could say four words of English but all of a sudden she cried 'shark!' Two hundred yards from the beach, the girl shouted *shark!* And two alone on a pumped up inner-tube on a deep turquoise sea.

Back on the beach, she toweled her body down and could not stop laughing. It was only a joke, her eyes said. Jimmy tried to laugh, knowing how hard the water would get from then.

Some memories are the kind you have to be by yourself to understand. The melody bugging Jimmy is the girl's voice. Her voice was homing waves. Then she explained. 'The shark, it's no problem, you can't daydream the sea.' That's what the translator said as the girl explained, laughing in the sun.

Back at the hotel her watermelon was cool on the table. But that melon was too smooth, too cool, just too quiet. It was waiting as she upped from the bed. And when her knife prized it, opening a slice, a slim slice, something flashed. Instead of only melon, something to do with the sea flashed. It was not a melon slice. It was the vermil-ion razor of a coast-shark.

Chapter 36

Harold Shipman got it in the knees today. Should have been the neck. Or his balls. Instead of the judge doling out life for murdering those 15 old people, they should take all Shipman's four limbs. And use the dullest knife.

Going to your doctor to fix something, then Shipman jumps out the bush with a syringe. And maybe this mad doctor has killed 200 people already. Nobody can say.

So far the millennium is a bad let down. Nothing's changed. Talk over global warming is big on the news and that is one picture nobody can deny. So instead of only a Shipman, mad medic in England, a Shuttleman could be waiting to happen. Or a Rocketman.

South Africa is willing Jimmy to go. But not for the country. It would be because Agnes is there. Some days, Jimmy gets bad headaches over Agnes. One morning she'd rolled over and Donna had a face that was too much like Agnes. How will this pan out? A trip to Cape Town might have to happen. Soon.

Jimmy plays Ellington everyday. Today it's easy listening, time, listening to Ella Fitzgerald sing the duke. *Oh lady, be good to me.*

Donna was born in London. But her thing is that her own children should get born in Jamaica. That's what she says. This visit she will spend quality time with some Maroons. In England, not many black folk understand Maroons. Most people of colour here do not know Maroons are mystic black folk eked from runaway slaves that defeated the white man in Jamaica. Now Donna owns a plot of land not so far from one Maroon place. The lady is twenty-nine. And in Jamaica twenty-nine is no age at all. Time with Donna surprised Jimmy. Everyday of that first millennium week was hour upon hour of it. Getting what she's got. And he realized. Things would be easier having a woman like her. For one thing she knows music. Not jazz, but knows music from inside. Nathan tells it, saying a woman that knows music saves time. And the way Donna talks. That woman can use straight English, or she can chuck down in Jamaica patois like she was born there. She might stay with England. All Jimmy should do is say the word. No rush, but that's the thing. To him, the rest of it is simple. That woman can cook. Seven, eight millennium days with Jimmy at the flat and Donna cooked so nice.

Donna cooked the whole island away from the tenement flat. Then one day it got serious. No condoms that day. Condoms run out. But all Donna said was let's go with the flow. Her eyes said she got the score but wanted to go with the flow anyway. Her eyes said it's more sincere with no condom in the way. And that's when the best part started. It was with four days to go. Four days of Jamaica cooking, and four nights of the acest bareback riding a man could ever have. Donna knows about Agnes.

Agnes must get told about Donna. Not everything, but enough to say a little something happened. Jimmy will not tell Agnes that Donna was like the sole woman in the world, how she got the flat to sing old-time Jamaica songs.

Agnes is a Cape Town woman. She will stay South African. But just maybe. Well, she could settle in England; but the reason would be huge. That's what her letter says. Agnes is smart. She got a first in civil engineering from King's no less. And somebody like that would earn five times more in England. But Agnes lets that ride. She's doing merchant banking in Cape Town. And at twenty six, she comes from a family with five brothers and sisters that, along with their mother and father, depend on what she can earn. Agnes can see things. With one letter she sent a hundred photos of Karoo. Karoo is a mystic place in South Africa. Even from the photos the place is set. The letter calls it the surest place on earth. Visions can take place in Karoo; a place big enough for towns and villages and wider than wide. Karoo a place where troubles get clarified. Jimmy was cut by that. And now he goes back to the letter to search that sentence. Looking at the photographs, nothing can be this beautiful. Not this pure, this simple. Whoever first named a circle had the same feeling of simple and pure things. In a song, the full moon was the first circle. Or was it the pupil in a woman's eye? Spiritual goals get set in Karoo. And now and then a solo tree steps up in the landscape, a tree that a leopard can shelter from the sun. Afrikaners used to believe they owned the place. Bullnecked rednecks believed that it was them who discovered the mystic of Karoo. And until recent times, redneck had power so only their folk could live big there. Now all that has changed.

Jimmy phoned Donna. Then phoned Agnes. And talked, promising to visit Karoo. Photographs are only paper, she said.

Chapter 37

Geraldine and Jimmy the only ones. Nobody else from their intake still at Homes. But a split will happen. Soon. From the first day back after Christmas, Geraldine declared door canvassing is no longer an adventure. She wants to work from base. And now she can go for it because Clive is growing the telesales team. She can hit the phones to sell furniture.

But she wants to go to Ireland. Wants to get back with Brian and maybe settle quietly in rural County Clare.

And that's because in England the countryside is getting too slick. There's more than 33,000 listed farm buildings but about a third of them already been converted to residential for city folk. And that is so hotch-potch, so often out of place, she says, so hick Range Rover and urban moron descending but never seeing the wood for trees.

A new intake. Jimmy a supervisor now. Colette turns a crew of eight over to him. And this will hike the money. He can not lose. If recruits drop out then their canvassing leads go to the supervisor; if they stay, then the supervisor gets a piece of their commission. In three months this could mean Jimmy saying goodbye to work and getting back to score music.

He the top predator now, the do-it man. All the k-cs want their leads from him. And this is a big puzzle. But not to Geraldine. She says this is down to the way Jimmy smiles; *exotic* is the word she used.

But Geraldine wrong. Dead wrong. Mostly Jimmy is not smiling. What this guy's doing is smile-the-smile. The doorstep is only pretence. The man that used to have huge dreadlocks is smiling-the-smile, despising those people on their doorstep. For every two or three like Geraldine, 20 resent him. And that resentment can be up front or way behind the line of sight. It's easy to hate the smug, the patronizing. And that's most of them.

What's happening to England? England can be more than where someone was born. Or less. Granite and sandstone is solemn here. And seashells are knowing, austere and collectable. And the open countryside in dun summer, the English countryside pacing the long length of a motorway and never getting short of breath. And Patrick Moore doing astronomy on TV. And Radio 3, they play jazz as well as classical on that channel. Some of this is too hard for talk, yet it claims a hold. Then again. England does not invest in Jimmy. Nothing but talk happens.

People of colour know. They want to reach out, to be neighbours, to get on with life on a level playing field. Quietly at night, they mull over what to say if they could talk to someone white.

Smug English are easy to take. They the ones that are up-front, always get to the point; sometimes they even know you know, so you get ceasefire, even a handshake. But the patronizing ones, what a different game! They have the best dentists. Smiling their own smile, saying 'Welcome!' But lying through their dentist.

For Jimmy this often happens on the doorstep. And, in a way, that makes it easy to play. Easy to talk spiel. Easy to smile-the-smile then send a k-c to take them down. Any crap, and Jimmy smiles the smile. They never know it but he's taking aim. Aiming with that smile, someone will fall. And that's because the k-c comes along with a body-bag disguised as a briefcase and collects all their money. A gut full of it. Every penny they can find. And every penny they didn't know was there. That's the payback. And along with the sweetness of that is the commission, the wafting readies, the golden wedge.

Smiling-the-smile is hard. Not the same as pasting a smile. If Jimmy tried to explain smiling-the-smile it would be a lazy E-flat, more arpeggio than chord. Trying to explain smiling-the-smile, Jimmy goes to the keyboard and slams down a chord. E-flat. Then tries E-flat minor. He can not put it into words. But when somebody smiles the smile, all the time they think 'Hey, arsehole, think I belong in Brixton? Yeah? Well, go shit yourself!'

Wagner playing in a house sometimes as somebody wonders about the black chap on their doorstep. Or they play Schubert. Pink Floyd is one hot favourite. And Barbara Streissand is the one they like to play in a hypocrite house, wanting to believe the black chappie on their doorstep is simple, wanting to believe that because Jimmy black he can not wait to get back to whoop loud music in a tenement. And want him to stumble, not speak. And can not take the fact that this guy talks in well formed sentences. And none of them would ever believe that maybe Jimmy could one day out-music any living modern composer in their heart. They want the black chappie to talk dub. But Jimmy knows what they do. So what

130

he must do is simple. It's smile-the-smile time. Hard.

But sometimes. Well, sometimes it's just plain impossible to get away with it. Now and then somebody's seen that *smile* before. Somewhere on their travels they've seen that smile-the-smile, maybe on a Caribbean beach. But mostly a doorstep hypocrite never gets the true meaning of a lean black man smiling the smile on their lily white.

Smiling-the-smile fills Jimmy's pocket. Clive's sales-spiel shovels money to the smile-the-smile man. And every k-c white, every one a clean-shaven white guy with suit and tie, so no chance somebody ever yell 'Black mugger!'

Geraldine, what would she say to this? In summer she will head for a beach. And live nine removes from Jimmy's world. And yet. She once invited him to her mother's house in Hertfordshire. A detached place, part-rural, inch quiet and coppiced with a proud little lake. And fox hunting takes place round the woody.

Mulling, Jimmy turns off the music.

First thing is the middleclass homeowner. They put on a show. They have to be big on their doorstep, always on top. Even when working the doors with Geraldine, working exactly the same streets together, Jimmy was pulling more money than she ever made. Must be a good reason for that. Talking light with Geraldine one day, the chat shifts to how more money came Jimmy's way and she said the explanation was easy. She told a story. Middle class English people are the world expert at pretence. Yes, they never let on about the problem they have. Except to one another. And only now and then.

Jimmy listened closely to Geraldine. This was not about cash flows and stiff upper lips. Sometimes there's somebody having a hard time. Sometimes a door opens and there's no attitude, no disdain in a cynical eye. Only pain. But then the eye always blinks. Because they have a black man on their doorstep? No. Geraldine says no. This is not about black or white. Middle class people are like that with strangers. Even a white stranger, someone white? Yes, even someone white. How's that? Well, it's the stranger they react against.

Jimmy wants to believe this. But disbelieving easier. And always safer. Geraldine tries one more time. Yes, she says, it can be anything. Like someone with a funny accent, or something simple as personal space. Like standing too close when you talk? Or too far.

131

Of course, being black gives the stranger quicker. But that's only because the black stranger sticks out. Sticks out like a sore thumb.

Chapter 38

One rainy day, all the canvassers collect in the telesales room. They listen to hot telesales pros calling punters down the line. Every canvasser gets a turn on the phone; dud punters on the line, but on the call-list for a rainy day. You pick up a phone and sell a window to someone you can not see. But zap!

Way out the blue, this never clicked for Jimmy before. And that's because being on the phone can get weird. Nobody knows who's on the line; you talking glass but you get to *be* glass. You invisible on the phone. Punters don't know Jimmy black.

Werner Heisenberg was way ahead. By the time he was 31, they gave him the Nobel physics prize. That was 1932. Jesse Owens was 19. And Hitler 43. Three neat primes: 19, 31, 43.

Werner said the velocity of a particle can never get logged the same time as the dot-space of the particle. This is one square deal in the round universe. Physics calls it *the uncertainty principle*. Particle after atomic particle, not huge like golf balls with Tiger Woods soldering them on the green. But too small to ever get seen. Except by the right equation. Small, small, having names like *strange*, or *charm, up, down, beauty, truth*.

Way down where the whole cosmos cranks down to basic byte, no African or Jew. And no Aryan. So a Jew is only what Adolf could see. Maybe Stephen Hawking is for real. Or he just plays air-guitar with that wheelchair.

Iron filings on a clean surface will close down a magnet. And that was magic, strange, spooky. Till the right equation got there.

Timbuktu had a huge library before Oxford university ever got its first book. And somewhere, right now, is somebody working moonbeams like a tanner with cowhide.

A seeing man listening a radio can not see more than a blind lady. And if some tune like Fantasia On Greensleeves is playing, coming down the radio quiet and polite, but affirming, then few sighted folk ever wonder who plays that sweet music; and even then they never think the player might be a person of colour. Vaughan Williams! Folk just say the name and, abracadabra! Only white.

Chapter 39

Today the workday changed at Homes. To catch more homeowners at home, canvassing will happen from 2 till 8 o'clock now. The first hour at base is still the same, still doing role-play.

Casting out, Jimmy eyes one lady recruit. She a timid woman. Their eyes meet. Her eyes look from some place very far. Agnes is another hemisphere from here and this woman makes Jimmy remember somebody's eyeing Agnes in Cape Town; somebody there wants to marry Agnes down. But this little woman is here now. And Jimmy will make a play. She looks frail, wears her neck low because she's nervous. Maybe she's a single mother. Her eyes say she's tired, weary eyes saying she could do with somebody to help her vision. Somebody should tell the score, tell of the game at Homes; she will not make money here. The canvasser game is too swerved for someone afraid. Somebody should tell her go now, get a fixed deal. Nathan would do that. Nathan would never let a woman suffer for money. Years before, even when there was a stay-away court order, Nathan delivered maintenance money to Jimmy's mother ever Friday evening.

Geraldine yapped it. Because of the tape she plays at work ever day, everybody knows Jimmy does music. And someone in telesales is big on jazz, a guy doing telesales here knows swing through to post-bop.

Colette in a cut mood today. The boss lady hands a peach each to everybody in the role-play room. And as usual she takes charge of role-play. This is no drama society, but everybody glad to clown around before going to front the upper-lip doorstep miles.

Coffee in hand, Colette sets the room. She checks it again. Seeing everything. And stops here and there to talk of Lancashire. It was in those parts that the spinning machine was invented. But now there's only empty mills. She was there last weekend. And checked out foothills of the Pennines. And took the train from Preston to Accrington. And the beech was too thick to reckon. And the oak was like at anchor, holding onto England. She could talk it all day. Her grandparents are from Lancashire.

She gets round to Jimmy. "Salty stuff."

"Sorry?"

"Your music," she says. "Geraldine lent me your tape. Hope you don't mind."

"Course not. How'd you get on with it?"

"You just might make a name one day, my man. *Some* talent. Shall we get your autograph now?"

"Well," Jimmy grins, "I can't find my pen."

"You're very talkative today!"

"Nothing personal."

"What's wrong?"

"It's a long day ahead and I've got things bugging me. Hard to explain."

"Give it a whirl."

Jimmy blank. Pans the room, slowed down, taking in every new recruit. One by one. One by one, the look in their face is the same look that was on his own face October when he first arrived here. Innocent anticipation in every face. Somebody should turn them away.

"Try!" Colette says, reminding him.

"What?"

"Tell me about your music."

"In what way?"

"Where you want to go with it."

"Well, it's quite difficult. I sort of, you know, _"

"Cat got your tongue?"

Quiet, Jimmy gazing Colette. Watching her eyes. Seeing her red mouth. Her earrings. And the lazy peach in her hand. "When you compose, it's a burden. Huge weight. You hit on something and, bit by bit, it sort fits."

"The magic happens?"

"I wish!"

"Oh, come off it! Stop being so coy. You're very vain."

"Well, that's when the worry starts."

"Why?"

"You worry because the piece wants to bite you. You're thinking this is it, this new piece is the business!"

"And you're hoping nobody's done it before."

"Yeah! How did you know?"

"It's very jazz, your stuff."

Jimmy turns fully to the woman. One minute back he was wanting to get away, set a distance, supposing she would not know how clarinet is different from a sax. But dead wrong. Two peaches juggle in one hand and she sips coffee with no sugar.

"Know any musicians?"

Colette winces. Shuffles a peach to Jimmy. "Since you ask," she says, "I happen to know quite a few. No, don't look surprised! I know some first-rate people."

"Rock music?"

"Popular, jazz, classical."

"Jazz, *and* classical?"

"You look devastated!"

"Surprised."

"What did you think? Think I'm just some greedy so and so, is that it? Is that what they say about me?"

"I didn't figure you for classical music."

"I was there myself, once."

"Singing?"

"Violin."

"*Violin?*"

"Yes. And I *know* a composer. My onetime partner is a composer."

Wanting a quiet space, Jimmy nods. He gives back the peach. And scans the room. "So, you know the graft. You know the heartbreak."

Across the room the timid woman smiles at Jimmy. But something else there. Hurt in her eye. The ache in every recruit is like fog in the room. How to tell them? The whole thing a mug's game. They saw the same serial advert in the jobs page: *£1000/ week. No experience necessary*. But no more than two will make half that money. And even if seven or eight will still here after two weeks, then three leave by the third week. That's when Colette takes the basic pay away. After two weeks everyone pulls commission only.

Canvassing for commission is a mug's game here. The slim timid woman will disappear in the ground. And she thin enough already. And Colette, what a surprise she's so into music! Her earrings big and dumb as a horseshoe.

"How are you finding the job?" she wonders. "Making lots of money?"

Jimmy looking hard at the new recruits, hard at every face. He survived here. And way ahead now. But most of these will never

136

make it. "The job? Yeah, it's something to do, puts money in my pocket. What can I say? You pay me, so you know."

"Well, you might try being a little more up for it. You could say it's going great."

Jimmy blinks. "It's going great."

"Let me tell you a little something," Colette puffs. "Think where your bread and butter comes from. Remember that. Never knock money. Never!"

She turns from Jimmy and scans the room. Checking. Measuring every face. And measuring again. Checking space. As she turns back to him her eyes dart this way and that. Colette runs a drama group on the side. It's fringe theatre and other heavy commitments. And if it wasn't for this family obligation to Homes, she'd be a theatre producer full time. Today, her red Maserati bleeds to the afternoon.

The sky was overcast all morning. But through the wide window of the role-play room the weather looks set now. The sun shines for the first time this afternoon. And, talk is, one day Colette upped from the office and went straight to the bank. Then walked into the Maserati showroom with a bag of cash.

Jimmy shapes his two hands, shifting his long fingers this way and that, shifting till they exactly fit round the image of a low crouching thing in the parking lot. And now his hands cup a new red gleam through the window. Colette's Maserati like a scarlet rose in his hands. And she standing close.

"Like it?"

"Sorry?"

"The car," she says.

Jimmy nods, weighing the car. "It's like a song. Kind of a sad song, though."

"If it's money that's bothering you, if that's what your little hand trick means, then stick around. I guarantee you'll make what you want. Late spring, early summer. Good dosh, I promise. Then you can go off and do your composing. Zings in spring around here!"

Role-play time. Colette dances to mid-room and drags Jimmy by the hand. She shrugs her jacket. And quickly takes the part of someone seriously put out by the ringing of their doorbell. The room gathers round.

137

"I'm busy!" Colette, the-woman-at-her-door, pouts. "I'm washing my hair, or can't you see!"

Jimmy bright eyed. "So sorry to disturb you, but I knew you were in. I just didn't want to face my boss and say I'd left before giving you the good news."

"The good news? Ooh, you're from Littlewoods Pools?"

"I've brought something really exciting!" Jimmy continues, polite, but talking past the invitation to chitchat. "Homes, Homes & Homes are sponsoring home improvement in this area. We're looking for the right sort of homes."

"So, you're not from the pools company? What a blow! By the way, what's the right kind of homes?"

"The right kind of homes is so easy to explain. It's homes with the proudest owners. Many careful homeowners in your area will put a proud smile on the face of their property. Some will use a fresh coat of paint."

"An overcoat? Well now, what colour paint would you suggest?"

"Any colour you like," Jimmy grins. "But honestly, some homeowners will go a step further than a coat of paint."

"Come off it! What are you trying to sell me?"

"Because your home is one of the loveliest in this area, this one-off sponsorship allows you to select any glass related product. Anything you like!"

"Like what?"

"Double glazing, for one example. Arctic-proof glass. Or a beautiful conservatory. We will install you a conservatory for a full fifty percent below list-price!"

Hands on hip, Colette throws back her head and laughs. She laughs the laugh of a flirty doorstep woman. "Well, handsome," she says, "I think there's something you should know. I, er, don't own the property. I'm staying with family for the week!"

The role-play room laughs. Bad laughing. It's Jimmy. Committed a mickey-mouse. Huge mistake. Yapped, but forgot to check if the woman was the homeowner. And quickly Colette gets back to being Colette; strict, but something like kindness in her eye. As she leaves the role-play room her jacket rides her fluid hips.

Today's role-play was a free laugh for the recruits. Loosened them up, freeing them from mind cramp before hitting the road. Laughing now, everyone innocent with hope. But their face will wrack despair in days, at most a week. The timid woman gets near to Jimmy, very close.

"That woman likes you," she says, shy.

Jimmy cut by the flat Manchester accent of the woman. "Which woman?"

"Colette."

"*Colette*?"

"She fancies you. She was trying to tell you with that role-play."

Jimmy knows the timid woman's toughing it out. That's why she here. Her suit fits neat, but should've got binned a long time. Her nails are manicured but not painted. "No work in Manchester?"

"No real work to speak of down here, is there? I've done this commission lark before. They're all the same. You get a bit of a basic to start, but that's how they rope you in."

"Ever worked doorsteps before?"

"I'm not a canvasser. Tried it once. I was still at college and _"

"College?"

"Furniture repairs, nothing academic."

"How did the door-knocking go?"

"Terrifying. You just want to turn and run."

"Then why bother with this one?"

"I'm here to do telesales, but that's next week."

"Then why role-play the doorstep?"

"It's Colette, she said I should do canvassing this week."

"Which crew?"

"I might get put in yours, you never know! How long you been working here? I'm Carmen, by the way."

"Three, maybe four months. A job like this, well it's not for everyone."

"You don't like it here?"

"It's not that. You kind of lose track of time. But, yeah, telesales is where they make the serious money. Don't know that much about it but some guy in there is a monster."

"A big-hitter?"

"Yeah, earns 150 grand a year."

"*150 grand*?"

"So they say. Been in London long?"

Knowing she should be somewhere else, Carmen sucks her teeth. On 20th July 1969, Neil Armstrong said 'The Eagle has landed.'

139

The lunar module from Apollo 11 had just touched down on the moon and Carmen was two weeks old. Her Jamaican mother was still toying a nursery rhyme, *the cat and the fiddle, the cow jumped over the moon.* And Buzz Aldrin was quick with a slide rule. Buzz had two PhD degrees and in space he was celebrating Communion from the chalice a preacher at his Pentecostal church gave him. But to Neil, the great memory of all that was not only walking up there; as the lunar module was getting closer, the corona of the sun was visible round the limb of the moon, and now he says that it was hard to think of lovers serenading this same moon while guys from earth were walking round up there, kicking moon-dust, planting a flag. Neil says the sky was not blue but black; and the weirdest part was that the whole thing was more like daylight than night up there, and the surface of the moon from the lunar module looked just like sand; he was almost expecting to see girls in bikinis getting ready for a swim. The surface of the moon is really black and grey, but Neil in the lunar module thinking it was like beach sand.

Jimmy tries again. "Been in London long, or is that a secret?"

"No secret," Carmen smiles. "Been here a week. Hey, the silly thing is I was born in London. We went to Manchester when my dad got a job up there. You're from Liverpool yourself, aren't you?"

10 to 2. Time for the road. But everybody still hanging their coffee cup. Jimmy and Carmen have started a chat, knowing everybody looking at them.

The weather is nice, she says. Jimmy twirls the plastic cup, wanting to stop the small talk. Carmen wondering how come no one else of colour is here. His fingers click, counting in Ornithology, Jimmy says it's a Charlie Parker track in his head. And these finger-clicks cut with Max Roach on the track, Max on the drums doing Jimmy's talk. Carmen can sense it because she turns to him, knowing. 'Naughty!' she says. Yeah, this woman got that right. And who would not want to be far from this place a day like today, like on a boat looking at the ocean and listening to Ornithology. Or be alone with Carmen. She's never heard of Max Roach. But wants to know why Jimmy is obsessed by boats. Because, he says, the sea is where you keep your feet on the ground. As she laughs, she surprises the rest of the room to hush and gaze. Jimmy likes that. Likes them looking at him and Carmen, but looking only from the outside. He
140

tells Carmen if there was no Charlie Parker to listen before arriving for work, it would be hard to hack this job at all. Charlie was in a madhouse once, a place called Camarillo, and because of it, folk thinking they got rid of him. But then Charlie cut some of the greatest tracks music will ever see; Relaxing At Camarillo is one such track. Jimmy tells Carmen about the smile-the-smile thing on the doorsteps. Turning her back on the room, she reaches over. A woman with quiet eyes, touching his hair.

"You like my hair?"

"It's a nice head of hair," she says. "Makes a change, doesn't it? Everybody's got locks these days."

"Time for brains," Jimmy grins.

"I'm not the brainy type."

"Wig."

"*Wig?*"

"Yeah. Wig is what bebop guys called brains."

"Camarillo," she says, serious again, "I don't know why, but it makes me think of chocolates. Not like a mental hospital at all."

"You don't get it!"

"You patronizing me?"

"It's obvious you don't see where jazz fits."

"I don't think you know me well enough to talk to me like that!"

Jimmy wants to relax the woman, quietly says, "Why telesales?"

"That was quick!"

"What?"

"You give up too easily."

"I hate conflict," Jimmy grunts.

"Then how're you going to survive?"

"I *always* get by."

"You sure?"

"Yeah. So, now you know."

"What you say is not what's in your eyes."

"Lady," Jimmy grins, "why do you want a job in telesales?"

Carmen blinks. "Well, there's this neat little wind-chime on Edgware Road, I've got to have it."

"Happy wind-chimes!"

"So, this is you? The patronizing man?"

"Sorry."

"For what?"

"For bugging you."

Carmen was on jury service last month. Somebody in Manchester shipped too many mobile phones. Made just one trip too many. And it was hard seeing the way tears welled in the guy's eyes when the sentence came.

She fixes Jimmy by the eyes. "You've been spoilt! Too used to getting your own way."

"I can't believe somebody would want to go after a wind-chime."

"Jesus, you really *have* been spoilt!"

"What's the real reason?"

"It's a brilliant wind-chime. Gorgeous, old."

"You're not a hard-up single mother?"

"*Me*, with kids? No way! Kids are what my mother had."

Jimmy lights a smoke. "Well, I think they call that the blues."

"How do you mean?"

"Paying for stuff you can't buy."

Carmen nervy now. She no longer wants to talk. "Look," she blares, "I need a job!"

Somebody should tell this woman, say 'Go get a job somewhere else.' Jimmy wants to say the right thing, say the business here is a mug's game. But this is where the daily bread comes from. And the woman might wonder how somebody can give advice but not take it. In a set tone, he hints at this. And does it in a way that's fair for all. "Why *this* place?"

"This place, that place! They're always going to hustle you. In telesales they don't have to know you're black."

"Yeah, you with that northern accent!"

"I mean, you get to London and phone up about a job, then _"

"When you get there it's a shock."

"Yes!"

"They can't connect the black face to the northern accent on the phone."

"It's a joke, honest."

"Noir cinema!"

"When's it going to stop?"

In telesales, Carmen can hide. She's done the hide game before. She says Jimmy has almost lost the Scouse accent. Like some folk that move away from Liverpool, Jimmy gets along some place else. Like Simon Rattle. Simon wields a conductor's baton for talking no

Scouse.

Carmen pulls a photograph of her family. It's she, her brother, mother and father. This snap goes everywhere she goes. She calls it her private little piece of the other Bayeux Tapestry. The *other* Bayeux? She laughs. Jimmy says she's kind of nice. Behind the quiet, she's so set. Better than that, she seriously nice. He tells the woman of the composer. And straightaway her heart jumps; she wants to know what a composer's doing selling double-glazing. Her family used to have a greyhound in Manchester. They used to race it and lose money. In one minute he tells her the works, why he's here.

Carmen looks up at the wall-clock. Then turns to him. "I'm not into jazz."

"You don't have to be. I bet you listen to nonsense."

"Look, I'm only trying to help. I don't think jazz is folk music."

"That's because you don't know jazz. No Brixton overcoat can hide it!"

"You sound like my brother. Listen, if they haven't got a cozy little name for what you do, then they don't have power over you."

"Wise lady, what would you suggest?"

"Do something they know."

"Something *they* know?"

"That's how it works."

"Do what?"

"Compromise. Smile and compromise."

"Standing round trying to be St Paul's cathedral?"

"Be serious!"

"I'm dead serious!"

"Can't you compromise?"

"How? Get a flat in Brixton, play reggae in pubs and do covers of the Stones?"

Jimmy watching Carmen. Watching her heart heave as she sighs. A wish dies in her eyes. She's no longer hunched with nerves. This woman was born when Neil and Buzz were doing that roundtrip to the moon. She's taller than she looked before.

"Try a compromise," she says.

"I've compromised all my life."

"Then go the extra mile!"

"And where's that road lead?"

"Don't turn your nose up at it," she says. "It's a start. You have to play the game. In this life nobody will lift a finger to help you if you don't give them what they want. If I was you, I would send my tapes to America. Better still, just go!"

Chapter 40

Knocking doors and smiling the smile, Jimmy wonders. It was that rap with Carmen.

America could be the place. Great music is there. Going to America would mean gigging the best, and meeting up with Bobby Delaney to do serious concerts. But Agnes. That woman would never want to know. Sending tapes to America would be one thing. But it would mean having to follow, going to live there. A year, maybe more. Agnes would never go to America. England as far as she will go.

Donna being a music woman means she would understand. She's happy in Jamaica now. And planting her land, two acres of good Portland ten minutes from the Rio Grande. That, and chickens and things.

Nobody in half the world would reject America. But being black and turning up with a big English accent and having to explain? And the way blacks in the south are still mostly poor and might as well be in o-gape Africa. But serious women in America. Most of the smartest black women in America. They have the opportunity. They do Ivy League or the Juilliard. Jimmy can not wait.

And that's the rub. With or without Ages, he would say hello to the American woman. He was fourteen when all of that got started. Lots of them will cry, Nathan said, handing over that first packet of rubbers. Ten years later and that's been mostly true. So far.

But Jimmy knows. Somebody like him attracts some of the awkwardest women in England; the race denial kind, the type of black woman never letting go of fairytales. Zeal in their face, the denial women sing the loudest hymns in church. The secular ones memorize cute slogans or go on marches, hoisting placards higher in the sky than the whitest liberal hoist. To Jimmy the weirdest woman of all was a social worker, the one liking to keep her brassiere on. She was licking ice cream from a blue saucer one day, gulping and gulping, saying he should write classical; compose proper music instead of jazz, she said. But at the other end of the scale he's been lucky. Some great women happen along the way. But something about him that brings trouble to a good woman. And something else.

One day Geraldine said it, saying she's never ever seen Jimmy

145

look at a white woman. She wanted to know why. And he told it the honest way. Apart from one afternoon with a Jamaican white girl, and that was when he was fourteen, there's never been a white girlfriend. The women are of colour, black, from light tan to steep jet.

Money wise, the take at Homes is cutting it for Jimmy now. That grand a week is still a way off, still not quite happening so far, but he starts to believe. Colette said money would zing from spring, and the take getting cozy.

Jimmy is not a natural salesman. And now he knows that knocking a stranger's door is only small time. It's cap-in-hand. And something else wrong. Twinges happen. More and more something like conscience happening. The predator-game is getting to be no fun now. Far from Brixton, meeting middle class folk on their doorstep is taking Jimmy to the soft England belly. This is a turning point. Some of these people live big, but worry all over them. The meaning of the job at Homes is starting to oppress. Two things could be true. It might only be with spiel instead of a condom, but on one doorstep journey a black guy is sticking it to middle England. Sticking it hard. And something else. For Jimmy, canvassing is getting like saying goodbye every time a door opens. He could be leaving for America. The solution comes straight out the blue.

One evening the fateful door opens. Before this evening it was only sales spiel on a doorstep. It was guff over glass. But knocking a door and knowing there's bull in what you say, that's a kind of begging. Some punters know this guy is lying, some make the connection between lying and begging. But the hardest part is one or two glimpse something that might even get called noble, but it flickers out the moment of smiling the smile, the moment Jimmy opens his mouth to lie. They know. And they want to spit in that lying mouth. They want to say the sales spiel on their doorstep is victim cringe.

Smiling-the-smile is victim cringe. You pretend what you are not, something far less than you, a shallow jive, something plain silly. On some of the more clued-up doorsteps nothing ever gets said about this. And that's a big surprise.

Now and then some white person is rooting for black people. Their eyes say 'Chin up, you can make it!' And in bare branches, birds twitter like hoists on oilrigs.

146

Jimmy slowing for a smoke. Must think.

First thing is what happened on one weird doorstep. It was a weird, weird. So weird, that maybe quitting the job must happen next. But it was the chat with Carmen. That was so set. All Carmen said, all she did not say.

To Carmen, too many black guys boasting how many woman have kids for them. And they the same guys that, well, nine out of ten do not support their own child. Kids should ask to get born; they should demand life. High in your head they must want life. You can not just turn up in the sheets. Because all that happens next is you only add to the list, the long baby-line having no solutions but only a gaping mouth. And so many lost, tiny and black; instead of being babies, they get like hatchlings begging worms from the sky.

Chapter 41

The message on the answer-phone plays one more time. The seventh time. The voice is part strict, part happy. It looks like bad news. Hand shaking, he dials the number.

"Lorna, it's me. Got your message."

"Jimmy?"

"Yes."

"*Hi!* Nice to hear from you!"

Nervy, Jimmy bracing himself. "Any news?"

"Guess what! Justin opened his eyes this morning. He smiled. We couldn't believe it!"

"Great news!"

"Well, yes and no. It was only a blip. But it's a good sign. He opens his eyes and next thing he's like 'What, me?' Then his eyes close again. The doctors reckon he can make it and we went again this afternoon. Too early to tell, but it's looking good. God, I can't take it all in. Funny, eh? How are things with you?"

Happiness is in Lorna's voice and, suddenly, Jimmy loves this woman. She's on a rush. Her brother still on life-support, having to get by on one lung, but they think he might pull through. That's the best surgery could do. And nobody knows for sure who did it.

"Me?" Jimmy winks. "I'm making out. This and that."

"You sound so far off. Anything wrong? You OK?"

"Can't complain. Picked up the phone thinking it was going to be bad news."

Lorna smiles down the line. "Listen, why don't you come over? I've got goodies going in the kitchen. Can do for two, honest. Great if you can come. Come round!"

"Well, _"

"Get yourself round here!"

Jimmy eyes the damp patch on his tenement wall. It's mildew that a spray could treat. But it looks bigger today. The wall looks like the mildew wants to eat through the wallpaper and get outside to mildew a sheer drop to the street. Mildew looking like wisteria on the tenement wall. Who wouldn't want to sip wine and chat with a woman doing her cooking one evening like this. Lorna in her flat, inviting somebody from high-rise mildew.

Jimmy gets the mouthpiece near. "Seven o'clock too early, too late?"

Lorna laughs. "Make it eight. And be very hungry when you get here. *Very* hungry."

Jimmy happy for Lorna. But does not want to visit. Things are still a daze. That weird doorstep thing yesterday is still spooky. And to-day he walked from Homes. Colette would have given him a chance, but Jimmy walked away with only half a stash. And that means only one thing; the quickest way to money from here looks like having to give music lessons. Or do gigs. But either way, that would be no music at all. Jimmy is no teacher. Hates people getting instruments they will never play even half well. Morons can not do jazz. They can not get from bozo box to improvise with light.

Colette was livid. After the weird happening on the doorstep Jimmy headed away, leaving the canvasser crew behind. A bottle of malt was in the flat. A whole bottle. One weird, one spooky door-step encounter was it. A moment of feeling something like mercy.

On TV, a crashed plane fills the evening news screen. And now the lush lips of the newsreader. A passenger plane is nose-down on the runway and a hundred lives in danger, but what's she doing with those lips? Sly levers! Her lips spread like clams. And all the time the plane with photographers round it, tending to the slew.

Geraldine quick with words. Sometimes she makes Jimmy say more than necessary. It's a struggle, him trying hold anything back. Geraldine probing all the time. But what happened to Jimmy yes-terday, the business with the homeowner, that weird doorstep thing, that is not something to talk over with Geraldine. So no phone call. No easy way to tell her what really happened. And anyway, who Geraldine? Alarm bells ring. Is Geraldine some kind of investiga-tor? A sneak? She could be undercover as a journalist, or reporting back to Trading Standards. Naked hard-sell is big. And everywhere civil liberties getting disregarded by sales onslaught. The sales game doing what it wants and calling it *entrepreneurship* and sip bubbly, laughing the laugh. Devious sales folk conning their way from the backseat of a car, or from a snatch & grab address in a business park. Rules fly. Eagles on spiel for thermals. Hands like talons in air. And that would attract fair-play institutions. The mark-up at Homes is huge. Clive goes to China every year, gets prefab at 5% the UK price. But customer complaints all the time now: hinges

149

fall off, panels warp, doors that will not open. On bad days, 8 or 10 angry customers in the reception area at Homes. But the sales side is the base line. Sales folk posing as customer-services managers, guys calling one another killer-closers; the kind of guys that sit down in punters' living rooms and won't leave, never taking no for the answer. One k-c stayed 10 hours in a couple's house, squatting their living room; they signed the deal just to get him out of there.

Weary, Jimmy starts a spliff. And eyes the damp patch on the wall. And mulls. Wondering. Geraldine a snitch, a snitch hovering? Apart from palaver about her marriage she never talks of herself. Yet she always wants to know more and more; about Jimmy, about how Nathan earns his living, why Agnes back in Cape Town instead of the big London money.

Nathan's hands have maybe another three years. But he still can build a ten-paper spliff. Perfect every time. But that arthritis, it will get so he will need a pipe instead of a spliff.

Hard for Jimmy to think. Geraldine was honest on the doorstep. She never said *customer services managers*, always gave it to the punters straight. Hard to think. Jimmy remembering their chats. Main thing was she wants to be with Brian so they can front open fires in village pubs and tip oak-strong ale. But now she in limbo, floundering at her mother's house; and later in the year their garden will give Hunza apricots. But one thing is ever permanent about Geraldine. That woman knows the countryside. And not just the names of birds.

The spliff sets aside. The phone grabs near. Time to find out. Time to find out who Geraldine. Jimmy just about to tap out the number, but remembers the clincher. Some days Geraldine arrives for work with fresh flowers from her mother's greenhouse. The phone falls back on the cradle. Half a whisky pours. Looks like Geraldine is who she is. Jimmy easing back with smoke and alcohol. Only the ceiling to look at. And wondering over Agnes, the thing about kids that woman wants. Through the haze he can see her eyes, like his eyes can meet hers down a carousel. Maybe this is only the spliff. Ganja doing spliff things. And yet. Agnes and her smile, like she was here now. That smile. And the back, the front and side. Jimmy knows. Something belongs here. Something owned. Agnes gone too long.

Upstairs on Pluto, the barking dogs demand a minute. Downstairs, heavy carpentry going on; somebody hikes a dull saw through cold timber. Jimmy quick to the keyboard. The sawing painful, but consistent, having a nagging beat. His left hand at chords, getting the chords right, comping the rhythm of that saw, and right hand hovers, waiting for clues. But nothing.

When the sawing is over, an electric drill chaws into flustered timber.

Agnes was never too jealous. Not too much. But she dreads venereal disease. AIDS is big in South Africa. And that's down to guys that will not use a condom. If Jimmy must go with some other woman while she away, then it must be condoms every time; that's what Agnes said. Her only rule. Jimmy agrees. But then. There was that thing early new year between him and Donna. And that can not go away. Maybe Agnes would understand. Agnes could look at Donna and how she's clean. Donna clean, inside and out. But Agnes would be jealous of Arleene. Women resent Arleene. They know she way ahead. Arleene's got no real brains to speak of, but way ahead as woman. Jimmy believes Agnes could be like a sister with Donna. And in some parts of Africa a man can have two wives.

For one hour songs of South African music play. Agnes sent this tape of five-part harmonies in a language Jimmy has never heard of. Songs that click. This is spiritual. African songs quietly washing over somebody in a Tottenham tenement. Like the ocean over gravel.

Jimmy wants Nathan to check this African music. Nathan personally knows South African musos, guys like Hugh Masakele and Abdullah Ibrahim. But the singing on this tape is deep, deep. Only Africa can play this. Jimmy phones, saying 'Yo!' And straightaway chocks the phone to the hi-fi speaker. Agnes said her five aunts are the women singing on these tracks. One is a lullaby, unguent, a mother in pain, Africa aching, aching. Sad Africa and a mother woman calling in the song.

All those years welding by day and playing jazz at night, but Nathan is nowhere. Before the all-clear to come to England he was playing serious jazz in Kingston and getting rated by everyone visiting the island. But jazz was never big in Jamaica. Nathan should have checked America.

Last week a white DJ on the BBC said something big. They have

151

50,000 tracks from South Africa that the apartheid regime used to play only to blacks: songs in Ndebele, and Sotho, Swazi, Tswana, Venda, Zulu. The white man in South Africa even applied apartheid to music. The good news is that the music got taped. And somebody saved the tapes. And now some of this music of South African black people will be coming out in a CD collection. They plan to call the collection African Renaissance. Alan Lomax will bring out a hundred CDs of that music, but they could get 10,000 CDs from all the South African songs they have on tape.

After ten minutes, Jimmy grabs the handset. Wanting to talk music now. But Nathan gone from the line.

Agnes is the other side of the world. Or Arleene, she should be here. She was never here.

Jimmy got woman fever. Bad. It wants a woman to cool it. And Donna in Jamaica. Lorna is a drive away but her mind is on terrible things. Where Carmen? Carmen! The face, that rude walk. No point to Lorna. A night like tonight Lorna got too much word. She will talk escalators and flake highs. And talk of her brother. But Carmen. Jimmy wanting Carmen in the flat. The place ready. Quick, he grabs the phone.

Carmen does not recognize him. Not at first. But then when she knows who, she's surprised. A distant woman. Glad for the call, yes, but surprised. Why? Jimmy should have guessed, she says. She lives with somebody; a calm reliable guy.

Chapter 42

Lorna is a white man's daughter. That is biology. She always talks about her mother, a black woman from Barbados.

One minute to 8 o'clock, Jimmy is wary outside a new peach door. A basement flat. There was nowhere to park, and it was a grim quarter mile from where the car slotted, but a woman is cooking here tonight.

The bell does not sound from outside. And he stands back, weary and wary, woozy from topic more than booze. Complex lights play the door surface. One play of light is shapes too intricate to name. Shapes looking like jazz chords under a fluid melody. A very pale outside-lamp syncs to an aloof streetlight. Light playing a cold evening in late February. The door half opens.

It's the smile. Only Lorna can do that. But she's worried already. Jimmy laughs.

Hand over her mouth, the lady looks shocked. "What happened?"

"What?"

"Your locks!"

"Oh that!"

"What have you done?"

"Got rid of them. Months ago. Walking around with that was like being a mascot."

"What?"

"Like being a trophy."

"You look so, you know, so *different*!"

"Should have been like this all the time."

Lorna can not decide. She wondering who Jimmy. Head turns this way and that, her mouth wants to smile. Her eyes can not connect with where Jimmy's going for fire; where can he go with no locks? So she stares at him, not at the stars over his shoulder.

Eventually, she turns and twirls. Slow at first. Indecisive, wondering. Then nice and easy. Lorna smiles into the evening. Twirling, relaxed. "I made the dress myself."

"Wanted something to go with the cooking, but this wine is all I could think of."

"Let's get in out the cold. You look so different!"

"Me?"

"You!"

"*You* look different!" Jimmy nods, stepping inside and taking a good look at the homely woman. She unnerves him. But it's warm here. And close. The hall-light fits like a hug.

"So, it's my kaftan that gets you?" she says. "That's what the gawp is?"

"Kind of expected you'd still be in that dark suit, the one at the zoo. I was gawping?"

"Okay, not a gawp exactly."

"Hope it was civilized."

"It's like, you looked like a little lost boy outside a bread shop."

"A bread shop is *not* me. Too basic."

"A car showroom, then. Settle for that? Ooh, close the door, boy. For my sake!"

Four paces down the hallway and Lorna dips into a room, her living room, but more office than a chill zone. Things are small and tidy. Two high-backed chairs look like bishops would want to sit. And maybe a woman bishop sits here, retired now. Jimmy knows something is wary about this space. Lorna's front room is what would please a sharp old woman; an old bishop woman could do her memories from here, her bric-a-brac long gone. A tidy old bishop woman could prepare for death here.

But then. A parachute is on the wall. It looks more like a rucksack, but this thing is hard packed for the sky. Photos of skydivers grin next to it.

The only disorder in the room is two carrier-bags. They flop up against the bookshelf, a jammed little library. A small flowerpot tucks between old parachute books on the top shelf. The flowerpot is empty, never used, never sustaining life. Maybe Lorna needs it this way, needing a prop, a handy symbolic; the lady wants to remember her feet on the ground. A mini hi-fi is posing on a shelf.

The sky is a weird place. Falling from the sky is not for everyone. But Lorna is never like everyone. She difficult. Her grinning face is in the skydiving snaps and, even with goggles on, her face stands out a mile.

Thud. A sudden thump between the shoulder blades. A hand slams Jimmy to the wall. So sudden, more than a nudge, less than a shove, but it stumbles him. It's Lorna's hand. Now it waits on his shoulder. But Jimmy will not turn round, can not get what's going on. Right behind him is a playful woman. But something else there.

154

What she mean by this? Her woman smell gets him, nudging. His finger hits the hi-fi pause switch and, as the sound kicks in, ice tinkles in a glass. Jimmy turns round and a tall glass is in Lorna's hand.

"This is brandy," she says. Her voice dips. "You like brandy? Well this is brandy mixed with cane-juice."

"Cane-juice chaser, or a brandy chaser?"

Bach's Goldberg playing on the little hi-fi. The music spreads over the tidy room like sailcloth spreading. Glenn Gould playing, a piano genie completing in the aria. To Jimmy, the playing is like the piano itself is in the room. Playing like this, this Gould guy some place way off, like on a shuttle, going on a solo to space, or coming back from far blue lights. This piano playing leaving everything behind. Music like this is what ears are for, Jimmy says. Glenn Gould like a monk-dervish in Lorna's living room.

"How'd you get into parachuting?"

"Parachuting? It's what we do. My dad was a paratrooper."

This hi-fi is skewed. Jimmy wants to listen Bach but the music plays through stupid speakers. Bach arrives, but late. Some nerd said astronomy the ultimate turning away, the purest reaching out. But the only thing stars do in nursery rhymes is twinkle. Or twitter like birds. And the only thing black holes can do is croak. Black holes! Those things are poorly understood. And that's because every sigh of light is info carrying the code of the whole world. But for now black holes gobbling up whole star-clusters like crows. Black holes always croak B-flat. They croak at fifty, sixty octaves below middle C; that's what somebody said, using quick equations for ears.

Lorna shouts from the kitchen. Jimmy shouts right back, saying enough brandy in the mix already.

This Bach with Glenn Gould playing, this the thing. Sitting in one of the bishop chairs, Jimmy could load up here. Music taking care of business in Lorna's neat room. A five-paper spliff would do it. But something else. Nothing senses can fix, not right away. Not the music. What here is maybe not even here. It's something else. The brandy ties into cane-juice; where did Lorna get the idea? Jimmy getting nagged by a scent. Troubling, an attar, faint in the room.

The woman! He remembers the smiling woman in Belem. She smooched one evening in a Brazilian cinema. The scent in Lorna's

155

living room is like the Belem woman: avocado, ripe, fresh, just like that Belem woman one Brazil night.

Lorna gets fussed with space. The only random space in this room is the screensaver on her laptop; random-moving, the word *ricochet* smirks the cold laptop face. And the hi-fi speakers! They should not be on the bookshelf, not on the same shelf together. They'd sound better any place else. But sitting in a chair that a bishop would design, that's part of the deal here. Jimmy gets back to the shelves to scan.

What does Lorna read? Some title should leap out, a topic with disorder built in. From the neat neatness of the shelves something should surprise. This a skydiving woman but only a bible shouts back from the shelf. A bronze bible.

On the top shelf a book on Monet looks different from the rest. Is this the surprise? Idly, Jimmy goes through image after image of teal Argenteuil. Blue-green, limber water every place. But no amber. Not like brandy in a bishop chair. Not like chasing cane-juice through a nighttime sluice.

Tucked between two books, a snap of Lorna falling from the sky. What's she doing now that her brother's in a coma? Fear death? That day at the zoo no parachute was in her eye. She was contained, a clenched woman. And her hand was beside Jimmy's on the damp steel buffering the lions' cage.

"Nice room," Jimmy says, as she comes back to the room.

"So, you like the music."

"*Great* music."

Territory rage! With no warning, Lorna's lips rip with anger. "What's this? What have you done? You've moved the speakers!"

Jimmy will try to head the angry woman off. "How'd you get into Glenn Gould?"

Lorna jumps over to the two speaker, and jockeys them round till back where she'd left them. "What?"

Stepping from the bishop chair, Jimmy will not do a shouting match. Better leave. Then again, she should know the facts. "It's the way sound works. There's science to sound. With two speakers you have to make them agree. A bit like dowsing rods. Or when your arms sync with your feet so you can swim. It's coordination, it's like _"

"Like lions getting it on?" Lorna says, mischief playing her gaze.

156

"Remember them at the zoo, mating?"

The quick mood change makes Jimmy realize. Lorna close to the edge. He already should know that, and should find some way to help. Say something to take from the pain she hides. In a stuttering motion he checks out the parachute on the wall. Then checks the computer screen. Checks the ceiling. But will not look at Lorna. "How come you went for Gould playing Bach?"

"I don't know, do I? That bit of Bach is the only classical music I have."

"People say things about him."

"Who?"

"Glenn Gould."

"So?"

"You don't want to know?"

"Not really."

"Then why bother listening to his stuff?"

"OK, OK! What do they say?"

"Well," Jimmy shrugging, "people call him disrespectful."

"Disrespectful?"

"Yeah, like he was some weirdo. Or a terrorist. Idiots!"

"What do they mean?"

"They have nothing to say about this guy, nothing real, so they say he's disrespectful."

Lorna lopes to the hi-fi. Removes the Bach. But her heart truly likes the music. Thinned voiced, she asks Jimmy if he'll listen to the Beatles. He wonders if she's got anything by Mary J. Who? Mary J. Blige, Jimmy huffs, saying Mary sings whole tenements away. Lorna does not play a Beatles song. Instead, she gets some John Coltrane going. And straightaway something starts. It tiptoes on the carpet. Music that straightaway wanting a woman to dance it. Lorna angry, but this music will change that. Coltrane paving the way. And Lorna slowing it down.

Jimmy half smiling. Even under a big kaftan Lorna's body can not hide. This is no lady bishop's room. Lorna with trouble in her meat now.

Wires connect tubes connecting her brother. And her mother, what's that woman like? Lorna said her mother has roots in west Africa somewhere. Lorna's lips do not pout. Her skin up from ochre, and her nose straight. All of that derives from her father.

157

From the waist up, only hair and the spacing of eyes tell of her mother. Jimmy nods; Lorna carrying one serious African woman butt.

The screensaver punching on the computer screen. The word *ricochet* floats from the music. Why of all the words did Lorna get that word? This who she? She mooches to Coltrane. She does not seem the kind to go looking for lions in a zoo. Jimmy asks if it's OK to smoke. Nodding, she grabs a video.

And soon hot Barbados on the screen. The video is Lorna and her cousins. Their skin near midnight black. Open blue water is only one minute from their house and, far out at sea, way past pale transitions of yachts, blue and yellow fishing boats unite the tide. Lorna doing a voice-over to the video, saying that some vacant days her cousins leave what they do to check the beach out. This video is from last July, she says; and what a great holiday! She brought back a bottle of seawater for her mother. Lorna simmering in her living room. This could be bad. She understands the quiet between herself and Jimmy. And quietly turns away. Melancholy in her eye.

Jimmy should say something, make the hurt for her brother less. He could talk music, but what is music? He won't mention what happened yesterday, the weirdness on a punter's doorstep. But it's tough trying to shake the memory of the punter's face. Tobacco ties the emotion of Lorna's room. The cigarette stubs out. The CD of Coltrane is Giant Steps. Coltrane playing, suggesting 'Take it!'

Lorna turns to Jimmy. "What's up?"

"How d'you mean?"

"You look lost."

"Not lost"

"Could have fooled me!"

Somewhere on a hospital ward, Justin. And faint sounds of blood. And chemicals propelled. His mother and two sisters go everyday with a father and a bible to read. Preacher-man's words are not the same as music. Music is stars twinkling, but preaching bluffs most ears. And yet. Coltrane preached through that sax.

"How'd you get into Coltrane?"

"Oh," she sighs, "it was a present. Somebody once gave me a couple of CDs and it was this Giant Steps and," turning wistfully, she hoists another CD , "this one, A Love Supreme."

"Coltrane was a mystic."

158

"Jazz, but not jazz."

"Yeah."

"What key is the music in?"

Jimmy's eyes dip to the floor. "It's my ear, I only have relative pitch."

"What?"

"I can't be sure what the key is. Not from listening."

"But you're a composer!"

"Yeah."

"How can you compose if you can't tell keys?"

"McCartney can't read music. Gershwin set everything down in F-sharp."

Quiet, worried, she clasps her hands. "What's the matter?"

"Listening to Coltrane makes me think."

"You want me to play something else?"

"No."

"Then what's wrong?"

"I hope your brother makes it."

Lorna steps to the hi-fi. Head shaking, she turns the music down. "Let's get Justin back on his feet, eh."

"The sooner the better."

"In Jesus name!"

"Well, yeah."

"Let's, er, change the subject."

"Your brother is all that matters."

"Tell me about your music."

"Music? That old headache?"

"How's it going?"

"I can't do the stuff I want."

"How d'you mean?"

"I get an idea, and then I get to my keyboard and, yeah, I can't do stuff away from the keyboard. I only have relative pitch. The great thing is absolute pitch."

"What's brought this on?"

"What?"

"You, I think you doubt yourself."

Jimmy shrugs. "There's people out there, proper ear freaks. They could figure it out."

"What the hell are we talking about now?"

159

"It's Bach and Coltrane. One guy leads to the other."

"What?"

"Wayne Marshall, he could figure Bach and Coltrane."

Through the kaftan, Lorna's hand guides skinny pantyhose over round hips. "That's a bit anorak, isn't it? *So* over my head."

"Anorak, well, maybe. But not a Brixton overcoat."

"Listen, this is what happened. After you phoned I was like 'Hmmm, will he like the music here?' You always go on about Bach, so, guess what? I went straight out and got this CD and it's Bach when you get here. That's clever?"

"Bach is different. No Bach, and maybe no eternal music."

"As in forever?"

"He was a music prophet."

"A *prophet*?"

"Yeah. The kind that's safer than guys walking on water, raising the dead."

In lazing butterfly motion, Lorna's hands roam the air. Dreamlike, her hands wander her good body space, looking for home. Hands that could be searching for something in the dark, like a lamp, or a dress with sequins, or the handrail of a rail-car. Jimmy lights a smoke.

"You never slow down," she says. "Can you relax for five minutes? With you, it's always 'Watch me, I've got another river to cross.' Let's take it easy, OK? Come with me. The kitchen is this way. Nice, yummy! Come with me."

Somebody walking in a winter field might almost step on a hare. But a live hare will bound high from that, bound towards the winter sky. And that's why the sky steps slow across fields where hares celebrate. Or so some old fairytale says, some old woman telling it upright in a chair.

"Bach" Jimmy says, "his partita music cuts to Coltrane. But there's nobody big enough out there for Coltrane to cut to."

Lorna's hand like a sister's on his arm. "Give it up, Jimmy."

Jimmy knows. It's happened again. This woman is a kind of healer. If she was walking down Oxford Street then just by touching somebody at a bus stop she'd make the bus come soon.

"OK, no more anorak talk. Not from me."

Lorna bites her lip. "Can you do me a little favour?"

"Anything."

160

"Anything?"

"Anything for a woman who can parachute over England. Sorry, what's the favour?"

"Don't go on about prophets. Slow down. I'm glad you came. I didn't ask you to prove God or anything. This is not some kind of audition."

Jimmy asks if Lorna knows who Wayne Marshall is. And big surprise. She knows about Wayne. Knows him as a classical organ player. And he plays Gershwin. Her mother listens to that. Her mother's family and Wayne's mother come from exactly the same part of Barbados.

But a bigger surprise for Jimmy. Heavy-duty, world class. Waiting in Lorna's hallway, and bossing half the space, a monochrome of Mike Tyson. Tyson on Lorna's wall. All head and neck, this is early Mike. He was only 20 years old.

Jimmy must understand. But jealous now. Who could ever get started with a woman that's got a thing for Tyson? Tyson's eyes almost smile. But it's a lion's gaze. No emotion, no moral store. Only function. Clear-cut life or death. In Tyson's gaze something is customized to gaze like dice.

Jimmy squares up to the photo. And, for a flash, would swap all he's got or could ever have. That means all hopes for music, all dreams of getting near to Ellington in the hall of fame, everything, the whole lot, just for one fight in a boxing ring. One fight. The thrill of walking away or dying. Doing everything in the ring. For ten fitful seconds he shadow-boxes the portrait on the wall. Tyson does not flinch. If anything, the gaze on the wall is more focussed. Tyson would blink even less if he was here in the hall. In the gaze, no flicker of tragedy waiting down the road.

Mildness is in Lorna's eyes. Not laughing. This makes Jimmy feel alone. Isolated, he turns back to Tyson on the wall. Some very neat writing is on the blank space below the neck. And next to the Tyson picture, another picture; Lorna in a photograph with two women. Tyson's portrait is like a mountain side over Lorna with her mother and sister in the photo. Now Jimmy knows. Lorna's mother is a nice woman. Her kind eyes, open face, a black woman with lips beautiful as sleep. And Lorna knows. Her eyes say 'I know it makes you uneasy.' Yes, her father is a white man.

The hall light is not bright. But bright enough to make out the careful writing below Tyson's neck. A safe little script, calm, saying: *Every ton can fly!*

With this, Lorna connects to the bulletproof man in the picture. Pain in her face. And pride. Quiet, her brandy glass tips to Tyson. It tips in a way that a white man's daughter normally would not tip it.

Her glass tips again to the pitiless gaze on the wall. "Somebody will do a proper biography one day," she blinks. "When they get it, when they see what they've done to this man, it'll be 'Oh, wait a minute, sorry, we didn't understand!'"

"Yeah. But it will be far too late."

"Well, maybe. Mr Tyson, this one is for you. Every ton can fly. Cheers, Michael!"

Chapter 43

Fresh cloves of garlic dive in blaring olive oil. Fennel seeds sizzle as she empties a bowl of prawns in the frying pan. This the place. The smell of the ocean here. Jimmy grabs a spoon. A slice of lemon clings.

The beads in her necklace annoy, dangling, and she flings it under the neckline. "It's prawn cocktail," she says, ladling plates on the little table.

Every ton can fly! Lorna's epigram for Tyson is tough but neat. Cruel, something biblical. The same words on the side of a jumbo jet, and no big deal. But under Tyson's portrait, toasting him, that's a different thing. To Jimmy, Lorna treats Mike Tyson like a load-bearing beam, like some affirming wall. Her wishing words look like a kind of epitaph. But too terse. She's a born-again Christian because her brother in his coma gives religion to her life.

Every ton can fly! Words the preacher-man might have said. Uncomfortable, Jimmy shifting side to side. Quiet, he turns to Lorna. Prawns cash in the woman's mouth and brandy flecks the front of her dress.

Every ton can fly! This is religion. Or fading road signs. This is to the ex-heavyweight champion of the world. It's like a law of alchemy. With women the swell of a pregnant belly is a law. But a heavyweight champ working a heavy-bag in the gym or deconstructing a warrior in the ring, that another law of nature. Without a Tyson every now then, only spoofs; nothing would be left to make a real woman's belly swell. From John O'Groats to Land's End, Timbuktu to China, guys would be no longer guys. Only anemic swabs would in a fertility lab. And already guys pushing prams while the woman slopes alongside with a spliff in her mouth.

Every ton can fly! This the epitaph to some wrought thing. Relentless, restless. It will not go away. Lorna dipped her glass to Tyson's portrait in the hallway. And somewhere in a kiln, felled beech trees lose their moisture right now. Some of the panels made from them will end up at Homes, Homes & Homes. Walking in beech forests must be a thrill, seeing wild things at stealth. And all the time supercars posing in suburban driveways.

"Yes," Lorna groans. "Every ton can fly. Even Brixton, believe me!"

Head spinning, Jimmy nods the pun. He tries a smile. But something nags. Maybe now a good time to talk of what happened. A whole new way of seeing happened on that last doorstep yesterday. Now looks like a good time to talk it.

Jimmy shoves aside the plate. "Somebody broke down in front of me." His first words for more than ten minutes. "A white guy."

"Broke down, as in tears?"

"Yeah. Huge eye-water."

"When?"

"Yesterday, about 4 o'clock."

"Why?"

"This and that?"

"What happened?"

Disappointing himself, he will lie to Lorna. Knowing what the reason is, but not really sure how to say it. His eyes lower to the ground. "Not sure."

"Everybody gets those. It's 'I know what I want to say but I can't say it.' Happens to me all the time."

"I wanted to sell double-glazing to the guy."

"So, what happened?"

"It was him and his wife. Their house is probably gonna get repossessed and all I did was talk bull about cut price conservatories."

"Try this," Lorna tots neat brandy in the tumbler. "Take a sip of this."

"I can still hear myself rattling on. Didn't get what he was saying. I wouldn't listen. I could tell something was wrong. But he had to spell it out before I'd back off."

"Listen, you're upset. Is it one of those commission jobs?"

"Sort of. Well, yeah, if the punters don't spend, you don't get paid."

"I'd sweep the streets first!"

If it was hazy before, then it's wide awake now. Jimmy awake. Being one type of music man means he is not a predator. A natural predator only knows the kill. The doorstep encounter left scare marks. But it's clearer now about the problem. He remembers the cold-blood stepping forward and the man and his wife stepping back in their own house. And him refusing to understand his own eyes. Clive would have been proud.

"Do I look like a predator to you?"

164

"As in 'There's some meat so let's grab it!' kind of thing?"

"Yeah," Jimmy groans, "something like that."

Clean fingers could run Lorna's neck. Tidy fingers could stroke as she sips that brandy thing. Maybe Jimmy can talk to her neck, talk some blues to the woman's neck. The seven sins are greed, gluttony, and lust. Then four more. But the big thing is light. A light that gets called morals. But the more morals you want, the less you a hustler. You can not be a predator if you are not even a hustler.

"Bit of a softie, aren't you?" Lorna chides. "Quite a sensitive soul, really. Music man, you are *so* sensitive!"

"Somebody crying never really gets to me. I can't believe I got affected by it. And all the time the guy's wife was only a step behind him in the hall. If I was there strutting away, like a bailiff or somebody, it would be easy to take."

"As in 'Nothing personal, just doing my job' sort of thing?"

"Yeah, something like that."

"But?"

"I was just a black guy. Me talking bull on their doorstep. That bugs me."

Somewhere right now in South Africa, or deep-south in America, somebody black pleads for sunlight. But only getting hellfire. Lorna homed in on that. Her eyes say it.

"*Just* a black guy?" she shrieks. Her eyes say 'I don't get it.' Her body disbelieves. Her hands raise with disbelief. "What *are* you saying? You're having me on! *Just* a black guy?"

"Don't think I don't know how weird it sounds."

Lorna shoves her glass away. She jumps ups. And kicks the sink cupboard. Then kicks it big and loud. Her eyes smolder on Jimmy. Hands clenched, angry, tight. She'd knock him cold. "I don't believe this!"

"I know. I know. I don't believe it myself. What I just said."

"Tell me one thing."

"Yeah, I know."

"Is you is, or is you ain't got uncle-tom sickness?"

Jimmy vaults from the kitchen stool. "Me?"

"You!"

"*Me*?"

"You come here, eat my cooking and insult me. Yes, you!"

Jimmy might as well weigh a ton. But one that will not fly. His

165

hands fall to his sides. Limp. They want to reach out to the brandy glass. But can't move from his sides. His eyes hurt. Eyeballs like sandpaper on them. The light in the kitchen seems to flicker, seems like made from candle wax. Somewhere in the night real candles will be burning in reverence. Embarrassed, his throat clears. Wanting to explain himself, his arms quietly spread, and, hoarse, hears himself talk. "No ma'am, ah is no uncle tom. Ah don't need no uncle tom medication."

Lorna's eyes are ice cold. Her head shakes and shakes. "The day at the zoo," she says, "you shouted after me. I mean, you were so sure. It was 'Look at this crap in the zoo, they can have it, it's not for me.' You wanted to leave with the lions."

"I wanted to get away. From the zoo, from every place. The planet. I didn't know where to go. There was captivity all around. Then I noticed you. But you didn't give me a chance. It ended up with a load of small talk. I wanted it to be me and the lions. Wanted to leave and take them with me."

"And now, you are *just* a black guy!"

On the little kitchen table two avocados and a pear. A ripe bunch of grapes sling over an earth bowl. Lorna gets a lemon from the draw and, quiet but still angry, slices it four ways. Then squeeze, and squeeze, drop by drop. Drop after drop in a jug. Neat cane juice follows. Diluting but not diluting. Mixing but uniting. A deliberate woman, she puts a spoonful to her lips. Patiently, other things go in the mix. A whole grapefruit first. Then a mango. And something else, hiding. Before Jimmy can talk, a half-tumbler of brandy pours. Lorna stares into the jug. A jug is one type of hug. Jimmy reminds her that he's driving, going by car.

Maybe that's what Tyson doing in the hallway. Maybe Lorna the kind of woman going to Tyson's portrait to check she can walk tall. Maybe her life too difficult. Jimmy wonders who stays overnight here, who gets lucky to get sugarcane on this woman's breath. But one thing clear. No uncle tom ever here. No uncle tom ever gets the chance. But.

"It's tough out there," Jimmy says. "Knocking doors, talking spiel to middle class English folk. It was only like a game to me."

"Till yesterday."

"Yeah, that punter yesterday."

"Nothing like that ever happened before."

166

"Not to me. Never!"

"Know what? I think you're at the crossroads."

"Yeah, tucked up in my Brixton overcoat."

"All dressed up and nowhere to go."

"That overcoat is a *weird* garment. We can't take this thing off. Every day there's this burden wearing you."

Lorna pours the jug. Numb, Jimmy gets a smoke. He remembers the look in the man's eyes. The pain, the worry. After one more step in the punters' hallway the woman's eyes welled. Hard, remembering. Normally that's what gets laughed at. Lorna watching cigarette smoke drool to rings.

Jimmy exhales. "On the other hand, I know what that bloke was thinking when he got that house."

"Their home is their castle. Him and the woman."

"They didn't want to live next to blacks."

"Right!"

"I can't stop thinking about it."

"Yes, yes! But what's new?"

"It's a bitch."

"What?"

"Trying to figure it. It was only him and his lady."

"And they were just kind of ordinary?"

"That's what bugs me. How ordinary they were."

Lorna shakes her head. Quiet, she turns to her glass. "Not simple, is it?"

"Not black and white."

Leaving the punter's house yesterday, Jimmy carried weirdness away. It was like the man's eyes were in his pocket, like glass where eyes should be. And the woman's vision; when the tears wiped away, her eyes asked Jimmy to leave behind the two smashed eyes of her man. He can not forget the punter's broken eyes. This was not supposed to happen. The job was to be only money. Taking down arrogant English folk was a bonus. Then again. Before the man's eyes glazed, a message was in his gaze; cold resentment in his eye. And that was definitely the spur: for Jimmy, it was 'Get the money, hard!' From that minute, that punter was going to get it in the neck, going to get a dose of how blacks pay everyday for what they can not afford. For five minutes it was great seeing that man ail. That was the bonus. The touchpaper. The

167

fireworks. But.

Somehow, it changed. Somehow everything changed. Yesterday things haywire. With no warning the man's resentment changed. Puzzlement was in his eye for a moment. Then puzzlement changed to strange. In the punter's eyes was a kind of trust. But the strangest part was what happened next. The man said Jimmy should be ashamed of himself. He could tell from the calculation in Jimmy's eye.

This the part when it changed. The man said that as long as Jimmy smiled the smile, he was just a slave. A slave? Yes, a small-time slave. Hustling, not running free. The man knows all about smile-the-smile. He was a teacher in a difficult innercity school and, now and then, saw that same smile on the face of quite a few black pupils. Talented ones do the best smile, the man said.

A searing guitar upstairs. In the flat above Lorna's, a Freddy King track. Eric Clapton covered this track when he was in the Blues-breakers with John Mayall. But strange things happen. Things only music can explain, or show. This track plays all the time up there.

Lorna sighs. "It's hard. People are people."

"Yes."

"Where will you get buried?"

"What?"

"What if you died here tonight," she laughs, "who would I contact?"

"Look, since simple stuff like death's on the menu, how about one little question."

"What is it?"

The guitar upstairs sears through the floor. It motivates Jimmy. "Well," he says, "it'll wait."

"Drink up, boy. It's not the end of the world, is it?"

"Know what that track upstairs is? It's Key to The Highway."

"Look, I'll tell you a story."

"No fairytales."

"No fairytales, promise."

"The truth, and nothing but?"

"The truth," she says, crossing her heart.

"So, it's a true story?"

"Where my mother works she's the only black face. Normally it's like 'Let's all get on with it, do what we get paid for.' But some
168

days it's 'Oh look, we have a cute little black lady here, ain't she lovely!' And when they have a headache, a bit of flu, anything wrong with them, toothache, anything, they go straight to mum, nobody else. They all go to her. Even the gents and ladies that wouldn't normally allow her the time of day. Then when they're OK again, guess what!"

"Yeah, she goes back to being wallpaper."

"So, what's that tell you?"

Jimmy's mouth is too dry. "Could be anything."

"Take a guess."

His hand fumbles the jacket collar down from his neck. Then toys with the cigarette packet. And rattles the box of matches, rattling. "It could be anything."

"Try!"

"They want a listener, a stooge?"

"They want nanny!" Lorna yells. Her angry eyes ask Jimmy. Eyes that say he's some kind of alien, a spy, and she does not rate him.

"What?"

"They want a black nanny. It's Oprah Winfrey they want."

"Oprah?"

"Who else?"

"I don't get it."

"Think!"

"What?"

"Think pain. Think aspirins."

"Jeez!"

"When pain time comes round, they want somebody to cozy-up to. So they wheel out Oprah. But after the grand emotion it's like 'Who do those blacks think they are?' Understand?"

Quiet, Jimmy nods. "Yeah. They're OK again and don't need your aspirin now."

"Bingo!"

"Listen, that Oprah, I don't think she cares. You're looking at one seriously rich lady. Worth billions."

"Richest nanny on the planet, big deal!"

"I'd settle for half a percent of that cool money. Any time!"

Lorna shakes her head. Disappointed in Jimmy. "Bet she gets one."

"What?"

"A facelift. Getting old, with nowhere to go but her toys. Gets a facelift."

"Before that," Jimmy grins, "she can come my way. The lady can adopt me. She can be my sugar-mama. All that dangerous money going to waste!"

"Listen, let's get real! A house in the suburbs is a big casino."

"What?"

"Some bloke getting tearful on his doorstep, living in a big house, what does that make you when he locks his door?"

Quick, Jimmy shuffles out a smoke. Lorna steps to him and, as the tobacco lights, she takes it from his lips. Inhaling an angry lungfull, she staggers on her feet. She does not smoke. Jimmy grabs her hand. And straightaway a torrent, electric teem. Raw, angry energy. For Jimmy, this business about casinos is hard to shake off. Folk in suburbia play their cards right. Some of those streets have the greatest houses, set for quiet dwelling. And their gardens often flex with calm. One afternoon a widow invited him to see hers. A listed detached house. She was just back from her son in Manilla and was never going back. Getting too old, she said. Her arms were pocked from insect bites. Her son married a local woman and now she had two little brown grandchildren. Perfect; just perfect, she said.

Canvassing, Jimmy never saw any black people in those swish spot, those Lorna *casinos*. But Geraldine pitched the occasional one or two black folk. Or so she says.

Something concealed about Lorna. And little by little Jimmy gets what this is. It stems from the tidy sitting room. Somebody as tidy as this is afraid of dying. Die suddenly, you don't want just anybody picking through your things from the mess you leave behind. So where you live must be tidy when they come to collect your bits and pieces. Lorna fears death from skydiving. This tidy little flat is a foil for the hair-trigger temper. Hard to believe. She flips then straightaway calms right down. And a big bible on her shelf. But not a traditional one. This bible is not solemn looking. Not black. The cover of Lorna's bible is mid-bronze, like charred tropical. Hot with ember.

Night waits the other side of the curtains and, in the street, people pass by on the pavement. And a slant light from the lamppost, drizzled on now. Something troubles this sitting room. The strange plant? Lorna would have gone to Kew Gardens instead of the zoo

170

that day she met Jimmy. They might never have met. And him being here, now, thinking Lorna nice looking. But something gets in the way. It pulls her up short.

She is not the kind of woman to domesticate. The evidence is in her hands. Hands that are not fulfilled. Hands like that are the type that fluff a concerto. A failed Rachmaninov coursed through her hands.

"You OK?" Jimmy says.

The woman steps closer the plant near the window. "You don't like it."

"To be honest I don't know what to like. Look, your furniture is not what this is about. There's heavy-duty stuff bugging you. There's things that you don't face up to."

"Things?"

"Yeah."

"Like what?"

"Things!"

"Like who am I?"

"Yes."

"Anything else?"

"Not really."

"Then what's the problem?"

"Well, now you mention it! Yeah, there is *one* question."

Lorna laughs. "Like can I lend you a million?"

"Well, _"

"Two million?"

"I'll get to the point."

"Pull the trigger, I won't blink. Promise. Talk to me, what's the question?"

This a black woman with a white father. Rare in England. Nathan believes that a mixed-race woman with a white father can be a big problem; more time, she will borrow her mother's eye and look straight past a black man.

Chapter 44

Lorna always talks of herself as black.

"Does it ever bug you?"

"Does *what* bug me?"

"The part where your father's a white man. You think about it, don't you? How it works. Is it easier with a white father? Ever get to discard that Brixton overcoat?"

Something sets in the room. Here, sudden, it arches over Lorna. Settling over the whole woman, it has no flesh. Or name. And if she move, even one tick, then her skeleton crumble. If she so much as blinks then her bones turn to powder.

The tidy flat is not the secret. Something cryptic here. Jimmy steps close. His finger dots the woman's nose. Her eyes flicker. They recognize him. Her mouth puckers, lips part. Her mouth is dry. Whatever she say, nobody would hear. What's her name? Something escape her lips, a half-sentence. *What*? Man Friday?

She turns away. "Robinson Crusoe copped it. It was in the sand."

Jimmy grabs the woman's shoulders in his worried hands. "That's bullshit they made up!"

"The sand said 'Hey, look where he's going. Let's go there with him.' Understand?"

"This is bull. A fairytale!"

"It was the footsteps, they copped that first minute of madness. Juices flowed."

"Woman! That's only a story. A fairytale some dreamer wrote!"

"And, what, all we have is a load of reality now?"

"You tell me."

"I love my dad. But that's not what you want to hear, is it?"

"I don't know your family. I don't even know you."

"White's got nothing to do with anything. We don't wake up and think 'Shit, there's this stranger in the house, a white man, got to get away.' No way!"

Jimmy turns from pain in Lorna's eyes. From her pained brown eyes. From the emptiness in eyes. But something else. Emotionally hemmed, he must leave now. In two strides, steps into the hall.

"No!" Lorna says. "Don't go! Stay for ten minutes. It's only me."

Jimmy at the front door. But stalling. Something connects him to Lorna. Maybe it's the memory of lions in a cage, the lightning and

172

thunder that came one summer day in a zoo. Turning back down the hall, he sets the overcoat back on the hook.

Lorna tired, ground down. She would talk to someone tonight but knows. Jimmy does ten calming press-ups in the woman's hallway. Knowing she's watching. Hauling up, he moves to look again at Tyson's portrait. Quiet, she stands beside him.

"I don't understand this."

Hands behind her back, Lorna standing like a longing shopkeeper. "Sir," she sighs, "can I help you? What don't you understand."

"There's mystic stuff going on. The way Tyson is full of himself. Cocksure. This guy's going to jail but he can't see that far ahead in this photo."

"Glad you like it!"

"Tyson is too hard to figure. Then there's why you even have his picture in the first place."

Of the women who discuss this, Lorna is not the first to see more to Mike Tyson than bozo war machine. This a portrait of a proud Mike. In the picture he was top of the pile the instant of becoming the youngest ever heavyweight champion of the world. But nothing is in the picture that would one day get called guilt, nothing showing a man they claim grabbed by force materials he could get ten times better for nothing. Whatever happened in that hotel room, it did not have to be rape. But.

A few years later, Evander Holyfield should not beat Mike Tyson. But did. Evander went to the fight with a religious belief, saying 'No rapist will ever beat me.' And all the time his eyes were dead sure. His eyes fixed on Mike. And maybe that was it. Tyson got spooked by the *holy* in Holyfield's name.

Mike got to religion in jail. But Evander dominating him at the weigh-in to the fight was so total that when those two heavyweights got into the ring, the man to lose was the one with the bigger burden in his heart. Tyson got a beating. Lost fair and square. And in the return match he was starting to hit Holyfield with dynamite. But then his demons got untied. Demons up from inner-city hell, freaking him. Watching that was pure anguish for most people. Tyson got scared of losing this time. Had nowhere to go if the second Holyfield fight should end the same way as the first fight. He was hitting Evander with bad punches, evil intent, bossing Evander with speed and power. But demons talk, they talk shortcut. And straightaway Tyson bit down in Evander's ear. Biting one piece clean off. All that was left of Tyson was him spitting demons and Evander's ear.

In Lorna's soft hallway light Jimmy gazing the picture. And maybe if it was somebody older, instead of Jimmy, maybe that somebody would know. Sometimes demons burn blood. Passing through the toll gate, blood can get glory with itself. Or get a demon to talk it.

Jimmy turns to Lorna, the woman with a bronze bible. "Think Tyson did that rape?"

"*Rape*?"

"Yeah, that rape he went to jail for."

"How would I know?"

"You've got his picture on your wall."

"What are you getting at?"

Chapter 45

Lorna has weird people for a neighbour. Her neighbour wants to know if she can baby-sit their cat this weekend. But she gives it to them straight: last time round was a one and only one-off!

"You know," she says, closing the front door, "you take somebody as they are. It's what's inside."

"Tyson raped that girl?"

"It's not 'Oh, come see how clean *my* cupboards are!' Who's to judge?"

"Think Tyson raped that woman?"

"No, I don't."

"White folk have a *big* problem with Tyson."

"Listen people who have a problem with Tyson don't get it. They don't really have a problem with him. Their problem is closer to home. It's what happens. Grace is the answer."

"*Grace*?" Jimmy laughs, turning to the taut portrait on the wall. "What's that?"

"It can make a ton fly."

In the 18th century, John Newton was a slave master. John murdered African man by the boatload. And unleashed cold blood devil sex on African women. Demon lust. And then he pens Amazing Grace, a tune black America would cut to a gospel anthem one day.

"Grace is like a jet plane?"

Lorna's palms glide up the wall. They run the mat surface of the wall like half expecting a Braille definition there. "The best way I can describe it, well, grace is selfless. The complete *opposite* of selfishness."

Right now in Jamaica it's early evening. Donna is considering turning Catholic. She can talk catechisms and penitence all day. In her last phone call she talked penitence.

Jimmy checks the time. "Grace, make a ton fly? *How*?"

"Without grace, it's 'The table is over here but where's the dinner?' Get it?"

"Lady, I keep from religion. I'm not religious. Not anymore."

"Is that a smirk?"

"I don't believe in religion, OK? I stay away from it."

"And that makes you superior? Well, you are *not* Mike Tyson. Mike didn't have grace, but watch this space."

Lorna's hands take from the wall. They move like doves' wings in air. Jimmy knows. He must not quarrel with this woman. Instead of tucking up with safe women, Jimmy getting into talk that often ends with quarrels. One night, and it was way past midnight, nearer dawn, Arleene asked him to leave. That was three weeks ago. She was tired of abstract talk and heartless bouts between the sheets.

In the warm pinch of Lorna's hallway this talk should stop now. Abstraction should stop here. But what should happen next will not happen tonight.

"Are you being sensitive again?"

Jimmy frowns. "I don't remember the name of the girl."

"Which girl?"

"The one that said Tyson raped her."

"Oh, her!"

"Yeah."

"It's Desiree. Her name is Desiree. Some kind of beauty queen, or whatever."

"You a feminist?"

"What's a feminist?" Lorna grins.

"That lot couldn't believe their luck when Tyson messed up."

"Lot?"

"The closet racists."

"And feminists are the same as them?"

"They knew they'd get him. The racists got the feminists all wound up. They were outside the court, picketing outside the Tyson trial. Ninety-nine percent of them were white females."

"And *I* could be part of that?"

"Tyson had just one way to go. Desiree must be a retard if she thought white women cared spit about her. She was just their pawn. A bit of a feminist yourself aren't you?"

"Bit of a feminist?" Lorna shrugs. "And a bit white?"

"They got on their soapbox for Tyson."

"Well, yeah."

"Don't fudge me! You know what I'm saying. That's why you have the guy's picture on your wall. Stop playing games!"

"People have a problem, so they get up and preach."

"Who's preaching for Mike?"

"Well, there's always a few Roman candles out there."

The doorbell rings. Lorna's hands settle her hips. Her eyes say she will ignore who's at the door. Even if who's out there can hear her talking in the hallway.

"What's a Roman candle?" Jimmy says. "Sounds sad."

"When your parachute fails."

"What, in this day and age?"

"Anything can fail."

"Don't they have a failsafe?"

"Some days you're up and, God, it's like you could live up there forever."

"Like in a dream?"

"Yeah. You're in the world, but not in it, if you know what I mean. You remember all sorts. What Christmas presents you got. Or the presents you give. Then before you know it the ground comes at you. And, Christ, if your parachute fails you are toast!"

"That's a Roman candle?"

"Yeah."

"It doesn't scare you?"

"Not if you don't think about it. What's your thing?"

"Aquaplaning."

Ignoring the doorbell, the third ring, Lorna turns to Tyson's picture. "You know, there was this video at training camp. It was somebody filming his own jump but the chute didn't open. So the film was like 'Watch me film my life story.'"

"A rhino polevaulting from the sky."

"Some people won't take parachuting for what it is. They get carried away and can't wait. It's 'Hey, look at me!' But you get used to them."

In the flat upstairs, Robert Cray's guitar takes a solo. And another guitar playing on the track, wanting to rip the ceiling apart. Got to be Albert Collins playing that way. But Lorna does not care. She with Tyson. Her right hand strokes the burdened brow in the photo. Tyson's brow fevered with suffering. And the woman's hand tracing, veering the glowering ton of neck.

"It's the neck you like?"

"It's that old testo thing," she says. "Stupid to wish all the world's testosterone was in Mike Tyson's neck. Christ, that's so stupid."

Jimmy steps to the photo for a closer look at the fight mechanic on Lorna's wall. "A Roman candle?"

Lorna knows this guy can not walk on water. And Tyson is not

177

even a champ now. But. Something about him makes a serious point. And a woman connects it. The flat upstairs tilting a serious, serious guitar. A ship on the calm ocean would keel that tilt. A guitar playing Natural Ball at full volume now. The solo is only a run of pentatonic cliches, Jimmy says. But then. There's all the rest Robert Cray does with chords. Great chords. Jimmy dancing in the hall, chanting 'Play it, bro, play it!'

Lorna would dance. She moves a little. Shy moves. But won't get close. Woman scared of what she wants. Scared to get what she could. But Jimmy knows. She ripe tonight. The next thing that should happen is it. It should happen right in the hall. This the time to stop talk. A night like this somebody should get into this woman. And guitar music playing the ceiling.

Lions do not rape. A boss lion will have more than one lioness. Being a predator means flesh, grabbing limb from limb. And devour. What they say about Tyson and rape means nothing. Desiree was lucky. She got to tell her Tyson night, or lie about, but tell it from high in prey-heaven. And that never happens on the plains.

Folk talk civilization. And the first ordainment is *the rule of law.* But they never mean justice. Where the rule of justice? One rule brings Tyson as a beast; a rule playing him in a cage. And another rule saying Tyson can take all the meat he wants, wild and fresh, but the rule-maker gets to watch. And that's because there's got to be a rule-maker to get the best ringside seat. In a boxing ring the ref never even counts to ten sometimes. The fight can go the full distance and you see what you see. And sometimes what you see is not what the judges see. And then you ask 'Who referees the judges?'

But with a man and woman, well. This a different game. Man and woman alone one night? In a room high in the sky, together, alone together, late, late, at night? Like Tyson and Desiree in that midnight hotel? Well, you ask yourself what you want to see when you yourself got nada in that hotel room.

Jimmy's head shakes. "Desiree was a *wicked* bitch."

"Well, I don't think I'd go that far. Wicked is a bit strong. The bible uses that word."

"Wicked was taking Tyson's balls, castrating the guy so white folk could gloat."

Lorna is a woman at home. But her head some place else. Like in a hospital ward. At the bedside of her brother. Her throat clears. "I

178

wasn't there," she moans.

"Then you better tell somebody, quick!"

"I'm just little me. What can I do?"

"Tell the ones that want Tyson's balls."

"I look like I know such people?"

"They want guys castrated. That means they want *my* balls. Guys everywhere."

"Slow down, please! You're going too far. This is not a casino game."

Reaching for his coat, Jimmy grits his teeth. "Not a game? Where'd you hear that?"

Urgent, Lorna's eyes say she can not talk this any more. She grabs Jimmy's arm, spinning him round. "I'm not kicking you out. Let's get a coffee. It's fresh-ground. Ready in five minutes."

Chapter 46

"This is bollocks!" Clive storms into Colette's office, shakes a fist at the wall-charts. Both hands raise as if to prevent the sales peaks avalanching off the charts.

Colette stubs her smoke. "Can we do this later?" .

"All it bloody takes is a new bottom line! New bottom line, or new sales manager!"

Jimmy gets the smokes from his pocket. And leaves the room. Best wait in the corridor while the storm blows. Clive does a wardance some days. Some days the boss man's voice kicks walls around here. His voice chocks the building. But Colette is cool, easy. This one-way thing could take a while. Jimmy lights up in the corridor.

A week since being at Lorna's flat, Jimmy back at Homes. But not for canvassing. Not any more. That gig is for tougher folk. Door canvassing is for the type that can smile the smile all day long. Rain or shine. Colette giving Jimmy one last chance. Though he'd see what happened that last day of canvassing, it would have been the sack. But she relented, gave out a huge lecturing. But this is it. One final warning, she said, saying normal people don't walk from money, especially when things going so well for them, and especially not while supervising others and getting cream from their take. That's what she said. Then she got sentimental.

Colette has a sweet spot for any artsy. Jimmy knows that. All the while Jimmy plays Colette out, knowing that. And now if the interview clicks he will do a stint in telesales. Colette agreed to give him a go at it. But too much is at stake, so a formal interview will happen to make sure. The interview will be a toughie, she said.

Geraldine talks about big money telesales people can earn. All you do is sit with a phone in your hand. Unreal. But for Jimmy there's more to this than money. And that is being invisible. In telesales somebody invisible all the way. A great thing for a lone. And that's because the sun can not bounce. Invisible, but not like a pebble that skims water to sink under its own weight. No Brixton overcoat is ever visible down the phone. Not with Jimmy wearing it.

Lorna talks of her family. Talks of their trip every year to the Northumberland village where her father was born. Her family gets a great time in the safety of that essential home; every summer it's
180

simple fun, being near invisible on the village green. The invisible part comes from Alan Stanley. His white skin is magic round the black wife and kids. But sheep outnumber people by five to one in Northumberland. And maybe, just maybe, the folk there realize this, so never bother talking herd.

Wanting to be invisible, you want it to be by choice. In telesales no need to smile the smile. You talk this and that, like cars or the weather, but no doorstep agony on the phone. If you invisible, you do not get like Oprah Winfrey. You do not soak up white middle-class pain to get a billion dollars but no respect. Oprah should know by now that she a nanny. White folk bawl to nanny. Oprah's got money enough to fling in the sea to make a new continent rise, but getting no true respect. The richest nanny in the world, but her place in the nursery; that's what Lorna says.

In the corridor outside Colette's office is a quiet now. No storm blowing. No Clive scowl. Clive huffs by, heading for the Bentley.

Colette's office is smoky warm. The boss woman swings in a chair with a reputation for irritating visitors; the way the chair's new leather squeaks. It's the kind of place a cat would curl up in. Bad kitty, lazy with spite, nudging sleep.

She is bleary eyed. "Sit yourself down."

Jimmy looks long at the woman's earrings. To him those earrings look like plates. They would be the biggest on a market stall, twenty steps oversize, looking like fish in yellow water. A big octopus would want them. Or they could pose high in a rural kitchen.

Clive's theatrics did not faze Colette. Studying her face, Jimmy can find no evidence of the insomnia she's supposed to suffer from.

"Play cards?"

" Now and then."

"What do you play?"

"Three-card brag. Or a bit of poker."

"Ooh, three-card brag! Deuces wild?"

Jimmy shrugs, wanting to get more conversational but, to tell the truth, dreading the mind-games to get through here. This should be the part where the interview takes off. But Colette is always kind to him. And anyway, she the boss. "No, no wild deuces for me."

"Why not?"

"I don't understand."

"What?"

"I can't see how card games relate to telesales."

"Ah, telesales!" Colette purrs. Her hands collect a wad of business cards on her desk and, slow, deliberate, she shuffles them. "Gambling, well, gambling and sales are the same sort of thing, really. Different sides of the same coin. I'll tell you why. It's about winning with the hand you've got."

"How's it work?"

"Eager, are we?"

"Can't wait."

"Oh good! So, let's get there. What sort of money are you looking for?"

"Well, I'd like, I mean, it would be great if _"

"Don't be shy!"

Geraldine said money can get crazy in telesales. Somebody in the telesales team here earns three grand a week.

"I heard a thousand a week happens quite a lot. That would be great."

"Only *one* thousand? Well, now! That's only middle-lane here. We've got three guys, hot shots, they make a grand each in a very *bad* week. Make a lot, a lot of money. One guy's a bit of a gambler. Earns a fortune."

"A fortune? That's a lot of money!"

"Think of a number. Then multiply it by your house!"

Jimmy laughs. "I live in a tenement."

Colette checks her watch. Her head shakes. Business-like, she ups from the chair. The paperweight on her desk is engraved with the Ferrari prancing horse. She will trade up to a Ferrari. Even though her Maserati is brand new. She scoops a trail of ash from the desk. Jimmy sits up.

"I'll tell you a little something. At Homes you're completely self-employed in telesales. We'll stake you with a basic, a little something while you find your way, a month, six weeks. Then you're on your own, got that?"

Jimmy getting hopeful. Geraldine warned him what questions would impress Colette but he does not remember them. "How much is the basic?"

"Wrong question!"

"I was only trying to evaluate."

182

"You say you play cards, yes? Well, you don't ask that kind of question. Not if you want to win!"

"Sorry, how much is the commission?"

Colette gets back to her chair. And, watching Jimmy, coolly begins to relax. Her body dips. And a cigarette is quietly alight in her mouth. Jimmy lights up.

"That's more like it!" she winks.

"I want to earn big."

"Listen, we only talk reality around here. We talk of the commission you can earn."

"I want to get as much commission as possible."

"When you start selling, the first fifty grand gets you five percent. Then ten percent from there. You could be looking at telephone numbers! Fancy it?"

It's the way Colette gets the message across. That's what bugs Jimmy. It sounds too easy. Like anybody could do it. But the great thing with telesales is there's no doorstep smiling-the-smile. Games on the phone, yes, and deference. But they have to imagine. The punter must imagine. Jimmy gazing at the boss woman. Gazing her dark brows. And watching the inclination of her eyes. She's doing to him what he used to do to homeowners on their doorstep. Colette is the sizzle business. And the steak. She a kind of preacher. But money here takes the marketplace to a set kingdom come.

And then Clive. She wants to trump Clive. Telesales was her idea. And it's so successful already it drives 60% of business at Holmes. Nothing must escape. Listening as she explains, Jimmy gets set. He takes as much of Colette as can get seen. Got nothing to do with much, but somebody could get the colour of her underwear here.

In telesales nobody knows. No ethnic lilt in Jimmy's voice. Over the phone this is business. Donna said the desire for God is written in the human heart. And she talked of love, hoping for happiness. And that Ferrari paperweight on Colette's desk is the size of a tropical something, like a grapefruit in evening sunshine.

"Hi, Jimmy, hello!" Colette whoops, her hand waving in Jimmy's face. She leans across the desk. Waving. "Hello, anybody home? I know you're in there somewhere!"

Jimmy backs from the reverie. "I was thinking about doorsteps. It's ugly out there. But I *was* listening to you."

"Still thinking about canvassing?"

"Well, yes. But I definitely want to move on."

"We're all tinkers in this life. One way or another. If it makes you feel better I did it one year myself and it was *gross*!"

"Are you giving me the telesales job?"

"Let's take it from the top. Let me tell you golden rule number one. Hard-sell is out, finished! Those days are *so* yesterday. The next phase will be more, how can I put it, organic? We're not giving up on our homeowners. But we want the business sector. We used to have quite a few barrow boys in telesales, but from now we'll only have graduates. Any background. History, science, anything."

"Theology?"

"Well, no. Come off it! God sell home improvement? Come on!"

"Music?"

"Yes, yes. You did a music degree, didn't you? Yes, that's right. Well what we can do with that, what that means, music means you can develop a theme. It means you can listen. Listening is 95% of sales. Not patronizing you, am I? What do you think? Any questions?"

"To be honest, it's only about the money. The more, the better."

"Heard the one about musical cows?" Colette giggles. "You know, cows have their favourite tunes."

"Their own juke box?"

"Ooh, cows with their own juke box!"

"They produce more milk listening to music?"

"Correct. So, play the right music!"

"How's it work?"

Colette checking her watch. She's irritated. "Look, don't come the prima donna with me! I'm trying to help you. I don't have to do this. Let's cut to the chase. You want money, you want a job that won't browbeat you. Well, you've got it."

"Honestly, I want it."

"Communicate, Jimmy! Listen and learn. Understand that, and it's done and dusted."

"When do I start?"

"We'll set you out some targets, but it's a numbers game."

"I know what that means. Saw it in canvassing. It's fishing."

Colette's eyebrows crimp. Chatty earrings clatter her cheeks. "No, not fishing! Telesales, let me tell you it's as tough as it gets. What you have to realize is for every two hundred phone calls, you might

184

get a deal."

"That's a lot!"

"Two hundred calls and a hundred and ninety-nine end in zilch. Oh, you might get lucky and sell one little piece of kit when you least expect it. A thousand calls can go by. Two weeks can come and go. Three weeks, and nothing!"

"That sounds dispiriting."

"The big hitters have it in their guts. But they prepare, prepare, prepare. Sounds familiar?"

"I think so."

"You *think* so?"

"No, I get it. Who will I be talking to?"

"Players," she says, dry.

"But who are they?"

"We talk to company directors. Regular guys. Far more chatty down the phone than face to face. All you have to do is get past their secretaries."

"I hadn't realized."

"Hadn't realized, what?"

"Talking to the secretaries before getting through to the boss."

"Look, this is your bread and butter. You with me? You get polite with the secretary, that's how you get put through to the boss. It's a game. You think money, money, money! Got that? Beats doorsteps, yes?"

"Yes. I mean, thanks. Thanks for giving me the chance."

The new reception girl is Clive's daughter. She does not like guys grinning. And dropped out of university because she couldn't hack it. She tried telesales. But bombed. She will inherit Clive's share one day. Bonfires could burn in Colette's office. Something more than tobacco hangs in the air. Another lung full of smoke exhales as she leans back in the chair.

"The chances you get with me!"

"I won't mess up. Honestly."

"One false move and you're out!"

"Sure."

"Go home and come back tomorrow."

"How does furniture get into the business sector?"

"What do you mean?"

"Company directors don't live in their offices."

"They don't? Let me tell you, those people don't *stay* overnight in the office. But that's where they live, believe me. They live in the office, honey. Nine to five. They're all egotists, dogs by another name. They want a home from home. Tasteful bits and bobs, screens, discreet one-offs, even wardrobes. We make and fit. And of course there's the people who work from home. Even some very big hitters, top finance execs, hotshots, lots work from home."

"I still don't get the part with my music background, I don't see how it helps. I can't phone up some accountant and talk rhythm or counterpoint."

"No, no. You wouldn't get two seconds with that. No, honey. You will have a chat with the top man. We give you a script, don't worry. We'll train you up. It'll take about a week. Then once you get the feel of it you can go from there, you know, cut loose, improvise, do your thing. No, a music degree is fine."

"Politics graduates."

"What about them?"

"They the best at telesales?"

"*Politics*? We've had a couple of those here. Very revealing. It was all book with them, no imagination. Hands always in their pockets. No, this job is about flair. If it's in there it will come out, I promise you. But we can't carry you. You have got to *want* it. The bottom line is you must deliver. You make money, we make money. Simple, or what?"

Jimmy gets a clutch of A4 gloss magazines titled 'Homes, Homes & Homes' that the woman points at on her coffee table. And quiet, he moves through March/April, the current edition. The magazine shows furniture, wood-panels, desks, partitions, chairs, everything that wood can make. This is what's getting sold down the phone.

"What's the average cost of these things?"

Colette checks the time. "No, it doesn't quite work like that. With some bits of kit you're looking at a few hundred quid. A reception suite could do you for a hundred grand. We did one suite for 380 thousand. Depends."

"But there must be bozos on the line as well as clever people."

"Don't worry, we'll go into all that tomorrow. Any thoughts?"

Colette wants Jimmy to make it. And not just in telesales. She knows where he wants to be. And he knows she roots for him, wanting him to arrive. And she never talks of race.

She blinks at the copy of Portrait Of A Girl on the wall. A painting that reminds her of business goals. "It's by Modigliani."

"So, I get a percentage of every thing I sell."

"Correct."

"And I could clear a grand a week?"

"That is down to you. We've been through that. Look, the deal gets better and better. As you go on you get at the perks. *Oh*, the perks! How much you make is how much you *want* to make. Got it? If you want to win then you *do* win. But you have got to *want* it. Want, is not even close."

"Who else sells furniture over the phone?"

"Oh, just a dozen other outfits. Does that bother you?"

"No."

"Why?"

"I rate myself."

"*That's* the spirit!"

Jimmy nods. "It's going to be great while it lasts."

"Ah!" Colette shrieks, grabbing her torso. The boss woman looking like she could do a rough aerobics work out. She stubs the cigarette. "Let me give you a little bit of advice." Her voice dips. "There'll be days when it will get tough as old nails. When that happens, and it happens to everyone, don't go talking of quitting. Not in the salesroom. And *never* in front of Clive. Remember that! Look, nobody gives a toss for the artist and his dream. Nobody understands vision here. Don't go on about your music, your vocation, or what have you. You can't sit on some high horse, you know, like all of this was just so much slumming it. Don't say I didn't warn you!"

"Then what do people talk about around here?"

"Deals, deals, deals! And then more deals. Money, money, money. What's left, well that's your restaurants, your trips abroad. The usual suspects. That's how to do it. If you make decent money then you spend it. And there's a right way to spend money, believe me!"

Instead of the ten minutes set for the interview, Colette gives Jimmy a whole half hour. This makes him welcome. But wondering why.

Chapter 47

To get a clear head after the interview, Jimmy walked in the park. A quiet walk. This park a good place to be alone. Wide open air. Far from a tenement.

Going through the park gates he was thinking of Agnes. Mulling the chats they used to have here. And then remembered that quibble in her walk. One day she was wearing very high heels and Jimmy heard a woman moving with dark footfalls, making him wonder if something was wrong with her heart, like a bug was in her chambers. Laughing, Agnes said her heart was way out past the horizon, she could run down a gazelle. One afternoon Jimmy got her to walk one more lap round the park. It was the only way. That hitched rhythm in the woman's walk stays with him now, making him lonely this morning in the quiet park. Remembering.

A solo painter here. A one-armed painter sitting at the pond's edge in the park. For five minutes in clamped morning air, gazing over the shoulder of the artist, somebody's got the blues. The painter stipples a paintbrush to dun drawing paper. His grass is grass. And his trees, trees. Only the bird does not sing. And somehow the landscape splits away, splits like to tapers. This one-armed man quietly preparing fault-lines of summer already. And somebody saying summer is more than a season and a half from here. The artist turns back to the paint, saying the birds they hear singing somewhere remind him of ambitions, the kind that twitter in a domestic cage of finches. People think birds are only singing? Well, maybe they do bigger things, songs that could match astronomy. Birds do astronomy? Birds claim whole tracts of England. They can claim it with little melodies in a tree. And the whole thing stippled down on dun drawing paper by a one-armed man in a dank park.

Walking from the artist and his work, Jimmy wished for wrapping paper. Weird, even to himself, but he wished for one acre of brown paper. Enough brown paper could wrap all the trees in the park, right to the gate, the place where they strew fresh gravel. But this would be a fable. Joining sections of life with make-do cellotape, a bad mistake in a public place.

And now, mulling over the months of canvassing. Mile after mile of cold tarmac. But a few fair minded people were out there. Sometimes on some of those doorsteps, neat conversations took place, even heartfelt. And talk of jazz. Talk of how jazz is puzzled by gibe.

One retired civil servant encouraged Jimmy to keep composing. Somebody else said that Lullaby Of Birdland was composed by George Shearing, yes, a blind Englishman. A woman who traveled most the world said that racial problems are not so bad now, not like before. She said that because of hardcore race segregation fifty years ago, even Charlie Parker used the back door to get into Birdland, the nightclub named after him. Yes, the one that inspired George Shearing's tune everyone knows.

Chapter 48

Jimmy must hear Agnes. The voice. The whole world in that woman's voice sometimes. A blue sky laugh. The phone rings and rings, but nada. Nobody in that Cape Town house. Or nobody that answers the phone.

Alone in the flat with just the keyboard to kick, he must get a 10-paper spliff right. Ten tenement dogs will bark any time now. Bad dogs will bark the building down. That's what happens everyday. And right now maybe Agnes is jogging in a Cape Town park.

Jimmy mulls Colette. Maybe it's only the sound of her earrings, them going from tinkle to clatter, clittaclatter, clittaclatter. Earrings should not do that. But the worst part is the mute flesh, her earrings cascading her flesh. One evening Colette got to her car and, as she looked up, one quick look up at the window, caught Jimmy gazing.

Seven o'clock in the evening, Jimmy phones Geraldine. Money to be made at Homes, but it looks like a hard road up ahead. Maybe now the time to pull out from the dive; something addictive in the air, like maybe a Roman candle. But who would not go for it?

Telesales can not be like cocaine. This money game is a game where being invisible plays. And yet. This could get vulgar. Somebody could end up dry-retching for hours at a time on a floor somewhere, alone, miles from music and home.

Geraldine laughs. "How did the interview go? Will you give it a try?"

"Yeah. I'll definitely go for it."

"Thought you would."

"Think I'll be any good?"

"Probably sell in your first week."

"How much are you making?"

"Oh, it's not too bad."

"Yeah, yeah. How much?"

"A goodish deal every three weeks. Not complaining. On average I make the best part of 500 quid a week. I can live with that. Did I tell you there's a mutation?"

"A what?"

"Somebody in the office earns three grand a week. Only an average, but it's *three grand* on average! That's before his bonuses, trips

190

to Hong Kong or whatever. Odd little guy, turns up in jeans and cowboy boots."

"You've told me before."

"Did Colette mention him?"

"Yeah. That stuff is true, then."

"True, blue."

"I can't believe it!"

"Yes, I know. The really amazing thing is it happens right in front of you. You know, in a jabbering little place. It's not even that. It's more a psychiatry workshop! One bloke deliberately turns up in shoes with holes in the bottom. Everyday I say a little prayer."

"What's telesales really like? Somebody earning that kind of money?"

"Money?" Geraldine's voice echoes round the handset. "It's not the money, my innocent. It's the one-upmanship. That's what they're about. Some people have just *got* to win. That's why the gambler chap is tops. It's the chase. Some of them stand on their chairs when they sense the kill."

"Somebody talking business on the phone and standing on a chair?" Jimmy laughs.

Geraldine can not explain. In the sales office she's in a foreign country. A place with strange customs where the locals speak to phones all day and only ever really speak to one another when wanting to gloat. As she winds up talking of money land, she gets excited by something near. It's a vase. Her sister finished it just this evening. A shelf will get specially made for it but, for now, it gets parked on the piano. Nothing was ever like the aquamarine as the aquamarine in the vase. Her sister jokes about it, pretending the aquamarine vase is blood from thimbles of a thousand royal dwarves.

Jimmy must cut through the reverie. "How many women in the sales room?"

"Two, including me."

"Carmen, the other one?"

"Who?"

"The shy black woman."

"Oh, right."

"What's she up to?"

"Gosh, you are *so* out of the loop! Sacked. Colette got rid of her. Our dear little Colette is frequently a cheerless bitch. I was coming

191

to that. I'm not sure you could handle the ego stuff. Don't hit your target, and you're out on your ear. Colette slings you out."

Chapter 49

The tone in her voice was too sad. Too plaintive. On the phone Lorna wanted him to come round later. And now Jimmy arrives the woman wants to talk the world. The whole shebang. But not her brother. The hospital said Justin slipped a little.

There's always gravity. Want to talk gravity? That's boring? Well, if gravity was even one little bit less then orbits of the planets would be helter-skelter round the sun. Lorna is bored with stars, saying she wants real life. Real, like what? Something personal.

Sipping black coffee, Jimmy mentions the rape. Twenty years ago one cousin came to England from Jamaica and that same week she got raped by a nightclub bouncer and committed suicide.

Lorna covers her eyes. "My God, that's terrible!"

"Yeah, a feather from nowhere."

She gets the brandy bottle. But does not open it. Quietly, turns to Jimmy. "Every ton can fly, right? So maybe feathers can try."

"You mean angels and stuff?"

"You know, Mike Tyson was in Brixton a few weeks back."

"You went?"

"Yes."

"How was it?"

"Fabulous! Absolutely fantastic! In the crowd and so near him. He unhinged the place."

"Yeah, I watched some of it on TV."

"He was so happy. Teasing the girls, shadow boxing with the kids. And, well, he's not as big as you'd think. See him on TV and it's always 'Get in my way and guess what happens next!' But he's just a boy, a friendly boy."

"They never want that guy to be just a guy They want a freak show."

"He had a great time in Brixton. Loved everyone."

"You his sister, or what?"

"There was so much love in his eyes. *So* much love. Hard to explain it. It wasn't what I expected."

"Hendrix had to burn his guitar," Jimmy says. "They wanted the freak. They wouldn't make do with the genius. You ever seen that video of Hendrix at the Isle of Wight gig? When the set is over he chucks the guitar into the ground. I mean, bangs it down! Then he walks. Dead three weeks later."

Lorna bites her lip. "Tyson set fire to his own heart. It's 'Here's the ashes before I die!' And that's *impossible* to live with."

TV of Tyson in Brixton showed him in a crowd swell. But the way Lorna talks makes Jimmy realize. Before, it was too vague. It never got spoken. And maybe only because she a white man's daughter. But this is crystal now. You identify with Tyson or you want him mocked. That's what happens. Some people understand this fork in the road. But black guys from sport have fridge-loads of money and get Ferraris and slots on chat shows, but most of them are triumphant bozos. Or hypocrites foisted as role models. And the worst part is that compared to real talent, most so called role models are only third rate anyway. Tyson shuns the stench of that. That's why they bring him down. Lorna reckons the poor guy maybe never even wanted to be a boxer in the first place, maybe Mike was only wanting to be someone plain, like a farmer, a hard working human tending cattle or growing barley. Or a small-town photographer snapping squirrels and trees.

Jimmy says even a teddy-bear could fight Mike now. Tyson was the last of a breed. Mike can no longer fight. Mike Tyson does not want to slay the head of any man. Looks like the show all over for Tyson. Anybody can beat him now. But where were they when he was a lion? Yeah, quaking from the safe side of the cage!

Tyson a man with no home. And that hurts. All the time. As a person of colour you have no St Paul's Cathedral you designed. No Newton, and nothing you own like the Statue of Liberty. Nothing is there for you like even a thoroughfare such as Oxford Street.

Guys like Mohammad Ali and Nelson Mandela own real-estate. And that is when folk are proud of them. And Jesse Owens and Duke Ellington. But Mike Tyson getting denied. Lorna thinks her bible is clear, saying grace is divine courtesy. She talks like she was a disciple of preacher-man, claims that flake highs is what black guys in Britain get. Flake highs is what happens if you don't get to heaven. But who gets to heaven?

This woman can quote from the bible, talk like she was at the Last Supper. But too much sissy in that for a man to use. You'd just be walking round with grace in your pants and something called etiquette polishing your shoes. And how far down the road would you get with that? You'd catch your reflection in your polished shoe one

194

day and, man! You yourself would laugh.

Jimmy must skip religion. They have good stories in the bible. But then you get a virgin giving birth and dead folk getting resurrection. And nobody asking how come all that was only in the Middle East. How come preacher was not from Africa? Or China? Or India? The pope asking forgiveness for how the Christian church violated the rights of ethnic folk. And the Catholic church itself was wicked to Jews, century after century.

Lorna brings biscuits back to the sitting room. And pours coffee. But no brandy tonight. Sitting on the carpet, she looks up, smiling.

The day Tyson came to town was up there. Brixton was it. It was the 21st day of the first month, new millennium. Bop, bebop!

Brixton's got rude-boy in a de street. But Tyson a de daddy. By a long mile. The closet-racists played a cold hand. They did not want Mike in England in the first place, so got their line ready. And the first thing they did was get on-side with someone black, somebody big-time. And only one name was big enough. And that was Ali. The woad-managers chose Muhammed Ali and made a point of mentioning how welcomed Ali was when he was in Brixton years before, saying how he was then as well as now a model to us all. Tyson is a pariah, Lambeth council said, saying 'We must prevent Tyson from coming here.'

But the taxpayers of Brixton knew. The council got two woad-managers to look in the face of Brixton, fully expecting to see a trusting fool. Even after what happened in '81 with that riot.

Tyson was smiling all the time. A wry smile, Lorna says. The crowd was surging, wanting to get near the ace. And nobody sane can deny him. The crowd shouting 'We love you, we love you, bro!' Black folk going to Brixton to see the Tyson man, saying his pain was their pain. Way out loud, everybody shouted that in this world only one pain.

But the woad-managers wanted a freak show. They could not prevent Tyson from Brixton, but they wanted to watch. But watch from a safe place. They wanted him inside a cage, to have dominion on him like some animal. The woad-managers wanted Mike to get obliging and smile, wanted him tied up to a big uncle tom cabin to be the black obliging. No matter how much death or earthquake, famine, war, loss, no matter what, Mike should tilt like uncle tom

195

tilting on the TV news screen.

The woad-managers said Tyson is a rapist. Keep him out the country, they said; we don't want him walking up and down. But what if Desiree was white? What if she was white? It would have be gloves off time! No civic gardenias for woad-managers to run to and tend pretend.

Lorna talks like she's back in Brixton that Tyson afternoon. And, as she talks, Jimmy could be walking the same streets. And checking the area for lore.

Hearing that Tyson was going to be there she hurried from her desk. And twenty yards from the tube station, heart pounding for release, breath riding the bustle, she was pressed up to a tight-packed market stall and, for something to do, trying to get release from her heart, grabbed something. It was sugar cane. Nine yards of cane from an old woman running the stall. As she cut the cane to lengths, twenty-seven even lengths, the old woman smiled a huge Caribbean. Someone in the crowd yelled, saying Tyson coming round the corner. Quick, a crowd crush. It could have run wild, but straightaway everyone realized. They knew the woad-managers wanted folk to stampede. Everybody realized the woad-managers wanted to see the crowd get like an animal. So folk toned it down to discipline.

But it was hard to wait. Tyson was just round the corner, moving it, getting close. The old woman selling Lorna sugarcane asked if anybody could imagine Tyson sweating his guts out as a slave. Tyson, cutting cane? Picking cotton? Getting whipped? Wearing out every day? They'd shoot him first, she said.

Lorna reached down into the carrier bag to touch lengths of heavy cane. The cane was supporting her. Maybe it was only by a forbidden sweetness, the endgame of tooth decay, fire provoking blood to instant energy. Black slaves gone forever, ripped from their continent to produce sweetness. Slavery was a lifelong stint. Seven days a week, 14 hours every day. Man, woman, and every child from five years old. Lorna tells their story.

"Hold it!" Jimmy says. A half cup of coffee pours. But something bad. Not details, and not the blues. Not even gospel. Nothing with a name. Not yet. Something sad here.

Lorna nodding. Her hands smooth a blank sheet of paper. "For every ton of sugar, a slave died."

"Hold it!" Jimmy hollers. He can not go on. Coffee is a riddle. Sugar a serious problem now.

Sugar is every place, Lorna says. On the plantations sugar got down from cane in three forms. First was the heft, the black molasses, stuff you can eat. Next, the brown shades of sugar, all alluring, giving coffee tables round the world their name. Last, comes absolute white; that the phase taking slaves down by the grave load.

"What does that tell you? You writing this down?"

Jimmy can not answer. Not in the woman's eyes. In her gaze a lifetime hurrying. Her eyes know. Her mouth moves. She talks of Atlantic Road. In the heart of Brixton a road named Atlantic Road? She was hurrying along Atlantic Road the day Tyson was in town. She and twenty seven heavier and heavier cuts of cane.

After Tyson left Brixton the crowd split to fives and sixes. And ones and twos. She decided to tour the area. But refused a lift from somebody; she was not getting into a lime-green convertible in cold January. Atlantic Road is a peculiar name for a road. Not a place to accept a lift in a strange car. A lime-green pose car.

Despite the bustle, Atlantic Road pays homage to a bad time. A lame. That road got named after a part-lame ocean, part penitent. And with Tyson in Brixton, Atlantic Road was big regret. A tomb of ocean graves. Millions did not survive the Atlantic from Africa to slavery.

"Hold it there!" Jimmy yells, shifting from the prim bishop-chair. And hauling weary to his feet. Wanting to leave.

Brixton's got a street called Atlantic Road? A place with a road named that should be on the coast, a promenade facing the ocean. Maybe the folk in Brixton can hear the ocean on Atlantic Road. Maybe they can taste a tide coming. Get salt in air instead of sugar.

Chapter 50

Sharp in Lorna's gaze, Jimmy gets over to the bookshelf. "Think your brother will make it?"

Her eyes indicate the snaps of skydivers on the wall. "Take a look at those."

"Who am I looking out for?"

"The guy with the cigar. The photo on the right."

"Who is he?"

"That's him. It's Justin. My brother."

Justin Stanley. To Jimmy, Lorna's brother looks like everybody else in the photo. Looks white. Even to Jimmy, even to someone accustomed everyday to the spread of black types, Justin looking white in the photo. Nothing in the face. Not like a white face turning from the sun or tanned. And no white face in shadow. Only Lorna's brother. Justin is dreadlocked under his safety helmet, she says.

Justin's lung stopped a screwdriver in the gang fight. And that halfway explains his coma six months already. It was a race fight. A black v white business one alley night. Lorna mentioned the race part already, but now Jimmy can see. Yes, it's possible.

Possible that in the thick of the fray, panic was in that wrought-iron alley. Guys wanting to get away. Or rushing to get more involved. So Justin could have got confused for somebody from the white gang. Could have been a black guy who got him. By pure mistake, Justin may have got a weird deal from the fight. And some black guys walk with screwdrivers not knives.

"Doesn't look very black, does he?" Jimmy says, wanting to be casual. But mulling. Heaps of what-ifs to this story. But Lorna would not want to hear. Not simple. Jimmy lopes back to his bishop-chair. Maybe Lorna knows.

Brixton is a place having streets with more jolting names than Atlantic Road. Streets named after big time English poets. Guys like Spenser and Shakespeare, Chaucer. Poets that would hit weatherproof verse today. Chaucer Road is the sneaky one, the ironic. Lorna's eyebrows raise. Chaucer was that guy who penned the Canterbury Tales, right? So? So those archbishops at Canterbury, they have serious tales to tell their god. *What?* Christian kingdom after kingdom poured innocent blood in the ocean. African blood. What? Yes, the Church of England. It used to have slave plantations in the Caribbean. *What?* The Archbishopric of Canterbury had slaves. *What?* Yes, for one example try a plantation in Barbados. The Codrington plantation. Check it out on the internet. That's the same Barbados where your grandparents come from. Your black grandparents. And the Church of England had billions invested in South Africa. During the apartheid days, the church backed mammon. Even today, the church has a priest living in a mansion named Lambeth Palace; a man calling himself Archbishop of Canterbury. How come a priest, a preacher-man for these days, how come he live in a palace? Lorna's eyes blear. She can not answer. Over Jimmy's shoulder her eyes seek the bible on her shelf. But Jimmy does not want scriptures. Lorna knows that. And anyway in England only one person in 200 goes to church on Sunday now. Some bishops already say the church here will be dead and buried less than 40 years into the millennium.

Lorna remembers being only yards from Tyson the day he was in Brixton. After he left she was in a bad way. Dazed, confused. Then she saw a big portrait of him hanging in a market stall. And getting home she got it up on the wall. It's the same one in the hallway now. After the picture hanging, and it was late night by then, the idea of brandy with cane came out of nowhere. No man was in her life and she was asking herself the big question. First thing was why she was alone. A lonely woman with empty eyes and a brother lying in a coma and, now and then, opening his eye and saying 'What, me?'

The crowd was gathering for Mike Tyson. And that was because of group-woe, something never getting talked, never getting put down in writing but, somehow, calling up a saviour. Somebody bigger than life, but alive as man. The internet is too fickle to track down the answer. And the answer is not there anyway, never having got put down in writing.

Lorna turns to Jimmy. "Don't laugh."

Jimmy with nothing to laugh at, says a white dwarf is a star having gravity three hundred and fifty thousand times gravity on earth. But Lorna's eyes do not twinkle. Her eyes are hurt.

"What's up?" he asks, gently.

"Don't laugh."

"What is it?"

Her throat clears. "Tyson, well, he was a bit like that knight of the Red Cross."

"Who?"

"Promise not to laugh?"

"I will not laugh. Which knight?"

"The one in Spenser's Faerie Queene."

The knight is fiction. Yes, she knows that. But so what? The knight was grace. He was dragon-slaying in the Faerie Queene till no injustice was left, nothing big enough to provoke him. Tyson in the Faerie Queene? Oh, somehow! Spenser was real enough, calling up the knight to hook fair play in England. Fair play, by pure courtesy. And now a woman in a bishop chair saying 'That is grace.'

Bullshit, Jimmy grows. A big idea, but big on bull. Stuff so huge it can not fit any place. But her brother on a life support machine so maybe she could use a dose of fairytales.

Jimmy's head shakes. "Listen, Tyson had a fight deal. That's why he came. It was a fight contract that brought him to England. The guy came to beat up a British black boxer. And that was for money. Going to Brixton was from his heart, I believe that, but the thing in the ring was the bottom line. That's why he came."

Loss is in Lorna's gaze. She wants to hide. And Jimmy, trying for something to say, asks if her parents ever visit her here in the flat.

Bernice is Lorna's mother. A black lady born in England. At seven years old Bernice was supposed to go Barbados. Go back home. But little buy little, inch by inch, that plan got left behind.

Bernice was grown by a stock West Indian mother and father, a nurse and carpenter. And, as usual, they wanted a big education for their daughter. Bernice was dutiful with her books and, eventually, well, England displaced Barbados in their happiness

Then one day.

One day in her teens Bernice quaked in front of the TV. Shocked, afraid. Her mother and father quaked. Black and afraid in front of the TV, afraid to look. Afraid of the next sentence. Afraid of the last one. Enoch Powell was the main TV item that evening on the news. It was the rivers-of-blood speech.

Enoch quoted slick numbers from the Registrar General's Office, saying how five million or even seven million Commonwealth immigrants and their descendants will be all over England by the year 2000. The year Tyson came to Brixton.

Enoch was in full flow when the money in the rented slot-TV ran out. And by the time they got the right coins, Enoch was talking of how white people have become strangers in their own country. He said it, saying England was a place with such inner cities that a white person can not go as far as their corner shop without getting followed by wide-grinning piccaninnies.

Quiet, Lorna wipes her eyes. Jimmy lights a smoke. Voice breaking, she says Bernice still knows that Powell speech by heart.

Brokenhearted, afraid for weeks to go outdoors, like even getting to work or school, the family wanted to get straight back to Barbados, wanted to leave the lie of one mother-country, say goodbye for good. But something happened. Completely unexpected, way out the blue. A man called Tony Benn was on TV. Tony called on England, saying 'Remember fair play, remember.' Lorna says her grandparents could not stop sobbing because of that one man; Tony a special white man, they said. And because of him they decided to give it a go. Give England one more try. But only one year at a time. And keeping quiet. The plan was for Bernice to go back to Barbados one day to marry and settle. But even now, even after all those years, Bernice has never been to Barbados. Not even for a holiday.

Lorna does not know what changed her mother's mind. After the rivers-of-blood speech Bernice made a vow. Bernice and her mother got ground down by the Powell speech. And late that night when sleep would not come, Bernice cried. And was taking a bath and combing warm water from her hair. Then, deliberate, she drew blood from her finger with a safety pin. And vowed. She vowed quiet in the night. Vowed on the family bible. Vowing two vows. Hand on the bible, Bernice resolved never to settle any place in England. And the next vow was just as resolute. It was never to get anywhere near a white boy. And that was how it was.

But then. A few years later when it was boyfriend time she had a go-getter boyfriend, a black guy born in Antigua and into buying up and renting property. Everything was set. She was just about to leave her job to help out at her boyfriend's business so they could maybe retire by forty with a boat in the Caribbean. But something happened.

Way, way out the blue. Impossible to think. A square circle. Snow ablaze. No slavery.

One day the impossible happened. One day, loping into the dole office where Bernice worked was a Viking man. Smiling, he was in motorcycle gear . A man, not a blank white. A tall white man with a trimmed brown beard. But not one of the oppressors. Alan Stanley was striding through town. And Bernice married him.

Lorna turns to Jimmy. "I know what you're thinking."

"Yeah? What am I thinking?"

"It's the bit about *grinning piccaninnies*, isn't it. You're thinking my mother and her half-piccaninnies, aren't you?"

Jimmy shifting in the bishop chair. But wondering. "Is this going to be a sermon?"

There's one vow Bernice made. The one about never having a white boyfriend. Maybe she should not have made it. Not on the bible. That's the reason maybe why her son in a coma now, the bible taking her son away to pay that vow. Mystic business in the bible sometimes, bronze or black.

"The bible is used in church. And they use it in the courts."

"I already told you, I don't get into bibles and stuff."

Lorna shrugs. "Some people don't rate the bible. But it's like how much light you really want, understand? You get some people thinking 'Why bother with that scorching sun when I have a neat little switch on the wall!' You one of those?"

In two hours Jimmy and Lorna cover ground together. Talk most things. But it had to happen. Eventually talk turns to Stephen Lawrence. How come nobody ever gets even for Stephen. Lorna will not talk of guns. The bronze of her bible, is that anything to do with blood?

Gold for the winner, Jimmy says, and silver for regret, being just one step away. But bronze! Bronze for the blood you spill just getting to the rostrum at all.

"Where did you get that?" Lorna smiles. "That's *lovely!*"

"It's from this opera I'm doing. A jazz piece."

Bernice vowed on the bible. But with blood oozing from her finger. A bronze bible is not a black hole. But just as final. Lorna turned to religion after what happened to Justin and she can not talk about him. But weird, she can talk of Stephen Lawrence. Deep down, this woman talking the blues. Even Tyson would weep the way Lorna talks of Stephen.

Stephen is one antidote. A template. A black human fitting her brother with only small adjustments. Lorna talks sad, sad, sad. She was at a meeting one night and a chatty woman got up and said what Brixton is. The only thing Brixton's got going for it is, well, Brixton is no Eltham; that's what the chatty woman said, telling the meeting that if Stephen Lawrence was in Brixton and not Eltham that fateful night he would have been plain invisible. No maniac ever goes to Brixton to find somebody to hack. Somebody black.

A white man and a white woman tried to save Stephen. They were kneeling where Stephen fell in Eltham. The white man and white woman tried their heart to comfort him. The woman had Stephen's head in her white arms, kneeling down beside him in the night. And the man tried and tried. His shirt getting drenched in the youth's blood. The white man and his white wife knew the boy was slipping away. But they kept trying. Trying harder all the time. Trying, trying. They tried everything they knew. But. No dice. It was all in vain. The next day was just too difficult. The man with a big burden in his heart. He washed Stephen's blood from his shirt. Then searched and searched his soul. He just did not know what to do with the blood-stained water from the wash. In the end, he took it to his garden and poured it over a small rosebush.

Jimmy sad now. For a minute he can not speak. Quiet, he sinks to the floor. Stephen would have invisible in Brixton. Day or night. But in Eltham that fateful night, Stephen was in a Brixton overcoat.

"What the white man did with the blood-stained water, that was the biggest thing ever. The man's shirt is a shroud."

Lorna nods. "A holy shroud, to be kept safe."

"Got to find a place for something like that."

"But where?"

Jimmy paws the air. Exhaling hard. "I don't know."

"Then let's put it on the internet. Like a verse."

"Or we could get it into the British Museum."

Lorna is on the floor. So much, so much! She will not talk of guns. But something in her gaze. Her eyes look like ghost flashlights. "Yes, the British Museum could be the place." Reaching the bookshelf, she gets a poetry volume of Omar Khayyam. And turns the page. And page, and page, saying 'Stephen, Stephen.' Then turns back to the start. And softly, reads one quatrain. Two lines repeat from the verse, calm, makeshift: *And never blows the rose so red, as where some buried black boy bled.*

Chapter 51

At last, a sale! Halfway through the third week, a sale for Jimmy. Great sale for a novice. But two and a half weeks till today it was bad news on the line. Nobody was buying from the novice phone.

Telesales is one hitch. It can be whoring that ruins. But the phone gets someone invisible; and that phone whoring is never face to face. Telesales is horse trading. Anything can get sold. Even homesteads on Mars. Mountains bigger than Everest are under the oceans, but so what? On some shy Mars shore, plots of Mars are up for sale already. Plots overlooking what was the Mars ocean getting bought by myth seekers in Texas. And it is telesales jockeys doing the selling.

On the phone, five seconds to get a genie down the line. And then the seller can take all the time in the world; a minute, two hours, any old time. The punter tunes in for magic. And land-plots selling on Mars means no problem selling stuff to worming execs fifty or a hundred miles from London.

A brooding reception suite got sold to a private college today. Jimmy did the deal. The gambler and Geraldine were happy over this. The gambler took Jimmy by the elbow, saying 'This is where the party starts!' But huge jealousy was in the salesroom. The commission on Jimmy's deal is nearly four grand and, wait a minute, hey, that's serious wedge for a first deal!

Two minutes after the sale gets confirmed, Colette is in the salesroom. Big champagne in her happy arms. Beckoning Jimmy, she skits to the window. Her voice hits a sweet note. If that's a want, she says, pointing to the hardware in the parking lot, then it's the pick of the likes of what's there. But a word of advice to the newly baptized: the road to cars like that is where you travel alone, and light; no artist's dreams. Getting there means you have to really *want*. Chilled champagne pressing into Jimmy's hand as Colette turns to the room.

This woman flicks. Colette switches from delicate to callous. Like old snow. Jimmy's never seen this side to the woman before. Geraldine talked about it. But unreal seeing it up close. All the phones get downed. Except the gambler's phone. He's beyond the law here, the big earner with cowboy boots piling high on a desk.

This callous thing with Colette is like snowflakes in cold air. Or like watching the Thames from a warm apartment in Canary Wharf. Or being with a great woman watching the cityscape and seeing it tart as darkness falls. For Jimmy, the Thames was the thing one evening. It sapped. The onset of snow was so sudden. Snowflakes gathered on the window pane and the woman said 'What a world! My God!'

Colette turning ice. Jimmy's deal is only a tool to Colette. Because now she drives a wedge, using it to taunt people in the salesroom. Most of them only do mickey mouse deals anyway and here's Jimmy, she says, one of the newest people in the salesroom and gets a deal with four grand commission already. There and then two people get sacked. 'Get a job on the checkout till at Tesco's!'

Jimmy standing by a window. Chilled champagne in his hand. And Colette playing air guitar round him. She taunts the salesroom and goes through the door. The gambler laughs. Lighting a smoke, the high-roller says Colette's name should be up on the bonus board. Why? Every week the top two performers in the room get a bonus. And Colette should be one prize next week. That's what the gambler says. And Chardonnay, yeah, that's a dozen bottles for the winner. Colette, a prize? Yeah, the gambler laughs. Laughing old tobacco stains he says the runner-up should get a private striptease or then a hand-job from the boss lady.

In her own right Colette is the best actor. She the ace sales-jockey. Always selling new recruits a money fairytale, saying all they have to do is hit the phones and that it can be difficult, yes, but with big bucks up for grabs all they have to do is commit; and, oh, make a sale in the first three weeks. No debate about it. You sell in three weeks, or walk. Want money, or you looking for hiking boots?

Chapter 52

The salesroom at Homes is glass three sides. Exactly like it got designed to jolt the tea, get action from the sellers. Some days lightning threatens from an overcast sky. And days can pass when nobody in the room sells a thing. Not even the gambler. And that's when the bragging starts. Always somebody with a big tale, a hot weekend somewhere, or clubbing all New York or Las Vegas, or a depraved week sloshed in Zanzibar and old bazaars.

Then, sudden as lightning, somebody does it. By luck or design. And the lucky designer is the gambler here. The dash for cash starts all over. Cash, the cool, the drought-buster.

With a telesales crew of thirty, only four or five will ever make decent money. And only one in the top-man seat. The rest come and go. Start getting to know somebody and next thing they up and gone. The next cycle maybe lasts three months. And the big cycle can take six months to pan out. And all the time heavy footfalls on the way out.

Colette the boss. She never blinks to get rid of some hapless one. Sales charts never lie. Your name on the sales chart and if your curve falls then you tell the chart why. You will get more pity from the chart than Colette. But the lady, she's got one weak spot. She is a business leader, chopping down the salesroom like buzzsaws in a forest, but she a woman. A woman with a ding for the arts. Theatre is her thing. If music is there to play or drama to stage, then she the business. Jimmy taps into that. Taps into the soft spot on the flick woman. But the gambler says if she was ever to square up to another female, somebody with education, then Colette would lose. One somebody could be Geraldine; her bearing, education, how she talks.

Jimmy invisible. Eight hours a day on the telephone playing people that don't even consider the race of who is talking them. No ethnic lilt down the phone, Jimmy playing in a word city that is pure colour-blind. Like on a skateboard over graphite. The phone is it. And now and then will be some heavy Thespian to tend. Sometimes a woman is there to play. And that is pure fun for sales guys; especially if she the kind of slick wanting to excite, like a blind date, illicit, hot. Or only wanting to meet for lunch. But she plays down the line, laughing low, and somebody will suggest she should buy a little something; a boardroom suite would be great. That's how the game plays. And some woman directors can play nice, play blind intricate down the line. And to think, white folk invisible all the time.

The thing is talking blind. On the phone is blindness. Punters spending money with someone blind. And for Jimmy that is more than neat.

Some days the gambler ignores his phone, listening to Chopin on his Walkman. Shutting off from the sales noise, the gambler listens to Rubinstein play Chopin waltzes. Now and then somebody gets to borrow his gear and go for a smoke. And listen the A Minor Waltz, Opus 34 Number 2. This a waltz? Summer is only one season away. The heartache in this Chopin piece could be death arriving. And somebody wanting for death to be alone in a winter field with fresh snow. Jimmy agreeing with the gambler; winter death is the theme of this A Minor Waltz.

The gambler says somebody famous can die good. The whole world can watch a famous man die and from then nobody will fear death. Like the preacher-man dying on the cross? No, preacher was not the one. So maybe it can be a tyrant, a tyrant dying in public. One day a tyrant will walk to a gallows or firing squad and folk will get to see dying is no big a deal. To the gambler, that's what Chopin's A Minor Waltz means.

Sometimes summer is better with rain. Instead of sweltering, summer is sometimes better with wildness, playing with thunder, grabbing a sight of lightning. But summer is still down the road from the sales room. A whole season invisible from here.

Chapter 53

Jimmy got two letters from Donna this week. Mostly it was fuss about her diet. Donna watchin' dat body ting. But still doing that cooking.

Agnes should get a letter from Jimmy. Any man would want to spend a summer raining with Agnes. Then again. That woman could arrive from South Africa out the blue one day. Any time soon. Like one Saturday she turned up puzzling more than usual, arriving at the flat with curtain rods. And a Stan Getz LP was in the carrier-bag she had. Nobody had seen much of that disk, except in Poland, so there was new Getz music to listen in England. And in a Tottenham tenement. Jimmy will never forget. Can never forget Agnes fitting curtain rods at the window, him sitting back and watching that woman high on a chair with 8 floors down to the street. But that was one year ago already. In her last letter a man drops by at her uncle's house. And two times in the letter she talks how the guy's a big time finance manager with a voice like Paul Robeson. According to the letter, this guy even talks like Paul.

In one recent dream Jimmy watching a lion looking out to sea. And later in the dream was walking a seafront edged by blue neon lions. A cold coast at dawn.

Nathan collected a pile of Motown, every cut from the 60's and 70's. And Jimmy plays Motown all the time. Motown nice. Nathan said Motown was so beautiful *killed* Jamaica with sweet music. Talented folk. Smoky Robinson, The Supremes, Marvin Gaye. TV in the UK should do a whole month of Motown. That's what Nathan believes. And those old videos of the Supremes, to Jimmy it was Diana Ross. She the sweetest looking of all time. She was maybe 18 or 19 when doing Baby Don't Leave Me. That limber body, that long neck. The melancholy that was in her woman eye. Must be a woman like that now. Maybe Diana's got a daughter waiting for Jimmy. Maybe she' go two daughters to choose from.

"What would you like to see happen about your brother? I know guys that can deal with it. No problem."

Lorna gasps. "Violence?"

Jimmy quotes from his opera. "Lions don't roar at the sea."

Lorna will not reply. Worry in her mouth. The doctors say Justin dipped back, took a bad turn. It does not look good. And that is so hard to deal with. Lorna's mother goes to a faith-healer. And her father went out to the garden with his sledgehammer and shocked the shed apart. Alan Stanley roaring at the sea.

Jimmy at Lorna's flat for the second time this week. Hard to know why she turns to him. But she sounded bad when she phoned tonight. And now a pack of silence in her apartment, quiet, gazing at a bookshelf.

Lorna is ground down. Pain in her eye. She expects the phone to ring. She afraid. Restless in the room, pacing. She'd be better off at her parents' place. This woman wants someone to hold. But she would not want to boogie. If she was alone here she would read the bible. The whole New Testament, one more time. Maybe if it was soft and slow. But Jimmy is not the man for that. It would wreck this woman. She wants a man, not a wounded music man, not a fugitive from close.

Apart from Agnes, woman was only prey to Jimmy. Agnes was always different. She the woman somebody wants a whole tribe of kids with. And she is not afraid of that. Her destiny will not tarry when her belly swells per year. And now she at the ocean, in Cape Town, closing her eyes to watch her vision. And if anything remotely looks like a racial going by, then she spits straight past it.

Somebody must pay for Justin, Jimmy says. England is a white man's country but if you human you have to make room for yourself. Or why do handshakes? If you get hit, then you counterpunch. Three times as hard.

Lorna will not talk payback. Violence is bad every time; there's no limit to violence, she says. But to Jimmy this woman's got her imagination tangled. Her vision in a bronze bible, this woman can not see what must get done. In broad daylight lions in a cage and her bible's got no solution to that. She listens to Jimmy talk of neon lions in a dream.

Upright in her bishop chair, she turns to him. "Violence is out."

"Well, you *could* call revenge violence."

"What would you call it?"

"Revenge? Revenge is payback time."

"Vengeance is mine, said the Lord."

"I do not understand bibles and praying. Your Jesus walked on water but one of the disciples always walked beside him with a sword. What was Peter's sword for?"

"My parents want the law involved, OK? My father wants a public inquiry."

"And what will that do?"

"It will clear the air."

"Yes. But what will it achieve, beyond a bunch of talk?"

"Bigots are bigots."

"What's your mother say?"

"It was difficult."

"What does she think?"

"They had a bust-up over it. Dad was 'I told him those dreadlocks would drag him down.' You never hear my mother swear, but she got into that and I was 'Go ahead, let it all out!' It went on and on. For days, really."

Jimmy turns to the skydivers on the wall. Wondering. Lorna a sheep? She is no warrior woman. Not the type to walk beside a warrior in the race jungle; lady, you got too much bible! Lorna hopes to make the situation over Justin go away, to dream his coma away. But Justin can not dream. A coma a strange place to dream. Then there's the part that maybe Justin stopped the screwdriver from one of his own posse, another black guy. And way down from in the coma he said it again yesterday, said, 'What, me?'

Lorna a black woman. But part white. That ocher, that pencil profile. And she believes in a *due process*. But that stuff tickles uncle tom. If it wasn't for colour she'd be English all day. And yet. Something else. Mike Tyson in her dream. She switched a Guns & Roses photograph in the hall for Tyson; that what she says.

The screensaver idles in the room. The word *ricochet* annoys Jimmy. It shuffles the mute screen like a strangle cord, like somebody tossing rope from a nightmare. That computer is my friend, Lorna says. Why a word instead of a picture? Most people have a picture but she wants *ricochet*.

This is fresh coffee. Maybe this woman can catch her reflection in a coffee cup. One screensaver for Lorna could be a lioness; on her computer should be the picture of a young lioness playing tawny grass with cubs on the plains.

No mixed-race waver in Lorna. Nothing like the girl Jimmy was with. He was 17 then. And now remembers a bitch. The only good time was the day her syndicate clocked the lottery. The girl was hot

211

that day, beautiful with her own fire. But the next day spoiled all that. The first thing was a safari suit. Her share was four hundred grand and she was even going to get Jimmy a sports car. But getting a car from her would have been a bad move. Her witch-like would cramp the car from going fast or far. She was 18, frisk, always telling what was obvious: like 'Do you know it's Monday today?' But the stupidest part was the way she repeated how she mixed-race; even reminding Jimmy, especially when in a crowd. The bigger the crowd the more the witch used to say 'I'm *mixed race.*' She was never black; *black* was for black people. And though her father was black that did not make her black; no matter what, she said. A girl with bats in her head. But some people change. Maybe by now she shaping up from the lopside. She was in a Porsche Boxter the last time Jimmy saw her.

Lorna gets to her feet. "What's wrong?"

"You're you. I'm glad for that."

"Is that a compliment?"

"Yes."

"Thank you!"

"You're nothing like somebody I used to know."

"So?"

"So, nothing. There's no next move."

"Who was she?"

"A witch."

"What?"

"Probably lives in Epping Forest by now."

"A weirdo?"

"A witch. She never said black. It was always 'my father's people' and stuff."

Lorna's head shakes. "Jimmy, you want to know about my father. It's in your eyes."

"To know, or not to know."

"Honestly, there's nothing to talk about."

"Well, now you mention it, who is he?"

She straightens her back in the bishop chair. And grins. "Well, he's a brown-eyed handsome man. Tall. Quiet. Hard-working. A little difficult with strangers. I mean, he won't let anyone get too close. The two of you would get on like a house on fire."

"Then how come he does nothing about Justin?"

"Depends what you mean by nothing."

"Your dad should square things, that's what!"

"We don't know who did it."

"Think it's because he's scared?"

"*Scared*?"

"Yeah, scared he might find out something."

"Who?"

"Your father."

"What d'you mean?"

"Last week on the phone you said something about them having a great big bust up."

"Who?"

"Your father and Justin."

"Did I tell you that?"

"How else would I know?"

"Well, it was a long time ago. Ages and ages."

"Maybe it's still there, floating around."

"Well," Lorna nods, pushing chair, and her voice lowers, "perhaps there *is* one little thing. He couldn't take it when Justin came back with locks. They didn't speak for a year because of it."

"Back from where?"

"Justin was in Barbados for nine months and he came back with dreadlocks and a broad Bajan accent, and it was 'Look, this is the real me' sort of thing. *So* cute!"

"What about your sister? Where's she at?"

"How d'you mean?"

"I was thinking black people. Her stance with the black community."

Lorna gulps. Swallows hard. "My sister? Hmm, that's a good one. I can't make my mind up. Haven't you got anybody?"

"Like?"

"Brothers and sisters."

"People round me all day?"

"Family."

"Nah. I'm the only one. My mother didn't want any more. She wanted loads, but it didn't work out with my old man. It was not being sure what he was up to out there. With him, well, there could be twenty more like me. I've never asked."

"Don't you feel, isn't it lonely?"

"Yeah. I think about that. Would've been great if I had a brother. Or a sister."

"You can do a spliff if you want," Lorna smiles. "It's OK."

"What was with Justin getting a Bajan accent?"

"You'll have to ask him. I think I understand it, but he never really said."

"You sister ever been to Barbados?"

"In so many ways, it was a lot easier for her."

"How?"

"Can you stop making those little-lost-boy eyes at me?"

Jimmy taps the cigarette packet. Turns to the little bookshelf. Clumsy, alone. He knows Lorna watching all his moves. But then. Even on the day they first met, she was confident about him. Hard to tell why. But him being here tonight, comfortable in her apartment, talking family, she makes him feel alone.

"Want me to leave?"

"No."

"Got something on your mind?"

"Like what!"

"Your sister goes out with white guys?"

"That's none of my business. And what would it *ever* have to do with you?"

Jimmy wants a spliff. "Getting touchy in your old age!"

"Her boyfriend *is* white. Satisfied?"

"Bet your father jumps for joy at that."

"Like how? He doesn't run around chanting 'One blue-eyed boy for Elaine, one for Lorna.'"

"That's not what I meant."

"Look, I didn't even think about that till I was sixteen, seventeen. And then it was just black guys that I liked. Well, more or less. Justin's the same. It's always been black girls. It was easier for Elaine. She always made her own choices and, listen, she's not trying to be white if that's what you mean. She knows what's what."

From the flat upstairs someone playing Robert Cray. At full tilt. Robert Cray and Eric Clapton on stage was a great gig. Buddy Guy was there, and maybe the best blues ever on stage in England was at the Albert Hall with all three guys and their Strats touring the blues.

Jimmy exhales a billow. "How come your father's not in that picture with the rest of you?"

214

"The picture in the hall next to Mike Tyson?"

"Yeah."

"I don't want to get into that."

"Sorry I asked."

"No psychoanalysis, OK?"

"Me, a shrink?"

"You sound like a little therapist. With you it's like 'Wait, there's shit to uncover here.' Well, you're dead wrong! We're a close family. *Close*."

"I never had that," Jimmy groans. "It was only me and my keyboard. I've had nine or ten keyboards down the years."

"Why the big thing about my dad?"

"Just a thought. Not trying to snoop. Don't get diced."

"You ask *lethal* questions."

Jimmy ambles over to the two photos of skydivers on the living room wall. Lorna's father taller than the rest in the photo. A white man looking like an ex-boxer. Or military cop. Lorna watching him.

Jimmy turns to her. "Your dad's sister, is she still singing?"

"Not really. After the last tour, the band she gave it a miss. But that was ages and ages ago. Fifteen, twenty years."

"She do any studio gigs?"

"Yeah. She was very good. She auditioned for a Jimmy Hendrix show. It was 60's soul music back then. Black music, basically."

"Otis Redding and Sam Cook. I love that stuff."

"Wilson Picket. Got any of his?"

"Sam & Dave."

"Solomon Burke."

"Irma Thomas."

"Christ! I thought you were jazz, jazz."

"My old man is *huge* on soul. Crucial. He used to do session work, backed soul acts for years. I have a load of soul. And the Motown stuff he gave me."

"Motown? My auntie could give your dad a run for his money."

"Now you're going *too* far."

"Well, _"

"I'm not being racial about this."

"She made some soul tapes up so we could play them at Justin's bedside. Funny how it turned out."

"Yeah," Jimmy jokes, "after the soul excursion your auntie put

215

away her foolish things and went back to white."

Lorna laughs out loud. Her head shakes. "It was Newcastle, fool!"

"What's all that like?"

"My dad's family?"

"Yeah."

"Typical working class. Geordies. You've got to understand, everybody got caught up in black music in the 60s."

"And Elvis."

"The Beatles."

"The Stones."

"Yeah. Listen to the Stones?"

"Not really. The early stuff with their guitarist that died _"

"Brian Jones."

"Yeah. But I can learn from the Beatles. What's your favourite Beatles track?"

"Mull."

"Mull of Kintyre?"

"Yes. What's yours?"

"The harmonies in Yesterday, beautiful."

"But it's not your favourite?"

"I dunno. Yes, I think so. Some people go for Lennon, but McCartney was the greatest by a mile. Hey, I think She Loves You is way up there."

"The energy."

"And the teeny lyric. Those old songs were neat."

"Pure."

"Purer."

"Listen," Lorna says, "my dad was a biker bloke. He didn't just wake up one morning and think 'Oh, what a swank day, I'll just go down to London and become a fireman and, oh, hang on a minute, I'll end up with a black wife and three kids.' There was no grand plan. It just turned out that way, OK?"

"Sounds special. Like from a nicer world."

"What d'you mean?"

"It's the way you describe it."

"Don't you believe me?"

"Bet your dad's got a head full of stuff. Somebody like me could learn from it."

"Nice of you to say so!" Lorna snorts.

216

"I mean it."

"What?"

"Chas Chandler was from up there, wasn't he?"

"Up where?"

"Newcastle."

"I think so. Yes, that's right. It was The Animals, a blues band."

"Eric Burdon."

"He was the singer."

"That guy was *deep* into black music."

"Yeah, he got to sing with Otis Redding."

"I've seen the video. It was him singing with Otis Redding on Top Of The Pops."

"He held his own."

"Eric Burdon understood. He had relatives working in the coal mines and to him they were the same as slaves."

"There was no real excitement in the post-war years."

"I saw this interview. Eric says back then it was either get into black music or look for unexploded bombs."

"Eric Burdon and The Animals."

"And Chas Chandler was in the band. The Animals."

"So?"

"Hendrix probably wouldn't have made it here without him."

"So?"

"So, something's bugging you. It's obvious."

Chapter 54

Alan Stanley always cooks Sunday dinner. Looking at a recipe just
once, Alan will remember it years later. This man can cook English
or Caribbean. And that includes the biggest jerk pork to run-down,
ackee & saltfish.

Alan was always a calming influence. Lorna's father, if ever he
sees young guys squaring up in the street then he gets right in there
to keep the peace. As a young guy Alan never visioned a black
woman. The closest to that was a quick Vietnamese girl. She was a
daughter from the local takeaway and he used to meet her in secret.
But that did not count. And that's because it was when he was fifteen and they never went all the way anyway. It tickles Lorna that
her father once had a thing for someone from far Vietnam. And all
the time at home in the 50s and 60s, Alan's father was playing folk
tunes on the Hardanger fiddle; so much Viking blood in Northumberland.

In the flow now, Lorna talks it. She remembers her first racial.
When she was in was her early teens she tried telling Alan about
something her mother just did not want to hear. From the age of
maybe eight or nine, Lorna started noticing. She'd maybe come
across a black and white couple in the street and, next thing, they
smiled because of her, and only at her, making a beeline to wherever she was. Thinking about it now, well, maybe it was just by being close to her that the black and white couple would call up a
blessing for their thing. But when Lorna told him, Alan only
laughed. Her father said she was not a priest, and that anyway her
imagination was too far.

Her voice lowers. "Well," she says, "my dad is kind. Absolutely
fair minded. Always listens to both sides of the argument."

"The perfect man! Looks like you're used to having knights in
white tunics round you."

"My dad?"

"Yeah. You're proud of him in a mythic way."

"Well, he's got his own hang-ups. We all do!"

"My dad's got hang-ups. It's white folk claiming they helped cre-
ate jazz. That pisses him right off. But then that's not a hang-up, is
it? What's your old man's gripe?"

"Complicated. Even the rest of us don't go there. He'll be alright

218

for months and months, I mean ages and ages, then something happens and he snaps, goes on about asylum seekers."

Jimmy rattling the box of matches. "What about the big one?"

"Black people?"

"Yes."

"Call me black, don't you?"

"Course!"

"There's some that wouldn't."

"Mixed race sounds too clumsy."

"Clumsy?"

"Yeah, no music to it. Why, what's up?"

"My grandmother thinks *mixed* is a cut above black. Big deal!"

"Your white grandmother?"

"Yes."

"They all think that."

"They?"

"White folk."

"No, they do not *all* think that!"

Right from the beginning of English settlement in Jamaica, white indentured servants were only a heartbeat above black slaves in the pecking order; and way above all of the indentured whites were the black freemen. To Jimmy it was weird seeing white people born and bred in Jamaica, Jamaican white folk ambling along with the same delayed rhythm as black Jamaica; even laughing the same. Seeing something like that was a big surprise. And one day a white guy used huge teeth to rip the knife-proof bark from sugar cane. That was way past words. Even now, that's something to step way back from and laugh. Laugh it, out loud, somewhere like in Trafalgar Square. . Under the Jamaica sun the white Jamaican laughed and crunched that cane. And Jamaica white guys tend to hook up with Jamaica black women.

Jimmy's fingers snap. "Listen, even black people think it."

"What?"

"Loads of black guys prefer half-caste girls."

Lorna groans. "I know that sort. The blacker some guys are, the more they _"

"I've never met somebody like you before."

"Me?"

"Don't get prissy. You know what I mean. Your father's white. A white man. Even looking at you and saying *white man* makes me nervous. With you I feel I have to watch what I say."

Lorna's brow knits her nose. High, her eyebrows split like a hyphen. Eyebrows hesitating over high cheekbones. She nods. "Yes."

"Think Alan understands what that does out there?"

"I don't think it's 'Oh there's that Stanley bloke, the one with all those darkies in his house.' It isn't like that. Oh, God. I don't know!"

"Make your mind up."

"I know the facts, OK?"

"But you don't want to tell me."

"Listen! Anybody brings crap to my dad, they have to do it behind his back or they get a right fucking hiding!"

Jimmy must get a spliff here. Slow, gets a good look at the Lorna woman. And knows. She beautiful tonight. Her heart is full of pain. And her brother might die. But this woman beautiful tonight. And the great thing is she knows her stuff. She can explain things.

With race, two sets of white folk in England. Most can get vexed up by non-whites here. The first group wants blacks out, gone. They still waiting for a successor to Enoch. The second group is more sensible, wanting no more blacks in the country, but, just as true, wanting to give the ones here every chance to earn their way. Then along came Norman Tebbit.

Chapter 55

Norman attracts two white camps. And everybody using some version of the Tebbit test now. But only few saying it out loud.

Norman was key to Margaret Thatcher. The sliest one of all, and by one mile more smart than she. But he bald. And a bald head did not elide on TV. Bald-head was too close to the fear of dying, the electorate seeing that skull as a warning. So despite Norman being heavy-duty English and smart, he was too bald; even his own side called him *Chingford skinhead*. Margaret did not understand the vision Norman could see, and that's why there's them still loving her that loved her. Norman was a flyer, a big time RAF and commercial pilot. And when you stop flying at that level, well. That's maybe when you get the worse flake-highs of all. Or so Lorna says.

Guys get flake-highs. Talented white guys get it when passed over. But black guys get it all the time.

The Tebbit test is simple. Lorna explains. Norman says black people must commit to England. And the up-front commitment is to support England at cricket. *Cricket*? Maybe you're watching TV with your father and if the West Indies play England and your father was born in the West Indies and you born here, then Norman wants the two of you to root for the England cricket team.

But if somebody black is ever involved in a hold-up, or even chucks a coke-can in the street, then the TV is quick. The TV says *of West Indian appearance*. Or they say *black*. No matter where the guy was born. Or a reporter might say mixed-race. But where Norman when bullshit like that coming over? Norman says 'What else can they say?' But all the time he pays the big TV license fee instead of scraping loud crap from them Tebbit shoes.

"So," Jimmy winks at Lorna, "if I want to get called English I have to support England at cricket."

"For starters."

"Alan thinks that?"

"My dad?"

"What's he think?"

"He's obviously not a racist!"

In Voodoo Chile, Hendrix plays heavy nether. Hendrix going to chop down a whole mountain with the side of his hand. And Stephen Hawking, a guy in a wheelchair with galaxies in his eye that

221

his hand can not point at. Stephen playing wicked air-harmonica round black holes and white dwarfs.

Jimmy laughs. "There's all kinds of ways to be racist."

"What are you getting at?"

"I heard about this BNP guy, he's got a serious thing for ethnic women."

"No way!"

"I'm serious."

"You're having me on!"

"It's dead true."

"Then he's sick."

"Obviously."

"Got to be, hasn't he?"

"A psycho."

"A hypocrite!"

"Yeah."

"So what's the problem?"

"I can't see how a black woman can shack up with a BNP?"

"She doesn't know."

"But suppose she does."

"She *can't* know!""

"Or she's got a split personality."

"*He's* the one with the problem."

"Listen, the white man _"

"Not my dad!"

"Sure?"

"What d'you mean?"

"Explain to me how a racist white boy can lust after a black woman!"

Somewhere on a nerd's computer, pixels moving like waves from ocean to shore. Every dot on the computer screen moves round as pairs of numbers. One number can marry another number in pixel heaven. Even the ugliest shape gets a mathematical matrix. And a word like *ricochet* bouncing around like ants in the cave of a skull.

Lorna's mouth puckers. "Where did you hear about that sick BNP moron?"

"He only went with ethnic women. Black women or Indian. One Chinese. It was in the papers. I kept the cutting."

"Can you get me a photocopy?"

"First thing tomorrow."

"Sure you're not making this up. There's mischief in your face."

"I am *not* making it up. It was a load of guns, knives and weird flyers in his flat. They found a squad load of manic stuff. But I'm not accusing your father."

"Then why tell me?"

"That story only confirmed that I must play safe with white."

"Well, you're *so* off the mark with my dad."

"I need to play safe. I'm not accusing anyone. Especially someone I don't know."

"He's obviously got his moods. We all have. If he gets in one of those, we laugh it off. If there's cricket on TV, Justin is 'Come on West Indies, come on!' It's always been like it in our house."

Justin might not make it. Hard to say what accounts for who is who. And who will live till a hundred. A cat gets run over and a spinster sheds tears, pining in front of the seven deadly sins pinned to her wall.

"When you see uncle Norman, tell him something for me."

"*Uncle* Norman?" Lorna grins.

"Yeah. Tell him I'd root for England one day but only after it's OK for me to criticize the place."

"What, you don't like everything in England?"

"Think it's funny? Norman Tebbit would have a heart attack if somebody black moved into his little hamlet."

"Wow!"

"This is life and death!"

"Wow!"

"Unless it's sport, they don't like you criticizing stuff. The minute you open your mouth, zap! Unless it's sport or entertainment there's always somebody ready to tell you to fuck off, dead pan, go back where you come from!"

On one shelf on her bookcase, Lorna has a pride of books on slavery and colonialism. Along with reading the bible, she is deeply into what went on. At least, the way books say what went on.

She gazes her feet. "My mother's got a little remedy for that."

"Yeah, that Oprah Winfrey!"

"No, no! When bigots start she just lets them get on with it."

"Your dad having his tantrums, and she puts cellotape on her mouth? No disrespect to your mother, but I can't see how a black

223

woman could stomach that."

"My parents get on!"

"They don't quarrel?"

"Don't be ridiculous! Everybody does flare-ups. It's not 'That's your side of the house, keep your thoughts to yourself.' It's a man and woman, 27 years together."

Looking past the skydivers on the wall, Jimmy notes a book on the slavery shelf. It's by Olaudah Equiano. "I'd be worried with a white girl."

"*Why?*"

"I couldn't tell her I got called a black bastard. Jeez, you'd have to be a cretin to live like that!"

"As long as *she* doesn't call you that."

"I couldn't get home and moan, not to a white woman."

"If she loves you, then _"

"I still couldn't tell her. I'd feel weird telling her."

"She can *not* be guilty for somebody else."

"What happens if I was out with her somewhere and racist crap comes over. What happens then? I'd have to be a serious thicko to live that way."

"Not my family!"

"Never?"

"Never!"

"Then congratulations."

"*What?*"

"You obviously get to live a fairytale. Congrats, lady."

"What is this? I mean, it's like a game to you. A vicious pack of witchfinders at the door. You're talking about my parents, you know, my mother, human beings, been together 27 years!"

Astronomers have pictures of the hot early stages of the universe. And most people have albums of their family frolicking the seaside. Big time physics looks for gravitons, heartbreaking particles too small to ever get seen but which would explain the sigh of this whole universe and its business. But for now, gravitons only live in equations. And one equation can cover the smallest things and stuff big enough to munch stars. Equations are kinder than folk can ever be.

Jimmy stubs the smoke. Weary. A nervous cough, a tobacco cough. The room is a pinch. The night a pinch. He turns to Lorna.

224

"I wasn't getting at your parents."

"Then what's your problem?"

"It wasn't personal. It's how I talk."

"Talk? You obsess! It's like some kind of fixation."

"Look, I've met some ace white girls. Way up there for talent. Looks. But it's never come down to anything with one. There's no way I could be out some place with a white girl and somebody call me a black cunt."

Languid, Lorna pulls at her hair. Thick Africa hair. Ponderous, she takes to the bishop chair for comfort. "It's different from the outside."

"I'd *never* take that chance. Never!"

"Not if you love someone?"

"*Love*?"

"People go round imagining. They make things up. All sorts."

"I don't think I'm making it up if I get called a black bastard."

"Things happen, even like you say. But there's none of that between my mother and father."

Jimmy flicks a smoke ring. Then a lazy punch through it. And checks the time. A jazz band at the Jazz Café tonight, should be a great gig. Lorna nervy in her own apartment. Silent, she looks round at things. Looking at the size of the sitting room, her visitor, the bookshelves and walls. Jimmy checks the time again.

"There's something in the kitchen," she says. "Lamb with aubergines and honey."

"Not hungry."

"Three minutes in the microwave, and it's ready."

"I don't want anything. Could do with some live music tonight."

"Bigots are all the same."

"Yeah."

"There's traffic both ways. It's a two-way street."

Jimmy steps to the hi-fi. Coltrane there somewhere. John Coltrane can take it here, preach some modals. A Coltrane solo can collect all the echoes in a valley or room. Or it can slap pebbles through a stream.

In three minutes Jimmy snug again. Comfortable in a bishop chair, tucking into Lorna's cooking. But she only picks at her plate. This woman somewhere else. Thin voiced and distant, she talks of some scary thing her parents met.

In the early days when Alan and Bernice were out together, they sometimes used to run into young black guys that would call her mother names. Bad names. Out of pure spite, hurt names. The day Bernice knew she was pregnant with Lorna, they checked out a West Indian restaurant to celebrate. It was a cool summer evening. So happy. But they ran into hurt words at the restaurant. It was a crowd of young black guys, taunting. Bad, non stop. Alan wanted to ignore it. Bernice pretended it was not there, staying quiet, heart aching because of the sheer spite and jostling. To play safe, they made a dash for it. But not before their minivan got a heavy shower. Bricks and kicks rained down on the minivan. The whole side of the van caved.

Racial taunts got less and less as the years passed. Mercifully. But Lorna's last boyfriend was very wordy to her mother. He a dread-locks guy born in England but seeing himself as a Jamaican all day, talking Jamaica patois like he was born there. And his own parents, well, both mixed-blood Jamaicans. That guy had a hell of a racial hang-up over Alan. The business against her father was one thing. Lorna was sure it would go away. But one day the guy let fly. It was at her mother. A tropical word storm. Heavy-duty Jamaica cuss words flinging at her mother.

Jimmy ships the last aubergine slice. "What was the deal?"

"He came out with a load of rubbish and I thought 'Jesus, what a mistake this is!' And that was it, basically."

"Lorna, a lot of black guys think like your boyfriend."

"Ex-boyfriend!"

"Your ex-boyfriend."

"Thank you."

"Most guys feel a thing for the women of their race. It's natural."

"You?"

"It's what's out there. White guys, black guys. The bottom line is the white man taking what he wants."

"What are you getting at?"

"When I was door canvassing, there were a few people with their guard down. Nice people."

"White people?"

"Yes, I've met serious white people. No hypocrite crap. Most of them were women. But if their blokes were ever somewhere in the house, like having supper, then pow! When they realize their

226

woman's on the doorstep with a black man, they drop their plate and run to the front door. A world class sprint. You'd have to see it. Sometimes there's guys with food slopping in their mouth, and all I'm doing was explaining double-glazing!"

"So?"

"So that's what's out there."

"So?"

"So don't get upset if black guys feel the same way."

"Got it all worked out, haven't you!"

"Do I look like a PR man for your boyfriend? Let's drop it!"

"Why, afraid you might say something?"

Jimmy glares at the time. "Lorna, I've got to go. It's late."

"You getting sensitive again?"

"Not sensitive. Disappointed."

"*Disappointed*?"

"You think black guys don't have their own balls."

"What?"

"It's OK Tebbit drawing his line in the sand but black guys can't like who they like, they mustn't hate who they hate."

"Look! My brother had a screwdriver puncture his lung because he's black!"

"Then what d'you want from me?"

Lorna wants understanding. Steadying herself, she steps across the room. Slow, scared. Holding on the curtains. The thick drapes part and she peers into night. In one second the bomb on Hiroshima killed more than 100,000 people. And if a bomb like that dropped on London there'd be far more junk, but the same tears; that's what she says.

"What's out there that you want? What are you looking for?"

She tugs her hair, quietly arranging. "I don't know."

"So, what's up?"

"Don't know what I'd do if anything happened to Justin."

"With everything I have, I wish him back to your family."

"Can you stay for ten minutes? Ten more minutes. Will you stay for five minutes?"

What can get said that would help this woman? Hard for Jimmy to say. And no point him sitting here, getting pulled down like glue.

He steps from the chair. "Let's do a nightclub. There's a serious jazzman in town tonight, a sax player at The Jazz Cafe. Up for it?"

Lorna's thoughts are too fragmented. Quiet, she turns to Jimmy. And will make a little space for the night. Tough she does not say it, her sitting room is no longer safe. Jimmy grabs his coat. Lorna is first to the front door, looking back and tugging on her overcoat.

Chapter 56

Only standing-room in the pub. This early on a Sunday afternoon
the crush bigger than normal. Looks like more than just one thing to
celebrate here.

Lorna waves her glass. "Happy birthday, happy twenty-five!"

Jimmy twenty-five today. Boozed, clinking glasses, malt whisky
to brandy. "Twenty-five is scary."

"Twenty-five is great!"

"Blink, and you're up the road all of a sudden."

"Compose anything to celebrate?"

"Nah. It would be too self-conscious."

"Painters paint themselves."

"Can't see why they bother. Hey, let's get another round."

"What have you got against painters."

"Only the ones that do self-portraits. You want to be looking as
far as possible, so whatever's out there is too far to be looking at
yourself in a mirror all day."

Lorna blinks. "What's it like to compose? What's it compare to?"

"Me?"

"Yeah."

"I can only talk for me."

"Talk to me!"

The barman plays in a folk band. And all the time having sots
round him in a pub. Desperate to quit pulling pints, he wants to get
gigging in the big time. For now, wouldn't mind tweaking Lorna
but thinks she Jimmy's woman.

"Well," Jimmy grins, "let's see. Composing, right?"

"Yeah."

"How I do it?"

"Yeah."

"When it gets going, for me it starts with something nagging.
Nagging and nagging. It's kind of in your head, but not in your
head. A bit like somebody passing in a car and they wave, but you
don't get to see who and so you spend all day figuring it out, then
you get a phonecall and you're too embarrassed because you didn't
think of them at all. Disappointed, even. Make any sense?"

Lorna has brandy in both eyes. And a little something else. The
barman gets it. Sees clues in Lorna. That she is only a woman, not a

sorry sister over a comatose sibling. The barman can see a great looking woman. But Jimmy in soft-focus about Lorna. In denial, finding talk where today talk should be the last thing to find. Like the lion puzzle.

One answer to the puzzle is straight out the blue. And all in a packed out pub near Embankment. The reason lions don't roar at the ocean is because facing it means turning from all they need. That's what he says. Lorna does not care.

She wants to know where music comes from, what makes jazz what jazz is, how somebody can even compose at all. Any muso would tell her the same thing. Music only comes when a soloist gets going, improvising. Miles Davis a good place to start. Musicians turning up at a studio to record and, every time, Miles only handed out scraps of paper. Atom scraps. No bigger than a Rizla paper with their part in gist. That's what some great players say about Miles, guys like Wayne Shorter and John McLaughlin.

Lorna orders another round. "Miles Davis was 'Take this, now show me!' Was that it?"

"No! It was 'Let's see what *we* can do with this.' Huge difference!"

Colette wished Jimmy luck on Friday. And early this morning a call from Germany. They said thanks for the music. It was great. Jimmy got away from telesales and connected with Germany all day yesterday, leading a start-up jazz orchestra in Dusseldorf. The money was a joke. But the buzz! It was all down to Geraldine. Her mother was born in Germany. And Dusseldorf is a one-off. Arriving there, the first thing was getting to a rowboat. Then breathe some air, not swabs. Then taking a piece of quiet Rhine sunset, rowing slow. Sunset was a very quiet evening. Somebody could have rowed off into swabless night.

In Jamaica a whole tribe of white Jamaicans live in St Elizabeth. They blue eyed, and know they Jamaican, but also say they are German. The Rhine is mystic water. For Jimmy, no ancestral spirit was there to greet; no shades laughing before forcing a loner below dark waters to drown there.

"Let me know," he says.

"What?"

"If you change your mind, naturally!"

"What," Lorna groans in her glass, "shall I change my mind
230

about?"

Jimmy only half-sober. But FULLY clenched. "Justice for Justin. Street justice."

"Same answer as before. *No* violence!"

Next to Lorna, a man and woman talking of Martian poetry. They mention Craig Raine. It was him who delivered. Fluttering as it falls, the pages of a book become a bird swooping from Mars. The man writing his thesis on Martian poetry.

Lorna tugs Jimmy. "Let's get away from here."

"Deal."

"Hungry?"

"Could eat a rhino."

"My place?"

Chapter 57

All afternoon a child's smile was on her face. The kind of smile an innocent child smiles. Jimmy watching the woman cook. And listening to talk of her family, the Barbados part and the white half in Northumberland. She remembers family holidays, them tucking into potato & onion cakes her grandmother still makes. Her mother always takes a thermos flask for their treks in the dales.

For as long as Lorna can remember, the family goes every year to stay with her grandparents. They live in their own cottage and it's 400 hundred years old. And the festival they have on the 4th of July up there with Alan helping the bonfire on the village green. Alan crisp at folk-dancing; loves bagpipes, Lorna says.

Nobody ever says boo to the Stanley family. Never, ever. Never a trace of racial. But then. That's because everybody knows. Alan is sixteen stone and way over six foot, a fireman and ex-paratroop, not the sort to play games if his family get messed with. Things would maybe be not so good if her father was black and her mother white. Lorna discussed it with other mixed race folk. There's always more anxiety coming from white people towards a black and white couple if the white partner is the woman. Mixed-race, their white mothers could live for years getting called a wog-loving whore.

This summer the Stanley family was supposed to take fresh photos at Hadrian's Wall. Looks like Justin will not be there. The Stanleys will not go north this summer. Alan Stanley the only white man in his house.

Lorna rounds the coffee pot. "Black or white?"

"Doesn't matter."

"What's on your mind? If you have something to say, say it!"

"I've got a little question for you."

"You want us to get married?" she laughs.

"How did all this happen?"

"What do you mean?"

Jimmy tries again. "How did your parents meet?"

Lorna shy, quiet. Coy now, she giggles. "Well," she says, "are you ready for this?"

 "Comfortable in my chair."

"Once upon a time there was a mummy bear, and a daddy bear and, no, didn't I tell you this?"

232

"Yeah, but tell me again."

"One day, this big loping Geordie bloke swaggers in at the office where a young black woman works. A huge Viking in motorbike gear. And, well, one year later I was born."

One more thing Jimmy must ask. Yes, she remembers that thunder at the zoo. The sky-wide terror? Yeah, hard to forget it. Laughing, she hits out at the hi-fi. And fumbles CDs like someone in the dark. Eventually a huge piece gets going: Coltrane plays Naima .

Lorna is like flames in a fire. Blues in the woman. She moves like a blues solo. And, well. What? Bounce. Yeah, yeah. One more time. No, dat ting is no fluke. So, one more time. Yeah, bounce. But slow this time. Then invert. For Jimmy, the doorway is too soon.

What did Lorna achieve by going to Brixton the day Tyson was there? She grabbed a bundle of sugarcane. And got near to Tyson. But now she in a loop, daydreaming of grace, dreaming of a phantom knight, a saviour. And crying herself to sleep. To Jimmy all that is down to too much bible. Bronze, and fairytale.

He sits up as she comes back to the sitting room. "Lorna, there's serious stuff out there."

"Is this going to be about race again. You never stop!"

"Let's talk about the weather then."

"Cyclones are a cunning breed," she laughs.

"What?"

"I really don't want to talk about race, OK?"

"Did you and your brother ever catch tadpoles?"

"What?"

"Did you laugh when he picked his nose?"

"What?"

"You don't want to talk about race, so I thought of something more interesting."

"Thank you very much!"

"White people define the world."

"Oh, come on!"

"When did racism get solved?"

"What do you mean?"

"They define everything."

"Bits and pieces, yeah, not *everything*."

"Some days it's like the planet's all hemmed in."

"You being sensitive again?"

"There's bozos out there," Jimmy says, "some really thick idiots."

"Yes."

"Some days you can win that fight if you try."

"Yes. They're a dwindling breed."

"Think so?"

"The new mood will put paid to them."

"New mood? What's that?"

"Live, and let live."

"I don't see that."

"Look again!"

"What about the folk behind the scenes?"

"*Who*?"

"The middle-classes, educated English people bulling you in their image then expecting you to be grateful for William Wilberforce."

In 1790, abolitionists bugged and bugged Parliament. But in vain. The pro-slavers waving the bigger stick. The price of slaves in the West Indies was a rocket. And British war-boats upped the Niger River to kidnap more Africa. More slaves.

"It was Thomas Clarkson," Lorna says.

"Who?"

"Wilberforce only tied a few loose ends in parliament."

"Without him it would have been another hundred years."

"Wilberforce was a racist."

"*What*?"

"He was all for abolition, but he thought black people could only ever be trained up to be servants."

"Where did you get that?"

Lorna nods at her bookshelves. "Take two of those when you go."

"I hate history books!"

"Thomas Clarkson and Granville Sharp, they were the real abolitionists."

"Hey, what about the blacks? Runaway slaves! They defeated Napoleon's best troops in Haiti. In Jamaica there's the Maroons."

"Please, give Thomas Clarkson a chance."

"Why? Those guys were only offloading guilt about Africa."

"Steady on!"

"Hypocrites always start with the same crap, how slavery was there before the white man turned up."

234

Mandela talks of being a slave in his own country, 'having no strength, no power, no control over our own destiny in the land of our birth.' And that was in the 20th century. But few records survive of slaves in America and the Caribbean; African men, women and children, a hemisphere from their land, the continent of their ancestors, languages and cultures.

Lorna bites her lip. "Take this book with you," she murmurs. "It's by a freed slave, Olaudah Equiano."

"Black people did *not* grab Africa with a flag."

"Slavery was a human failing."

"Then where does the name-calling come from?"

"How do you mean?"

"Black bastards, wogs, coons _"

"Bigots!"

"What?"

"Racism comes from bigots."

"And where's bigots come from?"

"What do you mean?"

"Rape!"

"What?"

"They snatched black folk to slavery, built their estates from the profits, preached lies from the bible."

"Steady on!"

"They lied!"

"There were certainly a few who _"

"Lied! They lied, lied! Said it was some god gave them authority to *civilize* Africa."

"You're going too far."

"Where is there to go?" Jimmy says.

Tonight, somewhere in Africa a moonbeam opens on a baby. That child is right next to another crying through hunger. The village they live in will bake in morning sun. And their mother will go to the river.

"Else when," Lorna whispers.

"What?"

"Live, and forgive."

Jimmy standing beside the skydiver pictures on the wall. Angry. Trying to get calm, he checks the face of Justin. And looks vacantly at the room. Then looks at Justin. And wants air. Wanting air. And

235

could conjure a jeep and get to Africa, head from north to south. But turns to Lorna's ochre. "I'm thinking of leaving this place."

"England?"

"Yeah."

"*Leaving?*"

"Give somewhere else a try."

"What's brought that on?"

"I've had enough. My old man thought by now it would be better. Not great, but better. Time to move on."

"Where would you go?"

"Jamaica."

"And do what?"

"Or Africa. No fuss."

"*Africa?*"

"Yeah."

"Sell mobile phones? You'd make a packet!"

"Nah! I'd head for a village, somewhere in the Sahara, learn about camels and donkeys, trade figs and dates."

"Don't be ridiculous!"

"How?"

"You'd be out of your depth in the Sahara."

"I don't know where my ancestors come from in Africa, so the desert would do it. Woman, the Sahara is deep. Deep, deep. I was meant to be a nomad."

"Dream on!"

"Or America."

"And there aren't race problems in America, right?"

"Hey, they only want uncle toms here. No disrespect to your old man, but it's people like him that get in the way."

Lorna's teeth clench. "I wouldn't mind if you eventually stopped bringing my father into this."

"Then I'll just borrow your cellotape, put some on my mouth."

At night, the desert shrugs its shoulders. The Sahara repairs the arid winds. And old caravan routes that are now modern roads. Cave paintings showing that more than 7000 years ago rivers and cattle as well as wildlife were in the Sahara. But the history books don't want to mention it was Africans doing the farming, the paintings, the medicine and embalming.

"Tell you what," Lorna sighs, "it could be you, the lions and me leaving together."

"This is *not* some joke."

"But you want me to approve."

"I don't care what you do!"

"Race relations *can* work."

"That's what they say in the bible?"

"You can't just walk away!"

Straightaway, Jimmy decides in Lorna's unblinking eyes. "You think I wouldn't understand if a lion speaks to me?"

"I don't have the answer to _"

"Yeah, you read your bible."

God wanted Abraham to prove his faith. So asked him to slay his son. So the god in the Old Testament did not know everything. Because he already would know what Abraham would do. Or that god was a theatre-director god, moving Abraham round like stage putty. Justin Stanley has a mother that broke her vow on the bible. The same Justin in a coma tonight, saying 'What, me?'

Lorna's eyebrows raise. "By the way, you never got round to explain where you got your name from. Jimmy-Lines, eh?"

"My name is my name."

"Now, now. Don't get defensive!"

On the hi-fi, Coltrane cuts chunks of air with a sax knife. Lorna got the CD as a gift, but she likes Coltrane anyway. Maybe Stephen Hawking listens to Coltrane. Because somewhere in that sax is the sense of a machine big enough to accelerate particles to grand unification. A machine big as the solar system.

Jimmy laughs. "It was my grandmother."

"Your granny named you?"

"Sort of. A map fell out a dictionary and it was covered in lines my old man had drawn. My grandmother was over here visiting, and she just said 'You have to call this boy Lines.' So they called me that for five minutes. But my mother said it should be Hendrix."

"Hendrix Dell?"

"Yeah, that was going to be it."

"That's how the Jimmy part got in the mix?"

"Yeah."

"What's she like?"

"My grandmother? *Big* thing for Miles Davis. But the map was so mystic they had to go with the flow. My old man just let the whole

237

thing ride."

"You get jazz from your grandmother?"

"Yeah. My old man was a world class trumpet player. Jazz. But all he got was duff gigs. I went to Jamaica and one day my grandmother grabs hold of me, looks in my eyes and comes out with 'Go with jazz, boy, and women will look for you.' Stunning!"

"Does she play?"

"She's dead now. But she used to whistle."

Lorna can see. She knows Jimmy now, watching him gaze to a longtime. That visit to Jamaica was with a crucial lady dying. Out the blue the old grandmother decided to die. And it was too hard to watch while her body got lowered in a grave.

"Do they call you Jimmy, or Jimmy-Lines?"

"They all say Jimmy."

"Jimmy-Lines is on your birth certificate?"

"Definitely. But it could have been Moses."

"*Moses*?"

"What a pig that would've been!"

Lorna fights it back. She wants to laugh. Giggling, stepping back, giggling silly in her hands already. "Moses? They were going to call you *Moses*?"

Jimmy must lie. Tagging with the bible could get too embarrassing. "Moses, as in Ed Moses."

"Who?"

"You don't know who Ed Moses was?"

"Don't think so."

"Athlete. An all-time great. Gold medals every time."

"Oh, him!"

"You were thinking Moses of the bible?"

"Well, he's the only one I know."

"Yeah. A true original."

"The ten commandments and _"

"My name would have been down to Ed Moses."

"Moses, eh? Got a ring to it, hasn't it? Moses of the Nile."

"One day I'll check out that river."

"Well, Moses," she laughs, "if you want to leave England, guess what? There's this bit of water, we call it the English Channel. It's not too far from here. Come, you can let me watch. Let's see you wave your wand, you know, like you did at the Red Sea!"

Chapter 58

The salesroom is where it happens. But some people should not be here. Not a place to hide. Emotions will not conceal failing to sell. Great weather in the top-man spot, but in the next chair can be drought for weeks.

And somewhere, far from this, a whole tribe withers. Tropical people who can not pull rain by crying. Some days the gambler can forget money. The gambler listens Chopin on his walkman and forgets. And alongside the deal-making is idle talk in the salesroom. Chit-chat. Like over holiday spots. Or debauchery down a bad alley. But getting back from anywhere and England is always beautiful. Everybody says that same thing.

A big poster in the salesroom. It has a whole wall to itself. People turn to it for relief. The new people always go up to it right the minute they get here. Everybody agrees; the picture is like something from a Beatles' song. It's like Norwegian Wood.

Some days Colette hums Norwegian Wood in the salesroom. She made the poster from a snap Geraldine brought to work one day. Trees stroll around in it. On overcast days that poster looks like floodlight shimmers, light that drops down to patrol shadows, a neat tree drama with light wanting to out-fox shadows. And the whole scene coming from a little snap taken at the bottom of Geraldine's garden.

On bad, bad, days, desiccated, times when selling is just not happening, Jimmy will switch off and imagine. Money is down the phone but he can vision things going on in the poster: some days it's a dream over women, the type that would walk on the well-kept lawn backing to the trees. Beautiful women. Beautiful, watching swans nudge the moon's reflection in the lake below the lawn. Ace women. They discuss the scope of desire, or what could ever have led anyone to suppose all swans white. The poster scene is far from Brixton.

Some days somebody should not be here, not selling spiel and furniture down the phone. Some days music wells up, and somebody should be at a keyboard alone. But not to fool around with white keys alone, like a lake strewn with white swans only. Some days are pure polychrome. But the salesroom is not the place to count swans. Money the thing here. And a little something else.

Somebody hooked to the game. Hooked to play invisible on the phone. And by the time telesales gets a camera feed, Jimmy will be long gone.

Seven weeks into the telesales job and a weird day comes along for Jimmy. Way out the blue. The windows of the salesroom got cleaned this morning, just like that bible thing about through a glass darkly.

Jimmy on the line to a punter one whole hour today, trying for a sale to St Albans. The man's son died in a car accident and every time Jimmy got near to close the deal, the man talked of his dead son. No matter what gets said, the man brings grief down the line. He could use a new office suite, but wants to talk grief. Thirty grand of furnishing he could buy but the man wants to talk loss. And all the while, the whine of a stacker-truck going by. A stacker-truck whining down the line. Bad business was in the St Albans voice. He is a non-believer but going to church now and then. Jimmy wants to steer the call back to the office-suite. This punter could fork out on a whole warehouse if somebody would listen him.

Any telesales day is this type and that, solicitors or accountants, engineers, fund managers, all types to sell to. And all the time the punter is like blind because Jimmy is not visible. And that explains what happens next.

The day the glass of the salesroom gets burnished, the day the call to the St Albans man, Jimmy gets a whole new set of dice. The man from St Albans says his son was driving back from London one night but had to swerve in the dark. Trying to avoid someone at the roadside, but swerved straight into a ditch and got killed. And for months after that there was the dankest grief. Crying out loud. And even now, four years later, he still gets the same nightmare. And that is always of moths. Colossal, fetid moths, settling round a pool of urine.

Jimmy no longer wants the sale. The man's story is too occult. Backing down, Jimmy wishing the man well. Saying goodbye. And just about to put down the phone when up comes a weird report.

The St Albans man says his son swerved into a ditch and died because of only one thing. If it had been a white man at the roadside, his son would have seen him in time, but it's not possible to see black people in the dark.

240

When she's in the salesroom, watching, Colette always sits behind a glass screen. From a master phone she can listen in to anyone making a call. And she tuned in to the end part of Jimmy making the call to the St Albans man. The man believed Jimmy white. It would have been easy to put the record straight but Jimmy said nothing. Something was crying out to get said. Fact after fact cried out not to get denied. But Jimmy said nothing, was bleeding inside a Brixton overcoat.

Half past three. This the end of the road. Jimmy can not go on. Not at Homes. Colette saw the flaw. A bad business. Quiet, he gets all the personal things from the desk. This the last time to play invisible here. Colette still watching. One day she bent over so somebody could see her bosom bloom.

Jimmy rings her extension. "You get your kicks listening?"

Colette got into Jimmy's private. But not as a woman alone with a man. What happened with the St Albans phonecall means she knows. This white woman knows. Colette has a key. From now she can take her key and get straight to where somebody of colour is just trying to get by. And all because Jimmy a dreamer, playing invisible down the line.

"It's not like that at all," she says. "It's not about kicks, believe me!"

Jimmy hangs up. And waves goodbye in the salesroom. Moves to the poster on the wall. One last look at the wall poster. Last look at mystic light playing beech on the wall. Nobody understands.

Colette is in the corridor, waiting. "How I get my kicks, is my business. And it is *not* with a telephone!"

"How would you have put it?"

"I run this place. Have you got the *faintest* idea what that means? It's not a party. I told you that. I told you what to expect. That's the way it works. It's not about being pleasant pals. It's about *money*! You make money, Homes makes money. That means I have to listen to what goes on in there. If I have to use a stick to keep it ontrack, if that's what it takes, then that's what it takes!"

"Then how does that square with being a voyeur. You didn't have to listen to everything!"

"Voyeur? I am a voyeur, am I? Then tell me who was acting the *wonderful* psychotherapist with that man. That poor, confused man. You knew there wasn't a deal, zilch, but you kept him going. That

241

poor man!"

"I didn't want to hang up on the guy. That's why I let him go on. I wanted him to get it off his chest. But you, it's like you get energy from listening. I wouldn't want my money that way."

"You know," she says, backing away, head shaking, "you are a *brand new* one. Never seen the likes of anything like you. You made seven grand in, what, six weeks? Now you want to kiss goodbye to fifty grand a year. Sixty grand."

Jimmy studies Colette. Trying to understand. Wanting to understand the woman, the salesroom boss, a millionaire white woman. Wanting to know why she tries to explain herself to a young black guy in limbo. He thinks her earrings look like stale brass, earrings looking like ocean anchors with hard bluish-white petals. Colette standing tall in the corridor with small hands on tailored hips.

Jimmy nods. "I'll get by."

She offers a smoke. Jimmy is like at bay, wondering. Would have been a cinch to tell St Albans the facts. Nobody should pretend their identity. To be black and born in England is the easy part. What did St Albans hear? A confident English voice. Jimmy's voice. Colour did not figure. But the default colour is white. And this can only mean that England is not yet a black man's home. Not yet.

Race just won't go away. It was in the salesroom all the time, but Jimmy blanked it everyday. In salesroom talk, he talked like everyone, talking the same swagger but blanking the racial. Two guys there always deliberately started talk meant to exclude him. When chat in the salesroom turned to asylum seekers or Britain uniting with Europe, that was the big excuse those guys jumped at, saying how Europe the homeland of the white man. Talking so Jimmy could hear, one guy said liberals that count black people as Europeans are the same nutters that look out their London window and expect camels in the street.

Colette fondles her lighter, looking steady in Jimmy's eye. "Why so defensive? I'm trying to help you. But I can't drag you back in there."

"When did I ask you to sort out my life?"

"I don't have to do this. Weren't you supposed to give this your best shot? You need the money. I know you do. *You* know you do. Walk from this and you won't get the same leverage somewhere else. You'll do gigs, of course you will. But that will be goodbye to

242

your true music. Want that?"

Jimmy knows. This woman was always good to him. So many times she went out of her way to help. And that's because she knows. Colette knows what it takes to be a music one. But the phonecall to St Albans was too difficult. This woman white. Because of one phonecall, somebody black can not hide from this woman.

His hand extends for farewell. "Don't think I don't appreciate what you're trying to do for me."

"Funny way of showing it!"

"That money I made here will take care of business."

"For a while."

"It's the way I want it."

What if it was not Colette? What if one of the camel-fanciers had listened to the St Albans call? Jimmy will not go back to the salesroom. But it would be ace to ask two guys in there if they fancy camels by the street-load, or just one at a time. And the salesroom poster! A mystic stretch of trees.

Colette lights a smoke. "All right, OK. I know where you're coming from. You must be by yourself. You want your music. Wish my life was that cut and dry!"

"You don't look too decrepit with what you have."

She pulls hard, getting huge tobacco from a long drag down. Her eyes blear. "Will you come to the theatre next week? Still got the ticket? The music is by a friend, I told him all about you. Come."

Chapter 59

Lorna phones Jimmy. She alive, upbeat on the line. "I just got a great Bessie Smith CD. Listen to this!"

Bessie Smith crooning St Louis Blues down the line. Bad regret. A woman alone, singing low and slow. *I hate to see, de evenin' sun go down. Hate to see, de evenin' sun go down...*

Lorna butts in, saying a blues concert playing at her flat tonight. Leaning back on the old settee, Jimmy checks the meaning of her words. Asks if the concert is just for two. For two?

The lady does not reply.

And now he wonders what happens if the concert goes on past bedtime. Humming along with Bessie, Lorna likes the phone. Humming, laughing. A good sign. So now Jimmy asks if will stay the night. Serious now, she admits it. Yes, the thought had crossed her mind. So? Well, maybe it wouldn't be a good idea. Not tonight.

Lorna's getting there. Little by little, slow, slow. But not ready. And she sings it. "Yes, maybe some other night."

Chapter 60

Rain this morning. All morning. And pigeons set fitful and grey, cooing on a window ledge. Nobody would swap these opaque pigeon songs for the full deal of a nightingale. No one sane. Someone alone, quiet, stock still, watching pigeons blip globules from a window pane. Then a bad downpour. And a loner backing up, slow, alone, stepping back, reluctant from the window into the old solitude of the flat. The vision in the windowpane looks like it knows. To Jimmy the weather is like that day last year when Agnes was on her way back to South Africa. And today as the pigeons retreated from the pelting, a lone man frowned.

Agnes. That woman should be in the flat. She would help make sense. Jimmy playing Minims at the one tempo that inertia sustains.

A week and a half since leaving Homes, he must get what happened. The man from St Albans should have been told: 'Listen, I am black.' Mulling at the keyboard and failing again today, nothing getting set. Chords resolving easy at the keyboard, but no music. That last day at Homes, that last phonecall was trying not to embarrass the St Albans man. Trying not to deepen grief. But maybe Jimmy stayed quiet because of something else. Like maybe passing for white down the phone. And that is cold pretence. That is a white face comparing itself to a black face in headlights. Like on a dark night in St Albans near a ditch. And Colette. Why the boss woman listen to the St Albans call? Jimmy wanted to be invisible. But sick now for trying it.

Music is no help. And religion is worse. A god that is supposed to be all powerful but allows one race to deny another just so a preacher-man can redeem. What, dis? Somebody gets a stroke may lose the use of arms and legs. Or somebody can talk glass instead of words, seeing things going wrong but can not talk it, like wanting to witness the door but only saying 'Close the window after you.'

Rain is not pretending. Rain insistent. It licks on the 8th floor windowpanes. Chilly water. Swathe after swathe. And across the way one of the tenements getting demolished. This is bad noise, bad, pitiless. Birds swoop to challenge that bulldozer goring down the stanchion where they have a new nest.

Geraldine calls Jimmy from Clapham Junction. The rain is scatty there, she says. And lots of people. Most in plastic raincoats. All sorts of colours. And bundling umbrellas or capering through the wet junction roads.

Great time for somebody with a diary, she says. Somebody with a lyrical way with words could make a go of a day like today. She made a good sale this morning. A really good one. And now must get herself steadied, get a coffee, a double cappuccino, laughing down the line. Then a quick dash home. Well, it's quite a hike to Hertfordshire, so must get a taxi or rely on a trudging train. Why the rush? It's the theatre tonight, remember? Jimmy did not remember.

"No more doldrums," she says, admonishing. "Just get yourself to the theatre tonight. Come on, see you later at The Chair!"

Colette was always good to Jimmy. So seeing her again could be it. He could say thanks face to face. Or don't show, write her a thank-you letter. But something strange. And this was not possible before that St Albans phonecall.

Turning from the rain Jimmy knows a new danger. Nothing to do with other folk. But racial odds, inside, knotted. Being non-racist is natural to Colette. The salesroom always kills race-talk when she around. But this woman now owns a key to a private. A key she can never give back. Nothing like a door key; you change the lock or get the key before they copy it.

Colette stumbled on Jimmy concealed. And now she knows. Seeing her again might answer it. Jimmy will know from her eye, know if the secret safe. Or maybe she's already laughed it over a half pint of lager somewhere. Or she's like the white couple that adopted a black child and one day they went into the bathroom and the child was scrubbing and scrubbing itself with bleach.

Jimmy must see this woman. See her eye. Those eyes will tell. The theatre ticket flips like a coin. And rain starts. All over again.

Chapter 61

Lavender in the foyer. A trace of lavender in the small but chatty place. And nice women. One woman is like candlelight. Some with no man beside them and looking like they ready to play cards or get cut from a market. Colette is in shimmering aqua-green, standing cozy with a man. As she steps close, kisses his beard. Geraldine does not know him, but lavender is the scent she wears tonight.

"So, you got here!" Colette yelps. "You look fit. A bit hungry, perhaps. But let me stop. This is the guy I told you about. Kevin, meet Jimmy. Jimmy, Kevin."

Colette takes Geraldine by the arm and moves her away. And in one minute Jimmy knows this the right place to be. The foyer of The Chair is evening emotion. But not a place to pretend. Kevin did the music for the play tonight and, as they chat, Jimmy can see the talent. Colette was right. This guy one of the chosen. A huge talent. Talking quick and easy, Kevin hates the airwaves because of all the risk-free music that plays. Hates flatfoot melodies, callow bozo harmonies. Kevin is forty-five and last year he made the shortlist for the British Composer Awards.

Jimmy can tell. This place is safe. Nobody here wears day-glo. Respect in the air. Somebody says gypsies are it and, if it wasn't for the start of the performance, two composers would talk and talk. But they swap phone numbers and agree to get round a piano one day.

Lavender is Geraldine's bling. Set after a shower, tonight lavender deftly on her body.

Snug between Colette and Geraldine, Jimmy checking out the play. And tries to blank lavender from one cozy near. But a secret, something nighttime. In the dimmed theatre light a low laughing. It comes from Colette. Laughing low, she thanks some secret thing. And on stage a gypsy girl plays. This actress being a gypsy, playing with light, doing gypsy; but she looks like Colette used to look at nineteen. The dance, the dance. The way the girl moving, not mere dance, more like floating a pagan land. Colette wants to be the girl on stage. This her secret for tonight. She could be a back-up for the gypsy, knowing the girl's part by heart, knows every gypsy move, miming in a polychrome gypsy line. The girl is a tart. And the part in Colette that wants to be the tart in the gypsy girl.

When the she quits the stage Jimmy wants to call out: Gypsy, you should be doing it tonight; you could take all this night with no pretending. But this. This? This place sets real with fairytale, like a spiteful hand beckoning. To Jimmy, this place is strange. A place where applause happens by a single hand only.

The stage is empty now. Only the sandy landscape there, dimmed low. A place where weather gets punished by ritual gypsy dance, and violins play.

During the first act, Geraldine's arm was in Jimmy's. And for a while her head sloped to his shoulder. This was comforting. It was like a sister. Jimmy should have had a sister. Guys with sisters normally have better lives, they understand women better. Jimmy was paying Geraldine no mind. But something else. Intimacy was there. A longing. He'd never thought of Geraldine as a woman woman. Not till tonight. But the evening can not disguise one simple: for tonight, and only tonight, Jimmy feeling how nice it would be alone with Geraldine. And not just at the theatre watching a play. Not as pals for the evening. But for the rest of the night. The lights go down for the second act.

Geraldine a married woman. Separated from her man. But for tonight she's spliced with lavender. Vacant, she toys with her wedding ring. Jimmy blinks, confused by the motion of the woman's hand. Her hand sliding the ring finger, willful, sliding back and to, again, again, deliberate and tight.

Suddenly she tugs him. Holds him by the shoulder. Looks him in the eye. And he knows. She cannot forget the ring. Not even for a night. Keeping the faith, she affirms her wedding ring. And maybe even the ring remembers. The small theatre drops a notch. The same enchantment, but a smaller place suddenly. The gypsy girl is heartless. Even sunflowers would not bloom when she sets.

Colette, Jimmy and Geraldine. Not part of the cast here but part of something. And now they leave their seat, awkward, quiet. Geraldine does not look at Jimmy. Not once. And he avoids her eyes anyway. The foyer is too confining. Time to go. Time maybe to go get a quick drink then grab a cab.

"What a good idea!" Colette says. "Lets all go for a drink. There's a lovely little spot. Two minutes from here."

Geraldine will not go for a drink. She must catch a train. And with

248

a strict goodnight the lavender woman goes alone into night. Jimmy alone with Colette. In nervy night air, with a trail of lavender disappearing into night, Jimmy has nothing to say. Lighting a smoke he looks over what Colette wears. And compares the ocean of the dress to her suits at the office. Her dark eyes will not go away. Her eyes compel like the gypsy gaze. But how can a woman way past 35 ever understudy a girl 19?

Colette has sleep in her gypsy-eye. "You're not really up for a drink, are you?"

"Well, I never usually drink on rainy days. "

"What's the matter?"

Jimmy dizzy, cut off. "Have you, er, got a clothesline in your back garden?"

The woman lights a smoke. Her head shakes. Quiet, nighttime swings the soft folds of her dress. A weave in cool aqua, the dress is like a swerving ocean. It shimmies like a jazz score.

Chapter 62

Red wine is served. Lobster piles on the plate. Colette doing quiet damage to wine. The restaurant lighting here is ambient, very low.

Something moves on the plate. It's the lobster, something in the lobster. It longs for the sea, longing for ocean quiet for the last time. To Colette this does not matter. The lobster is dead. But cut lobster muscles move it. This is no problem, she says; everything comes from the sea at one time or another and a lobster probably does not have a lot of brains to start with. That's what the woman says, sipping wine.

Colette pours herself and Jimmy free. But only half a glass each at a time. This lobster is quite dead. And the lighting is so nice, so low here, she says; yes, nice and restful. In this nighttime lighting, a man could reach out and touch a woman's lips, quietly part them, run a finger over them. Jimmy was thinking maybe she was too old before tonight. Or just because she the boss woman. Or maybe because of more worries.

Thirteen years between Jimmy and Colette, a single mother, millionaire woman, a doer. The wine is very near, generous, getting poured by a mystery woman. At the last half-glass each, she pours hers back in the bottle. Then back to her glass again. And straightaway another bottle of red wine from the waiter. A mystery woman, a confused guy, and lazy wine. And quiet chat as streetlights flicker. Two hours go by.

Jimmy surprised. Can not understand how easy it is to talk with Colette. Even talking politics. But the best part is how there's music to talk. And talk is Duke Ellington tonight. The restaurant should understand the Duke. Ellington connects their life. Duke was the composer man that played great piano. Some jazz folk say Duke could out-Monk even Thelonious Monk. But the Duke scored natural feeling. Colette is shaky on this. So Jimmy scats Ellington rhythms, hums the melody to Mood Indigo. Her fingers tap. She likes it here. Likes this. And Jimmy segues to Sophisticated Lady. Yes, her lips say. Want some more? Yes? Well, this is Cotton Tail.

Tucked to wine, relaxed in soft restaurant light, but somebody should hire a coach and take the folk here for a drive through Brixton. Then maybe they'd get a better feel. For Harlem? Even Jimmy would get wide-eyed. He one black individual that's never been to

Brixton. Could be the likes of a Cotton Club is there already. Ellington changed music. And Colette a blue woman, fondling a wine glass.

More wine. A man and woman aimless now. Ellington was a global womanizer, Jimmy says. And Solomon a king with a mile of women. But so what? Even the English weather gets a shout in the restaurant here. And talk of the theatre. Talk of money. But money talks for itself. Colette never plays the lottery, saying the lottery is for dreamers. And talk of travel, New York, restful beaches that croon the Pacific. And the sun has maybe only 5 billion more years to burn bright. Jimmy and Colette talk and talk. But never a word of the St Albans phonecall.

Could be, it's the restrained light. But chatty gatherings at other tables in the restaurant seem just right. At one table they talk of TV; especially liking the Antiques Roadshow, saying how unmissable it is, that it is spiritual uplift, and, yes, the Antiques Roadshow is better than church on Sundays. Well, yes, because there's always some new adventure up the road, isn't there. And that's because the road winds and never ends.

A glass of water. Red roses are in the table vase. They could be getting dangerous being so full-on red. The waiter is a part-timer here; by day, a postgrad physics student and hooked on old Startrek tapes. He never wore the Captain Kirk suit handed down by his grandfather, and even now they can't find the right ears for the one and only Mr Spock anywhere. Startrek was what made him choose physics; not the big cosmics of warp speed, but particle physics. Wiping the water jug, the waiter says there's more to water than smooth transparent. Water is quicker silver than thoughts. And yes, magnify water under a microscope and that's a new ballgame. Ballgame? Sorry, no pun intended. Because what's way down in the microscope are things like footballs moving all the time. And that's not all. The whole cosmos is made of the smallest particles; tiny stuff, attracting when close together but repelling if pushed too close. Colette and Jimmy standing now. She the distance of a hand from him. Her eyes are dark. The darkest eyes ever in a white face, Jimmy says. Except if gypsy is white. Colette sips one last water. Ready to go.

The Maserati is rose-red in night light. It squats on double yellow lines and, as they approach it, Colette hands Jimmy the keys. This

his first time ever in a Maserati, let alone getting to drive one.

As they get going Jimmy can not help wondering. He wonders who Colette. She curls easy in the passenger seat and, through every one of eight speakers, Roy Orbison lamenting on Blue Bayou. Her eyes close. If the guys at the office could see her now. If the camel-fanciers could see Colette in the passenger seat of her own car with Jimmy at the wheel.

Bad horses in this engine. The Maserati's balance is sure, sane, wild horses tamed to the handshake of a friend. Jimmy gearing. And in the car the bouquet of woman, part perfume, part sweat. And the scent of new leather. Colette does not speak. She looks straight past the hard-raked windscreen into frangible night. And perhaps if she talks, utters one word only, then Jimmy would divert.

The taste of red wine lingers. And in the car nothing that can get said. The car threading a night of bad horses. Horses harnessed and trained to race hard.

Colette could be more than one woman. The first woman is the easy; tonight she like a top-20 song, laying into senses. That woman will remember the St Albans phonecall. But the second woman! She naked, alone, like in a cold attic room with a skylight to old unloved outdoors; that woman is too scared of eternity and will not bother holding the image of a man hiding in a telephone.

She does not wear big earrings tonight. "Want to take her for a spin, really let her go?" she says, stroking the dark dashboard loom. "Let's go for it. Let's do the M25!"

The car pulls up at traffic lights. And Jimmy notes two delicate earrings, small, discreet, tender turquoise laced with silver. But the wine. Her eyes are clear but anxious. These traffic lights are the giver of a do, she says; lovely lights unpacking gifts of traffic in the night. And someone driving the car with nothing to say. Not with words. The Maserati bolts.

Colette, gypsy eyed. "What gives?"

"I was thinking how, you know, neat this car shifts."

"What's the problem?"

Jimmy must lie. Quiet, he turns the music off. Time to think. To decide. "No problem. A bit too much wine, that's all."

When it comes to women, guys in Jimmy's family are the hunter ace. Nathan and his brothers bring down some of the greatest prey in town. But for about a year Jimmy's been trying to walk from all

252

that. Maybe this is down to Agnes. Or maybe it's Donna, the gap in her front teeth when she smiles.

Now Jimmy can see. Plain stupid to bother with a woman unless she can ding. Slowing the car, he remembers the first visit to Jamaica. He was fourteen and every day under the Jamaica sun was listening to Thelonius Monk. Or understanding Bud Powell more and more. Then out of nowhere Nathan's mother died. That was hard to take. The sea was old turquoise as a wise old lady died. But the big image of Jamaica is folk having blood from all over. Full blood black, and full Chinese, full Indian, white. And then the mix. Folk mixed from every race. And the white girls that are born and living in Jamaica, they move with the same wait-state as the black girls. Woman in Jamaica hypnotize guys. And a Jamaica woman is woman dat mek time. And all that in a couple of strides. Jamaican women move by the moves only a reggae beat can show. But wait, only jazz can tell it! Jamaica woman mooch more dan woman wha' live a Englan'. Jimmy wanting there to be jazz to a woman. And not just any woman. Weird, but the only intimate thing with a white woman was with that Jamaican white girl. And that was more than ten years back. The white Jamaican girl was set. She had never been to England and she and Jimmy spent a week in teens, chatting, circling, finding out. And that was it. Jimmy born in England, with a snapped Scouse accent, and the girl born in Jamaica and talking a heavy-duty Jamaican brogue. One afternoon towards the end of the visit they walked hand in hand along the beach. And stopped at a quiet place.

Colette removes her earrings. The scent of sandalwood somewhere. A low scent, like from the clasp of sprites. The earrings rest in the cushion of her lap. And magic, night-light in a gift of silver! Earrings flash like fireflies.

Jimmy saw fireflies flashing on a verandah one warm Jamaica night. Maybe the Jamaican white girl visited England by now. Her letters stopped after about a year. And maybe by now she's managed the three children she said she would have. Colette wanted four or five.

"Cat got your tongue?"

Quiet, Jimmy's head shakes. The car slows. Nighttime slowing down, way down, earrings together like magic sand in the woman's lap. The car stops. "I don't want to go for a tear-up on the M25."

"No?"

"And I don't want to go back to my flat. Too untidy."

"Then, what?"

Jimmy looking back at the woman as hard as she looks at him. "I'd like to get to a hotel."

"Tired, are you?" she smiles, pretending. "Had too much to drink?"

"No. Not tired."

"Too drunk?"

"Not drunk."

"Then, what?"

"We should find a room. Some quiet place."

Chapter 63

"What's wrong?" Geraldine quips. "You don't seem yourself."
   Jimmy more asleep than awake. "We, er, went for a drink."
   "You ended up in bed with her?"
   "Well, _"
   "Talk about hypocrisy! She was supposed to be a witch, you know, gorging on the hapless unemployed. Forgotten?"
   "No."
   "Then what happened for Christ's sake?"
   "Last night?" he groans, reaching for a smoke. Unable to explain. Still trying to make sense of what happened. But must level with Geraldine. "I honestly don't know. What a night. You're not going to believe this. Nobody would."

First thing last night was getting a hotel. The arriving. And checking to make sure. Then checking again. Every pocket. Then checking one more time. But no condoms. Not one rubber.
   Having to mention it was bad, embarrassing. But he said it, saying they better go get a packet. But she was aching to use the ladies' room and, squeezing his hand, said she'd better book them in while he goes to find the things. So it was back in the car. Back to the night. Alone on the road. Alone with a lusting Maserati. Motoring nice and easy, dicing bursts of speed. Then backing off to check the rearview. And then something strange. A mystic deliverance. Freedom was never like this.
   Maybe it was the expensive car, because only few people can afford it. Colette's car. After a minute the emotion was else; it was the emotion that soloists get when a jazz band hits a groove. The kind of groove saying 'Play it!' The car was willing him to try it, try anything. And the next thing was the streets. Streets ad-libbing through the steering wheel.
   And the moon! Lambent, slung low, looking generous, nothing like a satellite. Streetlights were heavy as paperweights. With all of that, there was time to think. Thinking of the actors on stage earlier at the theatre. And the street was so silent, bruised by wandering, no applause coming from their old tarmac keeps.
   And somewhere the other side of the world, wild flowers were crackling like fire; somewhere where fever talks to flesh and cinch

255

with stars. And someone in a zip sports car was thinking of the owner, imagining by now she was taking a warm shower back at the hotel. Hard seconds. Gunning scarlet to the car. Hard down. Gunning, wanting to get this thing on. Then a quiet quarter mile. Going through light traffic, breezing. Then moving it. The car was slicing open land when the carphone rang.

Colette was sultry. Her sultry voice said 'Hi, hon!' Then said it. She said Mr & Mrs Core have booked into room 15. *Who*? Mr and Mrs Core.

The car shot into a clump of lights. And, like a wish, the night was giving back a quick late-night chemist, still open, like maybe it was waiting just for one somebody to come. Jimmy the one. And in one minute owning a smooth silk packet. The glacier on the attendant's face did not matter. Jimmy going back quick into night with a quiet grin, breezing the car. Whatever the attendant was thinking, nobody was going to a hotel to watch Colette hang washing on some arctic clothesline.

The air was pure air. Clean air. And traffic scant. Traffic was like two ships in a hundred miles of ocean. And Jimmy moving, afloat, knowing Colette was looking at the world-sized moon from the hotel window.

Bang!

On the zebra crossing! One inch from the bonnet! How'd the car stop? Out of nowhere an old man on the crossing. The face of a confused old man. And garish beacons flickered, mechanical orange in the night, flickering in the old man's eye.

Jimmy shaking, climbing from the car, trying to act steady. But the old man only shrugged. Not speaking, the shrug implying that what nearly happened was already enough said. Without checking the road he moved away. Taking his time and, eventually, he disappeared round a turning. Nobody could push a wheelbarrow full of pottery the way that old man walked away.

But no one witnessed this. Nobody else was even a mile away. And by now Jimmy was far from safe, gazing back at the car. To him the Maserati was like a tart after a red bout of frenzy. Hazard lights blaring, driver's door agape.

Still shaking, he was on the move again. Slow at first. Not sure. Wanting to hang back. Then thinking of the woman. Taking it. Surging a while. Thinking of Colette. Wondering if she the kind of
256

woman whose eyes stay open while getting claimed. The night was blue, diminished. That near-miss at the zebra crossing was too close a shave. And now it was heading back to the hotel. Motoring the Maserati hard. Going to get into one fastidious lady owner.

Then panic! Sweat. Cold sweat. A weird thought. One recent dream is with grass having evening cargo that will not suffice for lions unless zebras get blinded by stars. Stop the car!

Only two minutes before this the Maserati was a wild cat. But the red car changed on the crossing. It looked like a lioness more than a woman, a lioness crouching a fresh kill of zebra. That was no zebra-crossing. The Maserati was a lioness tearing zebra meat apart.

What would have happened? If it had been a real accident instead of a near-miss at the zebra crossing, the old man might have died. The police would've arrived. Then instead of Mr Core hurrying to consummate Mrs Core, the night would cut Mr Core. Dead or alive. And the moon would have seen. The full moon. And Jimmy was not Mr Core. Colette used her name at the hotel but he would have had to give facts to the police, exact details, starting with who owns the car and how come he was driving it.

Every black guy knows. The Metropolitan police can be the law. Or they a psycho with blood for dice: all they would've seen was a bullet car and somebody driving in a Brixton overcoat. Chances of getting to leave in one piece would have been nil.

But something was in the old man's face. The old man could tell. He knew Jimmy was no Brixtonite gazing the moon. Then again. The man from St Albans: where was the moon the night his son died?

The car phone rang. Ringing and ringing. Jimmy wanted to tell Colette. Wanted to talk the turmoil. But he lied. Saying the car was out of petrol. What will you do, she said. Jimmy lied again, saying he'd have to flag down a passing car and get a lift to a petrol station and find a can, get back to the car, then back to the petrol station and, finally, to the hotel. Forty minutes, he said, lying to the black handset.

Lying to Colette was not good. But something big was happening. And it was not only keeping faith with Agnes. Last night was moonlight and somebody very spooked on London tarmac.

The exact instant Colette asked where Jimmy was, and if he was lost, that was the instant he knew. Going back to that the hotel was not possible. Do what there? Get snug in a room? A room reeking from legions making do down the years. A hotel room was not the place to be. It would have been only like a seat in a theatre, a place for watching drama, a knotted fantasy.

Jimmy was lost. But not in any way that Colette would know. Not like being lost that a map could cure.

The engine fired. The tank was a quarter full, but what had to happen next needed a full tank. The only way ahead was a drive to Liverpool. Get away from London. Get north and laze the night over the Mersey, watch it ebb and flow. Somebody can be born and bred there but not go back to Liverpool except now and then. The Mersey on such a night would be water with fish frightened of fire. And maybe a prostitute coming up for air in moonlit tide.

Soon the Maserati was heading north. Breezing the motorway. Taking it easy, staring at joy. Colette's car was a red lady pounce, taking no prisoners, going north at night.

One hour up the motorway everything was lost. Jimmy remembered a quick pang for Geraldine at the theatre. And thinking how Carmen was glad with her man. Lorna a woman in purdah; a lonely woman with a bronze bible praying for a brother. And Colette. The way she poured that wine. Silver earrings sparkled in her lap. And her scent lingering in the car closeness. One more hour passed.

How come she don't call? Maybe she guessed. Because of that phonecall to St Albans the lady knowing a thing about him nobody else knows. Nobody white. And nothing he could ever say or she could say can remove it. Colette will always own one part of a private, owning it like some artifact. And no amount of physicals could ever undo that.

150 miles into the night. Motoring hard. But, suddenly, changing his mind. No longer wanting Liverpool. Remembering how somebody once whispered to the Mersea, how the murky water got cross. The water listened to a whisper but did not reply. Only spit. Liverpool was a slave port for three hundred years. It used to spit African cargo. And in some fairytale, Poseidon fetching up on a desolate shore to vomit now and then. And somebody in a red car turned back last night. Heading back to London.

Where to go? Drive to Brixton? Walk in Brixton at dawn? How would Brixton help? Maybe run into somebody there, have them wonder where he'd been all the time. Caged lions are at London

Zoo, and he was somewhere between lions and Brixton. And that was no particular place. And all the time Colette in that hotel room, warm, showered, alone, wondering.

Jimmy arrived at the hotel half past five in the morning. And scribbled a note. Then slipped the car keys and note under the door of room 15. Then walked away. Walking fast, and faster.

A door opened. In the narrow corridor Colette called a name. She called the name again. Jimmy stopped. And that was because the carpet was like Velcro now. Colette called his name again. But now he can not turn round. Can not move. And the next thing she was standing face to face, puzzling, looking him steady in the eye. The note was in her hand. Wounds in her eyes. She asks him, saying 'Tell me yourself.' What? The point of the note, she said. Wooden, pointing, Jimmy heard himself say 'The note is what only some loner can understand.'

Ten minutes of blear talk. Then a man and woman leave the hotel. Together but apart. In steep estrangement. Nothing was clear. That was the weirdest part. Two people confused. Or it was like somebody that witnessed their own birth. Not from a video years later, but right in the room where it happened.

To get a clear head Jimmy decided to take the bus home. And in early morning air Colette disappeared down the hill in a taut redness. Between this man and woman is nothing to talk about over a drink. Because then it can get dismissed as alcohol takes hold. This is different. This a man and woman looking, but seeing from mirror shards. In one shard a woman naked and out of sight. And a ballistic sports car in another part of the mirror. And a man with hands deep in the pocket of a Brixton overcoat.

Sad in the quiet early morning air he was at a bus stop alone. And listening birds sing from a churchyard.

Some women on the bus looked Turkish. The rest were African women. At every stop another one or two got on. And at the end something like thirty African women on the bus. Africa staring vacant at the street. African women sitting huddled in their own arms. Those women were going to early morning cleaning work, or getting back from it. What else they do in England? They see allure here. And nobody knows the compromise. Woman after woman, lost and lovely. And washing London toilets to get by.

Key in the door, the 8th floor flat was like safety. It was far from

259

the street. And Colette, that she arrived at her house and checked her daughter was OK, then kicked her shoes. Though she listens to classical music Colette is not the kind to have Grieg on tap, especially not the A Minor Piano Concerto. She is not the kind to close her eyes and listen to woods and fields. And yet. She always hums Norwegian Wood; a nice tune, but only stubble next to Grieg.

Jimmy got a grim image in the bathroom mirror. Scary, hassling. Maybe Colette will keep the note. Maybe she squats down by her dressing table to gaze the mirror with no place else to hide. And then. Something out the blue.

It was Mozart. In the early morning light he remembered Mozart Remembered a Mozart keyboard piece. The Sonata in A minor. And playing it quieter and quieter. Then built a spliff. Then played it note for note.

Then it was 8 o'clock. And a flop to the bed, watching the sun take control. And was still far from sleep at 9 o'clock when Geraldine phoned. Her sister-voice was on the line. It was not Colette on the phone. And that was a surprise.

"Sorry," Geraldine apologizes, "I didn't mean to get you out of bed. Sorry."

"It's OK," Jimmy yawns. "Trust me, I feel better for running last night past you. Weird, wasn't it?"

"Why didn't you just tell her?"

"What?"

"Why did you write a note?

"Because I didn't want a load of awkward questions."

"Like?"

"Like if I had a problem with my manhood."

"Your *manhood*? Haven't heard that one before!"

"The state I was in, I couldn't face Colette," he says. But must lie now. "I couldn't face feminist wisecracks so early in the morning."

"You poor thing!"

"I don't need patronizing, OK?"

"Well, lots of those women are still out there. But I don't think Colette is one of them."

"Which women d'you mean?"

Geraldine grins down the line. "Your pin-up girls."

"Who?"

"Your blithe feminists," she says, giggling wide now, losing control, giggling.

"*Who*?"

"The feminists."

"Feminists?"

"There's still a few militant ones out there. I heard they're still kitted-up for parties. Pretty balloons, this way!"

"I'm not in the mood," Jimmy groans. "Got to get my head round what happened last night. The last thing I need is stupid parties and balloons."

Geraldine laughs. "Then stay right where you are! You wouldn't want to be at one of those feminist things. Not really. I hear they blow their balloons up by farting into them, so keep away!"

Geraldine laughing loud down the line. She makes Jimmy want to laugh. And soon enough he's glad for someone like her, thinking it would be great having a sister like Geraldine. She understands.

And yet. And yet. Too hard to tell her the reason for the note. Maybe it's the phone. Face to face is better. Over the phone it's too anonymous.

Chapter 64

Hendrix was in a Burberry overcoat when Nathan first witnessed him. It was September '66, only a week after arriving in England. Nathan was already here a year by then.

That first sight was in Soho. Noon in a dingy club. Hendrix was having a quiet drink. Twenty three years old and to die in four years. A serious, shy guy, having a quiet drink. Nothing like the fireworks-wizard on stage. That grey London afternoon he was chatting with a versed guy called Mitch, a set drummer. Mitch Mitchell had a head full of Curtis Mayfield and soul. Nathan was the only other black guy there, three years older than Hendrix, and getting ignition for a studio gig.

Hendrix had distinctive eyes. Like from another place. Nobody in England ever saw anything like him before. Not just the big hair and funk clothes. But that guitar. And not just showman guitar. But that dread beauty, playing so alien but straightaway clicking. Pure human blues, but from some place else. Harrowing but beautiful guitar. Hendrix had humble eyes. And was more connected than any bishop.

Folk did not get it, Nathan says now. They munch the glitter, so they never did get to who Jimmy was. That if only they ever had let him really play he would have played blues like never going to get played again. Even now they listen him do a blues like Red House, thinking that is it. But that was only Hendrix to start. Or there's them that listen him play All Along The Watchtower and the wise ones get some kind of clue. They see a place no guitar from here ever went before. Or since. A flight to the beautiful place, the eternal home. The jawbones of a donkey got used on All Along The Watchtower. Two jawbones and two acoustic guitars. And maybe even Bob Dylan did not know what was fully caged in his own song. Not till Hendrix set it free.

Hendrix was right-handed. But always played leftie on guitar. They did not understand why he was so shy about his singing. Tracks like All Along The Watchtower got taped where Hendrix was behind a special screen in the studio. Like he was hiding. But really he was somebody not wanting to get stared at. A genie not wanting to get watched singing from the bottle.

Something like that happened to Terry Waite. Terry got back

from five years as a hostage in Beirut and for a long while had to eat alone. He was the Archbishop of Canterbury's global envoy before that, a huge guy, tall like a ladder, over six foot eight, but shy for food after five forfeit years.

Jimmy all alone. So maybe this the time to sing it one more time. Sing with no fuss, sing: *There must be some kind of way out of here, said the joker to the thief.*

Chapter 65

Geraldine guessed. She arrived with a taxi-load of shopping last week. And the first thing she did was throw her coat. Then arranged the place, corner to corner. Then came out with it, saying this the time for Jimmy to move on. And said that thinking of lions is not the way at all; lions are truly mysterious, yes, but staying indoors and daydreaming of lions is what even pussycats did not do.

Jimmy laughed. Geraldine will always make him laugh. The two of them laughed together one hour. And played music. And laughed some more. As she left, she invited him again for a weekend at her mother's house in Hertfordshire.

Thinking of lions is not so weird. For five weeks it was Colette. Hard for Jimmy to forget Colette. Hard to forget not going back to the hotel that night. The whole thing started at the theatre. In the ivory light of the foyer Colette kissed a man. A face kiss, her lips quick on a bearded face. But watching the play was when it started. Colette cooed like she was the gypsy girl. Jimmy wanted to go where the girl was going in a gypsy life. But where was that? The girl was not real. She was only playing a stage. And what a part she played that night. But the way Colette poured at the restaurant, the dark eyes, pouring wine, and looking exclusive across the table as it poured. But all the time at the restaurant it was the gypsy girl. Then that trip in the car. Looking for something. Steering a red bullet halfway through England. Maybe it was looking for the gypsy, looking for a woman nomad. Only a nomad would recognize it. And sometimes the roadway ahead is way more road than the way ahead. But only a gypsy understands the longing, the ache. The girl was a nomad in the part playing on stage. A gypsy owning no land. And somebody in the theatre and then the motorway, getting lost, puzzling over whether there was any place in particular to belong.

Jimmy in the flat alone. Trying to figure it. Trying music. Listening to Brahms. Listening to the Hungarian Dances day in, day out. Then one day trying them in reverse order, listening the last dance to the first, over and over. And at last things started making sense.

The woman on that gypsy highway was not Agnes. With Agnes somebody can rely on dread precision. Arleene came close, but says she wants a man that loves her. Then Donna. Donna so set; but a

264

woman like Donna would domesticate Jimmy.

The gypsy! A gypsy woman can grow things. Or just ups and leaves. Jimmy looking for a gypsy lady. As the Hungarian Dances played, the gypsy girl was always in the first dance. Even in the second dance a gypsy female starts fire at evening. And she will undress in G minor, carry water in D minor. Colette was always in the third dance. A nighttime gypsy gazing over wine at a ceiling tilt.

Chapter 66

Dashing out, Lorna trips over cables on the floor. Suddenly the night. Night is like a mare she must reach her hand into and deliver a foal to the world. But not quite. This the wrong way round. The machine got switched off. Justin dead.

Lorna phoned eight times, she said. And this makes Jimmy feel ghostly, wondering why of all people she wanted him to talk to. The phone rang and rang. But in a way all this is high ceilings. You dead and buried, so your ceiling is ground level; you have people upstairs in the life bungalow.

Pharaoh was the greed. Pharaoh wanted to check the god of Moses. So he bossed the builder to make a platform high enough to get up there and see. And *that* is what you call flake-highs. But Justin dead now.

Jimmy called New York. Bobby said the Minims music is the thing, but telling Jimmy one more time that lyrics about a blind lady must stay clear of bible talk; do that by June, and it's all systems go.

What was so special about Lazarus? Millennia before Lazarus, Pharaoh's builder got a solution to the god puzzle. Seeing that the god of Moses was too far to see, Pharaoh's builder did a runner. And the great Nile runs like forever, till one day that water dry.

The Sahara was green. Till seven thousand years back, it was green. African people were living there with farming and medicine, and even built the Sphinx and had mummies a thousand years before Egypt was even born. But then the whole Sahara turned to powder. And now Lorna's brother will get a tombstone.

For a while Justin was coming along. He looked like getting back. His mother arrived at the bedside with a faith healer. And doctors arrived with more doctors. But now him dead. Lorna's brother dead. And the preacher-man's words will not turn that round.

Chapter 67

Round Midnight non-stop, playing four hours already this evening. Not a tune that could derive in tenement Tottenham. They have a big-time football club down the road from Jimmy's flat, and a nice share of women live in the area. And tricksy streets.

Round Midnight is waterfalls in a silver city. This music plays and waterfalls cascade, water falls from umbrellas and yellow cab windscreens. And that never happens so neat in Tottenham. Rain falls here all the time, but this place is not downtown New York.

Round Midnight is a tune from '47. Monk was the same age as Jesus Christ on the cross. Monk walked the piano keys with ministry, comforting the sick and healing the lame. But not raising the dead. Justin dead.

A grand piano should be here. Where? Maybe on a grand piano a new idea could come along for Jimmy; an urban song, 90 notes for Justin. But no grand would get through this 8th floor tenement door. They would have to assemble it piece by piece. And if a grand piano was in Jimmy's flat, Lorna would have had no electric cables to stumble over yesterday.

Art Tatum the man. He the acest piano player ever. Seeing Tatum play, even Rubinstein could not believe his eye. Rachmaninov could not believe anyone like Art Tatum was in the world. And Paderewski, one more ace piano player that did not believe it was possible. Happy philharmonics, guys!

Weird, they can just switch off your machine then do some quick paperwork. Then say you dead.

Bud Powel was ruler of bebop piano. In a way he was like Justin. Bud was maybe only twenty when he nearly died one night. It was the New York police. De police lik Bud wid blow after truncheon blow. Blow dat mean fe kill. Police truncheon golosh Bud because him black. They left him in a gutter to die. Bud was in hospital for eleven weeks, and lived. How did Bud survive? Down the years his heart was breaking all the time, remembering. And in a way he was a dead man that night the police got him. But Bud was resurrected, alive but lame, a human wobbling in and out of mental institutions but set the rest of a life.

Listening to Bud's Bubble is wince-time for any piano player. Two years after that police attack, Bud managed this recording in

1946. And the bebop drum-breaks say 'Hey, put those truncheons away! Bop, bebop! Yeah, give drums a try. Look, see what you could do. Bebop! Don't mess law-and-order, bop!' That's what the drums say. The piano runs a laughing drizzle. Bud's piano saying 'Hey, catch this. Hitch these little rain drops high!'

Justin got disconnected from the machine. And deep down in that coma, before the machine got switched off, Justin opened his eye one last time and said, 'What, me?' And now his woman has given birth. A child Justin will never see.

For one hour Jimmy at the window, wondering. And Miles Davis! He played so consistent. So much space. Space impossible to lacerate with neon or police. Even gunfire. But nowadays jazz getting like furniture. Jazz getting to be backyard fire. Stupider and louder.

But listening to Miles, listening the Kind Of Blue album and checking out the Freddie Freeloader track, and no backyard noise will frustrate. Some people say this and that, saying Miles dropped Bill Evans for the Freddie track because no sophistication was required. But it's simpler than that. Bill could not play the blues. And Freddie Freeloader is space-wide blues with Miles on trumpet to spare.

To some people Kind Of Blue is like being on a boat. And that because something is so cut with the ocean, music inching water wide open.

Miles was Miles because of space with people playing round him. And Coltrane. Coltrane can take one whole year to play a solo. On this track, Cannonball is talking to woman; the sax like driving along with a good looking woman in a country lane and chestnut horses running in a field, and the woman saying 'Slow it down a little!' The Freddie Freeloader track going and going.

Jimmy grabbing a spliff. The man at the piano on this track is talking private. And the rub. The Freddie track got inspired by the guy that supplied Miles. Freddie the cocaine man that used to supply Miles Davis. And the ocean can distill to more white powder than salt. But in '59, after the record got released, Freddie tripped through New York agile and proud. Freddie boasting. Telling everybody that it's him on the Freddie Freeloader track. On every street corner Freddie saying 'That's me, that's me!'

Jimmy was listening to Freddie Freeloader when Lorna buzzed yesterday. But something said 'Check the door, this could be seri-
268

ous.' And straightaway it was bad business. Her scorched tears, bad blubbing and hurrying out. She could not believe that that was it, that Justin's last words were to be 'What, me?'

Chapter 68

Going to public meetings is one thing. But no point to a march. Not any more. In the 60s and 70s Nathan used to do marches all the time. In the early days people of colour and liberal whites used to go along to this place or that. Their banners saying 'Freedom!'

But now marching is silly. They only mark time. Marches getting like this religion or that. And always beg the question. And that is where the marchers come from. And then the big question. And that is where folk think they going, especially if the weather bad.

One day of protest two summers ago Jimmy just got back from Brazil. The woman in the paper-shop was beautiful, never complaining the rain. 'What's it matter if your clothes get wet?' she said. The proprietor got cups of tea. And outdoors it was banners of the marchers raising high and multi-coloured. Hundreds of them there, up high, alongside a famine for freedom. But right alongside the message was the cold eye outside; waiting in the rain that day were eyes tough as flint, jealous of tears.

Jimmy getting one more look at the leaflet Lorna left. She said what was what, but it was too hard to understand yesterday as she ran in and out of the flat. She was a blur, tripping over to leave. Justin's machine got switched off. And now the leaflet heavy as lead. Lorna's brother definitely dead.

How did it get to this? The doctors believed the worst was over. They talked a good chance to get back.

Jimmy wants a word, could phone Lorna to say 'Think of the good times.' But what's happening here is blankness at the keyboard. All the keys weird. The piano keys look like the damaged smile of a psycho. Diminished chords till the room. And ghosts walk in. They want the keyboard.

Ghosts hit the right notes every time. Ghosts get chords that say goodbye. It's OK, the chords say. It's OK. For one hour keys and ghosts get close, saying even suicide has another side; saying sometimes even waking up is a chore. Wake up for what? Brush your teeth? For what? Getting ready for another round of the smile game.

Quiet, ghosts quit Jimmy's flat. And somewhere in the manuscript pile on the settee is one piece getting worked more and more. A special. Music that dovetails. It syncs Bach's counterpoint with the flow of Coltrane. At the start it was only fooling with crunch, but now there's more fun to it than even ghosts gag at.

Nathan said Jimmy should get a wife. Why Nathan do a ting like dat? Ghosts get jealous, saying life is only couture. Life is getting to wear one mortal outfit or another: Chinese or black, Indian or white. What, even a Brixton overcoat?

Ghosts do white keys. Ghosts pretend to nothing. Then they try the black keys. What would Bach, Coltrane say? This goes on for one whole hour. In the end he arrives at a title for the piece. From now this is *Cobalt*. A Coltrane ghost and a Bach. Jimmy gets back to Lorna's leaflet. And reads it one more time. No blind lady or blind man could do this more.

7 o'clock. Getting late for the meeting. Jimmy set, saying good-bye to ghosts and folding the leaflet to tuck it neat in the overcoat.

Chapter 69

Bosworth Churchill Trass. Regional director of race relations for north London. A tall man, shaking his long black hands in the community hall. Most people here tonight know of him. But some leave the meeting even before things start. And only because Trass here.

Bosworth? Trass? Churchill? Race official wid a name like dat? Bosworth is not the kind of name not to laugh at. Bosworth is a quacker, duck contention round a mud pond. Bosworth overdub rap onto de old colonial timepiece. And a decrepit timepiece ticking where only a Bosworth can hear. The older people here try, still allowing. Because Bosworth on TV from time to time so they believe he talks for them.

Trass grins, handing out his business cards. "Call me BT. Feel free to call me BT!"

Lorna sitting with her mother and sister at a table facing the meeting. Longing in the mother's eye. The sight of dreadlocked guys connect her. Ease her worry. This is spiritual. But already agendas jockeying for prime time. Bosworth Trass the most visual official, the high sly.

One fierce black woman takes notes. Sitting next to Lorna and dressed in black, the woman jotting in a notebook. A young girl with a buttercup face caked with suspicion in the front row; Justin's girlfriend a widow now. Nobody escaping her gaze. A week-old baby locks tight in her arms.

This meeting-hall is a church already. People expecting a messiah. Most of what here is religious ritual: The messiah will come, give him time, give him time! Their eyes say it, saying they want a messiah to appear. Their messiah is belief and they believe something will happen; yes, *this* time. Even the younger people suspend what they know and sit lower in their chair.

Somebody talking of dogs. Dogs could hunt them down. The ones that got Justin could be hunted down with dogs. A jacket got torn on railings and they have the piece. One angry white woman says it. She says the jacket piece is enough. Hunt them down with dogs, snag them like a fox at your chicken-coop!

Sometimes they show fox-hunting on TV. Never the kill, only the chase. And the ritual starts blood-red jackets buttoned tight and well. But the cup is never only the fox. That show of horses running through fields and countryside is hinterland. Prime, protected, far from Brixton. In the chase, even the trees only ever get seen in the countryside. And horses. Hunter horses have a sky-load of go. And ruddy horsewomen pumping the air.

"Dogs will find them!" the woman cries. "Track them down with dogs!"

This a bad dream. Some people here can not be here. Two guys talking of Spartacus. They watched the video and gel with the part where one gladiator saying to the man he must fight 'You don't wanna know my name, I don't wanna know your name.'

England passing by in blankness. Blankness grabs Lorna gulping air. But not air. This a painkiller from what gets exhaled. Tears in her eye. But no memory. As she checks the dense room, nobody getting seen. Black people of every age are here, from every skin tone. And twenty, twenty-five white people that mostly female. A band of dreadlocked guys stand together at the back of the hall.

The woman in black talks for the first time. "Good evening. My name is Marcia Hosannah. I'm a friend of the Stanley family. I'm from the Society of Black Lawyers."

Quick, a white man from the front row. In one bound the man at the lawyer's microphone already. The next move is a surprise. The man gets a white kerchief from his pocket and dabs Lorna's eyes. Gently, dabbing. Then runs the collar of her jacket to fix it in place. A soft squeeze of her cheek, a nudge of chin, and this is easy. This is Alan Stanley. This the father of the family. Alan gets back to his chair without a word to anyone.

Eyes fixed to the table, the lawyer balks, sighs for air. "Thank you all for coming. I don't want to raise false hopes so I will come straight to the point. As you all know there have been no arrests. So this community, *our* community, we must spell out our own terms of reference. I repeat, no arrests!"

Lorna's head shakes. "Let's get on with it," she moans, turning blank to the meeting. She gets to her feet. "What's wrong with this community? We live here. This is where we live but it's like we want to walk round with torches in the dark, like we're too scared to turn the lights on. Know what I mean? What's Bosworth Trass got to say for himself?"

273

On the left flank of the main seating area Bosworth Trass up from a black swivel chair. "I will spell out what this is. You want to call it the terms of reference? That's fine with me. But first things first. There's no evidence of any systematic attacks on black people, absolutely no evidence at all. Nothing that would stand up in the courts. And that is not an excuse, it's a fact!"

Lorna slumps in her chair. "Tell us what you call evidence."

"Evidence is what you must have if the police are to act. You can't go to the courts with your empty hands."

But Bosworth knows. Everybody watching the hypocrite, catching the fidget. Only one swivel chair was in the hall and Bosworth owning it. This chair could be pendulum of some old clock, a relic from the old colonial office. The chairs in the meeting-hall from all over town, but where did they get a swivel chair? The chair swivels and talks, saying, *Evidence, spell it, police, spell, act, spell. Quite!* Trass will be a lord soon enough. Talk is, Bosworth getting to be Lord Trass of North London. And that explains why he's here. Trass come fe shore-up. To book woes that the race industry will own. This high-sly got the MBE last year to start towards the Lords.

Three in a pack. Or up to thirty when hyenas attack. And when the pack leaves, no evidence of prey. Hyenas eat the hooves. And eat the skin. And if the prey had horns, they eat the horns. And to get at blood in the blood-spattered soil where the prey falls those wild dogs eat the dirt where it falls.

Justin was in the alley. And even if what they say is true, that it was maybe one of his own posse by mistake, another black guy no less, then that is still part of the scavenger game. Because Justin was maybe passing for white by dread mistake in the alley light. Who is who? What, in some alleyway at twilight? Justin open him eye from in a de coma an' seh, 'What, me?'

The meeting-hall getting fetid. Astronomers have the big picture. But nobody listens to them. Folk get to a community hall or turn up in church to wait for it to happen. But only hyenas have anything to say. Nobody do nada. Nothing getting said that is not hyena talk.

Jimmy was a few minutes late. And looks at Lorna now and then. But the lady looks away. He will switch off from the meeting, imagine being at the keyboard. Eyes closed, this like at the piano already. Like up on the 8th floor at the flat. Limber hands taking the back of the seat in front. The left hand getting Bach's G Major from

274

the Cello Suite. The right hand spanning altered chords to run Coltrane's Mr PC. Sweat pours. And Lorna gazing.

Marcia is tall and pained. But holding her control. "Remember Stephen Lawrence, Mr Trass? Ever read the McPherson Report?"

Trass grits his teeth. "Evidence is the beginning of everything. Where's the evidence for your race attack? Where's the evidence for your institutional racism?"

"*Evidence?*" Lorna shrieks, drilling every heart. "You go for a drink with police officers, don't you Mr Trass. I hear you get drunk with them. Then what, take turns on the karaoke machine? That's what I call *evidence!*"

Jimmy can not escape to music. Not from here. Other sounds in the meeting hall and Marcia Hosannah a woman making guys disappoint themselves. The reason for the meeting can not prevent the woman's lips from lushing. And she ripe. Anywhere else it would be a different night. But Lorna in every heart. Tears well.

The community-hall is not home. But the April evening outdoors is just too anonymous for anyone to leave now. And yet. Most people know what will happen next. The only rub is the sight of a white man grieving a black man. Alan Stanley should say something. Or somebody give Trass a pasting. Justin only a stepping stone for Trass getting to the Lords. And only random noise here.

And to think. This business started with somebody waving a flag across the sea. A colonial cloth misleading folk. The colonial flag said 'Come, come to the motherland.'

Guys with Union Jacks were standing outside the meeting hall this evening. Skinhead laughing. And last week somebody from the BNP got a seat on a town council. This was the first time ever. It was in a little place called Bromyard & Winslow and because of a loophole in the law, the BNP man did not even have to get elected to claim a seat.

Flags can be big or small. The Union Jack can squint one eye or cover a city wall. But tonight people in a community hall still getting misled. Somebody should say something. Even in a voice that will falter. Even a whisper. But where black skin ever get to whisper? Enoch Powell mostly got his numbers right. But a blind lady getting here would have to choose; she could take a white cane and step past dog mess on the pavement, or step inside the community hall and listen bull.

"At the end of the day," Trass declares, and something like duck spit covers his mouth, "it all comes down to what you can prove."

Lorna jumps from her seat. "Prove? Prove what?"

"If society is to work for us all, then we have to give the law something. Simple. You have to do what the law understands. You can't run before you can walk."

Marcia grabs the microphone. Her eyes curse Bosworth Trass. "Just how many deaths will there have to be before we learn this walk?"

A gaunt black man moves to the center of the hall. Tall, old, bolt. This Kwame Urshell. Folk reckon Kwame was a black panther back in the 60s and 70s. Black panther, in England? Urshell knowing all about the race hypocrite. To prove a point he asks the women to check the business card they got from Bosworth. And all the white women and most of the light skinned women have two, three cards apiece.

Hush. Quiet. A sad, slow quiet. A Mexican wave hushing. Two by two, people realize. They realize just how difficult to see any man in the race industry having a wife black as himself. Bosworth has more than one reason for the big ethnic numbers. Nobody ever see him near any woman that would be black in South Africa. A tall woman from Lebanon going the rounds with Bosworth now. She is not here tonight.

Urshell takes the microphone. Too many black folk stalking skin. The victim is sista dumbo, brodda dumbo. Dem never know seh dem a de victim. They dumb to the footfall of the stalker man, the skin-tone man. An' dis happen all de time. It happen in a de race industry. You got skin stalkers that do teaching, skin stalker in entertainment, in sport, hypocrite dat talk multiracial dis and dat. But all dem do is run after light skin. Yes, instead of standing upright in the sun. Yes, the skin-stalker stalking light skin. Bosworth Trass top of the pile. But he is no fool, not with a big MA in Eng Lit from Cambridge. But come the time to some honest thing, anything that will use vision to chastise the oppressor, then pow! Bosworth quiver.

Everybody knows. One day the streets will call out race officials. But that day does not faze Mr Trass. Bosworth the slick. A race official saying how he proud being black and, in the beginning, he was convincing with this. But stray dogs grinned from his mouth.

276

Eventually. Even now race officials preaching, talking spit, talk *inclusivity*. But man! In private most of them running from their own ethnic. Urshell gets back to his seat.

Nobody knows for sure where this Bosworth from. But a herd of white women and light-skin getting fooled; woman after woman with galloping itch, watching the race official pinch to the Lords.

Chapter 70

Dull headache on account of the fuss, Jimmy quits the meeting and goes out to the night. Bosworth Trass turned Justin's death into agenda. And that pissed off everyone else. Or maybe it was only because Justin waiting to get buried that nobody kicked Trass to the ground. Or because there's always going to be a Bosworth, a hypocrite over race like a dog with bone.

Set in the night, Jimmy longs for something plain. Even coffee. Lone and quiet in the car, stopped at a zebra crossing now. The evening muggy with folk heading to a nightclub. And now and then a young Mike Tyson or a Janet Jackson pops among them.

Watching these people is asking for trouble. And that's because the next question that must get asked is 'Where they think they going?' And the question after that must be 'Where can there be to go?' Going to a nightclub, but really going on a march to nowhere. The nightclub is a meeting point. It collects flesh. Flesh that is blue with night. And somebody knows a dreamless night walking in a narrow lane and seeing moonlight reflect in a puddle.

Lorna is still at the meeting. That grieving woman. And Tyson. He could have been great. But things started going downhill for Mike even before the Buster Douglas fight in Japan. If the folk round him had respected Tyson, respecting the man, not the cash flow, then somebody would have said 'Mike, how can you beat Buster Douglas in Tokyo while you have a dose? Some bad whoring instinct dragged you to a whore, and now you have gonorrhea. Buster is no great fighter, but he a man!' Trouble is, from the start Mike never had the right gloves to box with. He never had gloves from the hide of that cow that jumped the moon. Yeah, that thing in the nursery rhyme. Hey diddle diddle, the cat and the fiddle.

Jimmy alone on the road. A loner, gazing the jostling passers-by. But sapped by what goes on in a rented box, the apartment tucked in the 8th floor of a slab-heart building. But there's always the open road. And the petrol gauge glowing the dark.

Chapter 71

10th April 1981. Bunny Wailer was celebrating his 34th birthday with friends but worried about Bob Marley. An IRA man called Bobby Sands was in jail but got elected to Westminster as MP for Fermanagh & South Tyrone. And a young man got stabbed in a Brixton pool-hall; serious blood flowed. Ronald Reagan had been shot 2 weeks before. Bob Marley was dying.

For too long the police used to stop and search every young black man in Brixton. To the Metropolitan police every black man was a mugger or a drug dealer. Every black man, every day.

The guy in the pool-hall was black and when the police rolled up they could have rushed him to hospital. But they stuck him in their vehicle and posed. Standing round, posing, showing who in control. Quiet, young blacks folded round and, seeing what was going on, they shouted 'Hospital, get him to a hospital!' But nada happen. So dem grab de guy from de police. And rushed him to hospital. That was the first day of the Brixton business that most people call a riot. Some people call it *the uprising*.

Next day was Saturday. Reagan was discharged from hospital and gets back to the White House. And the police in London claiming a Brixton cabdriver was carrying drugs. But all the time the cabbie was a family man staying well clear of drugs and folly. The police did not learn from the previous Brixton day. And when young black guys folded round this time, well, it was different. It was man intent. Dis time, a line get draw in a de front line.

Young and black, you going your lawful male business and then redneck in a dem uniform call you a thief, a mugger, a drug dealer. Sometimes they even plant drugs on you and you get called a race name with them guffawing like from a swamp, wanting your humiliation. And even now redneck police still expect black guys with cotton stuffed in their ear.

It was bricks and stones. That Saturday night of the 11th, that April night in '81. Bricks, stones and fire. Concrete on fire in the night!

Historians say the first petrol bomb got used on the UK mainland in that Brixton business. Vehicle and buildin' get bun down. They burned down in the street night! And it was no April shower that calmed things down, cooled the fire. It was water jets from a fire engine the police used. That was what cooled it. Brixton was old tarmac after the water hose, old and cold.

But from then it was no more shadow. Nobody hooking their finger round white cane, nobody blind. From then it was black man saying 'No way!' No more groping round the street, not blind! And now one young somebody out there somewhere, calculating how Newton's apple can ever fall from Eve's tree. A pissed-off young, sick of torture, sick of preacher-man in paradise watching hell getting spread by hypocrite and the black pastor saying 'Praise the Lord!'

Preacher-man went to the cross with a crown of thorns. And folk getting crucified in a Brixton overcoat. Between sunlight and shadow somebody will reckon the measure of empathy falling as light not tears.

And community relations. Now a big business called multiculture. Multiculture dis and dat. But nobody in the English countryside ever homing their paper in-laws in from the ethnic.

Chapter 72

The morning sun is high. Sunlight floating, getting a faint and fainter shade on every tree. And up and down, set properties define this road. Here every house detached. And lawns tugging the sun like a kite.

Jimmy on the road. Glad for how the countryside wakes up round him. Everything just as Geraldine described: 'You'll leave the turn-off and notice a bit of a smell for a hundred yards, then go past rape blossoming in the fields'. When he was canvassing for Homes, only a select few of those houses were exclusive as these. Some here way past a million.

From info by the Swedish Academy of Science, the planet is hotter now than at any time. They got their evidence from old Chinese books and tree rings in Colorado. And the bottom of the Sargasso Sea. And ice-cores in Tibet. Bad drought these days. And famine. And only Africa or India getting hit. But more time, well, this manmade climate will get to every place. Jimmy lights a smoke.

Two weeks since Justin's funeral. No flowers in the wreaths ever from a garden on Geraldine's road. Fire chewing tobacco as the car stops. So, this where she lives. This what Geraldine is from. She was only slumming it with that canvassing at Homes, no wonder! This quiet road is way past vision. Every house safe, slow, taking its time, watching the season in high spring.

Geraldine's heavy doorknocker slips, thundering into Saturday morning quiet. The noise is a mistake. Quick, Jimmy knocks again. Soft this time, like trying to atone. A dog barks. And the birds on Geraldine's road singing up and down in a sweet quiet, singing.

A quaint woman, assessing. "Come in, do come in! So good to meet you."

From how Geraldine mentioned her mother Jimmy was expecting an elfin, somebody well past 60. Instead, a woman of indistinct age at the door; a lady moving along but not quite demurring from polite smiling. And right behind, and near to unrecognizable under a green oilskin jacket, Geraldine grins in the hallway. A lady's bicycle is close to the kitchen dining room.

"So," the woman smiles, "you are Jimmy Dell. Well, how are you?"

"Pleased to meet you."

"I just this minute got back," Geraldine pants. "Dashed out to get fresh bread and a few things. You look tired."

"Was at Kevin's till late."

"Kevin? Who's Kevin?"

"The guy Colette introduced us to at the theatre, remember?"

Hand to jaw, the old woman ponders. Quiet, wondering. Assessing. Her eyes twinkle as she mentions blackcurrant bushes in the garden and how heavy with fruit they get in summer. Jimmy has never seen Geraldine this happy. This maybe the first time she's snug in her own eyes. This the woman who turned up at the flat unloading a mile of groceries and sorted the whole place corner to corner.

Geraldine laughs. "Find your way alright?"

"A doddle."

"Coffee? How about a nice mug of cocoa? I'm doing toast. Fancy a piece of toast? Half a loaf, if you want!"

Off the kitchen a conservatory. Jimmy thinking 'Big glass!' The conservatory is a Victorian design. And a great garden relaxing through the glass. Geraldine walking the floor in a girly mutiny.

"Mum's doing a bit of breakfast," she says. "Toast and cranberry. Nothing complicated. Oh, and a few eggs. Is that OK? Sit where you like."

"Did she already know the facts?" Jimmy says.

"What do you mean?"

"You tell her a black man was coming to visit?"

Geraldine's arms fall. Limp arms, speechless. Her blue eyes reach for the ceiling. Her shoulders raise. "Oh, come on! Are you going to be silly?"

"Well, I never know."

"Please don't spoil it."

Steam curls from the mug of fresh-ground coffee. And Jimmy knows. Geraldine's garden a fairytale. Gazing the lush he can see the garden is orchestra here. A full plate of toast on the table and her mother follows with a tray of cups, scrambled eggs and home-made jam. And white napkins, cutlery gleaming in sunlight. Jimmy thinking 'This is too much trouble.' But lying. He thanks Mrs Nash.

"Can't you call me Renate? May I call you Jimmy? Yes, of course. So, call me Renate."

Jimmy grabs a piece of toast. "Geraldine said you're big on pot-

282

tery,"

"Not pottery," Renate sighs. "That's Lydia, my other daughter. She's the one. But a long time ago I was quite handy with sculpture. Well, a bit more than just handy perhaps. But now it's my eyesight and, well, why go into that?"

Geraldine must set the record straight. Her eyes indicating a zany blue sculpture. "See that thing in the garden? That's my mother, that's what she can do. We call it Next Time. It won a prize when she was at art college. And winning prizes was a lot more difficult those days."

Renate blinks. "Ah, winning prizes!"

"Now it's just a free-for-all, isn't it mummy?"

"Like how?" Jimmy says.

"Nowadays you can just chuck your guts up in a bucket and there's certain to be a little committee out there to award you a prize for it."

"You must see the garden," Renate laughs. "We have some lovely wildlife. Herons in the mornings, and a few foxes roam about now and then. Badgers and kestrels. All sorts. Absolutely fantastic. Something all year round. Yes, we have some absolutely *lovely* moments at the far end of the garden. A real sense of wow!"

"I was thinking about working from home," Geraldine says. "I hate the travelling. I could sit in the conservatory and bring the phone out on a lead."

Renate grins. "Yes, and be quite naughty if you want."

"Sit in bra and knickers making business calls?"

Renate turns to Jimmy. "Why did you choose the piano? Or did it choose you? If I may say so, you look like, well, you seem more like _"

"A sax player?"

"Yes, that's what I think I'm getting at."

"It was never the sax. It was the chords, Renate. I got into piano because of chords. Piano makes you play chords. Melody is great, but chord work is deeper."

"I always think of you with a little mandolin," Geraldine giggles.

Renate curls a leg under her trim lady figure. "Any chance of a bit of music? I can't wait to hear you play."

"Right now?"

"No, no. After you've finished. Have your coffee, my dear. Bon

283

appetit."

Something the other side of the burnished conservatory glass. This thing brims of the tropics. Sipping coffee, checking out the mother and daughter team, Jimmy getting sedated with the garden quiet. And the way they have their lawn here, the hushed green, and, way down the vista, a half forest. Hunza apricot trees are out there. Geraldine had talked them all winter.

"Do you play much classical?" Renate asks.

"Classical? Yes. And romantic. Blues, atonal, jazz. Some days it's all one language with different accents."

Geraldine laughs. "What's the difference between classical and romantic?"

"Well, that's demo time. Let's get to the piano."

"Can't you say what it is? I mean, in a word?"

"Classical? Classical is like Beethoven or standard Mozart. Romantic is like Schubert or Chopin. Something like that."

Renate frowns. "But there are so many, many exceptions! The Moonlight Sonata, for example. Beethoven's Moonlight is very profoundly non-classical music."

"Romantic!" Geraldine says.

Renate agrees. "Or any of his sonatas. Thirty two of them, I think. *Deeply* romantic."

Jimmy sips coffee. And says that that example just shows the bottom line is only music and that anyway the Moonlight Sonata is a bad example. Bad example? Well, yes. Listen to it while watching the moon, understand the power of that C-sharp minor, and the magic disappears. All that's there with the moon shining is like a bunch of reindeer testing how thick ice is on a lake, getting more and more confident then, getting tired of testing, running onto it. Maybe it's the key of the piece; C-sharp minor may entice the drag in ice that reindeer love. Renate frowns. Old lady scowling tight, but promising she will try the reindeer image one moonlit night.

Music is like clouds, Jimmy says. Clouds? Yeah, breeze going through one way and you get nimbus or whatever, but another breeze will get you something else. Geraldine huffs, saying that that probably helps weather forecasters but farmers already know it in their guts. Jimmy looking out over the garden.

Six months after the event known as the Brixton riots, Stephen Hawking was in Moscow for a conference on quantum gravity. He
284

gave a seminar. But because they couldn't understand his wrecked voice, one of his students had to transpose his ideas. Wanting something to say, Jimmy talks a minute about Minims. Hums a few bars. Lorna said Mull of Kintyre is folk, but Yesterday could never be. To Colette, Norwegian Wood is up there with Greensleeves for folk.

"To do folk music," Renate says, "you just gather around and something heart warming happens."

"It's like knowing that that's a chair," Geraldine grins. "You know it's a chair even if you haven't seen it before. Folk music is like that."

"I think the young man knows that," Renate reproves.

Jimmy turns to Geraldine. "You mean, what exactly? That the guy fobbing me off from the festival was right?"

"Right? In what way?"

"Saying jazz is not folk."

"Is there one thing," Renate butts in, "just *one* thing about jazz why it is different from classical? I have so wanted to hear from the jazz side." She wants to change the subject, does not want fuss between her daughter and their guest.

Jimmy takes a deep breath. Where to start? No one place to begin. But in just one word, that word must be Africa. And the next word is syncopation. But the boss word would be *improvisation*.

Africa is too other for these white folk. Too awkward. And apart from Miles Davis, Jimmy will not talk too much jazz after bebop. Jazz means improvising, he says; jazz is rhythm, inventive quicksilver sound cities built on altered chords. Huge imagination. Improvisation is the purest music; the player knows and knows and will practice and practice for years, a lifetime, and, if you good enough, then the silent voice takes over. The silent voice says 'Speak for me, speak for me.'

This is hard to explain, Jimmy says. But one example might do it, like hit Renate's concert grand to show it. But Geraldine wants to do the whole thing in words only. Jimmy can not, saying words end where music starts. But. Renate mentions it, saying out loud that Beethoven was completely deaf at the end.

Jimmy nods. But says she should listen to what Beethoven did with the UK national anthem. Ludwig believed he was taking God Save The King to a neat place, but if a jazz musician was ever to cut loose with it then what Ludwig did would be only doodle-school. Renate is not convinced. Jimmy turns to the garden. This could get difficult. This can not get done without showing. That's the point. And yet.

A clue arrives. A good one. Bach could have worked this garden. Or Chopin. And Schoenberg would have made things happen here. This garden complete. Nothing can get added. This place is like from Beethoven, Jimmy says, like the Piano Sonata in C minor. But nothing here that Thelonious Monk would just sit back and look at all day. In a word, the planted blooms here is not jazz. No crunch, not here. Nothing a scarlet Ferrari could park beside and not seem weird. Not even Renate's sculpture. But how to explain crunch? Matisse could have painted and painted here, but there's nothing Picasso would have leaned on. The symmetries here are only two, three dimensional. Nothing here stacked like equations on-hold in the sky. Nothing like a clothesline with spacesuits flapping solar breeze.

Geraldine grins at Jimmy. "Bitten off more than you can chew?"

"Imagine water," he says, turning from the garden. "You get water doing its thing and a classical composer comes along, imitates water sounds, gets the sense and sounds. But there's still no idea what kind of water it is."

Renate's eyes doubt Jimmy. "I don't follow, sorry!"

"Imagine a boat out on the water," he says. "Classical music, romantic, that music can tell you there's some kind of a boat on the water. But if it's a speedboat, or yachts with multi-coloured spinnakers, then big trouble!"

"Nonsense!" Renate shouts. "I mean, well, _"

"Don't apologize," Jimmy shrugs. "Whatever you do, don't ask a composer to tell you the difference. But since you ask me, well I always think of boats. There might be the whole ocean to cut through, and lots of things can happen, but mostly you can't plan them. So if you want to bring home a melody then you'd have to be looking at jazz."

"Then where," Renate wonders, "do people like Stravinsky and Schoenberg fit into this?"

"Well, they're mostly in the same ballpark as jazz. But not quite."

Geraldine fills all the cups with more coffee. "What do you mean?"

Jimmy turns to Renate. "If you want a theme, then jazz is the most abstract form doing that. With classical you always have shapes you can name."

"Young man, I'm not sure I know what you mean."

"There's shapes, circles, squares, even a dodecahedron, but always with a name. But with jazz you're looking at things with no name sometimes. Chunks of the ocean have no name."

The phone rings. Let it ring, Geraldine shrugs. Renate chugs from her chair. She will answer it. Geraldine tucking into toast. And this jam is so homemade that half a jar gets downed, spoonful after spoonful. Jimmy laughing. And turns again to gaze the garden, grab some free quiet here.

Renate looks bleak. Coming back to the conservatory, she gulps her coffee. Must disappear. Only for a couple of hours, but urgent, must go. Jimmy must make himself at home. She'll get back as soon as poss, can't wait to hear him at the piano. She play? Well, she's been trying for fifty years. Jimmy says the jazz-classical thing is a bit like religion; one set of prophets always update an earlier set and people believe all over again.

Renate's head shakes. "Von Karajan used to drive the wickedest Porsche money can buy."

Jimmy asks if she's heard. Heard? Nigel Kennedy's done a CD homage to Hendrix. As she nods, accurate grey eyes narrow.

"Well," Jimmy grins, "there's more colours to jazz than a rainbow could weep at."

"Enough!" Renate laughs. Hands thrown in the air, a wistful look on her classic face.

Renate sixty four. Geraldine says her mother is a brilliant woman. She took early retirement as a psychology professor. Her father is sixty three. But looks severe; like he already seventy, she says.

The music on the radio stops. And a conversation in German starts. The talking is exact, coming from a shortwave set in the kitchen. Renate was born in Germany and it was through her that Jimmy got the coaching gig in Dusseldorf; the network of contacts paying dividends already. And because of that business with the Jews, smart Germans scared of labels these days.

"That radio only speaks German. I'll switch it off, if you like."

Jimmy glancing at the time. "No. Let it ride."

The blues show about to start on Jazz FM. And normally Jimmy can not miss it. Right now would be great to tap into it. Even for 20 minutes. Paul Jones fronting the show and still out there in his own right, still gigging the blues on stage, still playing good harmonica. The people that fostered Jimmy's mother have records by the Manfred Mann band, and she once got Paul to autograph a record sleeve.

Geraldine takes a seat. "Come to think of it, I can't remember that radio ever being tuned to anything else. My father didn't allow German anywhere else in the house. Can you believe it? I learned German in that kitchen, listening to that radio and talking to Renate."

"You speak to your mother in German?"

"Lots."

"Man!"

"Why the surprise?"

"If I wasn't here, you and your mum would be talking German?"

"The only time we *ever* do English is when she might say 'You can say that again!' Or, 'What a load of rubbish!' Ditties, really."

Jimmy is curious. "Your father is an army man, wars and stuff."

"Oh definitely! Retired now, of course. But still vigorous."

"They got divorced?"

"Separated. Bit of a bigamist when he moved in with the other one. She was way before my mother then he went back to her about seven years ago. It all came to a head. Some sort of minor aristo, Lady Zip of Buttons. Are you interested in this?"

"All the way. I'll take anything you tell me."

Geraldine points to the cigarette packet on the table. "An amazing, amazing, man! Lots to the bloke, lots."

"So what's the down side? He left you all."

"Leggy females!"

"Her nibs is a blonde?"

"Yes."

"Bitch toffs are always blonde."

"He's 'The Colonel' when Renate talks of him. Pretty scary!"

Chapter 73

One morning somebody answered the phone in Afrikaans. Agnes is fluent in Afrikaans. And Zulu, Xhosa. Not to mention English. And she can imitate Boers. She gets the same noise of a thick pig plowing as when Boers talk, or so she says. Part of the master plan under apartheid was that some Africans got forced to learn Afrikaans. Geraldine knows apartheid as a Reich in South Africa.

From the patio, the radio breaks into German again. To Jimmy something in the voice is too cool. Something too efficient, disciplined like topiary. If a bonsai tree could speak it would talk German. Getting freed from the eunuch of a thousand year rage, a bonsai would unload in German. Beethoven was deaf at the end, and some people think his later work came from a topiary that was his ears.

Jimmy turns to Geraldine. "What're they saying?"

"The radio? Oh, not a lot. Just a bit of muttering. Resentment about the arts. Don't you know any German at all?"

"Me?"

"Why not?"

"Not a word!"

"You did a music degree and you listen to Schubert, why would that be so strange?"

"Well, that stuff was at school. But speaking it or understanding it, that never cropped up."

"Well, here's your chance!"

"Why?"

"For one thing, you have a contract in Dusseldorf!"

"I like Dusseldorf. But they speak enough English there, the ones in the orchestra. And it sort of leaves them with something, me not talking German."

"Well, try sailing close to the wind. Knowing the language could protect you. There's still quite a bit of simmering going on."

"You mean the nazis?"

"Neo-nazis, or whatever."

"Hey, they can keep Wagner. They can keep all the punk Wagner they have!"

"All my cousins are in Dusseldorf. Lots."

TV gardening shows can cut tenement anguish. But Geraldine's garden is so else. Jimmy knows. Somebody could lay low here. Sometimes home is the image of home from home. And Stephen Hawking is home in a wheelchair. But where the puppeteer that parked a withered package in a wheelchair that can outsmart any puppeteer?

"This is the first time I've really noticed your details," Jimmy says.

"My *details*?"

"Yeah. I can see the German side."

"Oh, come on! What's changed about me in a few minutes? You've had a coffee. Noticed the radio is on."

"Don't know what it is. Could be your eyes. Your eyes never clicked before. The amount of blue you have. And I thought your hair was blond. But it's _"

"Platinum?"

"Yeah. Blondie blond."

"Depends."

"On what?"

"Oh don't be silly. Of course it depends on what I'm wearing. What else do you see?"

Looking across at Geraldine, Jimmy weirdly remembers Colette. Colette of the olive skin. A little black mole is on her cleavage and maybe her nipples brown. But Geraldine way north of that, her puzzling blue eyes looking at Jimmy. By pure chance he was in the same space as Colette last night. And that was the first time since that weird evening with the theatre. Last night was going great at Kevin's flat, working on the music deal, getting a neat collaboration. Then Colette arrived with her daughter. It had never cropped up before but Kevin was Colette's onetime. Kevin never mentioned it, except saying off-hand that she's a friend. Last night the whole thing got clear. Colette and Kevin lived eight years together and have a daughter. One day they even booked a slot at the register office. But been apart five years now. Seeing the full story, things suddenly made sense for Jimmy last night. He stood back from Kevin's piano checking the way Kevin played with the girl. Colette was chain-smoking at the far end of the studio. What did she do with the note? Their eyes met. A flicker of regret. Regret, quick but quiet. Something was there. And always going to be. But Kevin's studio was family space last night and Jimmy did not want to cut

290

the innocent teenage girl. Colette's daughter. Kevin's daughter. The girl was exactly like the Modigliani repro on her mother's office wall. It was time to go. Kevin picked up the vibes as Colette walked Jimmy to the car. Nothing was getting said, not till the engine fired up. Then Jimmy asked if she kept his note. No, she said, looking puffed, puckering, quiet, then saying he should try to check out a psychiatrist. He asked if she wanted to know. Know what, she said. Well, that theatre night he was shoveling the Maserati for all it was worth and, even now, still wondering how it would have been back to the hotel instead of driving away. Waving him on, she said 'Doubt is good for the ego. Life is a bore without a bit of wildcard now and then!'

"Jim lad!" Geraldine grins. "What do you see?"

"How d'you mean?"

"You were looking at me like you've never seen me before. So, what do you see?"

Jimmy laughs. "I see a surprise."

Chapter 74

Half past ten. Beside the patio two mimosas in full bloom. These things bloom like gold puffballs over the green garden sun-starved today. And somewhere in Portugal or Italy, far in the hot south, a lizard will be poking out a tongue on a tall mimosa tree. Jimmy says the chat on Geraldine's radio sounds like gyroscope talk; like spinning flywheels that hold in a stable plane no matter how their frames move. The morning striding round in the garden past the mimosas.

After leaving Colette with her ex and their daughter last night, Jimmy went for a night of malt. Sober malt whisky. And mostly the night was sleepless and definitely alone. By 4 in the morning the bottle was empty and the ganja clean out. But Cobalt was ready. This piece been jigged and rejigged and jigged so many times that now, well, no real reference in it to Bach or Coltrane.

Geraldine will go to Ireland tomorrow. So Jimmy here three weeks earlier than planned. She could go for six weeks. Or six months. So this might be the last chance for a tenement citizen to grab some quality garden time. The garden here says it could do with meeting someone new.

Geraldine promised a recovery day in her garden. And promised she would not talk of Colette. A washed patio here. And a washed breeze. And a table with three chairs freshened by recent ivory paint.

"Right!" she says. "Fancy a walk round, or shall we sit and talk?"

Jimmy blinks at the garden. "It's a lot bigger than you said. Never seen anything like it before. What's over there?"

"Oh, just half the world."

The lawn here could do a five-a-side football game. No. Not football. Not here. It would have to be bowls, something of a ripe age, or sedate. This garden and the 5-bedroom house is where Renate lives by herself. The old lady must be glad having her daughter back at home for a while. Geraldine and Jimmy go further from the house. Moving for outdoor solutions. A dog and two puppies arrive from where a wooden bench squats opposite a bird-box.

"We can sit here a minute," she says, checking the sky.

"I got the local newspaper on the way. There's something about a UFO."

"Yeah, something blipped in the clouds. But they only have smudged snaps."

"You believe that stuff?"

"Aliens?"

"No reason why something else can't be out there."

"If it's true, if life *is* out there, they probably need to get a bit of reconnaissance done."

At the far end of the property, birds singing high in a plane tree. Talk could be about UFOs here. But talk would blot. These birds are mystic enough. Jimmy could learn to listen here, listening to birds sing. This bird melody a flattened fifth, fluttering to the lawn, cascading trees, heading back to consecration. Then starting over. If this is England then where Brixton?

Looks like Colette was right. Sometimes the only real canvass is a wildcard. But all this is nothing to Geraldine; she's been in this mystic place most her life and not noticing.

Jimmy nods "Let's get back to the patio."

"Why, what's the matter?"

"This is too Zen."

"Zen?"

"I don't know why."

"You mean the quiet?"

"Yes, the quiet.""

"So natural?"

"Yeah. *Natural* is the word for this."

"Well, that's the point of having you here."

The huge thing in nature is its symmetries. By a mathematical tool known as symmetry-breaking, nature reveals some wondrous patterns to the heart and eye.

Jimmy turns to face Geraldine. "Thanks."

"Zen?"

"Yeah."

Birds have been around so long that there's one type in Borneo that mimics buzzsaws in a forest. And some birds imitate jets taking off or landing. So UFOs could be the next big thing for birds to mimic. But then, who would know?

Geraldine's outstretched arms indicate a clump of trees. "Recognize anything?"

"Don't ask me to name plants. I wouldn't have a clue."

293

"No, no. Look! Don't you recognize the trees?"

Something getting more and more familiar here, Jimmy looking round. The water, the trees. This like some place. But where? This Jimmy's first time in countryside England. Something like this can get seen from a motorway. Or the train. But being inside it is a different thing. Birds singing the landscape.

The far end of Geraldine's garden looks like the salesroom poster at Homes. But different lighting. Geraldine snapped a picture at dusk and Colette used a computer to make the poster suggest a whole forest. But instead of a lake, like the poster suggests, only a pond here at the beech edge. And light streams down through trees like from stained cathedral glass. After the phonecall to the St Albans man, Jimmy turned to that poster in the salesroom. But now, well, it's like gazing sunlight at play. The poster was a fake. No swans float on the pond. No swans here.

Silent, they go past flowers most people have never seen. And chat of work a little. And mention the hard facts of life causing them to meet. She says the past year's been very difficult. She feels a wipe-out, a total failure, having to come back to her mother's house. But that was nothing next to the ruin when her translation agency failed. The problem started after a breakneck advertising run: all the savings she and Brian had went into a website and a full page spread in Yellow Pages. She wants kids, but maybe Brian a blank. And tomorrow she goes to Ireland to find if anything meaningful still there between them.

"I suppose the house makes you think we've got a few bob," she says. "Not true!"

"Could have fooled me."

"See that vegetable patch? It is *definitely* no hobby. We haven't got two cents to rub together and I can't say how painful it was to come back and twiddle my thumbs. When I turned up at Homes I'd have cleaned the toilets if that was all there was."

"When I first saw you it was class at first sight. Aloof, but kind."

"Aloof?"

"Yes."

"Kind?"

"Yes."

"You've never said that to me before."

"There was no need. You always knew where you were going."

294

"What about now?"

"Pure class!"

"Are you pitching me? Are you trying to spiel me?"

"No. Class has got nothing to do with your plush house."

Geraldine getting misty-eyed, turns away. "You know," she says, "I've never really thanked you. I count on our friendship. Lots. I admire what you have. Your inner strength."

"My inner strength?" Jimmy laughs. "What bit of my anatomy is that?"

"You're very chippy today!"

"Well, you asked for it. You *know* you have class. It's all over you."

Petals on a flower will have a pattern. And normally that display is the start of the Fibonacci series. And a slave was a dice of sugar in coffee. Or stuffed cotton in one ear.

"Enough about me," Geraldine says. "How you, how's it going?"

"You mean Colette?"

"Hmm."

"This is the part where you weren't going to mention her."

"I don't understand any of it, the trade-off between you and that woman."

Birds sing the blues. And they can fly high; one day a military pilot was forty miles high and a flock of geese was up there. Birds will hop farmers' fields and somebody comes along with a shotgun and sprays the sky with buckshot. And that breaks their heart.

Jimmy yawns. "OK to smoke?"

"Bit late to ask!"

"No, not tobacco. Got to do a spliff."

A letter from Agnes alongside the Rizla in his pocket; a six page letter and a photograph from South Africa. But so far only the first paragraph got read: 'Sunday afternoon we went to the beach. The women assembled for traditional songs. I will send you a tape.' The letter arrived a week ago but Jimmy did not read it. He was all about thinking of Agnes, thinking of that woman wading sea water and waving from another continent. But it's the photograph. Hard to understand the photo with the letter.

"Someone on my mind, and it's definitely *not* Colette."

"Is it that South African woman?"

"Yep."

"How is she?"

"Me and her? No idea how it will pan out."

"Where does Colette come in?"

"Why mention her?"

"Because it's upsetting you."

"It's not Colette. Believe me."

Geraldine grabs the spliff. This the first time for a while that she will do a spliff. And now she pulls on it, pulling. And blows a bad smoke ring. Her smoke rings laze towards the trees. Jimmy laughing.

"Know what I think? I think you love your South African. Absolutely lost without her, but wish you'd slept with Colette. You should have, you know. A bit of been there, done that."

Jimmy wonders. Hard not to wonder how it would have turned out on that strange Colette night, that wildcard. One what-if was not leaving the flat that night with no condom. Or the linen on the bed, if it was clean that night. Or if no old man was at the zebra crossing nearly getting mowed down. None of that, and that woman would have got the ride of her gypsy eye. Now it's out of control. What was he looking for that would have got found in Colette? Up and coming black guy with cut music, was he only a kind of trophy for the woman? And all this because of trying to spare the St Albans man. It was not pretending being white. Jimmy can tell. That talk business with St Albans, it made the man believe it was a pure white-white thing. But maybe Colette herself was doing it, doing a black-white fantasy that theatre night. Or maybe she was only thinking Jimmy a man.

Geraldine's lawn could field a cricket match. The tapers of the fresh mown grass reach away, like wanting to set alight the whole countryside. Pass the grass, Geraldine, pass the grass!

Instead of Colette, instead of a white woman, what if it had been a black woman hearing Jimmy keep silent with St Albans? A militant black woman would suck her teeth. 'What a big-time uncle tom!' But. Most women of colour understand. They know how to set for a quiet life among the white.

"Can you live with it?"

"What?"

"Not sleeping with Colette."

Jimmy shrugs. "Sex is a weird thing. There's times it's like a

296

stowaway. Sometimes it's a bitch."

"I'll tell you how it is!" Geraldine groans. As she passes the spliff, her eyes stare into a new distance. Her voice dips. "Bad sex is like new clothes you don't want to keep but can't take back because you've lost the receipt."

"Yeah, I've been there."

"I almost started seeing someone. I was so missing Brian, missing out."

"Yeah, I know the feeling. There's been nothing going with me for three, four weeks now."

"Been using your hand?"

Jimmy exhales a yard of marijuana. Laughing. "Me? Hey, my piano wouldn't like that. My piano wants both my hands, it would get dead jealous."

"If I ever started seeing someone it would only be because I was sick of missing out."

"This going to be a confession?"

"Confession? You want one of those, do you?"

"Yeah, the dirtier the better!"

"Well hold on to your seat, mate!"

"Let's sit here. I get the feeling this is going to be dirty. Filthy."

Somewhere, nerds or only Stephen Hawking wondering how a butterfly can flap in a London garden and the weather in Tokyo or Timbuktu gets angry because of it. Geraldine's husband is a computer nerd. And it's computers that allow a dynamic cut to chaos equations. A woman can get a note from a man that can not blot the note she made of a phonecall.

Geraldine bites her lip. "One day, it was after Christmas and I went for a walk, getting away from myself, doing a bit of shopping, the usual. Then when I got to the checkout I had a packet of condoms in my trolley. I don't know how they got there!"

"Weird!"

She grabs a drooping flower, wrenching it from the stem. "You think that's weird? You have *no* idea what's out there."

"People are the ones. People are weird as weird."

"Artificial little distances. And *so* lots of posturing."

"Why the condoms?" Jimmy wonders.

"How the hell should I know? One day you find yourself alone and you don't want to, you know, blah de blah!"

297

"Why the condoms?"

Her fingers small, flick petals of a crimson flower in the air. "Condoms, condoms! Seen the one for women?"

"Yeah, I heard about that thing. Wouldn't want to meet it."

Geraldine draws her body to her arms. A small light in her blue woman eyes. "There's Fred and Gertrude, get it? Fred's sporting a canary condom and Gertrude's chuffed to the nines with hers. What a scream! Oh, wait, here they come. Can't you see them? Look, Mr and Mrs Flastic Puck! Anyone for ice-hockey?"

Chapter 75

Instead of Agnes, the photo must be one of her relatives. To Jimmy, this woman can not be Agnes. Her sister maybe, or her youngest aunt. But then there's 'All my love, Agnes.' signed over it.

The sun wavers a stark sky. And rooks screeching high in beech as Geraldine gets back from the house. Jimmy slips the photograph back to his pocket.

She sets a tray on the patio table and, following his eyes, looks out at the distance. "You seem miles away."

"Funny, an hour ago it was birdsong out there. Beautiful. How did rooks get into this?"

"Oh, the noise! *That's* what's bothering you? There's a different choir on stage now."

"Sounds like one of those stupid teen bands!"

Geraldine grins a girl's grin. "Fancy a riddle?"

"Riddle-me-dee, riddle-me-da."

"Yeah, that's it."

"You like all that stuff, don't you? Not so long go they would've called you a witch."

"How can a forest pine for Hitler?"

"Trees?"

"Yes."

"Pine for Hitler?"

"That's the riddle."

Wanting a joke betrayed, Jimmy sets the woman's eyes. But nothing in blue. Nothing blinks. "It's one of those head jobs, isn't it?"

"That's not the answer!"

"Is it a tattoo Hitler had, a tattoo of pine trees?"

"No."

"Look, there's no way I'll get it."

"Giving up, so soon?"

"Yeah, you'll have to tell me."

"It's about larch trees."

"What?"

Geraldine disappointed. "A forest can pine for Hitler when larch trees are planted in a pine forest!"

This the weird story of all time. Mystic, gothic, sick. But a true story. Jimmy toys with the bag of ganja, but lights a cigarette. Seriousness will happen here.

Just outside Berlin the old Nazis planted larch trees in a forest of pine. And every autumn for the past 60 years the larch turns brown against the green pine. They planted the larch in the shape of a giant swastika that can only ever get seen from the sky. And in a way it's like the Great Wall of China. That stuff in the forest is like Wagner, Jimmy says. Geraldine blinks. No, this is from now. Larch trees have been used for century after century to make boats, but in that forest near Berlin those larch were a kind of lighthouse. Yes, for myth-seeking Nazis in autumn skies.

Jimmy gazing down the tapered lawn. "Makes you think."

"Yes."

"Yeah, the things you can do with trees."

"Oh, they're gone. All chopped down. All gone now!"

"How come it took them so long?"

"Nobody knew it was there. Honestly, no one sensible knew. We can surf the chat-rooms, there's some really useful websites."

To Jimmy, Geraldine looks like emigrating. Why'd she tell him this story? This woman looking inside her heart, looking for German amnesia. Her mother is German.

But Jessye Norman sings Wagner. Because of something new in German theatre, they used colour-blind casting in Die Walkure, having a black woman as Sieglinde to mate in the forest with blond brother Siegmund. What's this? Wagner the man, rabid anti-Semite, boiling in his grave at Jessye. Wagner was weaver of blue-eyed art. Then how come Jessye? Well, she sings to colour blind the Aryan audience to a German fairytale. And Jessye the woman, a large lady leaving the opera-house alone as black. The ring, the magic ring! And Alberich the dwarf, maker of the ring, handing power to who can possess that thing. What? The ring, the ring!

"Know anything about trees?"

Jimmy wanting to do another a spliff. "Trees? As in the ones in my 8th floor tenement flat?"

"Don't be hateful."

"You've seen where I live. How would I know about trees?"

"Trees do it for me. For us all, really."

"Trees make me think of Mary J Blige."

"Who?"

"American singer. She can sing acres of tenements away. Sings
300

like she plants trees instead of growing concrete. She's about the same age as us, four years older."

"Lets swap."

"What?"

"Trees for music!"

"*What*?"

"Come on, for *one* day!"

"Where's that come from?"

"Look around. Take a good look around you."

"Yeah, everything to order."

"Yes."

"Discipline."

"Beautiful."

"But no jazz."

"Jazz?"

"With jazz, you'd be looking at something bigger than leaves."

"Conceited!"

"Or it's just me and my tenement full of trees, yes?"

"Got it all figured out, haven't you!"

"What?"

"Oh, forget it!"

"You started it!"

Geraldine beginning a low grin. "So, you want to fight? Well, I'm a judo black-belt and the lawn is over there."

"Woman! If I had a woman like you, I'd _"

"Watch it!"

Somewhere, maths and logic folk discuss orders of infinity. They like the fact that some infinities are countable. Geraldine is not interested. Her brow crimps as she turns to the countryside beyond the lawn.

"Can you always tell whether it's a man playing?"

Jimmy frowns. "What instrument were you thinking of?"

"The piano, anything."

"Depends."

"So, you *can't* tell!"

"What's with this gender stuff?"

"You can't tell if it's a man or woman. Go on, admit it!"

"Well, no, not with classical. But with jazz you're looking at a big difference. The boss players are guys. You always know who's who. Same thing with blues."

"Isn't that because you already know who's playing? There aren't too many, who shall I say, I mean, someone like, well _"

"Oscar Peterson?"

"Right!"

"You know of him?"

"I saw a TV piece. It was with Andre Previn and him."

"Some people think Oscar P is the man."

"Not too many of him around, are there?"

"Well, no. But it's not a total shut down."

"Then name me a woman."

"There's serious women in blues. And jazz."

"Who are they?"

"I wouldn't call any of them a genius. There's no woman Charlie Parker. And nobody on guitar that's a female BB King. But if you hear Sister Rosetta Tharpe, I think she's from the fifties or sixties, that woman played serious funky!"

"A black woman?"

"Yes."

"You're very proud of that, aren't you?"

"Proud?"

"Of your black musicians."

Libba Cotten played mean guitar. She performed till she was past ninety. But the big thing was Freight Train; Libba wrote that great track when she was maybe only twelve years old and some people say it is *the* theme of American folk.

"You proud of the white ones?"

"What a silly question!"

"But only when I ask it, right?"

"Only because you strut it around."

"And when I praise Bach or Mozart, what then?"

"Yes, I'd forgotten. Sorry."

"That's all black people have. Western blacks. If it wasn't for top musicians, them and the sports greats, we'd have nothing."

Geraldine sits back in her chair. Now the time. This the time to tell this woman. Tell the full story this time, no punches pulled. Jimmy will tell how Minims got turned back by the music festival.

Geraldine a good friend, but it's still awkward for Jimmy to talk with one white person about the racial white. The sentry at the music festival implied the millennium folk festival was for English white.

Turning from the garden, Jimmy starts his story. No spiel. Nothing like time being only one direction to space, or Stephen Hawking in a wheelchair hoping for gene therapy. Jimmy lets fly. Stuff that cuts through like a knife through butter. And when this gets said, only silence is left. Three miles wide. No Milky Way, no Galileo tilting, nobody seeing further by standing on giants' shoulders.

Lions were all over Britain before the ice age. And somebody having a recent dream of walking through a pride of sleeping lions.

Chapter 76

Geraldine pacing. Taking the ground. Wondering. Thinking hard. Pacing the patio, mulling. She could count every mosaic on the ground. "It's not the music. I think it's the title. They don't like *Minims for Britain*."

"When I first sent it off," Jimmy nods, "that's what it was called. But I changed my mind. I told them on the phone. That's why I rang. I said it's called Minims now."

"Minims, then! It still suggests immigrants all over the place."

"*What*?"

"Immigrants!"

"In the title?"

"Yes!"

"It's not about immigrants."

"Then why so defensive?"

"It's about people waking up, going for a better real."

"It's an odd title."

"But the French for minim is *blanche*."

"And?"

"If Minims was about immigrants I'd have called it something else, like Crotchets in Britain."

"What?"

"I could have called it Crochets."

"What's crochets got to with immigrants?"

"You're the grand linguist, and you don't get it?"

"No, honestly."

"In music, the French for crochet is black. Well, *noire*. So I could have said crochets. But Minims grabs all that."

Geraldine turns to the lawn. For a minute, it's like she's doing window shopping with a difficult someone; like maybe with a wayward nephew. A bill arrived last week from the hosts of her website. But the site will not be renewed. And she will be on a plane tomorrow. Jimmy gazing blank, does not look at the country-side.

Geraldine tugs his sleeve. "It's not how you explain it. It's what they think it means. Look, I'm going to speak my mind. Don't take it the wrong way."

Must be great living somewhere like this, Jimmy thinks. Stephen

304

Hawking would leave wheelchair tracks on the lawn here and somebody chase sheets of his papers before the breeze. Great lawnmower strokes.

Suddenly, an old reflex! Jimmy can not prevent this. Even if his jaws get wired shut.

Geraldine tugs harder. "Are you interested in what I have to tell you?" .

"Just don't say it's a chip on my shoulder!"

"Really got your hackles up, haven't you! What's the matter?"

"Brixton, it's all over me."

"What?"

"Brixton, it's over me like a psycho dog."

"Oh, stuff Brixton!"

"Yeah, wish someone would."

"Hope you don't think I'm trying to patronize you."

"You know what? The last thing I need is a pep talk. I could fill your house with all the 'Think positive, keep smiling' crap I've had!"

"Think negative then," she laughs.

"You should be so lucky!"

"Remember Clive? There was that silly 'My friends, no negatives please!' Remember that?"

Jimmy stifles a laugh. "Yeah, and his thick business motto."

Hovering the moon, all Neil Armstrong could think was girls in bikinis on a beach. Who can say how the dots got joined? Dots? Polka dot bikinis. Why'd a swimsuit get named after the place where they tested the atom bomb in '54? Bikinis on the moon.

"Know why I do music?"

"You're very, *very* good at it. It's so you."

"Good was the easy part."

"Never look a gift horse in the mouth!"

"Music is because I had to get away from words. I can live without talking."

"Don't be silly!"

"I mean it!"

"And when the phone rings?"

"No words at all!"

Geraldine yawns. Tired, she looks up at the upstairs windows. Wipes her eyes. Yawns again. "Fancy another spliff?"

305

"I couldn't believe a music degree would be up to here with politics."

"Plunks on the course?

"Plunks? What's a plunk?"

"Plunks is what call politicians in this house."

"I like that!"

"You had tone-deaf DJ's turn up on your degree?"

"Wish it was that simple! It was folk claiming jazz wouldn't be here without guys like Stravinsky. Some of them claim Stravinsky invented jazz and I had a moron saying there'd be no Hendrix without Buddy Holly."

"Oh, God!"

"Yeah."

"But isn't that, oh what's the word, flag-waving? I'm dead set against that. Who cares who got there first? What does it matter?"

Somebody must get the real story behind the Firebird; Stravinsky's score is big with ambition even now. And the man himself tried to tell it in a lecture called Poetics of Music. But nobody must hide behind a fairy tale.

"D'you know who Charlie Parker was?" Jimmy says.

"Wasn't he that chap they made a film about?"

"Played the saxophone."

"And drank neat iodine."

"Yeah, that's him, the one they called Bird."

"I remember the plot."

"Hey, that's another story. That film didn't get there. You didn't get the depth of the playing. You're looking at genius. The greatest improviser ever, the greatest."

"You're building up to something!"

"It's a load of bull claiming there'd be no Bird without Stravinsky's *Firebird*!"

"The film claimed that?"

"No."

"I think Clint Eastwood was getting at the man, the back story. You get the music from anywhere else."

"It's people who think they know. The ones who should know better, they're the ones!"

"Like, me?"

"Look, when Bob Marley came to England the BBC plods failed

306

him at the audition."

"What!"

"Seriously."

"Bob Marley?"

"They claimed Bob didn't know reggae!"

In 1724, Bach was getting down to the finish line with Cantata No. 90. That thing talks of fire and brimstone, even though guys like Newton and Leibniz already showed cleaner ways to the universe than gods and devils. Bach used 16-note chords in that cantata, a music sermon telling the second coming of preacher-man.

Geraldine's head shakes. "I know what you're getting at."

"What am I getting at?"

"It's obvious. You think Charlie Parker stands on his own two feet."

"Dead right!"

"Then why split hairs? Isn't it the music that matters?"

"Yes."

"So who got there first doesn't matter."

"It matters! It's slander. It matters!"

Geraldine pretends not to get it. Her eyebrows raise. "Slander?"

"Brixton!" Jimmy yells, pushing from the chair. He could turn from here. Leave. Or scatter marihuana in over this quiet green garden; enough seeds in his stache to start a ganja plantation.

"Why slander?"

"Because what they're saying is if you're black and talented, *really* good, then they must be the ones that tell you."

This quiet garden, this calm English place. It is not really where a hurricane would happen. Not where someone would decide to go barracuda fishing down the lane. The green reserve here is not where a bird of greatness might escape. Not from somebody's ribcage, even Stravinsky. What would Charlie Parker do? A bird of greatness would never escape from here. And that's because this place already free.

Jimmy grabs the ganja. "They say I have a chip on my shoulder. Claim I have an axe to grind."

"And *they* are always right, right?"

"They make sure people like me know my place. So they come with stuff like 'Just trying to help, don't take it the wrong way.' Any idea what I'm talking about?"

307

"No, Jimmy."

"Geraldine, I won't fill my head with stuff I can't own. How would I own this? Even if I clocked the lottery the people next door would resent me. They'd move out."

"Talent!"

"The only thing I own is the chip on my shoulder."

A bad quiet settles the patio. A word fog. Geraldine grates the coffeepot across the table and gets a full cup. Deliberate, she attacks the lukewarm cup. And, as she stirs, a clinking rhythm gyrates. A deliberate teaspoon on bone china. The cup wants to set the conservatory alight. Geraldine waiting. For a full minute saying nothing. Emotion in a china cup. This is mud. Not coffee. And now the woman sets the stirring so fast that a wall starts in the cup. Just like a circus rider on a wall of death. Maybe the coffee rider will escape the cup. Or collapse, die.

Now, she ready to talk. But not as anyone ever talked to Jimmy before. While the spoon trilled the cup, the spoon was Geraldine talking. But now she set. She will talk her mouth.

She slings the spoon. "What was all that about!"

"What'd you mean?"

"I'm a grown woman. No sand in my hair. I know you want to trust me. What stops you?"

Jimmy turns from the flowers in the garden. And from the woman. The mosaic tiles are eastern. Is jasmine out there in the garden? Some people live for jazz but have never seen jasmine, never holding the scent. Jasmine was always in brothels where guys like Jelly Roll Morton worked piano. And more than anybody, jazz was down to Jelly Roll. People in the know connect jazz with jasmine. They say jazz gets the name from the flower. Jasmine was in every brothel in early New Orleans and, with Jelly Roll splicing, it was the same time as Stravinsky doing a stint with Coco Chanel. Igor Stravinsky, serious music man shoveling Coco behind a bush in her garden. And that was way before the lady's perfume ever got to market.

Geraldine laughs. "What's the point of the story?"

Jimmy saying nada. Remembers why he's here, why she invited him. 'What are you doing here?' her eyes say.

"I wasn't trying out my frustration on you," he says. "I get wound up. There's spleen, it comes from all angles. If I think somebody's
308

having a go at me, telling me I have a chip on my shoulder, that stuff boils over."

"Listen, if there *is* a chip on your shoulder I'd be the first to tell you, believe me!"

"I'm saying sorry, OK?"

"Doesn't matter now."

"No, go on, say it!"

Since some infinities are not denumerable, then a map of any one of them would eat itself. The crockery on the little patio table is Renate's best.

Geraldine glowering. "I can never decide whether you believe in real people, or in nothing."

"Is that all?"

"What?"

"I thought you had a sermon for me."

"What I was trying to say, what I *am* saying, no, it's no use, I can't."

"Bet it's something sloppy," Jimmy laughs, "like I should settle down and live."

"Get a grip!"

"I am unhinged?"

"When will you stop feeling sorry for yourself?"

Jimmy gazing the lawn, out and out. Out and out. Geraldine starts on the table. She will clear it. Cup stacks in cup, saucer in saucer. And a soap-cloth in her hand. The woman drudging a table that was spick already. As if a blood-soaked stain there. But the table was always ivory, and no middle class brogue in a dish rag.

Chapter 77

Two o'clock. The sun loitering. The photo of Agnes shucks in Jimmy's armpit and, still gazing the lawn, he asks what would happen if a lion should suddenly turn up. Geraldine's quick eyes cut the garden. 'Where would a lion come from?' her blue eyes say.

"Black male, approximate age of seventy."

She does not understand. But wanting to be baited, says "Only seventy? Oh, right."

"That's what they said on Charlie Parker's postmortem report."

"What are you getting at?"

"Charlie was only thirty-four. Only a medically unqualified alien would think you're seventy when all you were doing was thirty-four. You can *not* look at a guy thirty-four and see some old man seventy. But that's what they did to Charlie."

"Music lives on, attitudes fade away."

"Get that on a banner sometime!"

"Love to! But what about a bit of consistency?"

"Me?"

"Yes!"

"I talk gibberish, or is it mumbo-jumbo?"

Geraldine shrieks. "There's that lion!"

"What?"

"Quick, it's coming this way!"

Jimmy over the table. Spins round. Sharp! No lion can be there, but he takes a look anyway.

Geraldine squints past the lawn. "Slosh for logic, mon frere!"

Jimmy is not jealous. Geraldine was one of the select few. She went alone to a sneak preview of the Tate Modern and the place was speechless. Or so she says. Art galleries are her kind of thing. And the Tate Modern is just the biggest modern art place anywhere; section after section, sectioning quiet air. When it opens the public will leave it in their will.

Her eyes sprinkle with mischief. "Did you vote for Ken?"

"Ken who?"

"Ken Livingstone. You know, that firebrand."

"What was the vote about?"

"Mayor of London. Where've you *been*!"

"Mayor of London?"

310

"What a palaver! London's got a lord mayor, and now they have Ken."

"Two mayors?"

"Silly, eh?"

"Who's the other one?"

"The lord mayor. But that's only ceremonial. Ken's job is to run the city, like the ones they have in America."

"No way I would have voted. No way!"

"Such a fuss about the Labour Party and Ken."

"Ken Livingstone?" Jimmy grunts. "What orchestra does he play in?"

"A little Stalin, are we?"

Jimmy can not kill. Not with words. Not like Geraldine. But things are not simple as she makes out. Rain clouds form. And weird what water can do. While there's somebody dying of thirst there's sure to be someone blathering in a swimming pool somewhere. And a lion laps water while a herd of zebra wait their turn. And only 90 seconds after the Big Bang the temperature of the universe cooled to one billion degrees. Somebody should hang these things together. Then talk down rain castles from the air.

Geraldine's husband comes from Dorset, from a place called Burton Bradstock having water meadows and the River Bride flowing though hills to the ocean. Cottage, after thatched cottage. Everyone knows everyone and, every spring, migrating birds shelter safe in the valley.

"What d'you think of Tebbit?"

"Norman Tebbit?"

"There's the Tebbit test. It's out there stirring it up."

"Yes, I know."

"Obviously, I don't agree. Strange thing is, well, I can see what he's getting at."

"I don't think he'd want your sympathy."

"I wasn't sympathizing. It's how cunning that stuff is."

"Can't we just enjoy the day?"

"Sorry I brought my tenement head!"

"No grand debates. Not today, please."

"It wasn't a debate. You have your garden. Your neighbours have theirs."

"If you want a yardstick," Geraldine grits her teeth, "then try Alan

311

Turing. Know about him?"

"Vaguely."

"Computing."

"Ah, yes! Artificial intelligence, wasn't it?"

"Yes, and, not exactly."

"So long as he wasn't a lion tamer!"

"He was our top man at Bletchley Park."

"Where?"

"Code-breaking in the war. Alan Turing cracked all the best German codes at Bletchley Park."

"What's that got to do with anything?"

"We'd all be speaking German."

"Bitte, bitte!"

Her eyebrows arch. "Kennst du das Land wo die Zitronen bluhn?"

"German?"

"Ja!"

"Hey," Jimmy laughs, "f I talked that arrogant bull I'd still be on the outside looking in."

"It was from a poem, silly."

"What's it mean?"

"Roughly?"

"Anyway you want it!"

Lithe, her body turns to the garden full on. "Well, I'd go for 'Oh, where's that country where lemons bloom?' Lush, isn't it?"

"Sounds like I should be grateful for something."

"I really don't see that. Lemons are *so* sunny."

"I don't feel grateful for the sun. Not nostalgic for lemons."

"Nostalgic?"

"I was born in England."

"Then remember that!"

"Then how come it's so easy for everybody to forget?"

"That's not fair!"

"Glad you see it that way. Lots don't."

"A few idiots."

Way out in space, on the inside of a spinning black hole, time travel could happen. And if a fat woman can see her toe then maybe she all ready to go. It was a genius called Kurt Godel. Kurt cracked it. Kurt was with Einstein at Princeton talking what can be known in the universe. Kurt showed that all true statements can never be

312

proved.

"How many idiots are a few?" Jimmy says.

"Three, OK no more than ten in a hundred."

"Then let's me and you go for a walk down your road. See what your neighbours think."

Geraldine bites her lip. "We always end up with the *same* old story. How many times have we been through this?"

Operation Sealion was what Hitler called the plan to invade and settle Britain. From Geraldine's garden in Hertfordshire, bales of clouds float the sky. And, way off, a sound like somebody shouting for help. But it's only a peacock. Geraldine's neighbour with garden enough for peacocks. And she once watched a girl struggling down a country lane in Mauritius, a tiny little girl with a man-sized tray of mangoes. So tiny. And she wanted to cry but her mother appeared out of nowhere, saying that she was her little peacock and peacocks don't cry. Turning from Jimmy to the lawn, Geraldine murmurs, saying Alan Turing was a bit of a peahen.

"Cherie, she's due any time now."

Jimmy did not hear. "Who?"

"Cherie Blair."

"Coming here?"

"No, no. It's due any time now. Their fourth child."

"Didn't know she was banged up."

"So, what will it be?"

"What?"

"Boy, or girl?"

"Listen," Jimmy yawns, "get to the point."

"The point is, you are scared of Norman Tebbit."

"Scared?"

"Alan Turing took the lid off something quite useful."

"Does it get me free?"

"Well, let's phone Brian. He's a wiz at this."

"Computers?"

"Let's give him a call."

"I don't want to talk to him."

"He's *very* good."

"Phoning him could lead to me talking about race and there's no way I'm going through that on the phone. Bet you know that Turing stuff anyway."

313

Geraldine looking like a little girl found out. A woman that can talk of poverty, or tricks in a cipher, but her eyes say she wants only one excuse to flip. If she phoned Brian she'd start by saying there's somebody visiting who can play the piano. Or she'd make baby-talk over their trip to the London Eye. Weird, but exactly the same number of Beethoven sonatas as glass capsules in the London Eye. Beethoven was way under 6 foot, but the London Eye cycling 450 feet tall.

Geraldine toys with the spliff. "Suppose, just suppose you ask a computer and you, well, _"

"Got stage fright?"

"Not sure I can do this."

"Can't explain Turing?"

"Don't want to get it wrong."

"This was your idea."

In World War 2, Alan Turing had a brainwave about a German cipher. But how to crack the code? First thing was sky-high maths. And thermionic valves that today any little pocket calculator could replace a roomful of. But the folk at Bletchley Park cracked the puzzle. And then they could really play. The codebreakers at Bletchley played and played. Those smart folk played war games with Germans. They laughed around, laughing at the codes, and at the difference in German between 'toads squatting in autumn grass' and 'Scheherazade fretting in silk sheets.'

Geraldine scuds the chair. "OK, here goes! Suppose you ask two people the same question and get the same answer."

"Could be the right answer, couldn't it!"

"Suppose it's a computer and a person, and you can't tell the answers apart."

"Ask a machine?" Jimmy laughs.

"What about the internet?"

"What?"

"We ask the search engine!"

"Well, yeah."

"So the software knows. Sort of."

"Yeah, like it's some kind of library assistant."

"All the librarians *I* know are real people!"

"And?"

"Obviously, it means search engines are intelligent."

"Three cheers for computers! Four cheers!"

"Don't be sarky, let me finish."

"What's this stuff got to do with me? The minute somebody like me gets close, think we've cracked it, that's when we get Anne Hathaway shoved in our face. Now it's Anne Hathaway's daffodils and some guy with a computer!"

"Haven't we done this anguish before? You never stop!"

"I visited Jamaica and they said 'English boy!' They were only teasing. I was born in England but it's like I should get down on my knees!"

"What?"

"I won't beg!"

"Calm down! Please."

"I can't live next door to Anne Hathaway."

"Who can?"

"Norman Tebbit."

"Look, that St Albans chap on the phone, he thought you were white. He couldn't tell. There's your proof!"

"Proof?"

"Norman Tebbit's little bobbin doesn't work."

"How'd you arrive at that?"

"Racism is what we see and hear."

"Hey, I don't need lessons in theoretical racism!"

"If your colour doesn't come into it over the phone then you're halfway there!"

"What if it was a white Jamaican that called the St Albans man?"

"Come off it! What's the chances of that?"

"I guarantee you if I knocked his door I'd just be a trespasser."

"What?"

"The man from St Albans."

"Him?"

"Him, and the likes."

Even arithmetic; no way can all the true statements in arithmetic ever be proved. That's what Godel's Incompleteness Theorem did. So a bunch of bishops learning to parachute will end the same way as politicos learning to polevault. Roman candles in the air. Plunks on a pole.

Geraldine frowns. "Are there no white people you admire?"

"English white?"

"Yes."

"Nigel Kennedy. Eric Clapton."

"Oh, come off it!"

"What?"

"Eric Clapton is only a rock guitarist."

"Ace at blues. Listen to him playing the blues. Especially with Johnnie Johnson."

"Can't you think of someone with more relevance?"

Alan Turing had brains big enough to keep Germans from England. But in the end that only paved the way for black people coming here. So in a way Turing did a Newton. Black folk attracted here like because of gravity. And, like Isaac, Turing had a thing with an apple: one guy seeing the apple fall, and wondering; the other guy laced the apple with cyanide and wondered no more. And then Steve Jobs came along and named Apple computers after Alan Turing. And the hard drive in all that.

Jimmy grabs for a smoke. "Relevance is a big word. Huge. But Humphrey Lyttleton cuts it."

"Who?"

"Humphrey Lyttleton. Jazzman, wrote a neat blues for Big Bill Broonzy."

"Try someone we all know."

"Scarman, then. Scarman was a great man."

Lorna rubs bleary from her eye. Blinks an owl's idle blink. "Who?"

"Lord Scarman, the guy who carried out the Brixton riots inquiry. You should get a copy. Serious stuff. Or Macpherson, bang up to date. His report on the murder of Stephen Lawrence. Serious white folk. But if it's *white* you want me to talk about, there's no greater human than Bach."

It was a big shock hearing white Jamaicans talk. Somebody first visiting Jamaica and it's big hearing raw patois coming from someone white. Natural, down-home. Jimmy remembering the day in Kingston when a white Jamaican was trying to imitate an English accent, and it was a black guy from England that the white Jamaican was imitating. In the quiet air from Geraldine's patio, checking out the quiet green, someone could wish their life away. And they have herons coming and going here. Foxes, yes. And badgers. But herons too.

Jimmy wonders what Geraldine thinks of Mike Tyson. Straightaway, her eyes narrow. Eyes thinned down with loathing. This woman does not like Mike. She says she's far too tired to talk of anything that might be to do with him.

Wondering in private, she quits her seat. Ambles to the lawn. The two puppies play round her as Jimmy mulls. This quiet garden, the night at the theatre, Geraldine's mother leaving with a question in her eye. A day like today is set. And a dithering sun making do. Geraldine lazing the lawn and missing her girlhood. And her visitor knows it would be great living a place like this. Or live some island where the only approach is by simple sea. But not *simple* like London to Manhattan, but some small place where maybe only a hundred people live, somewhere with no peeping tom with binoculars and no uncle tom with certificates in Latin.

Geraldine zigzags. Lopes back to the patio, wanting to talk. This unresolved woman telling her blues. The puppies are disappearing one by one in the baskets of strangers. Only two left now, and by this evening even they will be gone. She tried not to name them. Her sister will come later to take one. Well, Jimmy says, that's how it goes. But straightaway feeling harsh. Geraldine bites her lip. Jimmy and Geraldine are the same age, he is eleven days older. And after twenty four years they meet inside the tinsel world of Clive Core, the paunchy sales magician at Homes, Homes & Homes. But in late spring of 2000, they centrally alone. Looking for more than dreams and less than a promise.

"Enough gloom for one day," she says. "Let's do charades."

"Nah, let's do another spliff."

"Oh come on, be a sport. Let's do a bit of Orwell."

"Who?"

"George Orwell."

"Let's get a spliff going."

"I'm serious. Big Brother is everywhere. Venture anywhere outdoors, and we all have our images up on CCTV. In London the average person is on CCTV more than 300 times a day."

"What?"

"Three hundred times a day! Anyone for more cheese?"

"Jeez!"

In Germany they have a reality TV show named Big Brother. It's coming to the UK and, about a week ago they got more than 45,000 people here applying for 12 slots to get onto the first Big Brother show on British TV. A broadcasting fever, Geraldine says. Folk having TV cameras all over them. Getting a matchless view of their guts, 24/7. Hiking that fever of eye.

"George Orwell, scene one, take one. Ready?"

"Orwell got 1984 wrong," Jimmy says.

"At the third stroke, it will be 3:20 precisely, and time to sip your water! *Bleep, bleep, bleep.* At the third stroke, it will be 3:20 and 10 seconds, and time to eat your greens."

"At the third stroke," Jimmy shrugs, miming Big Brother, "it will be 4 o'clock and definitely time to leave the table."

"Imagine," Geraldine laughs, "what happens when it's 7:10 precisely and time for us to go to the loo, all six billion of us on the planet!"

Scatty laughing. They laugh and the peacock next door cries. Jimmy wonders what if the colonel should drop by and see Geraldine laugh so glad. See glad tears in her eye, having Renate's laugh and eyes. Jimmy thinks Brian is a severe dork, letting Geraldine go to pieces.

A bottle each of white wine. And fierce giggling in the Hertfordshire green. This is mid-afternoon. And the woman wanting to rustle something quick in the kitchen. Jimmy wants to check the garden. And haystack clouds loom. He will play piano when Renate gets back, but not jazz. In a recent dream it was lion cubs coming towards him. All this must mean something. But what? In this English garden overlooked by rain clouds, Renate's sculpture is a blue dream.

"I used to come here when I was little," Geraldine explains, guiding further in the garden, further from the house. "I'd just sit and pretend not to hear when they called from the house. I was a princess of France and Germany, with two sets of courtiers, lots and lots of dutiful people breathless every day. And over here, here is where they buried the king. He was killed hunting wolves one day."

"Wolves, as in Little Red Riding Hood?"

"No. A proper princess."

"Greedy little princess, then!" Jimmy jokes. "Why Germany and France? Why did the king have to die?"

"Can't remember the bit about wolves, I might have read something. Anyway my sister was doing German at school and everyday
318

I tested her vocab with the dictionary. Renate couldn't be bothered. And dad just said 'Bollocks!' And that made me feel sort of in charge. She's only six years older, but to an eight-year-old she was quite something."

"Until I went to Dusseldorf," Jimmy says, "Germany was off the scale. I never wanted to go. Ever. But Dusseldorf is a restrained place. Kind of industrial, but beautiful for a factory city. Maybe it's the Rhine, legends of spies and things."

"I love it there. But let me finish my story. Where was I?"

"The king died."

"Yes, yes! As a princess, I basically did what I liked. And that was *so* lush!"

"Like how?"

"Oh, like punishing the servants."

"Nasty little fairytale!"

"The king's daughter!"

"Nasty little king's daughter then. Sorry, I won't spoil it. Go for it."

"I, Princess Geraldine, had the greatest portraitist. He was a really young chap who always averted his eyes while trying to study my face. I was the king's cleverest child. And that made him change the constitution so I would rule instead of my brother."

"And then he ups and dies before you grow up. Jeez!"

"No not quite. I still got to rule. But, well," she stops, wistful at the grass, blue eyes narrowed, "want to know the sad part?"

"No fairytale ending?"

"It's my father. The other woman had two sons. My step-brothers. One's a speech writer."

Chopin would check out this place, Jimmy thinks. Chopin would sit this garden, but not with the clouds here today. Mauled by consumption and neuralgia, he went to Majorca to take sun. One quack looked at the stuff Chopin coughed up and pronounced him dead. The second doctor said 'Frederic is dying.' But Chopin still got those 24 Preludes out of his system. And all the time his woman looked after him. Frederic needing the sun, and his woman needing him. But his body was too dry, too wry. And then two journalist ghouls tried to photograph him on his deathbed in 1849. But Frederic's good woman kicked them back to the ghoul street.

Geraldine can not say the exact size of the garden. But years ago it was bigger. She ever listen to Chopin at night, the mazurkas or waltzes?

Two lime trees stand from the clump of beech. The leaves of the lime opened last week and she was waiting for that, gets to them now, choosing some just fallen.

"We'll have these in the salad later," she says.

"Dirty old leaves from the ground?"

"Where do you think potatoes come from!"

"Hey, I don't know food and stuff."

"Can't beat these leaves for garnish. Fresh lime leaves with new potatoes, a bit of salmon. In a week they'll be hopeless, tough old coins by autumn."

"You could do a Delia Smith on your lawn."

"Where was I with my story?"

"You got to rule after the king died."

"Yes, I ruled with great good sense."

"Kind taxes?"

"Of course. But then I blew it. I lost control to my husband when I challenged him to a race one day. What was I doing in a ball-gown? Tripped over and lost. So then I was the odd one out. In the entire history of the kingdom, the only ruler ever to lose it."

For Jimmy, this one weird day. Far from anything in the tenement. A white woman getting back to her childhood dream. Best thing for a tenement citizen is watch, listen to this green place tucked way inside secret England.

Weary, looking for the house, Geraldine wants to an odd-one-out. Jimmy wants to stay with the flow. Heaps to hold. But the lady wants charades. Let's do odd ones out.

Jimmy asks what would happen if somebody white should arrive now, that person the odd one out because of coming late? Or maybe Jimmy the odd-job because of colour. If the third person is a white man, would the man be the odd one? *Why*? Because a pair might be so gender as well as colour must get opposed. If female, say her own mother, how would odd-one-out work?

"I need a leak."

"Oh," Geraldine moans, "just do it over there. I'll be the other side of the shed."

Chapter 78

Far from Brixton, a peacock cries. Far from tenement fever sounds across the trees like a huntsman's horn. And not so long ago this place had psychos guffawing at a trapped thing, like a stag at bay. All of that a cosmos from the tenement. Here, no Cootie Williams playing trumpet in Duke Ellington's band. No Mood Indigo in this countryside. Only a peacock crying.

Jimmy calls out. "You OK back there?"

No answer from Geraldine. Rounding the shed, he calls again. But only a trellis. It divides a small secluded place where a tidy lawn backs into postcard blooms. Happy flowers, like they want to say hello. The whole thing like in a TV gala with sound turned off.

"Gardeners get stung by bees," Geraldine chips, "but honey tastes just as sweet!"

Jimmy flops on a flower pot and it breaks. This place could be Zen. And the thing about gardeners and bees, well. A spindle whirring on a godless universe, easy, serene, with no ambition. Only deeds count. And beauty.

To one tenement dweller it looks like the preacher-man enjoys suffering. And a garden called paradise when you die. Some people say flowers are the calling card of paradise. But who believes that when they can grow flowers like these. Blooms blowing in a quiet garden breeze, or flowers in a paradise of wreaths; simple choice from a tenement.

Geraldine's hands thick with soil. Some bouquets get composed to lie and little flowers will bloom from paving-stones in a ghetto but some folk deny that, saying those things between the pavement slabs are not flowers, calling them weeds. But. A solitary hand can point outside the Milky Way, or take cuttings from a garden, or clap loud enough. Even hold and hug.

Jimmy turns to Geraldine. "Gardening is kind of spiritual."

"Hmmm."

"It's better than religion here."

"On second thoughts, maybe you'd better spell that out."

"Gardeners prepare for bees knowing that bees prepare for them."

"Well, just don't call me honey!"

Jimmy living in a tenement, the woman's eyes look like she knows the antidote to bees' stings. Walking towards him, a whirring impishness in Geraldine's eyes. The roof and first-floor of the house focus through a vent in the hedge, like one arrow slit in a battlement. This Renate's secret place. The skylight was put there a year ago. A thread-fine drizzle now. Flecks of rain attract Geraldine's upturned face. Raindrops fall like faded notes on a score and her arms make a circle big enough to tame the whole countryside.

"Who's afraid of the big bad countryside?"

"Not me, lady. Not me!"

"You know, I'm a tiny piece of this. I hopefully have no bees in my bonnet."

Jimmy watching rain quicken. Rain saying, 'Hey, right now!' "Could be rain in a minute. Better head for the house."

"Oh, be a kid again!"

"What if I get wet?"

"Let's show you some *real* birds and bees. Come, let's do the rest of the garden. Rain falls any old time."

Hands signing and signing, the woman giving Jimmy a knowing tour of garden plants. Little Dorrits and striped Pickwicks, over here. To Geraldine *everybody* reads Dickens. But this drizzle getting in the way of book talk. As they hurry towards the house Geraldine points to plants Jimmy has never seen before, with names he's never heard of. Plants called Fritillary, dumb looking, heads look like bowing in reverence. And Tritonia. Wildflower. Dutch Hyacinths dab at walking knees, violets, dawn-tinted and whites, wanting to step from the border, wanting to chat. But only one way to describe what happens now. Rain.

Geraldine could play jazz. This woman can look at irises and see *baleful* and *pale, first-light, sham, incandescent*, and more. But most people catching the same irises see only white flowers.

Red irises might really be impossible to breed. But Renate wants to try. For quite a while the closest to red that gardeners get is the sludge-orange of the Fort Apache variety. Iris-breeders set up house with botanists trying to conjure a red. Even if it takes a hundred more years. But one iris is just for Jimmy: a black lovely, *Swazi Princess*. Geraldine smiles, her head shakes. And Jimmy laughing.

4 o'clock. The rhythm of rain shifting like antelopes. And a quick vegetable soup steams on the table. Restless rain, a torrent streams over double-glazing like bedroom curtain, nothing like a fountain.

The woman says the conservatory got added to the house in a fit by the colonel. But to a one living in a tenement, this quiet glass place is big as a house.

Jazz musicians have it. No colour-tone out of reach to them. They just know the chords to alter or invert, the arpeggio to cascade. Every word is in this woman's head for her mother's irises; as the rain falls she talks again of first-light, sham, incandescent irises.

A piece by Vivaldi, something in D-major playing. But what? Jimmy humming two bars as Geraldine brings the wine. White wine. She unwraps the wet towel from her hair. This is not good. This is danger. How to deal with this? Something here like the night at the theatre, a woman saying nothing. Rain launders over the conservatory and Geraldine's hair gets frizzed by towel. A bottle of wine on the floor between them. Hard not to want it. And want it all. White wine sloshing as she pours.

Rain strafes the clean double-glazing. And a woman here with her shoulders bare.

Jimmy peers through the pelter. "Think rain ever owes the land?"

"Owe?"

"Yeah, owe respect."

"*What*?"

"There's stuff going on between land and water."

"Yes. Evaporation."

"Not only that. There's respect."

"How can water owe respect?"

"You don't want to answer, then."

"Answer what? I mean, no wonder you didn't sleep with Colette!"

"What!"

"You torment yourself with abstract nonsense. What if this, what if that!"

"Better than wanting to be governor of the Bank of England."

Somewhere, someone picking lemons under a hot sun. And it was a day in Liverpool 25 years ago Nathan realized that lemons are great for lemonade but should not get squeezed to fake sunshine.

Geraldine laughs. "You wanted to run the Bank of England?"

"In jazz, you show respect. The greatest ones always finish with something more musical. Charlie Parker, Bud Powell. Vivaldi from classical."

"Vivaldi?"

"Yeah."

"How?"

"If you can forget the 200 years time difference, Vivaldi could pick up his violin and walk straight into Benny Goodman's outfit."

Geraldine steps from the settee. A peeved woman, swashing wine. "Absolutely *loathe* Vivaldi. Too much shirt. Do you know anybody who really appreciates him?"

"He was ace at improvising. Way ahead."

"Could you do me some improvising?"

"At the piano?"

"Yes, please!"

"Naturally."

She grabs the bottle. "Well, show me."

This a baby-grand. Jimmy checks the loud pedal and, with huge gestures, mimes an elaborate concert player. But something wrong. Lydia's vase, the thing with a blue-red hue that only the blood of royal dwarves could bleed. The vase posing on the piano.

The piano needs tuning. Only Art Tatum could play it. Jimmy says Beethoven was already deaf when he got a Broadwood piano from London in 1818. It was the way they explained how the Broadwood was made that made Ludwig warm to it. Geraldine's eyebrows arch. A blind lady with a white cane might remember white, but sighted folk see the white of the cane; that's the deal Jimmy says. Geraldine does not follow. So Jimmy says the piano is blind, he can not improvise it.

"Then let's smash its face in!"

"You're drunk," Jimmy says.

"Well, my libations are my affair."

"Let's get back to the conservatory."

"My piano defeated you. Heh, he-he-heh!"

"You want me to improvise on a big dud."

In the conservatory, Renate's sculpture shimmies through the cool wet glass. The chats that must have happen here! And still happen in German or English. Jimmy wondering.

Geraldine winks. "Still want to improvise? Let's see you improvise with this. Finish this: *My little glass is for wine, my _*"

"What do I do?" Jimmy laughs. "I'm not a wordsmith!"

"Improvise, you know, make something happen! OK, here we go:

My little glass is for wine, my _"

Dorks get off on words. And the biggest dorks on trains. The train trundling nice and easy but dork doing a crossword puzzle. Through the train window the countryside might be quiet like the calm ocean. But dork doing a crossword puzzle. Jimmy will not disappoint Geraldine. The rain making it just right for a parlour game. A drowned garden coming through wide double glazing and she tugs the pullover onto her shoulders.

"OK," Jimmy smiles, "let's try. *My little glass is for wine, my piano can hurt _*"

"*My little glass is for wine, my piano can hurt, but the rain on red grass _*"

"*My little glass is for wine, my piano can hurt, but the rain on red grass stains this woman's skirt.*"

Geraldine grabs the spliff. Her pullover swelling the glass room. Jimmy wants coffee. She says his hands look like clasped in the small of a woman's back. Quiet, careful, he steps away. Careful, moving to the rain glass. She will not see a bad ebony raised rough.

Chapter 79

The clouds spent all their emotion over Hertfordshire countryside. Wet and very green all over. And now the sun.

The letter from Agnes is tidy but, no matter what the rest of the letter could say, the photograph will not go away. "A great time to take that coffee."

Geraldine points at the conservatory carpet. "What do you think of my handiwork? That was little me. I did it myself. The stairs, the lot."

"Fantastic colour scheme!"

"Your type of thing?"

"Yeah. That blue looks so eastern, goes great with the cushions. You did great. The blue carpet cuts great to the green of the lawn. Looks neat."

"Not blue. It's turquoise. We got it in the sales and when it arrived the hardest part was to take that first cut."

Outside is light and bright. Breeze hovers the wash. And a camera is next to a flowerpot in the conservatory.

"Any film in that thing?" Jimmy wonders.

"Yes, I think so."

"Want a snap?"

"Hmmm!"

"I liked that spot by the trees. Or that place with the trellis. Got to get proof of this!"

"Proof?"

"Yeah, to show I was here."

"Sounds a bit ominous, doesn't it? Not planning to come again?"

"You know how I can get wound up."

"You *must* come for a whole weekend some time."

"Yeah, if you'll have me."

"Plenty of space. We can go for walks and pick Renate's brain, have her drool while you play the piano. That piano needs a good seeing to, someone who really can do it."

"Well, if you get back with Brian you won't be here."

"If only."

Geraldine kicks her flip-flops. And scoots outside to the sodden lawn. Jimmy will take the first turn with the camera and, as she skips to the lens, he can almost touch her smile. Set by the clear air,

326

her girly smile hurries from where it forget itself in luster. Just like she has never left this lawn for the world outside.

"Only two shots left. Want one against the house?"

"Got lots of those," she blinks. "Oh, I know! Let's do one together. Lydia will be here in a minute. We can get her to press the button."

"No delay switch?"

"What? Yes, I think there is a thingy. Not sure I can get it to work."

As Geraldine runs off to the house, Jimmy plays the lawn. And plays the dogs. Not what happens in the tenement, no tenement hounds here. Urban planners believe in land. And all the time in some lucky place like this, land getting sweetened by rain.

Geraldine stumbles back from the house and carries a bundle of newspapers. Different clothes, wearing a blue sweater now and tight jeans.

Just before the shutter clicks, they turn one on one. Geraldine smiles. She's never been to the dentist since she was twelve. Jimmy had never noticed before just how sad her eyes can be. For the next snap they link arms and wave at the camera. Then turn to the house, as if it could speak. This is big danger.

For Geraldine this is like the two Olympic skaters. All over again. The memory of them irritates her. In the memory, two swirling skaters leave a strange trail on ice. Their swerving image is hard to forget: the woman's perfume is quick, dashed on, nagging, seeping to the man's vaulting sweat. But it's their chitchats on the ice. That's the problem. Their heads are only sculptures on the sidelines. Their heads are the only bad part, two wooden flaws over empty ice. And their bodies. Their sinew body make some great moves, moves that redeem their wooden head. Their shadow on the ice is so deciduous, so thin, little, gliding down to the frozen wasteland in a stride. One dangerous parabolic glide; what a great move! Two hyperbolas on the axis; great move, *great* move! Olympic skaters dancing and dance, like water stencils maybe, crisscrossing in cold competition light. Over here, this way, this way, try the ice over here! Yes, you can do it, you can do it! Then they slip. The man first. Then the woman, trying to steady him. Flushed, ground grey down, they collect one another in a wistful glance. And in the dream they always zoom to the center of the rink, out and out. TV

327

images of two Olympic skaters never quite go away for Geraldine dreaming them.

5 o'clock. Renate phones. She's half an hour away. Geraldine is drunk. At the far end of the lawn the puppies have something at bay. She grabs Jimmy's sleeve to go see what the racket is.

Add one hour for trying to show what the piano can do, this means he'll be here till well past 7. He imagines the old lady's eyes, grey, flitting from her daughter to him, then back to her Geraldine. Renate sinew.

"What's white, covered in yellow, then covered in blue by evening?"

Jimmy does not understand. But that's Geraldine. A young mischief woman doing riddles. This puzzle nags him. "Say again?"

"Something white," she says, "it's covered with yellow in the morning, then blue by evening."

The answer must be the weather. Or a rainbow. Or a magic carpet that unweaves itself to improve the magic ride. But Geraldine says no, not a rainbow. And no magic carpet.

In music the lucky players have perfect pitch. And sound-tones can link to colours. But *yellow to blue by evening* is different. Geraldine woozy with wine. Jimmy admits defeat. The mischief woman grins. Then, way out the blue, and only for a blink, she points to her bosom under the blue jumper.

"My dear, friend, the answer is my female items. This morning I wore a yellow jumper and now I cover my pale mammary glands in blue."

"Jeez!"

"Hmmm!"

Jimmy nods. "Great riddle."

"Thought you might like it!"

"I do, I do!"

"Well don't count on a repeat. That was your lot!"

The London Eye got officially opened in March. Geraldine went for a rendezvous with Brian and they talked and talked. But all the time the Eye was glistening like a glass necklace on a giantess. And somewhere snowfall was heavier than usual. And somewhere rice was getting gathered in scant fields.

"Woman, you've had too much wine."

328

"Think I'm drunk?"

"You're tipsy. You look sad. Sad tipsy ."

"Think so?"

"Spell *Geraldine* backwards."

"Where's that bottle?"

"Where it should be. Far from you as possible!"

"Race you to the house!"

No time to think. Geraldine racing down the garden. Jimmy will chase. But his mobile drops. And, stopping to get it, remembers a story. They tell it in Jamaica. It's about a woman pirate a long time ago in Port Royal. That menacing lady always dressed like a man, everything about the way she used to hold herself was danger. Then one day she lost a sword fight on the quayside. But at death's door she just managed to rip the front from her shirt. Quick, the rip exposed the goods. The soft surprise. And her adversary was goggle-eyed, paralyzed with surprise. Her sword flashed and sliced the man clean through. And that was because the man did not remember. He was gaping like a man at a woman. But in one flash his adversary changed. And his life.

One bracing run to the conservatory and Jimmy slumping in the doorway. Way out of breath. Geraldine is safe with the day. She comes back from the house to the conservatory with a potted-plant in her hands. Shy, her eyes say 'For you! Today was therapy.' And a tenement dweller getting far from city fever. A pebble skimming water can slow down the ocean reaching the shore.

"I had a great day here today," Jimmy says.

"Glad you enjoyed it. Looking forward to more like it?"

"If you'll have me."

"Here," she says, giving him the plant, "take this. The petals of this little plant will remind you. It's long-flowering. Petals all year."

"I've never had somebody give me a plant before."

"Take care of it. Please."

Chapter 80

No more wine. The potted plant in Jimmy's hands making him think of sad things. Geraldine looks sad. His eyes say it. But she does not want to care. Sad women coming to England from eastern Europe more and more; some of them used to be scientists or engineers but now work in the hostess game, or even direct gigs in the night trade.

Geraldine promising to write, send photographs. Yes. Lots. Plenty of wildlife and landscape, solitude. She can not paint, but will walk with a camera. The door-knocker slams.

Straightaway, Jimmy on edge. Must get to the garden door. Must not seem too at home. Must seem edgy, not calm. Moving by quiet instinct to the door, sets the potted plant down. Grabbing a smoke.

In the body of the house two women's voices exchange. Glad voices, laughing exactly the same. And outside on the plush lawn, the dog and her two puppies play.

Geraldine grins. "This is Lydia. My big sister."

"Your *only* sister," Lydia laughs, offering her hand. "So, you are the single-minded composer, the jazz man!"

Jimmy nods, noting brittle purple nails. "Yes, I suppose so."

Lydia is not a woman that does small talk. Or eye contact. Not with Jimmy. She is taller than Geraldine. And will take a quick coffee then collect her puppy. And oh, will not intrude into the visit here. Jimmy mentions the vase, saying the colour unique but the shape is painful.

Lydia is thin. She wonders what a painful shape might look like. But any tenement dweller could tell it. Funny, but Lydia a bassoon player. Mozart is her special. Earlier today she practiced the full Bassoon Concerto in B-flat Major.

To Jimmy, Lydia talks like a game machine. To someone living in a high-rise, she just too big with talk. The wet garden looking bare from the double glazed conservatory. Geraldine is in the kitchen. And the sun! That thing shining now like it's set for the whole rain it did not prevent today.

Seeing the puppies on the lawn, Lydia shrieks. "Oh, look! There they are!"

"Mozart was only about five feet tall," Jimmy says. "And Stephen

Hawking is the size of a chair."

"I can't see mine," Lydia moans. "Where's *mine*?"

The London Eye is the highest observation wheel anywhere. It has a different motivation to skydivers or turbines. And some folk sit cozy in their capsule on the Eye, talking magic carpet rides and wiping tears of laughing.

"Gerry, I can't see my puppy!"

"Which one do you mean?" Geraldine yells from the kitchen. "There were only four. Those ones are the last two."

"Where's the one with the sad eyes?"

"The one with the blaze on his face?"

"No, no!" Lydia snaps. "The little nigger-brown one."

"Oh, that one!" Geraldine says, coming into the conservatory. "He was the first to go."

Jimmy smears a slow arc in the glass. The arc looks like new angels' wings. Angels have round wings. And this a near perfect arc. And the patio, the spot where the story got told of the swastika in a German forest. But. Time up. In this glass room, time cut, a tempo chit.

Geraldine beside Jimmy. Silent, her lips chalk white. A whey face topped by illness-enlarged eyes. Head dropped. Nothing anywhere is like this. And it is not religion, but the only word that will do this is *godforsaken*. Something godforsaken hauling Geraldine to itself. The woman can not talk.

A man from a tenement must not be here. Some cold thing in this place. Not anguish, not pain. But crowing over the gap between life and mortification.

Chapter 81

Urshell peers into the picture. His eyes clot. Large hands will rent the picture apart. His voice is thunder. "That woman is not for you!"

Jimmy just gets to snatch the picture from the old man. It was really Agnes all along. A phonecall confirmed it. Hard for him to disconnect from how she looked in London, but the woman in the picture looks like she's slackening her mouth to say 'Go on, try me!' And that's not how Agnes ever was. Even when the light low. This photo is cold change. But hard to argue over the old man's judgement of it.

Urshell's head shakes. "You have a difficult situation."

"I know."

"Want to do things right?"

"Yes."

"Then you can *not* move with a woman like that. If you want to get somewhere belonging to you, you have to tell the truth. A spiritual thing. That woman is a lie."

"A *lie*?"

The old man indicates the photograph. "A woman like that will get close, but only a fool would let that happen. A woman like that will use her tears to fool somebody, but one day she will betray a good man. Why let that be you? That woman barely awake but she shouting at somebody. You?"

For two weeks Jimmy's been trying to visit the old black panther. And now, after only five minutes, he knows the score. Only serious talk will follow. Plain talking. The problem with the photograph is huge. To put it back in his pocket will insult the old man. But leaving it on the coffee table, Urshell will destroy it.

Urshell is a Maroon. People like him get to a certain age and mostly will have vision in their soul. Maroons rebelled against slavery in Jamaica and, in the end, the white man was compelled to concede their demands.

Maroons never anti-white. But they are definitely for their own kind. To them, the endpoint of the black man's journey is still far down the road. This particular Maroon's been in England 50 years already. And that's maybe why he talks in three different forms. One is standard English. But most times it's a full-on Jamaican lilt.

The third form is a south London glottal, now and then.

And yes, he's conscious of that all the time but the whole thing just sort of crept up on him over the years. Fifty years? Man! Fifty years in England and he can not believe it, looking at Mrs Urshell and people calling her old. You know you old when a movie on TV that you watched thirty, forty years ago and the actors that used to be older than you by a generation now look young enough to be your son or daughter. But that is something a young man would not understand. And if it's excitement somebody's after, well, Urshell will not want to talk the time he was a black panther.

Jimmy did not resolve the Agnes problem. The whole letter got read, eventually, but that only confused things more. In her letter Agnes talked about getting deeper into the traditional culture. But the photograph a different story. To Urshell, this photo saying Agnes a traitor.

Agnes used to braid her hair. That's how it was all the time she was in London. But now she at home in South Africa, the woman going to a place of torture. She goes to a chemical hell-hole in some back street to torture that woman hair. And do it with chemicals or a hot iron. Why? To make it straight. *Why?* Because in her sediment eye, straight hair making her neater now. *How?* That the part where the lies start.

Something was always silent about Agnes. That woman has hair long enough to braid long, or pile high, or inflate to Afro. But to Urshell this straightened hair in the picture is torture, end of the road. This like somebody high up in a skyscraper crying 'Fire, fire!' But all the time what must get extinguished is inside their own head. Straightened hair is her fantasy? No, not fantasy; the old panther says those women are afraid. They run from facts. And because they have no place to run, they run to the sky. Like a mother ostrich shoving her head in the sand? No, not like a flightless bird. Like a pole-vaulter without a pole? No.

Well, what those women do is sing the blues; yes, what you can call a chain-reaction. And nobody ever seeing them without a smile. But, man! you want to cry because of the hopelessness. A woman slaying Africa through her hair, nowhere to run, so she running to her fake sky to cry 'Fire!'

Jimmy can see. What Urshell saying is simple. This is the old Brixton overcoat. Those women lost. So they button up tight in their Brixton overcoat and smile their sad smile waiting for a map. But Agnes is not even smiling in the photograph; the lady doing something else.

The old man's stout glasses frame his face. "Nervous times, young man. Crucial times!"

"Yes."

"Forty years back, a lot of black women would straighten dem hair. Fifty, sixty years. Those days you had just one show in town."

"So what happened?"

"Well, this is what you can call difficult."

"But there was that black-and-proud thing in the 60s and 70s. You hear it all the time in James Brown tracks."

"Yes, before you came into this world."

"I was born in '75. I listen to that stuff and it clicks!"

Urshell shakes his heavy head. "This thing, it is what you can call Samson and Delilah."

"Biblical?"

"Well, yes."

"I don't believe in the bible."

"A black woman murdering Africa by straightening her hair. And when you ask her why, man! Wid dat torture she tell yu seh she still black, in full control. But you know what? Some o' dem want dem head fe look like a bin liner, the shine-shine plastic bin liner."

"The bag in the dustbin?"

"Yu understan' dat?"

Jimmy turns to the old man. "Yeah, you're talking waste."

"Another generation lost!"

"Yes."

"Delilah destroyed Samson. But every time a black woman put a hot comb in her head, a black man turn into a mimic. Son, you must walk from that!"

The photograph is back in Jimmy's hands. The old man takes a shot of rum. Clears his throat. And takes the reading glasses in his hands to clean them. Feeling cut off, Jimmy mentions a weird set of images. Since the photo of Agnes arrived there's been a weird dream. A kind of nightmare. The images starts with being high in a glider and seeing women on a beach. A thousand women, standing still. The glider gets low, must get a close look. But then it's the mothers of friends. And, wait, friends' lady friends. Even his own

334

mother on the beach. The beach is loaded with black women. Only black? Every woman in the dream with laminated hair, or wearing a white a woman's wig to scratch. And the weirdest thing is how they all in that one place, on the beach together. Then the glider goes back. Lower this time. It's their eyes. Their eye tells of hurt. Only longtime weariness in their eye. They want to please, to oblige. But have only longitude for eyes. And cheerleaders stepping up among them, fingers twirling expert in false hair.

The old man grabs his heart. "That is a hell of a dream," he says, eyes cropped.

At absolute zero, substances can contain no heat energy. And it is only at a small range of temperatures that a fake can cause havoc. Jimmy confesses. Telling Urshell the dream is only a jazz-opera that will get fully composed one day. *Jazz*? Yes. Sometimes it's hard, because dreams dice with vibes. Then it is not a dream. Well, maybe it was only vibes at twilight.

Difficult for Jimmy facing up to what must get done. Agnes is difficult. She should be the one making the way easier. But that will wait. He turns from the photograph. And mentions the other reason being here to see the old man.

For a week, it was walking round with what happened that day in Geraldine's conservatory. Some days were like being a stowaway in the 8th floor tenement, like trying to sus security barriers at immigration control.

Anxious for a smoke, Jimmy must tell Urshell the whole story. But the old man does not allow smoking. Drink a jug of rum, that's fine. Get groggy on malt whisky. But absolutely no smoking here.

An hour after leaving Geraldine's glass and green, Jimmy was back in town. Back in the inner-city. And being glad, back in the safe old familiar. And saying a quiet 'Thanks!' to the streets.

Tottenham High Road was jammed. Saturday shoppers moving it along, but Geraldine's image was hard-wired. It was the crowds. Gazing at the crowds, trying for that one hue in somebody's face, a colour saying *nigger-brown*. The black faces going by had every hue; folk in colours from jet-black to Mediterranean tan. Jimmy looked at his own face in the rear-view mirror. But the bustle in the streets was too random. So the car stopped. And he waited. Waited, watching for that one colour. That fatal hue. People were going by, coming, going, hurrying and taking it slow. Black people along Tottenham High Road on a Saturday evening. Eventually, it had to happen. The evening shut down. Crowds dwindling to nothing and shops closing. Later that night it was being alone and doodling at the keyboard, whisky sloshed, and ganja cloudy in air. Then things got clear. All of a sudden things clear: whatever *nigger-brown* was, only somebody white could pick it out. Messing about at the keyboard stopped. Nothing known to music was big enough. The view of night from the 8th floor window was like fake star-ships. And whoring jump-if-you-want lights below. Crazy lights. Where were those cars going? Somebody, somewhere, would know. But who? No answer from the keyboard. Deep into night it was a search and searching, testing the keys. Minor chords, diminished, whole-tone arpeggios, minor, major, over and over, trying to get it. Trying to understand. One evening soon after they first met, Geraldine said she wasn't properly up to speed with race. Serious in eye, she said that that didn't mean there was any racial in her psyche. Well, when her sister said *nigger* Geraldine was where she at. She was the same place as her sister. It was 9 o'clock next morning when she phoned; on her way to Ireland, but wanting to square things. Jimmy listened to the white woman. It was Geraldine talking, saying this and saying that. But what point believing? After the call it was more confusion but, weird, remembering the good times. Remembering her kindness. This the difficult part. And that's because it's hard to tell. Maybe a word can be more than a word. A word can be something that sneaks up. Like a virus? *Nigger* may never get used directly by but it could all the time be dormant in a language-mind. But wait. What that mean? Clutching at straws, pulp psychology, mickey mouse? Somewhere a room full of field marshals and tone deaf philosophers shake their logic-beribboned heads. But Jimmy built a spliff. Cold fire, half-consoling. And he knew. Even if Geraldine never directly said it, she used the n-word: she recognized it as a label fit.

And that's because if somebody should suddenly shout 'Nigger!' and a street-load of people turn to look, then nobody that turns round expects to see a white man. But can any white say that after turning round they didn't see a nigger, that all they saw was a black man?

Chapter 82

Jimmy disbelieves. "*Good* news?"

Urshell says it again. "Yes, good news."

"Good?"

"Good news is there. You are what you can call lucky."

"Lucky?"

"Yes, the two parts of good luck. The private part of the white woman got restless with her public life."

"What?"

"Yu in a room wid no heat an' de white woman put yu in touch wid de fire."

"*What*?"

"The woman in the photograph, well, she put you in touch with the sun. To learn things like that, that is special. And," he leans over, shaking hands with Jimmy, "to know something like that makes you a very lucky man!"

"*Me,* lucky?"

The old man gets his glasses from the coffee table. And, shaking his head, his hands begin to burnish the lenses. Heavy lenses. Old hands, smudging, burnishing.

Jimmy blinks. "Trying to work out how I'm lucky."

"Anything was going on between you and the white woman?"

The night of the theatre. After picking up the condoms at the late-night chemist Jimmy asked himself what exactly was going to happen. Hurrying back to the hotel to get cozy? Or wage war? Was Colette going to substitute for Geraldine? Maybe that's why he turned back for a second packet after getting the first. But Geraldine is not Colette.

"No," Jimmy says, trying to sound decisive. "Nothing physical."

"Then what yu do? Play strawberry and cream?"

Jimmy does not answer the old man. After the rain in Hertfordshire at her mother's house it was while doing the photos with Geraldine that a twinge happened between them. For a minute a soft twinge on the wet lawn. For that minute, no longer friends. Only man and woman. But nothing got said. And maybe that's why nothing was said. Geraldine's conservatory was a place of burnished glass. And good white wine. And the really big thing must have been the conversations taking place down the years in that same glass room; down the years that family must have looked out at the seasons and bonded. Sipped tea, gin. Faced the wordless green of the countryside.

Urshell coughs. "Know something? Man, you turned into a white person to that young woman. The white girl. Son, your black balls got lost. Because *you* got lost."

"Turned into white? *Me*?"

"Watch TV?"

"Sorry?"

"You ever watch TV?"

"Well, yeah. Naturally."

"Then you have the answer."

Jimmy knows Urshell is no Miles Davis. But something spare is here. Something as sure about the old man as Miles was ever sure on a track. "Mr Urshell, I need your help."

"Son, let me try. You and the white girl, man! The two of you were like watching TV together. A nice little story."

"A fiction?"

"What you did with the woman was a story. But the two of you did not consider the players. You and she, playing a game round one another!"

"I told how it was, but you think something else happened!"

Urshell turns to the room. Jaws clenched. Gazing at the picture above the mantlepiece. "With commercial TV you get too much sell. Advertise dis, advertise dat. Shit left, shit right. But you and the woman, the two of you! It was like you fooling round in different parts of the city."

Jimmy leans from his chair. "How does nigger-brown come out of that?"

"When your white friend said nigger-brown, that _"

"It was her sister! It was the bitch who actually said it."

"When your friend agreed with nigger, that was always in the story. Always there. But you wanted a belief thing to happen."

"*Belief?* I don't get it!"

"Man! How do I get through to you?"

"If you think I'm too slow, I'll leave."

"Son, when I get under pressure, I mean *pressure*, what happens is one bad Jamaican to the rest of the world. That is my private self. Understand? The white woman was under pressure. Her private self

338

was restless with her public self. Simple as that."

"Me and her, we were only play-acting?"

"Playing, no. You can not watch your own back. Learn that!"

Geraldine always accepted Jimmy as a man. The story between them was always iffy, but always as friends. But then her language. That *nigger* word rejecting all black people. Rejecting him to the core.

Jimmy needs a smoke. "Mr Urshell, you said there was good news and bad news. What's the bad part?"

"Young man, you have what you can call a fantasy. Two of them. But you can let go if you want to let go."

"Two?"

"The first thing is Africa."

"Hey, I've never been to Africa!"

"A few young guys like you believe you can get inside Africa if you have a woman from Africa. Well, no man can get to Africa because of a woman. Not even a hundred women. Where," the old man laughs, "would little you live with one hundred women?"

"What's the second fantasy?"

"That is the easy one. Man, guys like you! You believe you can stop racial if you get fancy talk from middle-class white folk."

"What?"

"Listen! The big story of the black man is not slavery, not even what you can call *we shall overcome*. The great story of the black man is the dream a person will have. When people have the same dream, man!"

Above the old mantlepiece, Mandela's portrait is ever present. But somehow not really in the room. Overseer, seer. A father. Or patriarch. A grandfather, friend.

Jimmy nods. "Sometimes I dream of lions. Them, round me."

"Your white friends, they want to hear that? You, you know about that?"

Jimmy only half understanding. The old man getting too mystic. Too difficult. Too much twine in his soul. Too much to unravel. Somebody like Stephen Hawking can come along, someone with a safety string in the Minataur's labyrinth and soon everybody crying 'Stephen, show the way!'

"Got any white friends, Mr Urshell?"

"What?"

"Why'd you stay in England? If I was born somewhere else I wouldn't be here."

Urshell glares at the palms of his hands. His head shaking. Grey and wry. "England is a funny place."

"I couldn't be born somewhere else and get old here."

"Son, England will talk to you."

"Like when?"

"Well, everyone must give and take."

"We give, they take!"

"You have give and take going on out there."

"Yeah? Like where?"

The old man's hands clasp. Hands that remember pouring paraffin like wine, or striking matches in bed-sit rooms to dine. Urshell was in England before Tony Blair was even born. All those summers. And the rest of it. Seasons coming and going. Quiet, Jimmy wondering if hands like the old Jamaican's could ever have cast seedlings into England's winter soil.

Urshell slaps his knees. "One night, three years back, some white fellows are making a heap of noise out front. Evil noise. There must be six, seven of them. Anyway, I get outside to see what is going on. And, man! They have pissed all over the fence. Drunk. Anyway, I ask them to clean up the piss. One guy tell me seh dem can piss whe' dem like because it is their country. I ask him if the fence belong to him. Him seh 'No.' So I ask him who will clean the fence. According to him I must clean it. I ask him why. Him seh I must do it because it is my fence."

"You fronted a bunch of white boys, at *your* age? What, without a weapon?"

"Well, yes and no. All the time I had that old poker up my coat sleeve."

"*Yes!*"

"Anyway, my next-door neighbour is a white man and he could hear the commotion out front. He is what you can call an old boy, like myself, but him come straight out, him and a cricket bat into the night. And, brother! Dem tek one look, an' dem know seh my neighbour is the business. *Real* business. An' dem back the hell off. That was one of the most beautiful things to happen. Gets me what you can call sentimental. Anyway, I get back into the house and meditate on it. Yes, the fence can be mine."

"But the country is their country."

"Young man, that is England."

The fence can be yours but the land might not belong to you. The fence is where you keep things, in or out. Or where you show what you have. Or the place your neighbour meets you.

"Then why d'you stay?"

"What?"

"Don't you think living here is a cage?" Jimmy says.

"Where?"

"Living in England."

"*Cage*?"

"Yeah, a hold zone."

"Listen, I met my wife here. My daughters are born here, four of them. The second girl, she 'ave her own likkle business. The next girl is a bank manager. The next one doing finance with the council, and the last girl is a TV journalist. England give dem dat opportunity. If I had stayed in Jamaica maybe it could have worked out. But not so well. No, not so well."

"Five daughters?"

"Yes."

"No sons?"

"None."

"What's happening with daughter number five?"

Urshell old, grey. Ups slow from the chair. Old man remembering. Getting to a hazed place. "Alberta, she was my first born. That was in Jamaica. She came along before I left the island. My great-grandchildren come from her."

"Tell me about your friend," Jimmy says. "The white man next door."

The old man steps to the mantlepiece. "Well, what is a friend?"

"How d'you mean."

"Man, whe' yu come from! You don't know what is a friend?"

"Well, it's a weird question."

"So wha' 'appen?"

"I think it's someone you can trust."

"How many people trust you?"

"A few."

"How many people you trust?"

Jimmy twitching for a smoke. "Well, one or two."

341

"If you mess up, your friends absolve you?"

"You mean like forgive? Well, yeah."

"You, you forgive your friends?"

"Naturally."

"Then, young man, I have just one friend. And that is my fence."

"The *fence*?" Jimmy frowns. "The fence is your friend?"

"No fence, no friend."

"What?"

"Simple as that!"

"Then how come you stayed in England so long? Why'd you get old here? Why didn't you go back to Jamaica? Why not go back now? I do *not* understand."

Urshell already looking way past Jimmy. Years doing taxi-driving means he can tell. Somebody in a hurry is somebody you can read. Ambling to the door, he calls out to his daughter. "Annette! Bring some tea. Tea please, Annette."

Maybe only because of needing a smoke, but Jimmy queasy. The old man's unblinking eyes have not strayed from his. Reading him like any street map. A spliff, even a quick cigarette would help. And that's because of two black men talking of racism while willing to sip tea from a front room in England. And to make matters worse a helicopter circles overhead, its old propellers droning out unremitting noise. The 'copter sounds like it wants to land in Urshell's back garden. And spite, the way it hovers in the night. As it moves away, Urshell mentions it was a police helicopter. The old man makes a really strange request, asking Jimmy to guess if the pilot was a black policeman.

A woman comes into the room, a stunning Jimmy. She says a shy hello, puts a tea-tray on the coffee table.

Urshell is proud. "This one is my youngest one. This is the baby. The last one to fly the nest. One week from now and you will be a married woman, eh Annette?"

Jimmy knows the old man is watching all his moves. But his eyes can not leave the woman. She twenty two and, as she moves away, exactly one day older.

Annette directs her eyes at Jimmy as she grabs the door. "Yes!"

"Sorry?"

"The guy I'm getting married to *is* a lucky man. That's what you were going to say, wasn't it?"

342

Chapter 83

Urshell came to England from Jamaica in 1950. He was twenty four years old. His father a staunch church-goer and was in the air force during in the war, staying with England before deciding to settle. Urshell was supposed to become a tailor. And maybe even build cloth on Saville Row. But cutting cloth was way down the scale, too dull for the sunshine Jamaica boy. And every place he got a start they took him for a fool; some things he could do great they said he would still have to learn to do, but do it their way. So he quit. And moved around, job to job. Moving north, dawdling round in the Midlands, checking north and south. Then one day the wanderer turned into a van driver. And that was how the swerving started. High with miles.

At first it was only local wheels. Delivering this and that. Groceries, second-hand furniture, anything.

Then the big one. The bright nighttime. It was a job with a top Jamaican sound-system, carrying stuff all round the country. Nightclub slots, late night house-parties. In the fifties and sixties was deep anxiety over the war years. Vera Lynn was the voice, the mood. She did ballads that moved the national healing along. And, years later, they could not have penned *Don't cry for me Argentina* if it was not for Vera. Even now, she is deep down in the national reassurance. Folk called her the forces' sweetheart, so much heart was in those war-time ballads that lady used to sing.

Eventually, England wanted something else. Something hot and dangerous. But not war. And one new music was it. To start, it was guys calling their noise *skiffle*. But a few talented people happened along; cabaret guys like Lonnie Donnegan and Tommy Steel. And a black musician called Hutch was gigging in London. Hutch a jazz piano player with white folk wanting to party him all night.

Jazz in England was only smalltime. The radio played Glenn Miller. But Glenn's music had no snap. It was not swing. And maybe it was never even jazz. And then, on a local scale, guys like Kenny Ball and Acker Bilk happened along. But they never got to bebop. Bebop was way too difficult for most folk here.

Then again. Whether in England or Jamaica, most Jamaicans did not incline to jazz. Even Ernest Ranglin had to take his guitar out of Jamaica, get to America to set jazz-legs; same for Monty Alexander

343

on piano.

Jamaica got to independence in 1962. And black community after community developed in England. Jamaican music was the glue. And the buzz. Ska, blue-beat. And rock-steady was dancing it slow. Jamaica was in London, Birmingham, Manchester, Bristol. Every city. And the house-parties they used to have, man! And the she-beens! With Jamaican music it was the first time England ever got music in one private house that you could hear ten streets away. But all dat? Only innercity nighttime. Years and years.

Then the mid sixties. The whole sixties came along. But it was young white guys that made a difference. Some of them got far into Jamaican music. Black music in general. Those white guys turning up at the black clubs and getting serious in the whole Jamaican culture. Even now, UB40, white and black playing black music. In the 60s, Eric Clapton turned up at the Flamingo nightclub in London to play blues and learn Jamaican music from guys like Rico Rodriguez. And Prince Buster, Jackie Edwards. Eric the first white guitar player with a serious way of blues. English folk called him god. Well, till Hendrix touched down here in '66. Jackie Edwards was the mellow man, the Jamaican crooner on the England subculture; he penned two UK number one hits for the Spencer Davis Band in the 60s. Man, those days! Flamingo nightclub was the place. Prostitutes, pimps and other night folk coming out the night to wind down. And way before anybody was a hippy, Carnaby Street was the place for music into night; the nightclub in Carnaby Street had a Jamaican guy named Count Suckle running the show. And Georgie Fame. They had Georgie Fame gigging there. And he was a white guy that nobody ever remembered was white. White guys turned up at Jamaican house parties and learned 10-rizla spliffs, grooving along. And a good few dressed like Jamaican rude-boys. But all that was wallpaper to Urshell. He remembers noticing the white girls that turned up at every house party. Only one or two at the start, but more and more. And mostly it was runaways, sad females needing a place to crash. Or it was brute force nymphomaniacs looking for big black whammy. Some of those girls paired off with parasite black guys. Devious pimps.

Urshell has never been with a white woman. All the time he's been here, only ever checked black. In the early England years he was a serious Jamaican face-man and his looks pulled him along

344

from place after place. And that was to some of the sweetest black women on the planet; well, the ones here. Lonely nurse girls. And a face-man could pick off all the sly hairdressers and ambitious typists. Sometimes Urshell would go back to a nurses' home with one woman and find pure booty, woman after woman alone. And him! Working through them, one woman at a time, one wing of the nurses' home at a time. At one time he was even living in a nurses' home, sneaking in, sneaking out, shacked up full time with a nurse in her room.

The big communal was music. A good DJ of a top sound-system could pull heavy money. Jamaican music was bigger than white folk could believe, dazzling with nighttime and dark. And folk from other Caribbean spots. And folk from Africa. But it was Jamaican music doing the doing. And ganja.

Life was never peace and love. Serious ructions happened from time to time. Two guys fighting could be 'bout dis or dat. And Jamaicans fighting in the night would always end in blood. One man using a knife, another man used a bottle. Somebody else walk wid a razor. Urshell remembers one red night. Two Jamaican guys squared up over a woman and before the second guy could blink the first guy walked a knife across his eyes. Dropped to his knees, blood flow. Blood, calling on Jesus Christ. In the night, Jesus Christ. Blood was too purple in the night. Somebody lose dem eye, dem two eye in front o' yu. Losing sight, never going to see again. Man, that was just one night going wrong.

Nowadays you don't see guys bothering with the knife too much. Nowadays every psycho getting a gun. And the business is dem only use gun 'gainst another black man. White is like holy to them. Dem never shoot white. No matter how Africa get ransack, deny, no matter seh dem modda get crock by redneck, black shoot black. Or the obliging ones go to church to sing a hymn. Or appease on TV.

In the fifties it was different. Even as late as the eighties Jamaican music was deep down. Way down from a true heart. The black community was serious about itself. And even if somebody got cut, mostly nobody died. Not the way murder going on these days. Black murdering black. But back in the 60s and 70s, Jamaican music was the magic bandage. And to get to the best house-party, black folk coming from all over. Yes, yes. And guys standing along, meditating, alone or with spars. And ganja from JA. And, man! Sharash was something the police did not know back then; guys walking with a whole weight of sharash and the police search them but never understand. But it was the house-parties. And she-beens, party business wid Barley wine an' curry-goat.

Music was the thing. Jamaica music. And black woman from any place. The sweetest kind. Sweet black lady wind dem body. Music a play, an' de woman dem in a dem nighttime dress. And nutt'n was good as a woman wha' smile an' wind her body. Jamaican woman swerving her honey in the night. Nothing. And if the woman was right, you hold on to Jamaica all night! And wid all dat, yu smoke an' smoke. And smoke. And all the time the bass-line pounding the room, the whole house, the street outside, the next street. And the next street. Bass line pounding your *whole* life.

Jamaica bass line was heartache in your life. You longed for Jamaica, longing. And when you closed your eye this was no house-party, no shebeen. Man, this place was Jamaica.

It was Friday or Saturday night. The world could wait. Monday, it was back to work. But the rude-boys had different runnings; those guys used to do backstreet business, the type police investigate. But with regular work it was maybe cleaning a factory, or driving bus, or a white boy on a building site know your name but calling you John and tell you to unload that lorry.

Some people used to work seven days a week, having family back home, urgent money for shoes or medicine or pay rent. Or a man that was maybe forty-five might have a mother and father back home and four kids to send money to. But while the music play and a sweet woman smile her beauty across the room, that was what you looked to. And grounding with your brethren. To smoke, and smoke. Smoke Jamaica ganja wid yu bredren.

This went on for years. Way into the seventies. And the eighties. Then things changed.

Things got diluted down. And Urshell himself changed. Had to change. Got married. He remembered he was a Maroon. His duty to live clean. And after his third daughter was born, it was time to think. Time to accept he never might have a son. And the impact of that was him retreating from the way of the street. By then he was already past forty and not knowing he was to have two more daughters. And no sons. But in a funny sort of way, Urshell did not quit

346

the streets. Not all the way. Urshell was a bus driver for years. And the last years he worked as a taxi driver in London. Nowadays, it's trips to Jamaica, still learning, reconnecting with Maroon roots. Urshell was one time a dangerous woman predator. But things change. Now , an old man with five daughters and a head full of black folk history. Vibes master. An old man looking out the window and watching England go by. Then one day he will die here, never see Jamaica from under Jamaica soil.

Chapter 84

Anybody that can play every one of Chopin's etudes can play anything on piano; the huge technical answers, sheer keyboard sonority. Then again. Maybe *etudes* is not the word. And the same with lions; checking out lion attitude, talking to a caged lion in London Zoo, dreaming them.

Urshell is misty eyed. "Somebody that can dream lions? That is a one that will go where they must go."

"Sometimes I don't even know which way is which."

"Go a place a lion could respect you."

Jimmy nods to Mandela on the wall. "Like that guy?"

"Mandela is the great example. Just one glance, *one* glance, and you know a man that a lion will respect."

"Even in a city?"

"A man must be confident in himself. No circus lions. No funny blokes with earrings. No sun donkey!"

So far, this meeting with Urshell has been top seriousness. Jimmy here for two hours already. And laughing now, thinking of a donkey with a straw hat & dark-glasses, a donkey sipping Coca Cola under a bad sun.

"What's a sun donkey?" Jimmy laughs.

Urshell ups from the chair. "A sun donkey? Man, that is a black individual with blond dye. Red hair dye, yellow die, what you can call unnatural. Black man, black woman having that blond dye."

Learning a new language, Jimmy grabs at the smokes in his pocket. But in a strict no-smoking zone; the old man's eyes say 'Take it or leave it!' People of colour turning into thrill seekers. And the biggest thrill of all is denying the ethnic. All because of *black*. That word the big fake. It is not suitable for everyone with Africa in their blood. And that's because all people derive from Africa. Even the white man. Cosmetic this, cosmetic that, *black* getting to a point with no meaning at all. So it must go. It can not cope, can not describe some folk. Only bruised hearts and ethnic folly. No, not even bruised. Black and blue. Right now some women use skin lightening cream. They torture Africa to deny.

Jimmy respects Urshell. And that's why only the right answer will work. "Why didn't you go back to Jamaica?"

"You *know* Jamaica?"

"Never lived there. But I've visited."

"Let me tell you about JA. Every two years, myself and the family go out there. But the plan was always to go back."

"Then why not go back now?"

"Man, you move too fast."

"Is it that multiracial thing you like about London?"

"Son, you moving too fast."

"Jamaica is the place for multiracial. But you know that already, a lot better than me."

"Well, yes. In Jamaica you have what you can call a big mix-up. Black folk, white people, Chinese, Indians from Madras. Even a little Arawak blood in a few people."

"Arawak?"

"Arawak was the first folk in Jamaica."

"Indigenous?"

"Long before white and black."

"It was the mixed thing I noticed. It was everywhere."

"Maybe fifteen percent of Jamaican people are what you can call visible mix-blood. Twenty five percent have invisible blood. All over the island, mix-up wid dis, mix-up wid dat. We call them the brown Jamaicans. Calling everybody black, man, what a mistake! Jamaican brown people is what you can call a new folk. From Africa, yes, but not only Africa."

"If you went back to Jamaica you'd have deeper thoughts. You are a Maroon. You should be in Jamaica, living among Maroons. Not get old here and getting called a black bastard."

Urshell weighs a heavy rum tumbler in his hand. "Jamaica? That little island? JA is the most beautiful place in the world!"

"Then go back!"

"What?"

"You can take your pension from here."

"Snow on Blue Mountain. Humming bird. The sea."

"And honey women!"

Urshell turns to the door. His jaws clench. Then turns back to Jimmy. "Yes."

"Don't you miss those things?"

"Every day. Even after fifty years living here. Man, yu go a some a de smaller place dem and a woman a cook her food out in a de open. The sweetness of that will make you cry. The simple things,

349

son. The simple things."

"Yes, yes! But why d'you really stay here?"

"Why I stay?"

"Too difficult?"

"What?"

"Is it too difficult?"

"How?"

"Too hard to find the words?"

"Well, four of my daughters born here. And then I have my grandchildren that were born here. And, you know, you can get to like a place. You get to like a place that you live there for so long. I would miss springtime here. The leaves. Son, never take those leaves for granted. Some days is no place better than England.

"When I first came, it was what you can call different. We could *not* believe how grey things was. The sky grey. And the houses, even the birds was bleak! I used to beg my father, please send me back to Jamaica. And the weather. *Cold?* We had was to live in two rooms and those days, man! No central heating for working class folk. Black folk had was to have a paraffin heater on all day. Everything was grey."

"When you made your own money, why didn't you _"

"Which money?"

"Enough money from the van driving. You could have gone back and set up your own business. Why didn't you dust the grey and go back?"

"Well, after a while you realize. Things was not simple. The people here could smile. For a period of time you just did not notice a white person could smile true. Not smile. Dem was always in a hurry. *Morning! All right? Oh Good! Nice to see you. Bye-ee!* Man!"

"Yeah," Jimmy laughs. " It's the smile-the-smile game!"

"But you got used to them, you could get the true smile."

"Sure. But what about Jamaica?"

"Jamaica? Every time I go home I _"

"See, you said it!"

"What?"

"You said *home*. I knew it!"

Urshell smiles. "In Jamaica, people call me a foreigner. Even my own family. You get what you can call suspicion there. No, more a
350

kind of tension. A sort of a tension. Jamaican folk believe because you live in England you have money. Man, I have this cousin and dat guy do me a ting las' time I was out there. I and the wife was getting ready to get to the airport and this guy a look pa' mi shoes, him wan' me fe tek off me shoes an' gi' dem to him!"

"And did you?"

Urshell grits his teeth. "Another thing, in Jamaica they expect a man my age to go to church. But the noise! I could not stand the noise. Too much hand-clapping, people dem a shout. Wha' Massa God mus think!"

"Old man, I'm not religious."

"No. A one don't have to deal with that business in England. You don't have to go to church here. No sir!"

"And your daughters got a good education here."

"University education. One son-in-law is a science lecturer. Education, son. Education!"

"Education is *not* why black people stay."

"You, why yu stay?"

Jimmy grabs at the smokes in his pocket, stumbling to his feet. Then remembers. Sits back in the chair. And folds his arms. "It's weird, but I feel kind of connected here."

"Because?"

"There's things I have to do. And listen, I was born here. Even my mother was born here and they don't even know where her birth parents came from."

"I can not speak for anybody but myself, but mek a tell yu someting. A lot of funny business going on."

"That's why I've come to see you. You have the answer."

"The answer? Me? *I* do not know the answer, son. God will know the answer. You don't believe in God?"

"No!"

"A young man, so sure. God too big fe any man. Young or old."

"Then where was this god thing when black folk got scooped into the slave ships?"

In one gas-chamber crush, a chief rabbi from Poland invited God to show divine power, intervene, put things right, chastise the nazis and teach the world.

Urshell turns to Jimmy. "Well, my young friend, it was not God that wasn't there in that slave business. It was the devil that was.

351

Slavery was the easy part."

"What?"

"Slavery was the easy part of the black man story. The hard part up ahead, round the corner. A dog can shed yu blood. But no liar can repair history. Learn dat!"

"*What?*"

"A liar can not fix history."

"And this god thing is, what, the fixer?"

"You want my opinion, you have my opinion."

"God does *not* do it for me!" Jimmy huffs. "That praying, that dumb groping around, blind groping, asking for things from something that never answers back."

"Man, you lost your faith!"

"The New Testament says 'Wherever two or three are gathered in my name, there will I be.' Know that?"

"Yes, I know it."

"Then how d'you explain kids getting raped by priests?" ·

"Well, _"

"Raped!"

"Yes."

"Inside the church building!"

"Yes. Or a black congregation getting bombed in America."

"Yes."

"No, I can not explain."

"Old man, Mr Urshell, there's better ways to make it."

The mystic picture of Nelson Rolihlahla Mandela. It oversees the room here. In his autobiography, Mandela says 'i can not pinpoint when i became politicized, when i knew i would spend my life in the liberation struggle.'

Urshell's read the book. Five times. "Well, you have making it. And then you have *making* it."

"Where's the part where they don't call you nigger?"

Somewhere in a plush multi-millionaire house tonight, Margaret Thatcher revising her memoir. Or toying Vermouth and scrambled eggs, watching TV. And maybe her eye darts from the sideboard picture of her son to Tony Blair on Newsnight.

Urshell smiles, wry. "Sir, you are what I call a tricky customer. A tricky, tricky customer!"

"Because I don't believe in religion?"

352

"What about your future? You believe in your future?"

"How's that connect to getting called nigger?"

"For a smart person, you too sure of yourself."

"When it comes to my future, you're dead right I'm sure!"

"Then, I can not help you."

"You want me to go?"

"You known," Urshell grins, "one evening a few years back a white fellow ask me if black people have ten times as much boy babies as girl babies."

"What?"

"Yes, it was a bloke wanting to understand how so many black boys are with white girls. This was outside the London jamboree they keep every year for celebrity black folk. All the black guys, every one of them was with a white girl. I was in big trouble."

"Trouble?"

"Man, it was a throwback! Embarrassing. It was the black and white minstrel show. Yes, all over again."

"*Minstrel*?"

"A minstrel show. They used to have it on TV. That was from 60s. The Black & White Minstrels, a situation with showbiz white folk using black boot polish on dem face to pretend."

"*What*?"

"White folk blacking up on stage?"

"*Why*?"

"Well, that is what I mean by *making* it"

"How? *How*?"

"Dem used fe 'av diss white bloke a black up, Al Jolson."

"American, wasn't he?"

"Yes."

"The one blacking up to sing 'Mammy, mammy!' on stage?"

"Yes. A him wha' start dat."

"Yeah, and black entertainers cunked their hair. Nat Cole. Even Ellington. I've seen those old films. Man, black guys with smarmy hair gel!"

"That stuff was on the TV all the time, son. The minstrel show was every Saturday night and, you know, we would just sit and observe. But after a period of time a few of the black people born here said it was liberties, taking liberties, and dem get de show tek off de air. Yes, 1978."

"That's the part where nigger comes in? I don't get it."

"For an educated fellow, you take long."

"White people with boot polish on their face, *that* gives nigger?"

"No. Not by itself."

"*How*?"

"At the black celebrity bash, de jamboree wid all dem famous black guy, all the boxer boy dem, and the football players, the entertainment black people, all the black folk on TV, *every* single one of them arrived with a tuxedo and a white girl. Every one a dem. Man, it was minstrel town!"

"Minstrel fetish."

"That is how the white bloke believe black people must have ten boy baby for every little girl. Not one black guy was with a black girl."

"Maybe," Jimmy rustling for a smoke, "it was a coincidence."

"*Coincidence?* Son, three or four would be natural. Nine or ten would be what you can call this coincidence business. But it was every single one of them."

"*All* of them?"

"All a dem! All dem celebrity black guy, dem get into a money situation in life and dem mus' get a white girl. Dat ting out deh all de time. Black celebrity wid dem nightmare 'bout Africa."

In Israel, some people do not like the fact of being in the same Jewish ballpark as Falashas. And that's because the Falashas come from Ethiopia. And Ethiopia in Africa. In Israel, the Law of Return says if you Jewish anywhere then you can settle in Israel. But the Falashas black. And Israel still wondering how they can be Jewish. But all the while Israel accepted folk from what was the Soviet Union, hundreds of thousands of them, even when Israel knew by evidence that half those people can not be Jewish. But they white. Most people do not know Moses married a woman from Ethiopia.

"No dreams of lions," Jimmy groans. "Only pantomimes."

"What?"

"Mimics in pantomimes. Fake role-models. Duds with nightmares of Africa."

"Son, now yu dressin' a wound that will not heal."

"I'm trying to understand."

"This whole thing simple."

"I don't think it's simple."

354

"Then let's do it the hard way. Give me the name of one celebrity black guy with a black lady in England. One name!"

Right now in Zanzibar, and even some spots in Britain, some women wear the niqab. This veil was to protect them from the sun in desert climes but some city women say the veil is their religion. And maybe if a man gives a woman a rose, it does not have to mean seeing her mouth smile. Even galaxies wear veils. Until the right telescope comes along.

Jimmy twiddling, wanting a smoke. The old man says mimicry is to blame. In recent times it was guys mimicking Bob Marley.

"Dem believe Bob was talking to dem. Even young guys believe Bob was in some kind of talk with them, guy dat only know Bob by him photograph. But no man can know if Bob was talking alone. Bob was looking for his father. Bob never discussed that father business but some people could see what was bugging him. Good people know dat. Yes, Bob would meditate on why everybody in Trench Town have a blacker skin. It used to bug Bob."

Jimmy nods. "Yeah, my old man accuses the mimics. The false-heads."

"Dat false-head business start wid a record contract. Jamaica was a place where man used to walk the same street as Bob. Serious man, man like Bunny Wailer. But nobody was like Bob to a white guy name Chris Blackwell. It was Bob, him light skin."

"Chris is a white Jamaican. Exactly like Bob's own father."

"Chris born a London."

"But he was in Jamaica from childhood."

"Chris Blackwell come from a Jamaica plantation family."

"Bet Bob got the score!"

"Well, you know, man fe talk deep wid him own father. Dat natural. Bob talk when him sing. Rasta know dat, and it never stop Rasta."

"How do they deal with the mimicry?"

"Rasta over dat! Listen, every hypocrite must face up. Now a de time fe man up! Face the truth. Mimic fe look in a dem own face an' check if dem father look like Bob father, even like Bob himself."

"Man!"

The old man's head shakes. "Son, when you only have girl children, you have just one safe place in this life. Only one direction you can travel. One day you get old and you know what is out there. So you try to keep your daughters from certain type of guys. My daughters are black women, son. They would not be good enough for them tuxedo black guys. To guys like them, black women are not delicate enough."

"That's a load of bull!"

"Yes."

"That is not good. *Way* out of order!"

"Some of them your age. You never notice?"

"Well, you know, not really."

"*What*?"

"The music circuit, it's never the place. I never check out the audience. And the street doesn't interest me."

"Son, that is what I mean."

"Sorry?"

"Making it, or *making* it."

A quick pang. Jimmy remembers the twenty minutes with the Jamaican white girl. Even her parents were born in Jamaica. One day she will visit Worcestershire and Surrey. That's where strands of her family derive in England. But she, her flaxen hair was blowing the breeze and the sun hovering in the quiet afternoon as she showed one way up the beach. It would have been a lot more than twenty minutes alone together. But a boatload of tourists landed and fanned out.

"Jamaica, it's the other way round. If it's a black-white, then it's usually white guys with black women."

Urshell nods. "Yes. That is Jamaica. But below the surface, man! Jamaican people can have some of the *biggest* hang-up over race. Complexion, tings like dat."

"What about here?"

"England?"

"Yes."

Restless in his eye, Urshell turns to Mandela's picture. "Wicked business going on. This race business is not what you can call simple. Nowadays you have black girls that will never go with a black guy, not so much as look at a black man."

"In England?"

"Son, that race business going on all the time. Yes, more time with what you can call the darker skin women."

356

"What d'you they think they're up to?"

"Who?"

"Black women."

"How yu mean?"

"Think they're in denial?"

"Dem woman deh? Dem always a tell demself seh dem a mek it."

"Then they can stay the fuck away from me! Sorry, I didn't mean to swear. Not in your house. I don't mean to disrespect you."

Urshell shrugs. Weary, he hauls his frame from the armchair. "With some black women, black men are never good enough. Yes, you have black folk that hate being black, black girls believing that black men mean trouble. Their situation, man that is bad."

"Their situation makes me sick!"

"Son, you have black females that hate black men."

"*Why*?"

Colours of the rainbow? The sun is responsible for all that. And rainbows get chased by jazz musicians. All the time. It happens in nightclubs or any old hour. But in the eye of some people, daylight is only a donkey maze.

"Black women that can not deal with the truth, dem know seh if dem go wid black man dem wi' have black baby. You have a situation with black females running from their skin. Women that hate being black. Yes, any white bloke will do."

Jimmy gets to his feet. "Apocalypse."

"What?"

"Death, by fantasy."

Agnes looks out from her photograph on the arm of the chair. Agnes and her generation have the vote and, all told, at least 28 million blacks to 6 million whites in South Africa. That means you should be running the country in your image. Chemicals faking your natural hair means you do *not* understand.

"Who can spell out a fantasy? Yu?"

Jimmy shrugs the question away. The small tropical plant in Lorna's front room is a tease. A fantasy. From a distance the plant was like stitching. But it was real. And a solo flower flecked it like blood. She said it was from the Amazon somewhere but really swiped it from Kew Gardens.

"Fantasies are hard to nail," Jimmy admits. "But, hey, I'm not begging England. Not chasing tuxedos and white girls."

"Every man will have a fantasy one day."

"Maybe."

"Your fantasy?"

"I don't have a fantasy."

"The South African girl, what about that?"

"I think about the woman, I don't *fantasize* her."

"Son, listen. Because the woman is black does not mean she is not a fantasy. Yu no luv 'er. You do not love that girl. You love the *idea* of a woman from Africa. Some black guys have a fantasy for white. You have the fantasy for Africa."

"I've never been anywhere near Africa!"

"No man can get response from a continent. And," he laughs, slapping his hands, "which man can chase a whole continent round the bedroom?"

Talk here is depressing for Jimmy. Amusing sometimes, but depressing all the same. And that's maybe because it's true. Agnes herself accused him. She once said he was only checking her out because she's from Africa, not for who she. She was more blunt about it. Agnes said all he was looking for was a way to compensate. By being with a woman from Africa, compensation would follow. Jimmy did not understand. This heated little rap was in a music shop one day and, for a while, the other browsers got slackjawed, checking a hot-tongued woman getting serious.

"Mr Urshell, you think black people understand lions?"

The old man used to smoke. At one time it was 40 a day. And this is the part where he would reach for a smoke. Instead, he studies Jimmy. Over and over.

"Yes and no."

"What about English folk."

"What about them?"

"Think they understand lions?"

"Lion si human. Lion no si colour."

"Meaning?"

"A lion never bothers what clothes you wear."

Urshell is a London knowledge-man. London black cab driving. Fumbling from his chair now, his head shakes. A slow deliberate pacing, quartering and quartering the room. And studying Jimmy. Like maybe Jimmy a whole new kind of map, or comes from some place with no map.

358

After a hangman silence the old man gets back to his seat. "White people, they will mostly not want to think of anything like a lion."

"They shoot lions, put them in a zoo!"

"Then it is not the lion. The gun is the thing. Or the cage."

"Old man," Jimmy shakes his head, "that's like religion."

"Faith?"

"Bet bishops never dream lions!"

"Well, you know, things are never black and white. Many white folk are better than that racial stuff. I know English people who look at life the right way."

Chapter 85

The old man sprinkles rum on the carpet. His right hand on his heart. "Lions never get anything called nigger. Never!"

"I don't understand," Jimmy admits.

"See a lion, you run clear. Yes, free. De slave business can not get yu."

"That's *way* over my head."

"You are an educated fellow but, listen, if you understand the lion you can not fear a circus."

"Racism is not a circus?"

"Only a fool will perform."

"You never had to smile the smile?"

"Yes."

"Then you jumped to the ringmaster's whip, like everyone else!"

"I never have any nightmare 'bout Africa."

"Not trying to be difficult, but I don't get it."

"What?"

"Africa, nightmares about Africa. What's the point?"

"Those people all over the place. Why you don't ask them?"

"The sun donkeys?

"Black folk wid blond dye in a dem hair, straighten it. Start wid dem."

Urshell will never forget one nightmare. In one African war zone, children told him how easy it is to kill. Or chop limbs off. Kids as young as nine or ten. The thrill is bones. Human bones seldom refuse a machete; that why they bones! Those kids play the saddest game. They bet which severed limbs will jump round on the ground longest. Which legs. Which arm. No need for childish toys in child-crazed war spots.

Mandela's portrait on the wall keeps things calm here. The face alert, wry, smiling. But something distant in the eye; Mandela seeing far. To Jimmy the face looks oriental, smiling direct, but mostly eyes a long distance away. Africa, orient and far.

Urshell agrees. "Why I stay in England? Well, some of us hang around because we are what you can call lost."

"Folk with no compass? Nomads?"

"Nomad?"

"I *like* that word!" Jimmy says. "Nomad is me."

"That slave business. Black folk must look beyond it."

"Looking past the horizon?"

"Yes."

"Old man, there's too much denial. People in denial."

"What?"

"Living in the same England that made slavery happen. English people don't want to know. A few white liberals here and there, but they don't want to know. It's always 'That was long ago.' Yeah?"

"Coming from the West Indies to England was _"

"Tough?"

"Yes."

"American blacks don't have that problem."

"West Indies people have a situation. You can not go back to the sun and, well, we must move forward."

"Black man can not be a nomad in Britain! Where can you go?"

"Gypsy black people? No, son."

"That would be a *real* problem for English folk."

"Listen, you must hold down roots here. Move in city life."

"Like where?"

"Quite a few ambitious people go into business."

"Business? Anybody can do that!"

"Well, yes."

"Intelligent blacks want something more than a little business."

"As we go along, yes, we will get big-time."

"Merchant banking."

"Stuff like that."

"Hotshot lawyers."

"Lawyer?" Urshell scoffs. "Man, some of the weirdest people are lawyers. Selfish people. And, you know, ninety percent of them are not smart enough."

"Hey, blacks need black lawyers."

"Why?"

"How you gonna guarantee getting serious in court?"

"Son, lawyers talk. They have big talk, big talk, but most of them can not do even simple science."

"We want justice."

"What?"

"What else?"

"Justice is the easy part."

361

"Justice has got nothing to do with science. You don't need a physics degree to tell right from wrong. Put things right. And look at Margaret Thatcher. She did chemistry at Oxford, and look how she witched down on people. Even her own white people."

Urshell smiles. "The smartest person I ever saw, he was a man from Ghana, economics professor. And, brother! To him the only useful folk is the ones that do science. Or agriculture, engineers."

"Then how come he's mouthing off from his economics high and mighty?"

"That man, that honest man, walked away from that stuff. Went back to university for biology. Science is the place."

"Well they can call you nigger any time. It's in their cupboard. Never matters spit to them how educated you are. "

"Then who must get the education, you or them?"

Jimmy yawns. "People switching to science will take a hundred years."

"When white folk stopped using *nigger* every day, it was coloured people. Thirty, forty years."

"Now it's just black. But they still hit you with nigger."

"Yes."

"It was blacks in America making it OK to say *black*."

"That was the start! Respect was out there for the black man coming up."

"Respect? Old man, that was *way* back."

"Then keep up the folly."

"What d'you mean?"

"Folly is stuff you guys do."

"Music?"

"Entertainment is only relaxation, son. A smart person should be in a lab. Cure the sick. Reveal smart fuel."

Jimmy's eyes lower to his feet. "I dropped sciences at A level. Everybody can't be scientists."

"Music is folly. Politics is folly. Global warming going on. Bad, bad business. An' de politician dem, dem only know history."

"Yeah, or literature."

"Yes."

"Hey, Paddy Ashdown was a commando. A lethal guy with brains."

"Well, you know, the rest of them only know history. Dem learn
362

French. Tings like dat. But who de neck-back was Shakespeare? The folk running the country do not know the military. And dem don't know science. Politics is backseat driver talkin' piss-pot."

"Come on, Mr Urshell! They've got to be literate."

"You ever look in a dentist's eyes?"

"No."

"Man, a politician can sit in the best dentist's chair and talk the dentist's two living ears off."

Jimmy laughs. Driving a London black cab so many years, Urshell picked up half a world hearing science folk talk in the cab. And politicians. But who would ever have made time for Stephen Hawking if his work was in literature or politics. Or history. Even music.

"Nowadays, only piss-pot on TV. Vomit in the street."

Jimmy wonders. "What if, suppose you get what you say. Swap lawyers and politicians for scientists."

"Black lawyers, swap them for scientists."

"What happens then?"

"Respect."

"Pride!"

Urshell's head shakes. "You know, in the 60s we had good people. Black people with pride. That Afro thing was part of that. But look what that pride business did. Man! Look what happen to black folk since."

Chapter 86

No real account of what went on. The panthers in England are a mystery. The old story is people of colour here were getting like fresh gravel at a winter park gate; just like water-birds coming in from scree, blue with arctic to break the ice, the first immigrants that wintered here were just too cold except to start a song sometimes. In winter, England was vivid white in the countryside. Even now hedgerows pin back from surgery where ice-cold secateurs execute exact cuts in the firm. To the early immigrants the sight of grass was a summer of swabs. Or maybe it was never only grass. Maybe the colours on the grass were from a flock of parakeets that died, too thirsty at the grey edge of the pond.

Panthers could have changed all that. Panthers could have sent a shiver down that winter spine. But. Urshell will not want to talk anything as tense as black panthers.

Jimmy can tell. But there's nothing to lose by asking. Sitting tall, his throat clears. "They say a black panther movement was here in England."

The old man blinks.

Black panther. On 17th august '69, George Jackson wrote from Soledad Prison to his brother Jon, saying he added 5 new words to his vocabulary every day. *Africa.* Bobby Seale was talking deep with his own mother, saying the reality was that American black people will never go back to Africa. *Duel.* And that same year, and it was still 1969, Eldridge Cleaver challenged Ronald Reagan to a duel, calling him a sissy. Eldridge said Ronald could either accept the challenge, or simply call him Uncle Eldridge.

In his own sitting room, Urshell going through the gears. One old man going no place. Looks just like the UK panthers got coaxed off to a circus.

"Mr Urshell, I heard you were one of the black panthers in England."

The old man's eyes narrow, like hit by sunlight. His gaze a haze. Old man, remembering. Silent, he turns to old Mandela on the wall. Then turns to Jimmy. Peering forensic, his heavy glasses lumber down, quietly wondering if Jimmy one of the black recruits sent by government undercover to sneak on the community. Jimmy holding a cigarette but can not light it.

Urshell is resigned. "The folk at MI5 know all about me. So what the hell!"

"A black panther movement was here."

"Yes."

"When?"

"Well, it was the 60s. Late in the 60s."

"And it got profiled in the 70s?"

"Yes and no."

"Jamaicans?"

"Jamaica, Trinidad. This place, that."

"I heard it was Jamaicans."

"Jamaican people used to feel, well, sort of more ahead. But we put aside our squabbling."

"So, what was what?"

"How yu mean?"

"Who was who? Like, what was the level of being a panther?"

"Man bring to de table wha' dem 'ave."

"Some of the panthers were well educated. That's what I heard."

"Yes, the folk from Trinidad. Mostly them. Some of those people had big time education."

"I heard they were the biggest uncle toms on the planet."

"Well, you know, none of dem never understan' the white man. To folk like them, man, black power to them was the way to sleep with white. Live next door to white."

"Yeah. I heard that."

"We never had no real dazzle for white in Jamaica. That is why Jamaican people, we have the Maroons."

"And guys like Paul Bogle. Marcus Garvey. And that woman."

"Nanny, a warrior woman Maroon. Yes."

"Reggae. Worldwide."

"Jamaica all the way."

"How did you get to be a panther?"

Quick, the old man's jaws clench. Grinding now on a dirt-load of memory. If it wasn't for being indoors he'd spit. "Enoch Powell! Mr Powell was the devil himself."

"And having a name like that!"

"Name?"

"In the bible, Enoch was the father of Methuselah."

"One Enoch was the son of Cain!"

"Yes, yes! Yeah, I remember that!"

"Man, England was a tough place because of Mr Powell."

"The catalyst for the black panthers here, yeah?"

"Well, every black person could see how that gentleman was a very evil man. So a few of us turn into panthers."

"Who was the head?"

"Everyone."

"What?"

"Everybody in the movement was just plain Ivan X."

"*Ivan*?"

"Ivan."

"Ivan, like the Jimmy Cliff part in, what's that film called?"

"The Harder They Fall."

"Yeah, my old man's got the video."

"Ivan X was nutt'n to do with that. That film was in '72 and, well, the whole black panther movement was starting to stumble by then. *Ivan* was what you can call the first vanguard. Everybody was Ivan X. The pigs used to wage war. Dem arrest somebody and the only ting we seh was 'Ivan X!' Even the woman dem. Man, the women give dem name as Ivan X."

Bobby Seale's mother would have been a soldier in the Black Panther Party. But she told Bobby she was just too old. Then there was Kathleen, wife of Eldridge. And the thousands of militant black women in America standing side by side with guys. And as fully armed.

"Ever meet any of those Americans?"

"Like who?"

"Bobby Seale, Huey Newton. Bad panthers! Guys like Eldridge Cleaver."

"No."

"What guns did you have?"

"Gun?"

"The photos of those *dread* guys."

"Who?"

"American panthers. They always have heavy-duty artillery. In America, black power was it!"

"Son, listen. Black power was rebirth. And that is stainless any place. Nothing more beautiful than rebirth. For a period of time the black man was a lion. Mandela was a fighting man in Africa. But

366

we did not get any gun here."

"That's not what I heard."

"What yu hear?"

"I heard there was a place called the Black House."

Urshell wary, cold beads in his eye. "Well, there was maybe one guy. We had a half Portuguese guy. Half black. Michael X. Michael used to function from the Black House."

"Walked with a gun!"

"Yes. But only him."

"*Only him*?"

"Yes."

"Panthers without claws and teeth! What did you *do*?"

"Guns is not everything. The main thing was to get a basic education, learn what was the slave business. Everything run clear once you learn that. Colonial this and that. Never underestimate it. Dat stuff still out deh. England was never America."

"But they say nigger here. Not just in America."

"Dat worry yu?"

"Not only me!"

"Watch ya, read Black Skins White Masks."

"*Books*? What about the action, the real thing?"

"Well, a one can vision action. You have action, and *action*."

"No disrespect, but you're getting away from the point."

"And the point is?"

"It's what you did to justify being a panther. Calling yourselves Ivan X."

"We put things up for the community."

"What did you really do?"

"Organize."

"Organize what?"

"Legal defence. Organize the community. We had what you can call the project, buy bulk and cut the middleman. And get self-employed. Tings like dat."

"But what about the *real* action?"

"Like what?"

"Why were you afraid, Mr Urshell?"

"Afraid?"

"Afraid of guns, man. What's so terrible about a gun?"

"Yu no si wha' happen wid de young boy dem? Dem tek gun an'

a kill dem oneanadda."

"Not *that* type of gun."

"Which type?"

"The type where you refuse to get brutalized."

"What?"

"Where you refuse to have racist bozos brutalize you. Police still gang up on black guys, even beat them up at the station. My father said that that stuff happened in broad daylight."

"That was the 60s, the 70s."

"And the 80s. 90s. Now."

"Listen, I am not against police. My neighbour was a copper for 40 years."

"The white man with the cricket bat?"

"We go back 30 years."

Bobby Seale describes first seeing Huey Newton. Huey was tooled with a pump-action shotgun. And there's Jon Jackson, aged only 17 and using guns in a racist courtroom to try freeing his brother George.

"The panthers in the States, guys like Huey Newton, they told the cops 'If you shoot at me, I'm shooting right back.' *That's* the action I mean!"

Head shaking, the old man ambles to Mandela's photo on the wall. In one gliding move his hands swivel the frame round. Another photograph on the reverse. Two black guys. Dread guys. Dignified, dread. The picture defines a moment. It was on a victory rostrum. Each guy with a gloved fist in the air.

"This," Urshell nods, "is the *greatest* picture in the world!"

"It's those black power guys at the Olympics!"

"This is Tommy Smith. And this man is John Carlos. Yes, son. The '68 Olympics."

"The victory ceremony for the 200 meters."

"Start of modern rebirth."

"That's what I call panthers!"

"Listen, those two great brothers were not panthers. Dem do de black power salute, yes. But, man! Those boys are what you can call *greater* than panthers. Learn that!"

Jimmy standing now. When the picture got taken those two guys were about the same age he now. Their dread look, dread stance. They the anthem to the black man. Two, lighting a torch in the sky.

368

That's why they have their gloves on.

"Dignity, that is true power."

"But power denied."

Urshell's head shakes. "You wrong. True power will happen one day. And that is bigger than any gun."

On 5th December 1956, Nelson Mandela got arrested in front of his children at dawn. The smell of blood was in the air. Mandela was accused of treason. And the name of the arresting policeman was Rousseau. *Rousseau*? What? A policeman with the same last name as the 18th century French philosopher that said 'Man is born free but is everywhere in chains.'

"I can understand the clenched fists, but how come they bow their heads in the picture?"

Urshell's own head bows to his chest. His hands clasp. "John and Tommy? Those boys praying. They had to go back to America and the folk from the Ku Klux Klan was watching. There was still lynch mobs going on and Uncle Sam was glad for the medals but just turn a blind eye if dem get lynched. A situation where Martin Luther King got assassinated earlier that same year."

"1968?"

"Some of the black folk on the American team was uncle toms. Tommy Smith, that boy's own grandfather had been a slave. And Tommy, that *great* man, he was the one to turn the victory rostrum into a witness."

"Oh, man! *Please* don't say it was because of religion!"

"A slave can win a medal, but only a free man can own the shine."

In England too many vacant black folk turn up. Some of those black sportsmen are the first to drape in the Union Jack and flutter down the victory lap grinning, even when redneck hissing. It's one thing to run fast, or kick football. Or even box great. But if that's all you can do, if you don't have the principles, then you better just bank your million. And shut your hypocrite mouth.

Most of Tommy Smith's teammates say what he did on the victory rostrum cost them millions in sponsorship deals. But beyond winning a medal, or breaking a world record, what had those same black teammates done? Tommy and John changed something. For all time. And what could panthers do to measure that? What did the panthers in London do?

To Jimmy, Urshell looks like a really old man all of a sudden. He turns the picture round to show again the photo of Mandela.

"You realized you were not real panthers. That must have hurt!"

"No guns. But we used to drive parasites out the community."

"Who?"

"Lowlife black guys."

"Pimps?"

"Some of the brothers in the movement could handle themself, and the pimp dem used to understand that. We used to take a serious look at the toms, leaflet uncle toms with 'Dear Sir Lord Tom, straighten up and fly right.' Beautiful times! Then," Urshell stops, suddenly weary, clearing his throat, "then the dilution."

"I think you mean dissolution."

"The dilution."

"How did things fell apart?"

Nelson Mandela says Rousseau did not handcuff him that morning in December '56. Mandela was well capable of beating Rousseau to death. Or just give him a pasting. But allowed himself to get taken to the station.

"Well, the first business was money. Everything start with that. We had to have things."

"What was it?"

"How yu mean?"

"What did the movement need to get started?"

"Equipment. This was the 60s and some smart white folk was following Karl Marx. Early 70s. And that flower-power business. White girls burning dem brassiere in the street."

"But you had Marsha Hunt. *Fantastic* looking woman! American, wasn't she? I've seen posters of her and she was something else!"

"Yes."

"She was in Hair."

"That show? Yes, Hair was big-time and that girl used to *dazzle* the white boys."

"She had the biggest Afro in England!"

"But no respect for black men. That girl was the sign of what was coming. But folks was getting aware of serious black guys."

"Muhammad Ali?"

"Ali, Mandela."

370

"Hendrix."

"*Bad* guys. Great, great guys. Because of them the panther movement was like a magnet to English folk. High profile white folk."

"Anybody big?"

"Oh yes. Big time musicians, actors and _"

"You needed their help, that's life, but what did *they* want?"

"Who?"

"English folk."

"Well, you know, some of them was what you can call curious. Or rebellious. They had was to do something different, and the militant black people here was giving them a buzz! Some of the brothers in the movement were educated guys. So it was easy to talk, black with white."

"Sounds like white people wanted to join up," Jimmy laughs. "But seriously, how did they know where to find you? That was heavy-duty risks!"

"You know, things here was never underground. Everything was up front. English folk would help out. Good people. White people. Dem bring equipment, money. Tings like dat."

"What they did want?"

"How yu mean?"

"They gave up their time, gave their money, but what did they want in return?"

"Well, you know, when you look back tings not soh clear. The guys wanted to sit and smoke ganja with black folk, and it was always serious discussion with them, good talk. Good people, English people, brilliant guys. And the white girls, man! Those girls could talk. A lot of them was very smart, more serious than the blokes. Some of those girls could not wait to get to know the brothers. There was a lot of what you can call dazzle for black guys."

"Because of Hendrix and Ali."

"Yes, those great black boys that was out there. Dazzle. Middle class white girls did not care if a brother look like a jackass, they had to get some of that black man dazzle."

"*That* was the panthers here? Ivan X or whatever."

"I know. It looks bad."

"How could you allow dazzle to trump?"

"Allow?"

"Razzle-dazzle, bling-bling!"

"Young man, how old are you?"

"Diz, dazzle, bling!"

"What?"

"Hypocrites!"

"Who?"

"Your panther friends! Every Ivan bling X!"

In London the people calling themselves Ivan X were sipping wine and talking of silk sheets while reading Karl Marx, exactly at the same time Bobby Seale was lamenting the murder of members of the Black Panther Party in America. Government assassins were gunning panthers down. Dozens and dozens got murdered by redneck or uncle tom.

"It was only a couple of the brothers."

Jimmy turns to Urshell. "What?"

"Only a few of the brothers was going with the white girls."

"I heard the educated guys were the biggest hypocrites."

"Well, the movement couldn't hold together without educated people. But, yes, hypocrites was there. One guy resent the white girls mashing down the movement but then it was the same guy that was going with a white-looking Pakistani woman."

"Hypocrites!"

"Yes."

"The *same* guys begging to get on TV to talk black power."

"Yes."

Disappointed, Jimmy turns to Mandela on the wall. "Hard to believe how it works. You're talking bling hypocrites."

"Human nature."

"*Human nature?* That's why you didn't walk from the crap?"

"Me, personally?"

"Yes!"

Old, Urshell tries a smile. But he knows. All along the old man knows. He must deliver. For a while Jimmy the son he never had.

"Walk away?"

"Walk from the crap."

"Son, nobody could walk away. Everybody was up in the sphere. You would have to be there to know. The greatest time of life. And white folk had people you could respect."

"Like who?"

"The Beatles. John Lennon was a great man."

"Well, yeah."

"George Best."

"I hear he was the man."

"The boys out there that play football now, man, nobody in England good as Best."

"Hendrix was never big with black people here. Why not?"

"The black people here was into Jamaican music. A few Jamaicans used to have jazz records, but black in general did not know blues music."

Jimmy shrugs. "Hendrix was a blues man. But they baited him with cheap thrills."

"There was folk like James Brown, Aretha Franklyn. We loved that music here. The best record was Solid Gold Soul."

"An LP, wasn't it? My old man's got it. But the rest of that era was a lie, your stint with the panthers was a cheap lie."

"Well, no. It was not a lie."

"*What* was it?"

Chapter 87

Somewhere, on some colonial shelf is a book telling how black people got just too close to a Bunsen burner in the Garden of Eden.

Nelson Mandela talks about the value of education. The day in 1942 when he got his BA he was very proud. But straightaway a wise man told him. The man said that education was necessary but not sufficient, 'because no people or nation had ever freed itself through education alone.'

Jimmy's mother's foster-sister left Liverpool in 1970. She wanted to get away, wanted to do something real. She wanted to join the panthers. And at the start being with them was always heady-days. The life & death discussions, grassroots planning, the struggle and education classes on economics and slavery. Some of the classes were by very serious people from LSE. The panther movement was motoring. It was going the right place. Humming. But one day she realized. It was the simple things. Like a photocopier getting donated, heavy money getting donated by showbiz white folk. And all the time it was for nighttime service by the black spokesmen of the movement. Hard to believe how many guys called themselves black panthers but all the time had English women. They just did not get the contradiction. So she upped it straight back to Liverpool. Got back into jeans and T-shirts. And an honest quiet job in a car wash.

Jimmy could do with a smoke. Nervy, he turns to the old man. "I don't mean to disrespect you Mr Urshell, but _"

"Talk what you must talk."

"I don't get how you sat around doing small-time pretence."

"Listen, the movement was a grassroots thing. Everything happened so fast. Man, the movement was like a party. And with every jamboree there's folk that can not hold their liquor."

"People like you sat around watching black women get insulted. Was that the party?"

"No."

"What kind of fun was it?"

"Black people, we, well, you learn as you go along."

"Who was the sun donkey? Who was the minstrel? Hey, that's why we're still getting called niggers. *That's* why!"

Older than ever, wracked, Urshell clears his throat. "Well, that is only one side of the story. Most of the brothers had their black woman."

"We're going round in circles!"

"Well, yes."

"Why didn't you deal with the hypocrites, beat their brains out?"

"You know, this is not a simple business. Those guys used to attract rich English people. Educated people."

"The movement was supposed to be panthers!"

"Well, yes."

"Black *panthers*!"

"Yes, son."

"*Black* panthers!"

Urshell is too weary. An old man looking inside himself. Ground down. Trying for something that will square with freedom fire. But if he can not hide from somebody two generations down the line, somebody like Jimmy, how can he hide? He does not want to hide. Some flames are big as the Olympic flame. Some flames bigger.

"Sometimes, sometimes, you have to find out the hard way."

"Guys like you just get old. I need information, and all you do is remember."

"There was this particular brother."

"A tom?"

"He was in the movement. A big graduate guy. But that boy was what you can call a fool. He was with a brainy white girl and, well, for one whole year she suck de brother black wood. Then one day she call him a bloody wog."

"What, with the same mouth?"

"What you can call the precipice."

"What did you do? She was talking to *all* of you."

"I know."

"She was talking to the panthers."

"Well, yes and no."

"Man!"

"Son, calm down. That girl was talking to your generation more. Twenty, thirty years before her time."

"Sucks my cock and calls me a wog? I'd have shoved it under a bus!"

"You have a fire, son. We could have used some true fire."

"You treated Marx like he was a god, smoked ganja with dropout

375

English guys, and had the *nerve* to call yourselves black panthers!"

"A situation where some of the brothers were too tame."

"Yeah, scared of guns!"

"Guns was not a thing in England. Not then. Thirty, forty years."

"No guns, just white pussy and TV chat shows."

"Well, yes and no."

"That's why types like Bosworth Trass are out there."

"Well, you learn your lesson from that."

"Yeah, and the lesson is hypocrites multiplying!"

"The lesson is people of colour will never have a community. Not in England. All you have is folk with skin."

"Confused people."

"Everybody going dem own direction."

"But visible."

"Yes and no."

"The white man does *not* see it that way!"

"You get paid to talk for white?"

"No."

"In the old days some of the brothers could see what was coming."

"Guys like Mandela, they put their lives on the line!"

"The only struggle them educated guys was in was Chairman Mao."

"Who?"

"Chairman Mao. Socialism, communism."

Jimmy wants to cool it. He can see distress on the old man The panthers here did not get to the moon. Urshell has no place to go in his own home, except back to failed launch attempts. England can be hot in summer and they still do maypole dancing and candyfloss.

"I read somewhere that Mao's wife got beheaded."

Urshell wilts. His throat clears. "That was 1930, by a warlord."

"Think it's that beheading thing that was his allure?"

"Mao was still a young fellow and China was in a struggle. Years after that stuff, the Chairman was a good man to Africa. Folk in Africa get help from him."

"What did black panthers see in China?"

"The black struggle?"

"The panthers."

"Well, it was a big help to know what someone as big as Mao was

376

saying. We had study groups. All we had to do was change one word. Every time the Chairman talked *peasant,* we talked *slave.*"

"Or uncle tom."

"Well, yes and no."

"Toms are everywhere now."

"Man, that uncle tom business get ruction starting here. Serious quarrel."

"How'd the panthers deal with that?"

"We wanted it to hold together. Then, woosh!"

Instead of militant blacks, Urshell talks of posers. Black panthers in England were a knee-jerk to what was going on in America. The honest people got talked down by educated posers. Even America itself wanted the middle ground to be between right Martin Luther King and the panthers. But Rosa Parks did more than Martin and his bible. And in England they never had cotton or cane growing directly in the fields.

"No wonder there's nigger-brown!"

"Son, those guys were boys from the colonies. Most of them came from small little spots in the Caribbean, you know, glad to be here, walking round, do a little shopping in the big stores. In Jamaica we call them people *gladdy-gladdy.* Those guys was what you can call a gladdy-gladdy. Me along with them."

"Not panthers!"

"A panther will go where a panther must go, day or night."

Mandela says Robben Island was a place with no black warder. And no white prisoner. And for a long time all prisoners were forced to wear short trousers. Grown men, forced to the starched white warden fetish.

"How did you explain things?"

The old man pours a tumbler of water. And sits upright in the old chair. His heavy glasses slope from his eyes. His throat clears. "Nobody could explain something like that. The panthers in America got into big trouble, was breaking up. There was traitors among them. Police informers."

"*Informers*?"

"Son, when you have a black thing you always get somebody that will run to the white man and tell. Remember that!"

"Man!"

"Now, yu understand."

"Can't you tell who's who?"

"How?"

"Isn't there some kind of test, weed out the informers?"

"Religion."

"What?"

"Somewhere down the line you have to trust someone."

"I do *not* need religion to trust somebody!"

"The traitors in America, some of the panthers had was to leave America and lay low for a period of time. Some a dem hit Algeria, or Cuba. The police was starting to gun them down. It was a big shock. *Big* shock. Man, everybody in a daze. Over here nobody could explain none of that. Everybody was dem own direction. If yu buck up a one in the street, den more time de two a yu go yu separate direction."

"Yeah, hailing 'Black power!' What hypocrisy!"

"Well, no."

"What a let down. Panthers here were a bunch of mickey-mouse!"

"England is not America, son. Never was no need for no panthers here. England was always different. English folk different. After a period of time you realize that. You know, you must meet the Englishman with a different business, what you can call a higher understanding."

"Old man, you're losing me again. I don't understand."

"Nobody could believe Reagan becoming the president. And that has *definitely* got a big something to do with Michael Jackson."

"How?"

"Roll the dice, and you get one illusion."

"The up face, or the down face?"

"You get a B-movie clown becoming president of the US of A."

"Reagan?"

"Yes. And watch this! Roll the same dice and you get a weird thing, a black boy by name of one Michael Jackson. A black boy wanting to turn into a white man. A *weird* person. Yes, that little man nimble on the feet. But who can call that a black man?"

"Murder! Million upon million of people saw that man get killed, that young black man. Folk everywhere watch the murderer walk free."

A mystic thing. A white man calling himself Michael Jackson committed a public slaying. And that's because the man killed black Michael to put on his dancing shoes, along with his motivation, then went out on stage to celebrate.

Michael was brown-black. But now fake-white. Michael is white alabaster, more a computer Michelle than a man Michael. But way inside the junk Michael is bawling. One day he will dream again. Michael day.

The old man complains on his fingers. "Somebody could be African, or you mixed, or British black, all that stuff. Somebody was black as night or light as sunlight, but everybody was black. Simple as that. For a period of time we had to look at things that way. Not now."

"Black is cool," Jimmy shrugs. "I'm OK with it. No way I want to get called something else."

"Want my opinion?"

"That's why I'm here."

"Calling everybody black is, what? It does not liberate. With that Michael Jackson the whole thing gone up in smoke."

"Michael is ill, Mr Urshell. He got hit by a disease. It sapped the natural colour from him. I think it's called vitaligo."

"Disease?"

"Yes."

"Then it is a disease with a big nightmare 'bout Africa."

"Well, he can't help getting it."

"Even now that little man still calling himself black. Even now!"

"I think in America they say African-American."

"All black people are not African."

"Then what are we?" Jimmy laughs.

"Son, Africa is not a stain."

"Where's the part where *stain* comes into this?"

"Nowadays you hear all kind of business. People talk 'bout Irish-

American, or Italian-American. Polish-American. This and that. But dem never seh European-American. So who the hell is this African-American?"

"I think it's because they don't know. They don't know where in Africa the slaves came from."

The old man's sitting room all of a sudden too strict. Way too bare-knuckle. Definitely time for Jimmy to get a smoke. A tango with nicotine won't wait. Apologizing, he heads to the door, wanting to be outside. Must head for nicotine. And fresh night air. And somewhere in the house, Urshell's daughter playing Aretha Franklyn and singing it along. A honey woman getting married soon.

Amber light comes from the front room of Urshell's neighbour. Amber shining clear through the curtain. This is the English man with the cricket bat one drunken night. This man ever know Urshell was once a black panther?

The road stone quiet. Jimmy pulls back from an urge to knock the man's door. Nice laughing comes from his house, faint but set laughing. Maybe they don't watch TV in there. This man is the outdoor type, an ex-copper on the beat, and having a mooring in the Lake District. One summer he took Urshell on a slow car ride up there, touring round from Kendal to Windermere. The smell of juniper was drifting in and out as Urshell's wife gathered mosses for the rockery in her little garden. But wary; she was one old black lady thinking the ground would swallow her up as English folk watched and watched. But mostly that day was smiles. And buzzards were on high, soaring in the landscape, getting high on rabbits they gorge. To buzzards, rabbit blood is maybe just like gin.

Urshell is lucky to have such a neighbour, Jimmy thinks. And now somebody looking out at the night from the man's first-floor window. The whole thing just wants Charlie Parker playing it, faint but fluent. A night like this Charlie would pick up the sax and talk tarmac, talk that sax over rubber and boot-black, and solo over why star-filled nights tar lungs that sear for release. Urshell's neighbour is English as English come. Maybe he has never even heard of Charlie P.

Without Lester Young, no Charlie Parker. Lester switched from

380

drums to the sax and in no time nobody could believe the control, the tone, the scope. Billie Holliday said Lester's playing was the closest thing to singing that could ever be.

Urshell is not big on jazz. But he must know about Lester already; the ups, the downs, the cut. The genius. Jimmy wondering over laughing coming from the ex-policeman's front room. Smoke over, he gets back indoors.

The old man offers a shot of rum, asking about the football, the FA Cup Final was last week. Chelsea beat Aston Villa by the goal Roberto Di Matteo scored but Urshell missed it Missed the whole second half. But Jimmy watched it on TV. That was the last time this annual combat was under the old Twin Towers at Wembley. They will tear down the place and build something that will sit 90,000 folk down.

The great sax player? All ways to look at Lester Young. Lester a black man, but with green eyes and light skin derived from his Creole mother. *Green* eyes? Yeah. But green-eyes & light-skin or no, America still called him nigger sometimes.

The tar brush is big in America. If a redneck anywhere near then a tar brush better not fetch to somebody passing for white: even now, even if you have the bluest eyes or blondest hair, if that tar brush there somewhere, even way out of sight, then redneck talk what they say is your true colour, saying 'Nigger!' And that same America listened to Lester preach like a prophet through the sax, telling the big story, telling hope, anguish, respect. But that did not count for spit. Then again.

Lester's first wife was white. They had a daughter. But Lester never told anybody about his daughter. Her mother's all-white blood combined with Lester's part-white blood to such a degree that, man! No visible trace of black showed in the daughter. She absolutely passed for white. So maybe that's why she went her way, living as a white woman till she passed away in '93. Lester's daughter was getting away from something, living it her own way. But what was she really getting at?

Jimmy winds up the story "A whole lot of African Americans are out there who make a difference to the struggle."

"What is this *African* American business?"

"What d'you mean?"

"Lester Young, man! A pale-skin gent with green eyes. How you get African-American out of that?"

"Then *who* are the African Americans?"

"Louis Armstrong. Sydney Poitier, Eddie Murphy."

"Martin Luther King?"

"Yes."

"Oprah Winfey?"

"Yes."

"Colin Powell?"

"No."

"Colin is *black*."

"No."

"Mixed race, then."

"Yes and no."

Upstairs, the sound of Martha Reeve duetting with Marvin Gaye. This soft love song, so simple, so soft, two people no longer lonely. Urshell's daughter getting ready to fly the nest. And tonight she swoons down with Motown.

Who Berry Gordy? The big Motown man, the wiz, bringing all those great entertainers, the Supremes, Smoky Robinson, Martha and the Vandellas. And right at the end of that, it was Berry that got the Jackson Five. Michael was Michael. Michael was great. Michael was still a black man as late as Thriller. His whole family so good looking, smiling true, singing, dancing. And even now Janet is one sweet, sweet woman. Apart from messing her hair. Must have been great living through that. Urshell's daughter is a Motown dreamer.

Somebody like Lorna would not split hairs about who black. Lorna would tell Urshell to back off. But. Silly to just hang a Brixton overcoat on everybody.

"Why not say mixed race?"

"Why?"

"It's a fact, isn't it."

"Man, that word does not mean you connect with Africa."

Jimmy's brow furrows. "Then who is black?"

"People, you know, like Mr and Mrs Jackson. Those people are black."

"*Who*?"

"The mother and father of that little man."

"Michael's parents? What's the point? I hear his father's got green eyes."

"If yu look African, they yu African!"

"What's the bottom line?"

"Face to face with a lion, a white man will waste his time talking of niggers."

"Yes, yes, but what's the point?"

"The point?"

"Your way, and there's Africans and blacks. Then you've got something in between, people like Colin Powell with no name."

"Listen! You have a situation where white folk talk about something called *black African*. But nobody talking 'bout white African. White South African, yes, dat is cool. Or white people from Zimbabwe. But never white Africans. Africa is the home of black people, so *black African* is a tautology."

"A *what*?"

"In Jamaica patois," Urshell smiles, "things like a tautology is what we call a bang-a-rang."

Jimmy can not set. Urshell saying the same kind of thing as the camel-fanciers at Homes. Different intention, but the same kind of thing. Blacks from England and blacks from France, Belgium. And blacks from Holland, and where not. But just as nobody saying white African, so nobody can sanely talk of black European. Not yet.

The confusion so bad now that black-on-black violence happening all the time. The old man has seen most things in life, even saw one black guy call him a black bastard. And that was no joke. That guy was already dead. Well, kind of. Because only a dead man will be so dead that his dead head off-loads the one name that sickened him when alive. And it was nothing like American black folk saying, one on one, 'What's up, nigger?'

Thirty races of folk get called black these days. Thirty? Yes. Like the pieces of bible silver?

383

Urshell says it again. "Thirty types of black. You want to pretend?"

"Confused," Jimmy admits. "Not pretending, old man. I mean, it's like you want to divide people."

"If you do not know a thing, you can not divide it."

"Hey, *everybody* knows what black is!"

"You can *not* divide what was never united."

"I don't see that. What's the point? Guys like Mandela are still in the struggle."

"How far from London to Glasgow?"

"What?"

"Shortest route from Kilburn High Road to Stoke Newington?"

"*What*?"

"Collect different type of black folk, and, man! You will need a big room. A dance-hall."

Fed up, Jimmy ups from the chair. Weary. Wanting to leave. Wanting to talk to music, to get back to the flat and eke light from the piano keys. And yet. This old man talking what never gets talked.

Urshell's wife brings a plate of saltfish fritters. And two cups of coffee. She is definitely why Urshell never left England. With a wife like her, old or not old, a man could be any place and not notice. Small room, big room, in Africa, Jamaica. Any place.

Jimmy grabs a fork. "We could be looking at Noah's Ark."

"Calling all those people the same, *that* is the problem. You need a microscope to know some of them have anything at all to do with Africa."

"White folk say black and, hey, blacks call themselves black!"

"Black is a stain?"

"How d'you figure that?"

"Calling everybody black is like your dream dead. When you have folk like Lester Young, that is not African. That man's daughter can *not* be African-American. Even black. Even mixed-race. Somebody like she is plain white. Collecting her as black is plain folly if only a scientific can sight the tar-brush."

"Mr Urshell, you talk like a preacher. Like somebody from the bible. Yeah, like Solomon."

"Solomon had a black mother."

"Yeah. His father was Jewish."

"Yes."

"He called himself black."

"Yes."

"Then what's the problem?"

"According to the bible Solomon was wise, so I must be a fool."

"To be honest, I only mentioned Solomon because there's that cleave-the-baby-asunder in what you say."

"Solomon tell the Jerusalem women all about himself."

"With women," Jimmy grins, "that guy was it. The *big* boss. Solomon was the killer!"

The old man's eyes narrow. "Solomon was afraid."

"*Afraid?* That dread guy?"

"Solomon was what you can call nervous."

"Nervous?"

"Him tell the Jerusalem woman dem seh him black but comely. Black *but* comely! What is that?"

"The dude had 300 wives!"

"Those women, every one of them had to be true to Solomon."

"Yeah, their babies would get called black."

"Yes."

"Every night in Jerusalem it was ladies, frankincense and spice!"

"Solomon dip dat tar-brush deep."

"Bring it on!"

"Listen, a one must be honest with who you are. Acknowledge you are part African if another part is from somewhere else. No buts. Do *not* deny any part of yourself. Every part is worth the same."

Jimmy sets aside the plate. "How much is a part?"

"How yu mean?"

"Suppose you find out that you have, I dunno, ten percent of something else."

"If yu look African, then yu African!"

"So where do we go from there?"

"If a lion could choose a name it would not be Solomon."

"Nah, lions are happy with *lion*!"

Urshell sucks his teeth. "If yu African, you must be up front."

"Even if you were born some place else?"

"Even Jamaica."

"Brixton?"

"If yu African, yu African!"

"There's lots of pretence out there," Jimmy nods.

"Man, that is the baddest nightmare 'bout Africa!"

The old man slumps in his chair. Women of colour are self maiming everyday. Nowadays black women using white woman wig fe maim dem life. And that's because the community is more like what you can call a jail. Woman cry out. But only inside. Only from the heart. And that cry is the sad crying of all. Woman messing that hair, that Africa, some even bleach that Africa skin down. And who sees one real woman under the fake. Even their own children know them as dual: the one with distance in her eye, and the one in front of the mirror getting her stage hair right. Woman getting crushed by fake. Black woman becoming crushed petals. Man, dem is de crushed petal of slaves! Your hand reaching out, wanting a true woman, a sure end to your journey, but all that's there is a crushed petal. And crushed petals of slaves never quite bloom. Not where green grass in the countryside exhausts a whole jeopardy with blood.

Urshell's daughter in the room. Quiet, she clears the tumblers, cups and plates. She must say it. Too many young black guys internalize their heart. The bleed, the crush. Black guys getting crazy. And that makes it hard to find what is real. It rides like a runaway train. This sad, bad thing. But then, if a black woman can wear a white woman's wig into hospital to give birth, then what is real?

Chapter 89

"Black-on-black violence," Jimmy says, "it's the worst thing that can happen."

Urshell nods. "Yes."

"It's drugs and territory."

Young guys say nothing. Or they talk rap. Deep down, some suppose that if it's OK for Michael Jackson to slay a black man with a bottle of chemicals, then it *must* be OK for them to gun their rival down for blood.

Urshell's eyebrows twitch. "Drugs, son?"

"Territory, then."

"What is territory?"

To Mandela, going to Robben Island was like going to another country: 'Wc were face to face with the realization that our life would be irredeemably grim.' And they made him wear short trousers, this qualified lawyer fighting for freedom in his own land. And redneck in America still calling black man 'boy' and one from every thirteen black guys in a Yankee jail today.

"Territory is where you do your thing."

"Then trouble, brother. *Big* trouble!"

"What?"

"You young guys do a thing that is not life."

"*Me?*"

"Too much black guy have red eye."

"Yeah. Red, as in blood."

"If yu eye full wid blood, then blood is the territory."

Jimmy remembers something Mandela said. When they moved him to Pollsmoor, Mandela was now in a concrete zone; but he was missing *the natural splendour* of Robben Island.

In England young black guys fence down the community with knives and guns. Too many walk away from the children they beget, walking from family, from duty. Urshell says it again, saying even if you own the fence you do not own the country; you gotta own shares in the country here. Then you will look after what you have. Starting with your life, and your woman and kids.

Yep, guys with the red of eye arrive. And red-eye taking the cut from real work. The way of red-eye is being happy with second best. The only thing in a red eye is lung spit. Red-eye content to dude up in a Brixton overcoat. They go to the night to murder their own kind. Or slay at evening. Or in the morning. Any old time, dude in dat Brixton overcoat. And that because red-eye can not be the best they can be. How a red eye amount to great, even good? And all the time the woad-man laughing, content, content.

And, you know, rap music is part the blame. Rap music robs the world of world-class black boxers. The bigger rap, the bigger the bling, the stupider the fake. And nowadays, second rate boxers getting called world champion is one of the saddest things for anyone that ever saw Ali, or Ray Leonard, Marvin Hagler, Tommy Hearns, Aaron Pryor, Larry Holmes. And that rap robbery, that larceny, that's the least rap music will do. Man! Somebody wanting to talk like a machine gun? And call it music? That's the first level down. But how to get back from red-eye. Down in the basement, that's the third level down. Down where red-eye protecting red eyes from sunlight. And somebody will have a name that is not even a man's name. Red-eye can never look at Nelson Mandela to vision what must happen. In July 1990, Mandela was getting used to being free. He got back to South Africa and the death toll from street violence in that one year alone was already over fifteen hundred, 'more than all the political deaths of the previous year.'

Jimmy wondering. Quiet wondering. Finally, he must ask it. "Why did you take an African name?"

The old man wipes his old brow. And, slow, gets the glasses from their case. Vacant, his hands begin to polish them. Polish them slow. For a minute his brow troubled, thinking. Old man mulling. Nelson Mandela at Pollsmoor. They gave him meat and vegetables every day at Pollsmoor, instead of the gruel at Robben Island. At Pollsmoor they even let him have a newspaper and local radio; and it was easier for Winnie and the children to reach him there than at Robben Island.

The blacks in America have bad names for white. In England black people only have *white man*.

"You know," Urshell sighs, "when I was your kind of age I used to call myself an African. Not Jamaican."

388

"Afro-Caribbean?"

"I was African."

"Guys your age went through a back-to-your-roots feeling."

"Yes."

"The first thing was to change your name?"

"Yes."

"What was it before? Hope you don't mind me asking."

Urshell shrugs. "Errol."

"Errol?"

"Errol Fitzroy Urshell, became Kwame Urshell."

"What did your folks say, your mother and father?"

"My poor mother cried. My father was still alive so I had to hold on to Urshell."

"The next phase was Africa?"

"Yes."

"Whereabouts? You went alone?"

"West Africa. It was myself and two brethren went."

"Roots!"

"Yes."

"What was it like. How long did you stay?"

"Two years. Man, that place beautiful!"

"The land, the women?"

"Son, you would not believe African women!"

"Hey, I have a thing for those women. *Love* them."

"Woman wid dem big behind."

Jimmy grins. "Yeah."

"Then why you don't go and check the place out?"

"Those women didn't anchor you. You left."

"Well, yes and no."

"You left!"

"Yes."

"*Why?*"

"Well, you know, it was things. Lots of things, son."

Jimmy seeing the old man get queasy. Urshell is old enough to be grandpappy, and anybody should respect that. But a man's age is not enough. Not if that age is only to hide from something.

"Mr Urshell, what was the main reason you left Africa?"

389

"Well I would say it was the superstition. If it wasn't for that I would not have left. I just could not deal with the superstition. Somebody with a bible in one hand, witchcraft the other hand. Every ten mile a man call himself a chief, or a general, stuff like that. It was tough. I could look at my roots. Yes, all the while. Man, I looked into the face of folk that look like me. I belonged to those people. I belong to them. But I just did not know what to tell them. It made my heart swell. Those people could not talk to me, not *talk*. Everyone wanted me to praise England. Folk wanting to come here."

"The ones *you* met. The town people, maybe."

"Then go ask dem why dem come here!"

"Why?"

"African people, man! Dem 'ave dem own culture, dem language and _"

"Cultures!" Jimmy says. "Look, there's hundreds of languages in Africa. Thousands!"

"Den why dem come 'ere?"

"It's the towns-people, man. I think the ones that come here are from the towns."

"If you have some definite place you belong, you should be there. Travel, yes. But stay wid yu roots!"

"Studies."

"What?"

"At university the Africans I met were some of the most serious people on the planet!"

"Dem go back to Africa?"

"Everybody went back."

"Too many stay here."

"It's that colonial thing, isn't it? It's the same for them."

"Yu tek me fe a fool?"

"I wouldn't be sitting here if I did."

"Man, the African people have some place dem belong but still dem keep coming here to cry! Dem have dem language an' dem culture, dem family, dem history, the place where their mothers and fathers lived and died for a million years, but dem come a England fe shovel shit from redkneck an' bleat 'bout racism!"

Jimmy turns to Mandela's portrait on the wall. A serious man. Nelson Rolihlahla Mandela. A serious name. A name inside a name. But a difficult name. Hard to figure a man like that was maybe named after Horatio Nelson. A man like Mandela, the man who *is* Mandela on his own land, but a man who was maybe named by mistake after a sly slave-owner.

Urshell cleans his glasses.

Jimmy snaps his hands together. "Mandela, yes, but *Nelson*?"

The old man turns to the portrait. Quiet, he adjusts the glasses on his old face. He almost does not recognize his mentor on the wall. His eyes narrow. Silent old hands fold away eyeglasses. His eyes cloud. Voice lowers. "History will always rearrange."

"A man is not his name?"

"Yes, and no."

"What's the *no* part?"

"Son, it was the Greeks. Africa is a Greek word."

"Where did you get that?"

"Before the white man, Africa was Alkebulaan.

Jimmy yawns. "You should have stayed in the villages. I heard village people in Africa are it."

"Yes."

"Stephen Hawking describes supergravity, a theory."

"What?"

"The theory says particles having different spins are simply different aspects of the same superparticle."

"*What*?"

"What's village life like in Africa ?"

"Son, you moving too fast!"

"If I went to Africa it would have to be the villages. Or the desert."

"A young man can always have one more fantasy."

"I'd go to Mali and check out Ali Farka Toure, learn from him."

"And," Urshell smiles, "marry him daughter?"

Jimmy laughs. "What's it like to wake up in an African village?"

"Man, a family will be dirt poor, have one goat, and kill the goat so you can eat."

"Hospitality."

"Yes."

"Hospitality is not enough."

"Yes and no."

"How does *no* get into this?"

"That hospitality? Man! It was for the Europeans."

"Yeah. They snatched those people into slavery."

"Yes."

"And you, you went to the lands of your ancestors and moved around, enjoying that hospitality, but came back to get old here. Will you die here?"

Urshell can trace a part of his roots in Jamaica to a man in 1760. The man rounded up wild horses for sale. But by the weirdest of weird, that man was called Driver. Cudjoe Driver. So somewhere in the spirit world, Driver must have smiled at Urshell driving black cabs in London. Maroons believe in a spirit world they can talk to.

Urshell turns to Jimmy. "Because of that slave business, one day I realized something. I am from Africa."

"An African!"

"Definitely, that is plain. But I am a Jamaican. I belong more to Jamaica."

A night like this, a chat-room on the internet will be buzzing with motion physics. Very bright folk will be commemorating the fact that no absolute is anywhere for standing still; the calculation for the earth going round the sun is just as easy if the earth was standing still with the sun bobbing round it. The sun spits nuclear fire. The sun leans down on Africa.

"What are you now?" Jimmy laughs. "Jamaican British?"

"What?"

"British Jamaican?"

"African-Jamaican living in England. Getting by. Yes, living here 50 years."

"Old man, you will stay here!"

"Well, you know, you have to stand your ground."

"You must know your roots, who you defend."

"If all you know is what people talk then you might run when you must fight. Or fight when you must move on. Things like that."

"Like Mandela?"

392

Urshell nods to Mandela's portrait. "I hear what yu sayin'."

Jimmy coughs. "I worry about being English born."

"You want to be English?"

"Well, I dunno. Yes and no."

"That business could get funny. Bad, bad."

"It should be simpler."

"Son, that is a *long* way down the road. Your grandson. Your granddaughter."

A car-horn sounds in the night. A woman says hello somewhere in the street and, for half a tick, her voice could sing. This woman going to party the night away, boogie till dawn. Some lucky will hear that woman whisper tonight. Jimmy knows the woman is nothing like Geraldine. What's Geraldine doing? Staying in Ireland for all time? Sorting out what junked down in her conservatory?

He tells Urshell about one dream. The latest dream is two lions moving at evening along the Thames, one lion each side of the breezing river. The male lion goes to the water's edge. The lioness enters it, swimming across to him. In the cool London twilight the mane of the lion rising high on the riverbank., claiming the cool ancient river. The lion waits for the lioness to reach. And then. The best part. And that is lions walking the river, beside it, lion with lioness the same side of the river, moving along.

Wry, the old man ups from the chair. And says this is a simple dream, saying this dream is Jimmy with Agnes in mind. And straightaway Jimmy says Urshell should have Joseph for his name. Joseph? Yes, old man; Joseph, after the dream-sayer in the bible.

The old man stumps back to the chair. "Joseph is a big story. That Joseph story is too hard to carry. Want some tea, son? Rum?"

"Rum sounds great. But I'd best keep my head clear."

"Try some tea."

"No thanks! No more tea."

"A shot of water. Ice-water?"

"Listen, what happened after Africa?"

"Roots?"

"Yes. What happened when you got back. Why didn't you just go back to Jamaica, tap into your roots there?"

"Well, after Africa it was time to observe."

"*What?*"

"I was back to England, doing regular driving work."

"What did you see?"

"Years doing bus work, you get to understand folk. And then more years doing the black-cab business. Jamaica was too hard to go back to. Going back was to admit defeat. Then one day the whole business was plain. That lady was on the scene."

"Maggie?"

"Mrs Thatcher."

"*Mrs* Thatcher?"

"Yes."

Jimmy squints. "Sounds like you respect her, like she was something special."

"You know, that individual was a good woman in the early days."

"Like you wanted to, you know, dance with the witch."

"We watched the woman because, well, all my children are female and when a woman gets to the top you stand back and observe. She was what you can call a woman."

"She *hated* black people."

"Hate is a strong word. Bad."

"What would you call it?"

"The blokes in the government, man! Some a dem could not dance with a woman. You had a situation wid blokes a shelter in a dem office. Dem stoop low. A dat mek Mrs Thatcher get so high. Then everything change. After a year at Number 10, she was a big pretend duchess."

"A duchess over Brixton, Handsworth, and the rest."

"Yes, son. She badmout black people. 'We will not be swamped by immigrants!'"

"How did they rein her in? I hear she got sort of mellow towards blacks at the end."

"It was carnival."

"Notting Hill carnival? No way! There's no way that woman got influenced by carnival. Carnival is so *huge* on black."

"You never check carnival?"

"That tropical dice? Every year?"

"It was the white people. Carnival was bigger and bigger every year. Nobody could see how far you would go with that. But it was the white people saying 'We want the carnival.' Man, carnival was making you think new."

"Like you could be OK in England? Black and OK?"

"Yes."

"One phony weekend every year!"

Urshell's eyes close. His forearms take the arms of the chair. "Yes, son, I know."

The old man weary. A burden from the past. When carnival started, the mainstream physics community was thinking protons and neutrons are the base. But those people never bothered with a German called Leibniz. And now they know quarks are it. But even now most of them have never heard of the Monadology. Urshell is not a physics man. Jimmy is not a physics man, but knows enough. He backs down. It's too hard seeing pain on any old face, somebody admitting in their face that they have no real time left in this old world to see a happy ending.

When Duke Ellington got to Carnegie Hall in 1943, they listened his Black, Brown & Beige suite. And it was not just skin-tone, it was life. Mahalia Jackson sang it: *Black for labour, brown for black soldiers in the US army, and beige for American black music*. Urshell knows that. But only because Ellington cut Caribbean lilts in there with the suite.

The old man knows the Notting Hill carnival is only pain pretending. Pain hiding for a weekend every year. Carnival meaning meat. And something falls apart when a sweet black woman wears big bird feathers to wobble down the carnival road with a silver whistle in her mouth.

"Maggie, and the meat at Notting Hill!"

Urshell's eyes gaze the ground. "Yes."

"What about Tebbit?"

"Who?"

"Lord Tebbit. They must have freaked at carnival!"

"Yes."

Jimmy jumps from the chair. "You had activists in your day, but there's nobody out there now. It's like blacks can't wait to get patted on the head, like if enough of them know about the Tebbit test

395

there'd be queues 10 miles long, you know, them rushing out to show they can pass the good-little-black-boy test."

"Listen!" Urshell growls. "I check West Indies for cricket. And New Zealand for rugby. England is nice for some things. If you want a chance, England is a good place. But I am a Jamaican for Jamaica sun, and a Jamaican for Jamaica woman. I am a big Jamaican for Jamaica!"

"Did he ever flag you down?"

"Who?"

"Norman Tebbit. Did he ever get into your cab?"

"No. Dem have government transport fe dem people. I met the man one day, what you can call a polite fellow."

"Can't imagine him and you talking."

"Norman Tebbit is a very clever man."

"I didn't say he wasn't. I'm saying he's a big-mouth!"

"That man does no less and no more than anyone proud of their country."

"He's no friend of the black man."

"Listen, nowadays you can have a black cab any colour."

"Yeah, splashed with adverts. But what's that go to do with it."

"Lord Tebbit can ride in a red black-cab, or a green one, or a blue black-cab. Not to mention a black black-cab."

Jimmy laughs. "Yeah. What about a white black-cab with a black cabby? Get what I mean? It's the part where some city gent's waiting on a pavement and flags down a white black-cab, then gets something to talk about later, like 'I flagged a black-cab, a white one actually, and the colour was a bit off-putting but I didn't mind, had to get off my feet, then as I got to it there was this *huge* black man at the wheel. You have never seen anything like it in your life.' Jeez, what a riot!"

Urshell claps his knees. Shakes his head. Old man laughing. Laughing loud. Out loud. Laughing, bad. The old Jamaican folding down with laughing. And Jimmy glad. This is panto time. Serious laughing here. This thing funny. No, this bad. A black cabby, driving a white black-cab in London? Jimmy and Urshell chopping down with laughing. Bad, bad laughing. Impossible.

Urshell's wife bolts into the room. And their daughter. They get

396

two laughing madmen. Urshell wants to explain, wants to stop, tries to stop laughing, but can not. Jimmy worse. Can not stop this belly laughing. Laughing through pain now. Laughing getting close to clinic zone. But.

But. Seeing how the women are scared, Urshell gets to stop. He tries to tell why the laughing. But it doesn't take long. The women start. The part with the *huge black man at the wheel*, that the killer. And when one laughing winds down, somebody says something, anything, and the laughing starts over. This laughing, laughing. Nobody should laugh to death. Laughing this way, somebody could die. A white black-cab, with a black cabby? Somebody *definitely* dying here already.

Outside in the night, taxi drivers hustling for fares. And a rainbow arcs over the Rift Valley. The earliest nightmare of Africa was when Moses had a sister that got blousey because he married the Ethiopian woman. Then the Old Testament chastised her with a bad skin disease because of that nightmare she had of Africa.

Way past midnight, the idea of a white black-cab with a black cabby, this splitting the sides of four black people in a London room. Way past midnight.

In the end, the clock stops it. Tears of laughing in his eyes, Jimmy must leave. Buttoning his jacket he mentions Aristotle. Aristotle got away with mickey-mouse physics for over two thousand tears by believing that something had absolute position in space.

Urshell blinks. "Before you go, I will tell you about that dilution thing."

"How the panthers fell apart?"

"Yes. It is foolishness calling yourself a black activist nowadays. Too much what you can call conceit is out there."

"Deceit?"

"Deceit, conceit. Educated folk have stuff to talk. Anyway, a short while before I retired from the cab work I used to have this regular punter, a young black fellow. Him was maybe thirty-two. Born over here. Young fellow, his mother and father from the West Indies. Anyway, the first few times in the cab he was too uptight to talk to me. Then after a period of time, man! You could not stop that boy talking. The plum in that boy's mouth! Zeitgeist this, zeitgeist that.

397

Anyway, he was telling me about his white great-grandfather all the time. But when you looked at that boy, he was black as me. He was buying a little place in France and was starting to run between London and Paris every weekend, but man! A bigger uncle tom I have *never* seen! An' when yu get somebody dat young, you know big trouble up ahead. *Big* trouble."

Jimmy nods. "Sad!"

Urshell's daughter says, "Heartbreaking."

Jimmy moves to the door. "I feel sorry for the sucker."

"Son, I will put it this way. One year I used to have this white punter in the cab, a real city gent I used to cab nine, maybe ten times. Him never used to talk. Him just sit quiet, an' do de cube. You remember the cube? After five minutes I would drop him outside his office and that cube was always solved."

Jimmy glares at his watch. "What's the end part of this story?"

"Well, that city gent would always have the fare ready. It was always the right amount, always in the same hand as the cube. That gent would make sure the white side of the cube was pointing to me. *Every* time. Him never seh a word. That bloke thinks he was telling me something, but man!"

Smiling wry, Urshell's wife shakes hands with Jimmy. "Nobody," she says, "can put race back together like a Rubik's cube!"

Chapter 90

Lorna chants her list. "Tony Benn, Bob Geldof, Jools Holland, Paul McCartney, Ray Mears, Jeremy Paxman, Elvis Costello."

The list surprises Jimmy. To him, two names do not fit; two of these people could be big-time pretence. And more women should get listed by a woman. Some women. At least one woman.

"You sure?"

Lorna opens the car door. "Positive!"

"Hang on. There's one too many. You've got seven."

"Seven?"

"Yeah. It's got to be six."

"Oh, come on. If it works for six then even better for seven, eh. Come on, boy!"

"The rules say six, not seven. Got to be six."

"Then stuff the rules!"

"Why'd you bother playing?"

"Well," she shrugs, wanting a quiet life, "OK, let's have it."

"Strike one off."

Lorna grits her teeth. "I wouldn't know who to leave out. I'd feel like I was letting somebody down, you know. Wouldn't feel right."

"They're not here in the car, are they? They can't hear what we're saying. Come on, just cross off somebody. Anyone."

The morning air so fresh. The sea so calm. Quiet, sulking, she folds the list. And, as the folds get too tight to fold more, it unfolds. Lazy folds. Then the cycle goes. The list opens and closes like a baby concertina. Jimmy gazing at the sea.

"Tell you what, *you* cross off one! It's your game."

"You agreed the rules," he says. "You wanted to play."

"Look, we should be getting as much of the beach as we can. You know, before the hordes get here."

"Hey, just close your eyes and stick your finger down. Random elimination. There again," he remembers the serious point of the game, "just cross off the one you don't feel sure about. There's got to be one like that."

"I'll do you a deal. Let's do the beach before the noise arrives."

Jimmy lights a smoke. "What's the deal?"

"We go for that walk, I mean *now*, then I lose one name when we get back. How's that?"

Before this meeting up today, Jimmy and Lorna have not met since her brother's funeral. Time after time he picked up the phone. But words failed every time. Then sent a card of condolence. More than anything it was about not wanting to crowd the private space Lorna needed. It was six o'clock this morning and he was just about to turn in, but suddenly needed to know who was on the answerphone. Then steeled up, expecting Geraldine's voice. It was Lorna. And it was the whole world to hear that woman, hear that noonday voice. And straightaway he lost sleep-starvation. Lorna wanted to talk. Talk anything, everything. Maybe go for a walk somewhere; that's what the message said. And he phoned straight after listening. She did not mind the time, and it was nice to hear his voice, she said, and, yes, six o'clock was kind of early but it wasn't all that obscene because the sun was already smirking. What's up? Not a lot, a bit of this, bit of that. Then why don't we go for a drink later, maybe grab some pub music? Jimmy said the seaside would be better, especially with no crowds there. Why? Because the state he was in, the sight of sea water would fix it. And a model boat is in the flat, a yacht with mainsail and jib, but tired seeing it on the window sill. Any chance they could go now? What, now? Well, yeah, we can get there early, be the first ones there. Lorna asked if he's still driving that old, well, OK, that same old car? Yes, it's still going OK, but yeah, we better go in your car, he said. Better safe than sorry, she said. It was just after 7.30 when they got to Eastbourne. Lorna wanted to do a quick visit to Beachy Head. And Jimmy said all they do there is suicide; people swap stars in their eye to leap for mud. Beachy Head cliff gets more leaping than any place else in England. Lorna rubbed her eyes. Stopped thinking. Then turned back, headed down the seafront, alive, going past house after converted Victorian house of hotels. The car dawdled past the pier and the bandstand and, eventually, nudging to a calm spot over one expert morning sea. Strong coffee was in her flask. And they sat watching boats at quiet anchor, boats bobbing easy on the light swell, nodding feints to the wind. Just the sound of the sea was the thing. The kind of day a muso ace could sync, a jazz player, someone like Wes Montgomery. Or Tal Farlow. Players like that could splice loose ends a place like this, unleash wind-jamming on the strings. Life, more, yes, water.

Somewhere a woman by the sea is dreaming. She imagines the

same somebody again today, dreaming raindrops touching external worship of a togetherness. And in the dream the woman wants to be pregnant. And an emerald bottle is on a table. And a pale flower in the bottle. And pitter, patter, rain falling, rain, patter, slow. Rain saying something, saying 'Listen, hear water-slippers tiptoe a fairytale. Oh, anyone can hear. All you do is close your eyes and put them water-slippers on.'

Lorna laughs. "Water, on the guitar?"

"Yeah, Wes Montgomery says it with octaves. That guy plays the greatest octaves, huge block chords, lightning changes. You can *not* begin to believe the invention. Tal Farlow says it with single notes, stuff that just smiles before anyone can hear them, and then they really smile."

"Where's that come from?"

"A boat's a lot like a guitar."

Relaxed, walking easy, Lorna gets her dream. "How?"

"Because you need soundness of the boat before you test the waves. Same for music, improvised music."

"Guitar?"

"Any instrument. I feel like a bit of guitar today, that's all."

Lorna runs to the water. And turns back, saying, 'Boo, hiss!' Jimmy says this is no gimmick. You have to play music with no gimmicks, don't you know that by now? What, all the time you heard me say it? Yeah, Hendrix was still Hendrix on acoustic guitar. And he was Hendrix on bass. And you don't sail if you only wired to a tug or doing dry dock. A day like today and, well, somewhere else somebody's tacking closer to a distant goal.

Chapter 91

Jimmy forecasts the length of empty beach. Weirdly, thinking of old chats with Geraldine. Geraldine would use the empty beach. She would wonder. That woman would sus who was using this dry yet always wet place five, even ten thousand years before. And then she'd wonder who'd be using it a thousand years from now. Jimmy missing Geraldine. But will not try to square that with the killer word in her head.

Something Urshell said. The old man believes it will be four more generations before England is stable enough. Then maybe folk will get comfortable with colour, people of colour. The first sign will be talky whites. They won't want a TV studio to chat immigrants anymore. But the big sign is no black people running after *diversity* while hiding under fake kits; yes, like under a blond wig fluttering on ebony. And it will be a long time before a black person can arrive in a certain kind of car. Like a brand new Jag. Arrive in the city in a Jag, yes, but in the countryside do not arrive in a Jag and order a meal in a village pub and expect you won't cause hushed talk. Urshell says the Jag would pour salt into village wounds. Somebody black driving a Jag through old green England would be like foxes and hounds time. So if you go, then go in a mini. Or get there in Porsches or Ferraris. Why not a Jag? Because that motor is what the English gentleman drives in his English countryside. A hundred more years. That's how long for English folk to get used to a black man or woman with a yacht, even somebody having skill and heart enough to solo the ocean. They would have to win Olympic sailing gold. Then do it again. Or take on all the five oceans lone. But that stuff will happen one day. Or so one old man said.

Jimmy and Lorna watch the ocean. Quiet, together. Nothing to say. And as the sun gets higher in the sky, it opens something in Lorna. A little flower opens in her heart. This woman will never leave England.

Just think, she says, you can get in your car and in one hour be out of London sitting in the sand and looking at beautiful boats on the water. And doesn't Jimmy think that being able to do that is just too nice to leave and go any place else?

Jimmy must tell Lorna more about the visit to Urshell. The

woman looks at the sea, saying 'That old man is not a philosopher. He's just a retired cab-driver, right?' But then. She wants to know if Urshell looks anything like Mandela. She'd walk on water if there was somebody like Mandela, young, tall and wise. And nut-brown; one of his grandsons maybe.

"Well," Jimmy says, pointing the ocean, "Africa is over there. But the African diaspora is everywhere."

"What?"

"You and me, chips of Africa on this shore."

Lorna stomps the sand. "Not that stuff again! I am *not* an African, OK? I can't just offload the white part of me, chuck it in the sea."

"Hey, who asked you to?"

"I don't even feel *mixed* anything. If the world must brand me, black is fine with me."

"That's it!"

"What's wrong with black? We're all black. Christ, there's so many kinds of every colour. A million, million greens. Billions of blues and reds."

"There's big resentment. Huge."

Suddenly, her eyes pop. "No wait! What about a Rican?"

A what?"

"A Rican!"

"*Rican?*"

"Yes, that would do. Wouldn't it?"

"What's a Rican?" Jimmy says.

"Someone that's part-African. Why not? I'd be cool with Rican."

"You might start something."

"Must honour your mother and father, right?"

"Come on, who could say no to that!"

"Rican! And there's a good few Icans out there. And Cans."

Silent, Jimmy reaching for a handful of wet sand. In a way, Lorna agrees with Urshell. Not in so many words. And maybe not so much worry.

"You going to do a Tiger Woods?"

"How d'you mean?"

"Tiger calls himself a Cablinasian."

Lorna blinks. "What the hell is that?"

"It's an amalgam. It's caucasian, black, indian, asian."

"Jesus Christ!"

"Tiger's father is black, with bits of Caucasian and red-Indian."

"His mother is Thai, isn't she?"

"Yeah. In America orientals are asians."

Folk will understand the cut of *Cablinasian*. Except for the loudmouth, the malcontent. Huge loudmouth wanting Tiger to deny his mother and say African-American. Loudmouth wanting Tiger to falsify and shuffle round in a Brixton overcoat.

Somewhere, maybe in Polynesia, some people still use seashells for status. And it's easy to wonder. Shells from an English beach could be worth a fortune. Maybe the problem is branding. *Branding* implies that what gets branded is like cattle. Looks like people classified by cut is no bigger a deal than naming cornflakes.

Taking breeze from the ocean, Jimmy tells Lorna the meaning of the list. In a word, this is how to gauge race awareness.

How, for God's sake! Well, you pretend to be doing a party game then get somebody to name six white people that would never use *nigger* in anger. Well-known white folk. The closer your party gamer gets to doing the list in 15 seconds, the better the state of racial play. What if it takes more than a minute? Then they will only produce worthless paper. Screw that paper. Then what? Urshell did not say.

Because of Agnes, Jimmy wants the whole ocean. That woman so scared of flying she took being seasick all day for two weeks on a ship than just pack a suitcase, check her smile and catch a flight. She and Jimmy talked by mobile as her ship sailed away. He remembers her voice exactly: she couldn't see him at the quayside, so could he try waving both arms this time. There and then he was wondering if that woman would *ever* tuck in his bed again. It was because hurt was in her voice. She was talking the water, the ship slipping and sliding; menacing water, she said. Water was sliding and rolling like a mule on a slush hill. Jimmy remembering the ship turning from blue to grey, getting small, smaller and smaller, so small, and, eventually, too faint in the distance, too much wisp. A grey fog snatched it away.

And now he's here. In England still, walking a beach with Lorna. The breeze across the sea whirls. And gulls. Those birds pack breeze, and idle. And sails, furled and stowed. Boats lazing their cradle. And Lorna's shadow in step with Jimmy's. The cut of that

404

from the air! This man and woman going along the beach, but where they go? Lorna has her thoughts.

Jimmy thinking of the evening at Urshell's house. It was the old man's kind-hearted wife. As he was about to leave, the old lady slipped him a copy of Urshell's little booklet. Urshell penned a little streetwise thing and his wife slipped the photo of Agnes into it. Great old woman. She could see how the photo distressed Jimmy. And it was a week before he even looked at the homemade little booklet. But it stunned him cold, finding the photo of Agnes tucked inside it. But the photo was still bad, he still could not look at the picture of an alien woman. But could not destroy it. Sending it back seemed the best thing and he even started a letter to go along with it. But that was like a rotten fruit your hand picks in the dark. And then. Something. The new idea was to get the picture scanned into a computer, get the image of the straightened hair changed for natural. The computer technician was ace. He tried and tried. Trying natural hairstyles out on the photo. One style was Agnes with heavy braids. And she was beautiful again. Another style showed her with a part down the middle. But the one with the Afro! Yep, even the computer technician said it, saying that the Afro was the best style of all. And that's when Jimmy could see something wrong. It was wrong, wrong. It was like All Along The Watchtower time. Something was out of kilter, too wrong. No matter what hairstyle the technician tried, all that happened was Agnes and her fantasy for straight hair was getting replaced with Jimmy's own fantasy of her. And that was too hard for words. Replacing something false with something natural, and still guilty of fantasy? The technician said the best thing might be to do five or six printouts. But Jimmy took the photo and apologized. For ten days, it was moping. And thinking over why Urshell accused him of a fantasy. But finally it got clear. Could see what was wrong. Urshell was not wrong. But that old man was not right. Not quite. Jimmy knows now that this is no fantasy. Fantasy is not the word. This is affirmation. And even if *affirmation* is sideways vision, fantasy is not the right word. He was only longing for affirmation.

Lorna's footsteps in sync with Jimmy's, walking beside him and the easy beach. "What are you trying to affirm?"

"What d'you mean?"

"You were wittering away, mumbling."

"Must have been sleepwalking."

"You can't take your eyes off the sea. Fancy one of those yachts?"

Jimmy smiles. "No. And it's not about mermaids, OK?"

"Did you ever read mermaid fairytales, mermen, merchildren?"

"No. You?"

"As in, am I a mermaid?"

"Are you?"

"Can barely swim."

"Listen, let's talk."

"Yes."

"How have *you* been, how you been coping?"

"Me?"

"Lorna Stanley. What's up with that woman?"

"Well, I sort of kept to myself the whole time. Took a month off work. I couldn't face it. Christ, I locked myself in the flat. Most days I probably didn't even draw the curtains. It was 'What's the point!' I couldn't get it straight."

"That's why the message on my answerphone?"

"Yes."

"Why me?"

"Don't underestimate you! There was tons to get straight and I didn't realize how much there was. I couldn't face my mother. The night of the funeral we were all together at the house and that was the worst part. Nobody could accept it. You know, Justin was never going to come back through the front door and we broke down, cried and cried."

"Lorna, I don't want to intrude. I don't need to know."

Lorna's eyes mist. "Intrude? No. Times like these, well, some people are all over the place and they get counseling and then hang it all out. With me, I talk to you and it's 'God, now I understand!' Hope you know what I mean. I can't really explain it."

"Why couldn't you face your mother?"

"Too difficult. Awkward."

"I'd need to be close to my mother at a time like that."

"I know. I thought about it and, Christ! It was like cold fish. I was never able to just throw my arms round anyone. Even my mother."

"How did you cope?"

"I can't think. The only thing I remember is, I know I played it

406

non-stop. Played and played Mull of Kintyre. Played it non-stop. And the more I played it, the more it was 'You have to do this one more time.' I must have played that one song a thousand days."

"Mull of Kintyre?"

"Yeah."

"Why?"

"Because, because! How should I know? I can't explain it. There was only pain. And you're looking for affirmation, right? Try it. Try listening to Mull of Kintyre. Lock your door, get the phone off the hook, and Mull will sort it for you."

"I like the song myself," Jimmy says, "but no way a bunch of bagpipes would keep me from *my* mother. She needed you."

"I know, I know! It's doing my head in. I had to stay away, had to. I didn't know what was going on, thought I was losing it. And then I thought of Beachy Head. I listened to the shipping forecast. Every day I got a coffee and tuned in to Radio 4 and it was 'Viking, North Fitsera' Is it Fitsera? Well, something like 'South Fitsera, 40's, southerly 3 or 4 but occasionally 5, becoming cyclonic later.' Something every day like that."

"Lorna, slow down. I can't see where this is going."

"You can't? Then get a load of this: Occasional rain, then thundery showers, moderate with fog patches."

Lorna going to a place Jimmy does not understand. He's ready to head back. Get back to London. The solo with the sea is getting breached. Even with no one else on the beach but the two of them. Lorna is like a boat that was longtime on the seabed but at last getting given up by a storm. And now it's skeleton time. Bone getting delivered by sea-proof nylon cord.

"I couldn't face my mother because of one little thing," she says, talking to the sea. Sand trickles from her grasp like from an hourglass.

Jimmy lights a smoke. "What spooked you?"

"My family."

"The pain, you know, now that Justin's not there?"

"Things, there's things that never get said in families. And my dad, well. He's not the talky-talky kind."

"Him, finally accepting his son was black?"

"I think so. No. Well, yes. Something like that."

"The pain of that?"

"You know," she sighs, "Justin had dreadlocks. All his mates were black guys and nearly everybody at the funeral was black. Right up till the funeral service I don't think my father ever really wanted him to be black."

"White?"

"Don't be pushy?"

"Whitish?"

"No, I'm serious! He used to go on about how Justin looked like him, tall like him, and the same pointy-nose. On and on! It was always like if it wasn't for his frizzy hair, Justin was white. On and on!"

"What did Justin think?"

"Justin?"

"Yes."

"Thought it was a joke."

"As in?"

"The thing is, if you saw my brother in his motorbike helmet you'd never know he was black. Anything covering his hair."

Jimmy flits the cigarette to the sea. And turns to Lorna. "That is half a world from me."

Vacant, she scoops a lazy hand of sand. And sifting, sifting her fingers through. Then flings it at the waves. "Promise I can tell you."

"What is it?"

"I don't know who to talk to about it. Can I tell you?"

"Depends what it is," Jimmy whispers.

"I need to know if I tell you, then it stays put with you."

"Depends."

"Promise!"

"Who would I tell?"

"You won't mention it? Ever. Even to me. Promise me!"

Silent, Jimmy nods. Stands quiet in a whale of air coming from the sea. "I swear."

"Summer before last, my dad took snaps of him and Justin. It was such a graceful day. Just the two of them. All smiles."

"No!"

"You know?"

"I think so."

"What was it?"

408

"They had their crash helmets on?"

Lorna's eyes want the sea to borrow them. "Yes."

"You know, so Justin would look _"

"White! Look white. Yes."

"Man!"

"What else!"

"You sure? Are you one hundred percent positive?"

"What else was there! I was going through the family albums after the funeral, checking it all out, coming to terms. The snaps of my little brother. I was looking at all the old snaps of Justin and the family and in every picture my little brother's grinning his face off and I couldn't stop crying. When I saw the helmet ones, I'd seen them before, but something just clicked and I knew what they meant. So I took them out. Wanted to get rid of them, bury them somewhere. But then my dad comes into the room and I tell him I know what he's done, what the pictures mean. Doesn't say boo, does he! He's like 'You think you know it all' and I'm like 'No, but I wouldn't deny my own son!' And he gets so sad all of a sudden, weak at the knees. Then he takes them off me. And looks at them for a minute. Then he just sort of wilts, really. He looks so old and everything. Not himself at all and I started crying again. When he asks me what I want to do with them, I knew that was it."

"What did you say?"

"There's no way they're going back in the album, I said."

"Then?"

"He gets out his lighter and puts the snaps on a plate. Sets fire to them. We just sort of went numb together. Me and him watching the pictures burn."

Jimmy folds an arm round Lorna. But she recoils. Jumping back like she's been raped.

"Jimmy," she says, "you must *never* mention this. Not even back to me!"

"No, I will never bring it up. Ever. But _"

"But, *what*? You promised!"

"Well, why me? Things like that, man! You should keep that in the family. I've seen your father, he was at that meeting about Justin. But I don't know him. And I've never even set eyes on your brother. So I should *never* know this private thing about them. There's things that are too private."

409

Lorna wipes her eyes. "You can handle it."

"Why me, why didn't you tell somebody else?"

"Like who?"

"I'd tell the sea something big as that."

"The sea?"

"Why not?"

"Oh grow up!"

"The sea's got a bigger heart than me."

"The sea is a *lying* lump of water. Pickled, spiteful."

"What about your mother? It must have hurt her as much as you. She must have known about that crash helmet thing."

"Yes, she knew. I couldn't face her. I didn't know she knew. I looked at her and it was 'I have known this all along.' I couldn't look back. Justin dying, Christ! All those years and my dad's suddenly admitting Justin is mixed race. Black, or whatever."

"Black?"

"Yes."

"What's your mother say?"

"It really got to her. It was a bit of a problem, a lot harder than Justin dying."

"How did it turn round?"

"What do you mean?"

"Your dad, him seeing the facts."

"Oh, he just came out and admitted it. The psychos who got Justin must have seen him as black. My uncle had come down from Newcastle with a gun, a *huge* shotgun."

Jimmy pumps summer air with a fist. "Yes! Now you're talking! I honestly thought the guys in your family were passives."

"My dad? You're joking! He can be ice cold. When Justin was little he wouldn't tell if he got whacked. Anybody, teachers at school, black gangs, white gangs, my dad sorted them out!"

In the morning glare Lorna getting libation from the waves, the salt spray in air. Jimmy wishing, watching, listening to the ocean. The sound of the sea, the ocean in convention with the shore, ocean reminding him of one Ellington piece. Something tuneful but cut, playing. Somewhere a good instrument. An instrument within the waves. A solo, using the sea as a sound box, coaxing, getting plaintiffs from one horizon. What's Agnes doing? What does the photograph mean? Blue whales listen across the ocean. Way, way across

410

the sea blue whales in conversation. But the sea is no hearing-aid, not for the pangs of one man longing.

"What happened with the shotgun?"

Lorna bites her lip. "Oh, they sat around, you know, glowering. Staring at it. It was like that for a couple of days, a week, really. Then my dad talked my uncle out of it. It was 'Let's put our own house in order.' And that was that, really. At the end of the day they didn't know who to go for. And there was always that nagging feeling that maybe it was a mistake. I mean, one of Justin's own mates admitted using a screwdriver in the fight."

Today is a good-looking day. But the beach is no longer the place. Not for Jimmy. Not for Lorna. Not for a sad woman gazing yachts as they caper morning waves.

Out there the sea. Behind, everything that ever happened in England. The great and the guilty. Well, there's folk getting called great, national hero here, there, pioneers, but all the time guilty. Like Francis Drake. Sir Francis, what's he guilty of? He was a big time slave trader, a heavy-duty woad man, merchant trafficking slaves. You did not know that? What? Francis murdered black slaves, raped them. And stole their soul. Fifteen, twenty million African folk getting that done to them and England hugging a piece of the blood pie.

Jimmy asleep in Lorna's eyes. Dreaming the change. Today her eyes are the mildest eyes. And strange.

He remembers the jive in her apartment. The quip. Lorna gibed Jimmy over Moses parting the Red Sea. And now her eyes say she remembers what she said. Hand on his arm, she says sorry, saying she wants to move on from that. Is that possible?

"Are you free?"

"Free, as in not a slave?"

"Free, as in not involved with anyone," she says. "Are you still with that woman from South Africa?"

Lorna's body folds down to the sand. And slow, she gazes at the proud swell of sea.

Jimmy walks on, alone. Must think. The woman from South Africa? What if by some weird thing he gets back to London later and Agnes waiting in the flat? She took a set of keys to Africa. What's the point? Because it means I have somewhere I belong to in London. But anything can happen, what if you don't come back? Then you can change the lock. Tell you what, Jimmy said, just post the keys to the bottom of the sea. Agnes might arrive at the flat. Like by magic. Jimmy imagines her there, shy, and then she explains the photograph. Saying it was a joke. Yes, a joke! And the more she'd thought about it the more she realized if a man loved her then what her hair was like could not matter to him because she was not the same as her hair. Women play their hair, Jimmy, and it doesn't really mean anything if a woman straightens it. Even white women straighten their hair. White? Yes, some white women hurry to the hairdresser to rinse and straighten. But straight hair is natural to white, so the ones straightening it must only be playing bang-a-rang. Bang-a-rang? Jamaican word for *folly*. That's what he'd say, backing out the door to a woman getting to the 8th floor flat my magic. Weird, but Jimmy can not imagine Agnes singing the blues. She used to hum a lot.

To start, the whole Brixton business was only jive. 'Try Brixton!' was one more jive. Now things clear. The woad-man kicking hypocrisy round like any stray cat. Bob Dylan could sing that. Or Bono. Those guys can pick up their guitar and step to stage front. And just because of who they are, the way they toy the mic, they'd straightaway get to folk. And that's because it must be someone white. It must be white talking. Nobody really listening to somebody black talking of that racial. Only somebody white can tell woad the way woad. Somebody white must sympathize with somebody black before somebody white feeling shame. Even Mandela was too old before they'd listen. Only after he was too old was it OK to talk freedom.

A lyric in Jimmy's keeping. A surprise. Maybe it would be only like fodder for a crowd, like on a football terrace, but it could get used in a song one day. His fingers click. Ray Davies might have thought it. The rhythm easy. Borrowing the melody from Waterloo Sunset, Jimmy singing the lyric, singing low: *the blacks of Brixton, met the brix of Blackston, halfway to Leicester Square.*

Way down the beach, Lorna alone. She does not need the sea. She know Jimmy check her out? What's he doing? Being a new brother, something else? She listens footfalls in the sand.

"Remember the day at the zoo, the day we first met?" Jimmy
412

pants.

"I haven't forgotten. I'll *never* forget it."

"What d'you think happened to the lions?"

"I was thinking I'd go back one day," she says. "You know, go back to find out. Think we can go to the zoo together sometime?"

"I was thinking the same thing."

"Today? Look, I'd love to see them. I dreamed them one night and they were like 'When will you come again?' Funny, eh?"

Walking down the beach, alone now, Jimmy needing to be sure. Looks like things over with Agnes. Finished. Even in her own country Agnes hugging to a Brixton overcoat; well, she straighten her hair under that new South Africa sun. And maybe she's already got something neat going with a guy talking like Paul Robeson.

Jimmy mulling Donna. Next week will be New York. Flying to New York to get Minims on CD. Jamaica only a step from New York. Donna will meet Jimmy in Manhattan, saying she got a surprise and will fly out. Lorna is way down in his heart. But Donna deep in the soul. Maybe because of what happened with Donna; that hurricane the first time, and a peal of angels the last time. But only today on a quiet beach in England that things look clear to Jimmy.

Britannia in a white corset. Lorna saying America a two-way place. America a place with ace blacks at the top; ace black folk at the top in Wall Street and the military. But that same America is a place with sundown towns.

Jimmy grabs a smoke. "Sundown?"

"Yeah. A sundown town is 'Nigger, don't let the sun go down on you here!' You look surprised."

"What, in America?"

"Yep."

"These days?"

"Yep."

"Like where?"

"Towns," Lorna says, shrugging at the sea, "like Anna in Illinois. They still have rednecks there and Anna stands for 'Ain't no niggers allowed.' Hard to believe, isn't it?"

Lorna remembers a wild yellow-nosed albatross she read about doing weird things in America last month. It was seen near Martha's Vineyard. That albatross was like a vision, but real enough,

413

flying so far north of the equator. This type of albatross is from the southern hemisphere; the yellow-nosed have their home in the southern oceans and the only reason this loner was in America was trying to find a mate. A long-distance seabird, looking and looking, trying to pal it with gulls in Martha's Vineyard by sheer mistake.

Colin Powell was born in America to Jamaican parents and, if they'd gone to the UK instead of the USA, he'd have ended up as a sergeant in the British army; that's what Colin the 4-star American general reckons.

But Lorna loves this place. Even though her brother in the ground here, the lady loves England. And Jimmy can tell one thing. She definitely is not the type that will come along too often. And she closes in on some set thing in him. So maybe the rest is simple. With Donna, something deep going on. Donna the same beautiful as black olives. Jimmy remembering, contemplating that heavy woman on a plane from Kingston to New York. But. But that is next week. Because Lorna here. Today, right now. Lorna this side of the tripping ocean.

Leaving the Eastbourne seaside Jimmy and Lorna going on a journey. Getting back to north London, they could use the old road through Brixton and while away before crossing the Thames. Half a day getting left behind here. Like luggage. And in a way this is maybe how it was meant. Or they could stay with the beach to loll around, making small talk, see folk arrive with city-down eyes, and even get melancholy being a part of a sunny English day, toying in sand, laughing in sand; even building a neat sandcastle out of a ton of it. After all, every ton can fly.